Kaleidoscope

DIVERSE YA SCIENCE FICTION AND FANTASY STORIES

EDITED BY ALISA KRASNOSTEIN & JULIA RIOS

First published in Australia in October 2014
by Twelfth Planet Press
www.twelfthplanetpress.com

Design and layout by Amanda Rainey
Typeset in Sabon MT Pro

All rights reserved. Without limiting the rights under copyright above, no part of this publication may be reproduced, stored in or introduced into a retrieval system, or transmitted in any form, or by any means (electronic, mechanical, photocopying, recording or otherwise), without the prior written permission of both the copyright owner and the above publisher of this book.

"Cookie Cutter Superhero" © 2014 Tansy Rayner Roberts
"The Seventh Day of the Seventh Moon" © 2014 Ken Liu
"The Legend Trap" © 2014 Sean Williams
"End of Service" © 2014 Gabriela Lee
"Chupacabra's Song" © 2014 Jim C. Hines
"The Day the God Died" © 2014 Alena McNamara
"Signature" © 2014 Faith Mudge
"The Lovely Duckling" © 2014 Tim Susman
"Kiss and Kiss and Kiss and Tell" © 2014 E. C. Myers
"Vanilla" © 2014 Dirk Flinthart
"Careful Magic" © 2014 Karen Healey
"Walkdog" © 2014 Sofia Samatar
"Celebration" © 2014 Sean Eads
"The Truth About Owls" © 2014 Amal El-Mohtar
"Krishna Blue" © 2014 Shveta Thakrar
"Every Little Thing" © 2014 Holly Kench
"Happy Go Lucky" © 2014 Garth Nix
"Ordinary Things" © 2014 Vylar Kaftan
"Double Time" © 2014 John Chu
"Welcome" © 2014 William Alexander

National Library of Australia Cataloguing-in-Publication entry

Title:	Kaleidoscope : diverse YA science fiction and fantasy stories / Alisa Krasnostein, Julia Rios, editors; Amanda Rainey, designer; Garth Nix, author [and 18 others].
ISBN:	9781922101112 (paperback)
Subjects:	Science fiction.
	Fantasy fiction.
	Short stories.
Other Authors/Contributors:	Krasnostein, Alisa, editor.
	Rios, Julia, editor.
	Rainey, Amanda, book designer.
	Nix, Garth, 1963- author.
Dewey Number:	A823.01

Table of Contents

Cookie Cutter Superhero

By Tansy Rayner Roberts

Now that Joey was popular, it took twice as long to get from her French class up on the second floor, to the canteen line, and then to the table outside where her real friends were waiting.

Her new celebrity status was weird and uncomfortable, even worse than that first day of school years ago when she was surrounded by strangers prodding and staring at her left arm, every single one of them insisting, "I'm not being nosy, I'm just interested."

All this week, girls pretended like they had always been her friends, chatting about casual things in the hallway instead of ignoring her. So many of them found excuses to touch her—a brush of fingers against her hair or shoulder. She knew why they were doing it, and it was creepy.

"Oh, you are joining us, then?" said Willa when Joey finally approached. "Thought maybe we weren't good enough for you any more."

Joey gave Willa a Look. She could never quite tell whether she meant it when she was being horrible, or if it was supposed to be ironic. Best to assume the latter, because that meant they could keep being friends. "It's not my fault," she said. "I didn't ask for this."

"Poor baby," said Willa, and that time the sarcasm was really obvious.

"This is our last lunch," said Beck, who had been moping all week. "Our LAST LUNCH."

"It won't be for long," said Joey. "I'll be back in six months. Girls never last longer than a term." She groaned. "I'll have so much to catch up on before the exams."

"What do you need exams for?" said Willa. "You'll be famous. A couple of shoe endorsements, maybe a soft drink, and you'll be set for life."

Joey gave her a hard look. "I want to be a vet. That means exams." She wondered whether there would be space in her new room in the Sky Tower to keep up with her classes, or if it was a waste of time to even try. Could she hire a tutor or something? Bad enough that she would be months behind her friends—but she dreaded even more that the school would let her off all her exams at the end of the year and give her fake As.

"Six whole months," moaned Beck, interrupting Joey's sudden frantic thoughts about the horrible potential consequences if university gave her fake As too, because of who she used to be. Who she was about to become. She would be the worst vet ever. Animals would die.

This whole thing was a terrible idea. And there was no getting out of it now.

"Do you think you'll be a Legacy?" asked Beck, mumbling into Joey's shoulder.

"Oh come on!" said Willa. "Can't we talk about something else? Everyone asks her that. It's not like she even knows. The machine decides everything. Who's in, who's out, I bet it even picks a costume for you." She gave Joey the closest thing to a sympathetic look that she'd ever managed. "I'm more interested in Astra. She's pretty hot, and she's been in the team for a year and a half. How would it feel to be kicked out now?"

"Maybe you'll be the new Astra," said Beck, perking up a bit. "Her costume is nice, and she doesn't wear a mask."

"The girls never wear masks," said Willa. "They just change their hair color. Got to be recognizable for the sponsors, right?"

"Maybe Astra won't be the one to go," said Joey. That was the part she felt sort of worst about. She liked Astra a lot. She was way better than the last couple of Astras, who were boring carbon copies of the original Astra from five years ago, the posh one who now shilled for perfume companies. She was also more normal and down-to-earth than Magma, that crazy lava hero with the enormous rack, or Sigil, whose powers never had been properly explained, but wore the costume that put fear into Joey's heart, the one with strips of grey lycra and see-through plastic bubbles.

If she was going to be a Legacy, please please please let it not be Sigil. Costume redesigns never went well with the populace, and Joey was so not wearing bubbles.

The current Astra was tough and funny and had flippy blonde hair that always looked great. You could do way worse than being the new Astra. Except of course then everyone would go on about how Joey wasn't as good as the last one. That was the trouble with Legacies—it gave the media an excuse to criticize either you, or all the heroes with the same name who came before you.

Possibly Joey had been reading way too many hero mags lately.

She was trying not to think about the others, the men whose team she would be joining. They were just terrifying, all muscles and smiles. How would she ever fit in with them? How would she ever manage a coherent sentence in the same room as Surf, Shaggable Bloke of the Month in *Cosmic Magazine* six months running, or Solar, Bachelor of Steel, who was basically built of shoulders and handsome?

Then there was The Dark. She was going to be colleagues with The Dark. They'd probably have to have conversations with each other. It was all too big to fit inside her head.

"If you're not a Legacy," said Beck. "Maybe you'll be an Original?"

"That's rubbish," said Willa. "Much better to bring back a retro identity. There are so many cool female heroes who get ditched after a single term and never make it back as a Legacy. Remember Disco Doll?"

"Oh, not Disco Doll," Joey groaned. "I'm not defending justice in a mini-skirt and roller skates."

"No one remembers Disco Doll, Willa," said Beck, unusually sharp for her. "She was in the team before we were even born."

"That's my point," said Willa. "It's a terrible waste. All the Legacies lately have been recycling the same heroes from the last decade, with the occasional blast from the past from like, the 90s. No further back. Do you know how many awesome heroes there were in the 80s? In the first teams?"

"Yes, obviously we know, because you keep telling us," said Joey. "Do you know what else female heroes were doing in the 80s? They were sidekicking. Is that what you want me to try for? I could be Darkgirl, the kid sister to The Dark, who only fights the villains in pinafores and pigtails. Or Lady Surf, always riding a few waves behind my senior partner, and wearing a costume with his sponsors all over it."

"You'll be sorry when you end up as Astra 5, and no one ever remembers your name because the only obvious thing about you is that you're not her, or the one before her," huffed Willa.

There was a long pause as Joey glared at her and Willa stared at her lunch.

Two girls came over, the kind who managed to make the school uniform look extra neat and somehow fashionable. They wore three pairs of socks and very discreet tiny earrings, because that was the most you could get away with about being different in this school. The fact that they did it identically kind of wrecked the effect.

"You're Joey Marriot," said one of them, as if Joey might not have noticed.

"Get stuffed," said Willa. "Go on, hop away."

"Are you going to be a Legacy?" asked the other girl. "Do you know which one you're going to be? Will you be the new Astra?"

"I don't know," Joey said tiredly. "Leave us alone, will you?"

The first girl leaned in, speaking in a voice that was obviously trying to sound kind and concerned. "So when you become one of them, are they going to do something to fix your stump?"

"Wow," Joey said, ten minutes later as she and Willa stood outside the principal's office, waiting to be seen. "Talk about retro. You haven't done that since primary school. Hitting some kid for asking questions about my arm."

"Technically banging two girls' heads together is not the same as hitting them," Willa said primly.

"Pretty sure it's still assault."

"Well, sure. They got on my nerves."

"Are you going to follow around all the reporters who ask me the same questions? Because they're going to, you know. For months."

Willa gave her a sidelong look. "Not if the machines do give you a new arm. A power arm. With spikes on. I can see the action figures now..."

"They're still going to ask about it, aren't they?" Joey sighed. "Even if the machines give me eight arms and turn me into Octogirl, queen of the super squid people."

"It could happen, though, couldn't it? Everyone knows that The Dark was in a wheelchair before he stepped into the machine."

"Yeah," Joey muttered. "And no one ever talks about how he'll be in one again when the Lottery retires him." She held out her left arm before them, so there was no ignoring the way her wrist tapered into a rounded curve instead of a hand.

Her mum always said she should call it a curve, not a stump or anything ugly. She insisted that everyone treat it as a feature rather than a bug.

"I don't reckon I'd want a hand now," Joey said thoughtfully. "Remember when they tried to give me a prosthetic, when we were kids? It itched and I never got the hang of it, and everything took twice as long as just doing it one-handed. I'd already figured out how to do most things I needed to, by the time I was eight. They said I was too old. If I'd had a prosthetic earlier, I might have learned to do everything with it and not with my … curve." She shrugged. "Sixteen has to be way too old to learn how to use a superpower hand without making an idiot of myself."

Willa banged her head gently against the wall beside the principal's office. "Six months. Maybe even a year if you make it to a second term. That's forever. You won't be able to come back here to visit while it's all going on, will you?"

"I might."

"No, you won't. Because of leading supervillains to the school. You'll disappear into *Teen Hero Magazine*, and even when they retire you for some other chick, you'll be young enough to get a record deal or whatever."

Joey screwed her nose up. "As if. I'm not going to forget my friends."

"They'll be your friends instead. Your team. They all got stamped out of the same machine, right? So it will be programmed in. You'll be BFFs with the Cookie Cutter Superhero Power Club, hanging out in the Sky Tower and talking about, I don't know, wanky hero stuff."

Joey shoved Willa hard with her hip, and used her curve to smack her on the forehead. "I reckon I can still text you while saving the world. Don't be jealous of them. It's not like there's going to be any other girls in the team to be friends with, is it?"

Willa brightened. "There's that, I suppose."

There was a Sky Tower in every country that had a superhero machine. The Australian one loomed right over the Sydney Opera House, taking its place on tourist postcards.

Joey had not been inside the tower since a grade six excursion. She remembered stairs, whirling around and up so very high that Betsy Lewis had threatened to be sick, while all the boys pretended they were going to drop things from their pockets when they got to the top.

She'd met real live members of the team then. Solar, of course, and The Dark. Neither of them had changed in decades. They were joined by Speedster, not the original Speedster who died back in the mid 90s, but the young one with hipster glasses and thin dreadlocks that rattled when he ran. There was Beserker, the one who dressed like a Viking and used a power punch in battle. No one had ever brought him back as a Legacy. There were some hero concepts that just sucked too much to bring back. Oh and there was Lyrebird, the only girl, who was super flametastic and everyone said might be secretly hooking up with Solar.

That sold a lot of magazines, Joey remembered vaguely. Lyrebird had been popular—she stayed in the team nearly three years. That was almost unheard of for a female superhero. But she had to leave to make way for Sonara, who made way for Firework, who made way for Dragon Lady, who made way for Astra and Astra and Astra and another Firework, and Astra again. There was only ever one girl on the team, so they rotated faster than the men. They didn't have as many Legacies, either. They disappeared after their term, never to be seen again except as pop stars, fashion models, reality TV stars. I'm a Celebrity, Remember How I Used To Have Superpowers?

"Brought your costume then?" asked the freckled PA who guided Joey from the lobby with its gawking tourists, sandwich bar and souvenir shop, to the private lift used for the team only.

Joey gave him a blank stare. "What costume?"

"You know they don't provide them, right? You have to bring

your own. They won't let you in without it." He looked earnest, and Joey almost believed him in that second, despite the fact that she had done more research into the team and its rituals than anything else over the last two years.

"Don't be a dick, Mezza," said a voice behind them both. "Playing pranks on the new talent is the lowest form of humor."

Joey turned, and her throat closed over for a second or two as she recognized Astra.

The most famous woman in Australia smiled warmly and flipped her blonde hair at them both. She was in civilian clothes, a shirt and jeans with a silk scarf knotted loosely in her hair, and she looked amazing. Confidence and sunshine and power rolled off her. Joey had never seen such perfect hair before, even on television.

Astra smiled, and hooked her arm in Joey's. "Don't bother coming up, kid. I'll show the new girl up to the hero pad."

Mezza, obviously annoyed that he hadn't got to continue with his pathetic joke, sloped back to the reception desk.

"So," Astra said in the lift. "There will be cameras on you all the time up in the penthouse. Not just for today's media circus, but all the time. They're not supposed to be switched on outside official broadcast times, but they often are. If you need to adjust a bra strap or something, take it to the loos, or it will end up on a blooper reel somewhere."

"Thanks," Joey said quietly. Why didn't Astra seem to hate her? Was she pleased to be leaving, maybe? Joey had assumed she would be aloof and bitchy.

The lift took a few minutes to go all the way up the thirty-five floors of the tower, and in that time, Astra rattled off a bunch of other things that Joey needed to know. Tips and tricks for survival when you're the only girl in the team—and from some of her anecdotes, they weren't based just on her experience. Every female superhero had a duty to pass this stuff on to their replacement. "Oh, and don't let Vanish get you alone in a corner or a room," Astra finished, three floors from the top. "He's not good people."

"What about The Dark?" Joey asked nervously.

Astra flashed her a grin. "He's scary as hell, yeah? But The Dark is an okay bloke, deep down. He's not going to try to slip something into your drink, or feel you up in the middle of a burning building. Vanish is the one to worry about."

Joey opened her mouth to ask another question, but the lift door pinged open and suddenly there were lights and cameras crowded around them. "Here she is, our little star!" boomed a voice, and Astra got a bittersweet look on her face. She gave Joey a very stagey air-kiss, and then slipped away. Joey desperately wanted her to stay. For that short lift ride, for a few minutes, she hadn't felt alone.

The reporters were a lot like the girls at school, only she didn't have Willa to smack them in the face for asking questions like "Hey Joey, which superheroine Legacy do you most want to inherit?" "Hey Joey, is your costume going to be pants or no pants?" "Hey Joey, do you feel that this is a chance for you to finally live a normal life?"

Willa would totally have decked the jerk who asked that last one.

Joey winced into the lights. She found she couldn't actually move more than half a meter or so across the floor once she was out of the lift. They wanted her to pose and she couldn't quite bring herself to do that, but she smiled more broadly and stuck her chest out and did that thing she'd always done for pictures when she was little, where she turned slightly side-on and let her left arm rest slightly behind her hip so that she looked normal.

Once she realized that was what she was doing, she hated herself. So not cool.

Deliberately, she shifted again, looking towards a different obnoxious reporter who was asking her which of the hero boys she most wanted to hook up with (*Solar? Ew gross, isn't he old enough to be my dad?*). She brought her arm around so they could all get a good long look at the way her wrist curved into nothing instead of a hand.

Don't get hung up on what you haven't got, her mother's voice said inside her head. *Concentrate on positives, not negatives.*

If there was a pause in the questions in response to her showing them her arm, she did not hear it.

"Hey, Joey, what superpower do you want?" one of them hollered.

Joey looked right down the lens of whichever camera was closest to him. "Strength," she said. "A girl can only go so far with one-handed push ups."

They laughed, and took more pictures, and the tension broke inside her. She could do this.

Finally, the media sea parted, and a thin bald man in an offensively expensive suit came striding towards her, his hand out to shake hers. "Joey, Joey, Joey. I'm Clive Mandurah. Very glad to have you here. Nice for the Lottery to throw us up some young blood, eh?"

The crowd of journos tittered at that. Joey felt creeped out. Astra hadn't mentioned whether the team's manager was an okay bloke or not. There was definitely a "sit on my knee, little girl" vibe about him.

Clive's outstretched left hand, which was ready to shake hers several strides ago, finally plunged directly at her, only for him to realize in the last instance that he was aiming for the side where she was all curve and no fingers. He shifted to shake right hand to right with a cheesy grin at every single one of the cameras individually. "Come up here, my princess," he said with his teeth reflecting the glare of several spotlights. "Time to meet your team."

Joey looked up.

They stood there, all five of them, on a raised floor that looked like something off a chat show. Solar, wide-shouldered and powerful with that face that had been famous for so many decades, perpetually thirty years old, the golden sun god. Joey had always wondered how he got those muscles of his, if he was so strong. What did he have to bench press to build up muscle tone, planets?

Then there was The Dark, the second most longstanding hero of the team. He had been there since 1989. His face was masked and his long cape pooled out on the ground around his feet like an eternal shadow.

Around these two heroes of Aussie legend stood the more recent additions: Surf, the first indigenous Aboriginal superhero, who had resisted all of the PR attempts to make him look more "tribal" and had instead re-popularized the 90s grunge look of his Legacy, the first Surf, all dreadlocks and boardshorts.

Vanish, handsome and elegant and the one closest to Joey's own age, wore a retro stage-magician's costume, and there was nothing about him that screamed "predator". Joey was glad Astra had warned her.

Speaking of Astra, she was there too. She must have changed pretty rapidly as soon as she ducked out of that lift—but of course, they were good at that, weren't they? Astra's star-spangled leotard shone silver and blue in the bright lights, and while she definitely had a version of her costume that included sparkly yoga pants, today she was all bare leg, tits and teeth.

For the first time, Joey thought to herself: *what the hell kind of machine does this to people*?

"Time enough to chat with your new teammates when you're one of them," said Clive Mandurah, sweeping her onwards. "You've got a date with a machine, my little darling."

Everything went fast after that. Joey barely had time to look at the massive steel superhero machine before she was strapped into one of two glass-walled capsules that would transform her into a superhero. The other would retire one of the current team to make way for her. In the capsule, Joey could not move her head around. It was set up so that she could not see anything going on in the room, only a wall of screens broadcasting every TV station.

It was the usual scrawl that happened every Hero Day—a potted history of the machines that had appeared all at once in every country of the world in 1981, allowing humanity to create superheroes. Each machine created and retired the heroes, ran the Lottery which selected new candidates, chose which hero they would be, and made the final call as to which one would step down, to make room for the new.

Only a few aspects of the machine were actually programmable by mere humans. You could choose how often you changed over your heroes—or even if you did at all. The UK still had most of the team they had started with back in the 80s, apart from one or two who had died or resigned. In Japan, they changed heroes on their team every fortnight, churning through as many as they could of the millions of teenagers who wanted to be famous. Australia had chosen to follow the US system, with a changeover twice a year.

No one had told the machines that a team should only have one girl at a time—it simply turned out that way, nineteen times out of twenty, everywhere except Sweden which managed gender parity on average, and had at least twice had teams entirely made up of women. Willa always said that if you felt any doubt that whoever created the machines was a sexist bastard, all you had to do was look at the costumes it provided for female superheroes, and the way that every woman who went into the machine came out with her boobs several sizes bigger.

Joey could feel it starting to happen. She tingled all over as energy pummeled her body. Mysterious space radiation. Did anyone even know what the long term effects were of this stuff? What special cancers were superheroes likely to suffer from when they hit their sixties? Why hadn't she thought about these questions before she stepped into the box?

She concentrated on the TV screens, ignoring the distressing thing that was going on with her body, and the niggling worry that she was going to step out looking like a porn star. The screens showed Solar, Solar, Solar, smiling and flexing and lifting cars. She saw images of him with the first team in the 80s, and then with other teammates through the 90s and 00s. Romances with journalists, because who else did he meet except for heroes and villains? Solar's failed marriage to TV presenter Molly Mathers. All the good he had done, in the centre of the team.

Joey had never crunched the numbers before. If he was like, twenty-five in 1981, and that was a rough guess, then Solar had to be at least sixty now. Not old enough to be her dad—nearly old enough to be her granddad.

Did they usually put this much on the TV about him, on Hero Day? Everyone knew that The Dark was the cool one that got most of the media coverage, even though he refused to choose a brand sponsor.

But the screens continued to flash up history about Solar and his career, over and over, until gradually each of them flicked to a live feed here in the penthouse at the top of the Sky Tower. Ignoring the slow burning numbness that worked its way up her legs, Joey stared at the two glass-walled capsules of the machine. She could almost see her own blurred face in one of them, and the light building up from below, transforming her into something Else.

She did not, however, miss the sight of Solar walking with great dignity into the other capsule.

"No," Joey breathed, realizing finally that it wasn't Astra who was being kicked out to make room for her on the team. It was Australia's Greatest Hero. *They're all going to hate me...*

She shouldn't have opened her mouth. The light burned upwards now, more fierce than before, and every cell in her body screamed out as it flooded with power. The fingers of her right hand spread wide as light beams shot out of each of them, but Joey's eyes dragged down to her other arm.

She could see the shape of a new, perfect hand forming there, her arm tapering into it instead of the familiar curve. A second hand would be useful, normal, symmetrical. Basic.

Could she be a superhero without it? Did she want to be?

On the screens before Joey, an ordinary looking man stepped out of the machine and walked away. Gone was the big cheesy smile, the muscles. Even his ridiculous handsomeness had, it seemed, been provided straight out of the box. Cookie cutter superheroes. Perhaps someone else would get his handsomeness in the future.

Everything could be recycled, right?

How would Joey feel to have a perfect left hand for six months, and lose it again at the end?

How would she feel to have a perfect left hand at all? If she let the capsule do that, was it a lie that she had coped fine without it, that she had "managed her disability" with such good grace, as the counselors said?

Was she letting every disabled person in the world down if she took this the gift that the capsule was right now building for her out of light? Was she letting them all down if she did not?

Her left arm flickered, and the ghost of a hand disappeared, then appeared again. On, off, on, off.

Some people said you could choose what happened in the machine. Others said there was no chance, no option. Had Solar chosen to leave? Had the machine allowed him to retire because of some deep desire in him to be done? Or was she asking those questions to make herself feel better?

Joey stared at the curve-that-was-not and could not decide. As she hesitated, her new hand also dipped in and out of reality. Everything else burned, and she didn't even notice.

Yes—no—I want—I don't need—this is stupid.

She closed her eyes and screamed as the heat overwhelmed her.

I worked sixteen years to feel like my arm was normal. Isn't this cheating?

Also, I don't want my boobs to change. I finally got them the right size this year. All my clothes fit nicely.

Then the light was gone. Time lurched forwards. Joey found herself crumpled on the floor, gasping. Out of the capsule. She was out, though she didn't remember that part of it. The team stood around her, protecting her from the cameras. The Dark's cloak spread over them all like a fence of shadows.

Astra was there, holding Joey. Her blonde hair flipped back and forth like it was a character in a different story. "Are you all right?"

"I feel strong," Joey whispered back. She could feel it in every muscle, every limb, every cell. Oh, she was wearing lycra. That was new. It clung to her, all tight and soft. Her costume was mostly blue and yellow.

She stared down at her cleavage, wondering if she had been given any extra, or if that was just the effect of the lycra.

"Strong is good," said Astra.

Joey looked at the other woman. "You're still here."

"Yes," said Astra with a smile. "How about that? There are two of us now."

The Dark cleared his throat. "They want to know."

Joey looked up at him, and then across the penthouse to the machine. One word still scrawled across its screens. SOLAR, it said. That must have been a shock to them all. The journos were oddly quiet and restrained back there. "Where's my hero name? Who am I?" she asked.

"They want to know, mate," put in Surf. "Do you want to be Solar Girl, or Solar Woman? One of the jokers suggested Solarette but I don't recommend that one. Sounds like a nicotine patch."

Oh. Oh. A Legacy after all.

Solar.

Solar had never been a girl before. He had just been Solar.

Joey looked down at herself. No fake muscles, at least. She didn't know yet if the cookie cutter machine had made her prettier, or given her perfect hair, and the jury was still out on the boobs. But here she was, with one wrist that tapered into a rounded curve and another that was attached to a hand.

This, at least, was perfectly normal. Joey was glad that something was.

She could feel the strength coursing through her, crazy strength, and if she had the same powers as Solar, it would only take a few hours of sunbathing to build that strength up to planet-bench-pressing levels. The curve was a blunt instrument now, and she imagined smashing it through walls, tearing down whole buildings. No need to be careful with herself.

"Solar," she said in a low voice.

"You heard her," said Astra, louder. "She's Solar. No girlie version. Any of you hacks puts a 'Miss' in front of it, you'll answer to me."

"When can I start hitting things?" Joey whispered. Planets would have to wait, but she was so completely up for bench-pressing cars right now.

Astra gave her a hug, and a genuine kiss on the cheek. "Soon," she promised. They stood up and went to join their teammates.

"Hey, Solar," Astra said without moving her mouth, as they

all lined up and posed together. "Guess what? You're a sixteen-year-old who just deposed the most powerful man in the world. Completely no one is thinking about your arm right now."

Caught in the glare of the flashing lights and the cries of the journos (who were all shouting, "Solar, Solar over here," no longer using her real name), Joey froze for one brief moment, and then forced herself to smile.

First day on the job.

Seventh Day of the Seventh Moon

By Ken Liu

"Tell me a story," said Se. She had changed into her pajamas all by herself and snuggled under the blankets.

Se's big sister, Yuan, was just about to flip the switch next to the bedroom door. "How about you read a story by yourself? I have to … go see a friend."

"No, it's not the same." Se shook her head vigorously. "You have to tell me a story or I can't sleep."

Yuan glanced at her phone. Every minute tonight was precious. Dad was out of town on business, and Mom was working late and wouldn't be home till midnight. Yuan needed to be home before then, but if she could get her little sister to sleep quickly, she'd still have a couple of hours to see Jing on this, her last night in China.

"Come on, Yuan," Se begged. "Please!"

Yuan came back to the side of the bed and stroked Se's forehead gently. She sighed. "All right."

She texted Jing: *Late by half hour. Wait?*

The crystal cat charm, a gift from Jing, dangled from her phone. It twirled and glittered in the warm bedroom light as she waited impatiently for the response.

Finally, the phone beeped. *Of course. Won't leave until we meet.*

"Tell the story about the Qixi Festival," said Se, yawning. "That's tonight, isn't it?"

"Yes, yes it is."

Long ago, a beautiful young woman, the granddaughter of the Emperor of Heaven, lived in the sky by the eastern shore of the Silver River—that's the broad band of light you can sometimes see in the sky at night, when the air is clear.

She was skilled at the loom, and so that's why people called her—

"You skipped the part where you describe her weaving!"

"But you've heard this story a hundred times already. Can't I just get it over with?"

"You have to tell it right."

—as I had apparently neglected to mention: her works were displayed proudly by the Heavenly Court in the western sky at every sunset: glorious clouds of crimson, amethyst, periwinkle, and every shade in between. So people called her Zhinü, the Weaver Girl. And though she was the youngest of seven immortal sisters, we mortals addressed her by the honorific Big Sister Seven.

But over time, Zhinü grew wan and thin. Her brows were always tightly knit into a frown, and she did not wash her face or comb out her hair. The sunset clouds she wove were not as lovely as before, and mortals began to complain.

The Emperor of Heaven came to visit. "What ails you, my granddaughter?"

"Haha, you do that voice so well. You sound just like Grandfather."

"I'm glad you approve. Now stop interrupting."

"Oh, *Gonggong*, I'm so lonely. Living all by myself in this hut, my only company are my loom—*jiya, jiya*, it squeaks all day long—and a few magpies."

The Emperor took pity on her and found her a good match. The young man tended to cows on the western shore of the Silver River, so people called him Niulang, the Cowherd. He was handsome and kind and full of funny stories, and Zhinü loved him, and he her, the moment they set eyes on each other.

"See, I'm not such a bad matchmaker." The Emperor of Heaven smiled as he stroked his beard. "Now, I know you're young, and you should have fun. But now that you have a companion, please don't neglect your work."

Zhinü moved to the western shore of the Silver River to be with Niulang, and the two of them married. They had two boys, and there never was a happier family.

"Oh, no, here comes the boring part. You can skip it if you want to."

"No way! This is the best part. You'll understand when you're older. Now pay attention."

Every morning, as Niulang got up before sunrise to take the cows to their favorite pasture, Zhinü could not bear the thought of being separated from him. So she would come along. She'd put the two babies in two baskets draped on each side of an old, gentle ox, and she would ride on the back of a pure white bull led by Niulang. They'd sing together, tell each other stories from before they met, and laugh at the jokes that only they understood.

Zhinü's loom sat unused back at the hut, gathering dust.

Sunsets became ugly affairs. The few clouds that remained became tattered, wispy, colorless. The people laboring in the fields lost the beauty that had once lifted up their hearts at the end of a hard day, and their laments rose to the Heavenly Court.

"My maritorious child," said the Emperor of Heaven—

"What does that word mean?"

"It means loving your husband too much."

"How can you love someone too much?"

"Good question. I don't know either. Maybe the Emperor of Heaven didn't have enough love in his heart to understand. Maybe he was too old."

—"I warned you about neglecting your duty. For your disobedience and neglect, you must now move back to the eastern shore of the Silver River and never see Niulang and your children again."

Zhinü begged for reprieve, but the Emperor's word was as irreversible as the flow of the Silver River.

At the Emperor's decree, the Silver River was widened and deepened, and Zhinü forever parted from her husband. Today, you can see the star that is Zhinü on one side of the Silver River and the star that is Niulang on the other, their two sons two faint stars on each side of Niulang. They stare at each other across that unbridgeable gap, the longing and regret as endless as the flowing river.

"Why did you stop?"

"It's nothing. My throat just felt itchy for a bit."

"Are you sad for Niulang and Zhinü?"

"Maybe … a little bit. But it's just a story."

But the magpies that once kept Zhinü company took pity on the lovers. Once a year, on the seventh day of the seventh moon by the lunar calendar, on Qixi, the day when Zhinü is at her highest position in the sky, all the magpies in the world fly up to the Silver River and make a bridge with their bodies so that the lovers can spend one night together.

This is the day when all the young women in old China would pray to Big Sister Seven for love.

Oh, I know you want to hear more about the bridge of magpies. You love this part. Well, I imagine it's a lot of work for the birds. They probably have to go to magpie bridge-building school, and those who're a bit slow have to go to cram school for extra study sessions…

Yuan turned out the light and tiptoed out of her sister's bedroom.

On my way, she texted.

She made sure the air conditioning was set comfortably low, locked the door of the apartment, and ran down the stairs. And then she was in the hot, humid evening air of Hefei in August.

She biked through the streets, dodging an endless stream of cars beeping their horns. She liked the physicality of the ride, the way it made her body come alive, feel awake. She passed the sidewalks filled with people browsing past stores and kiosks filled with everything imaginable: discount electronics, toys, clothes, fancy European soups and cakes, mouth-watering sweet potatoes baked in tinfoil and fried, smelly tofu. The heat and the exertion stuck her shirt to her skin, and she had to wipe her forehead from time to time to keep the sweat out of her eyes.

And then she was at the coffee shop, and Jing—slender, graceful in a plain white dress and a light jacket (for the air conditioning), a faint whiff of the floral perfume that always made Yuan dizzy—greeted Yuan with that bright smile that she always wore.

As if this wasn't the night the world ended.

"Are you done packing?" Yuan asked.

"Oh, there's always more to pack." Jing's tone was light, breezy, careless. "But I don't have to get to the airport till nine in the morning. There's plenty of time."

"You should dress in layers, with something long-sleeved on top," said Yuan—mainly because she feared saying nothing. "It can get cold on the plane."

"Want to take a walk with me? The next time I walk around at night I'll be in America. Maybe I'll miss all this noise."

Yuan left her bike locked to the light post outside the coffee shop, and they strolled along the sidewalk like the rest of the crowd. They did not hold hands. In Shanghai, perhaps no one would have cared, but in Hefei, there would have been looks, and whispers, and maybe worse.

Yuan imagined Jing walking about the campus of the American high school at night. Jing had shown her pictures of the red brick buildings and immaculate lawns. And the smiling boys and girls: foreigners. Yuan felt out of breath; her heart seemed unable to decide on a steady rhythm.

"Look at that," said Jing, pointing to the display window of a pastry shop. "They're selling Qixi Lovers' Cakes now. So overpriced. And you know some stupid girl is going to throw a fit if her boyfriend doesn't buy it for her. I want to throw up."

"Not quite as bad as Valentine's Day," Yuan said. "I think the vendors are pretty restrained. Relatively speaking."

"That's because people aren't into Qixi any more. We Chinese always get more enthusiastic for Western imports, even holidays. It's a national character weakness."

"I like Qixi," Yuan said. She said it more emphatically than she meant to.

"What, you want to set out an altar under a melon trellis, offer up a plate of fruits, pray to Big Sister Seven, and hope for a spider to weave a web over the offering by morning so you'll get a nice husband in the future?"

Yuan's face grew hot. She stopped. "You don't have to mock everything Chinese."

Jing cocked her head, a teasing smile in her eyes. "You suddenly getting all patriotic on me now?"

"Your father has the money to pay for you to go to an American boarding school. That doesn't make you better than everyone else."

"Oh, lay off that wounded tone. You're hardly some migrant worker's daughter."

They stared at each other, the neon lights from the nearby stores flickering over their faces. Yuan wanted to kiss Jing and scream at her at the same time. She had always liked Jing's irreverence, the way she wanted to turn everything into a joke. She knew her anger had nothing to do with this conversation about Qixi at all.

Jing turned and continued down the sidewalk. After a moment, Yuan followed.

When Jing spoke again, her tone was calm, as if nothing had happened. "Remember the first time we went hiking together?"

That had been one of the best days of Yuan's life. They had skipped their cram school sessions and taken the bus to Emerald Lake, an artificial pond bordering several college campuses. Jing had showed Yuan how to set up her phone so that her mom couldn't see the messages Jing sent her, and Yuan had showed Jing her baby pictures. They had bought a lamb *chuanr* from a street vendor and shared it as they walked along the lakeshore. Her heart had beaten faster with each bite of roasted meat off the skewer, thinking that her lips were touching where *hers* had touched. And then, as they strolled through one of the campuses, Jing had boldly taken her hand: it was a college, after all.

And then that first kiss behind the willow tree, tasting the hot spices from the lamb kebab on Jing's tongue, the calls of wild geese behind her somewhere...

"I remember," she said. Her voice still sounded wounded, and she didn't care.

"I wish we could go there again," Jing said.

The anger in Yuan disappeared, just like that. Jing always had such a way with her. Yuan felt like putty in her hands.

"We can chat on QQ or Skype," Yuan said. She hurried to catch up so that she was walking next to Jing. "And you'll come back for visits. This isn't like the old days. It will be okay. We can still be together."

They had wandered off the main thoroughfare onto a less busy side street. The streetlights on one side were out, and looking up they could see a few stars in the sky. Hefei wasn't as polluted as some of the cities on the coast.

"I'm going to be really busy," Jing said. Her tone was calm, too calm.

"We can text every day, every hour."

"It's different over there. I'll be living on my own in a dorm. I have to actually study if I want to go to a good college. My family is paying a lot to give me this."

"Americans don't study that much."

"It's not like watching American TV shows. There aren't subtitles. I'll meet lots of new people. I have to make a new life over there, new friends. I'll need to be thinking, talking, breathing English all the time if I want to make it."

"I can text you in English," Yuan said. "I'll do whatever you want."

"You're not listening," Jing said. She stopped again and looked at Yuan.

"What are you trying to say?" As soon as she asked the question, Yuan regretted it. It made her sound so weak, so clingy, like a girl from one of those Korean dramas.

"I'm going away, Yuan. I told you this was going to happen last year, when we … started."

Yuan looked away so that Jing would not see her eyes. She pushed the image of Jing with someone else out of her mind. She cursed her eyes and told them to behave and stop embarrassing her.

"It will be okay." Jing's tone was now comforting, gentle, and that made it worse. "We'll both be okay."

Yuan said nothing because she knew she couldn't control her voice. She licked her lips, tasting the salt from the sweat of her ride. She wanted to wipe her eyes so she could see clearly again, but she didn't want to do it in front of Jing.

"I want to make this night a happy memory," Jing said, but her voice finally cracked. She struggled, but failed, to keep her calm mask on. "I'm trying to make this easier. Isn't that what you're supposed to do for those you love?"

Yuan looked up, blinking her eyes hard. She looked for the Silver River, and she remembered that in English it was called the Milky Way—what a graceless and silly name. She looked for Zhinü and Niulang, and she vaguely remembered that in English they were called Vega and Altair, names as cold and meaningless to her as the stars.

Just then, magpies seemed to come out of nowhere and gathered over their heads in a cloud of fluttering wings. While they looked up, stunned, the flock swept out of the night sky, descended over them like a giant spider web, and lifted them into the heavens.

Riding on the wings of magpies, Yuan found, was not like riding a magical carpet.

Not that she knew what riding a magical carpet felt like—but she was sure that it didn't involve being constantly poked from below by a hundred—no, a thousand—little winged fists.

The magpies would fall a bit below where they were and flap their wings rapidly in an upward burst until they collided with the girls' bodies. The combined force of all the magpies would push them up until the birds lost their momentum and began to fall away, and then a new wave of upward-thrusting magpies would take their place. The girls resembled two ping-pong balls riding on the water spout from a hose pointing up.

In the maelstrom of wings they found each other and clung together.

"Are you all right?" They each asked at the same time.

"What in the world is happening?" Jing asked, her words jumbled together from fear and excitement.

"This is a dream," Yuan said. "This must be a dream."

And then Jing began to laugh.

"It can't be a dream," she said. "These magpies carrying us: they tickle!"

And Yuan laughed too. It was so absurd, so impossible; yet it was happening.

Some of the magpies began to sing, a complicated, trilling, lovely chorus. There were magpies of every description: some with white bellies, some with white beaks, some with iridescent, shimmering, blue wings. Yuan felt as if she and Jing were enclosed inside the beating heart of some giant, flying, alien musical instrument.

Arms around each other, gingerly sitting side by side, they peeked out at the world below from between the darting wings of the magpies.

They were floating in a dark sea. The lights of the city of Hefei spread out below them like a pulsing, receding jellyfish.

"It's getting cold," said Yuan. She shivered as the wind whipped her hair around her face.

"We're really high up," said Jing. She took off her summer jacket and draped it around Yuan's shoulders. Yuan tucked her nose into the collar of the jacket and breathed in the lingering perfume. It warmed her heart even if the thin fabric did little against the chill.

Then Yuan berated herself. Jing had broken up with her, and she didn't need to look so needy, so pathetic. It was fine to cling to Jing in a moment of weakness, but now they were safe. Gently, she took her arm from around Jing and shrugged out of her arm as well. She lifted her face into the clear, frosty air, and tried to shift away from Jing, keeping some distance between them.

"Reminds you of Su Shi's poem, doesn't it?" Jing whispered. Yuan nodded reluctantly. Jing was the literary one, and she always knew the pretty words, suitable for every occasion.

A half moon, like a half-veiled smile, loomed pale white in the dark sky. It grew brighter and larger as they rose on the backs of the magpies.

Jing began to sing the words of the Song Dynasty poem, set to a popular tune, and after a moment, Yuan joined her:

When did the Moon first appear?
I ask the heavens and lift my wine cup.
I know not whether time passes the same way
In the palace among the clouds.

I'd like to ride up with the wind,
But I'm afraid of the chill from being so high
Among the jade porticos and nephrite beams.

We dance with our shadows.
Are we even on earth any more?
The silver light dapples the window,
Illuminating my sleepless night.
Do you hate us, Moon?
Why are you always waxing just when we're parting?

Like a dancer and her shadow, the two girls swayed, each separately, to a harmony as young as themselves and as old as the land beneath.

"So, it's all true," said Jing.

The magpies had lifted them above the clouds and leveled off. As they glided over the cottony mists, they could see a celestial city of bread loaf-like buildings, punctuated by spiky towers here and there, gleaming in the late summer moonlight in the distance: blue as ice, green as jade, white like ivory. The styles of the buildings were neither Western nor Chinese, but something that transcended them all: heavenly, the Palace of Immortals.

"I wonder if there really are immortals living there," said Yuan. What she didn't say out loud was her secret hope: she and Jing had been picked by the magpies for this trip to the heavens because the immortals thought they were as special a pair as Niulang and Zhinü—the thought was tinged with both excitement and sorrow.

And then they were at the Silver River. It was broader than the Yangtze, almost like Taihu Lake, with the other shore barely visible on the horizon. The rushing torrent roared past like stampeding horses, and giant waves as tall as the apartment buildings in Hefei pounded against the shore.

"Hey, don't carry us over the water!" Jing shouted. But the magpies ignored her and continued to fly towards the river.

"They're building a bridge," said Yuan. "It's Qixi, remember?"

Indeed, more flocks of magpies appeared. Along with the flock carrying the girls, they congregated like rivulets coalescing into a mighty river of wings. The magpies hovered over the water, with newcomers extending the flock's reach towards the other shore. They were forming an arching bridge over the Silver River.

"I have to take a picture of this," said Yuan, and she took out her cell phone.

The crystal cat charm dangling from the phone caught the light of the moon and dazzled. The magpies immediately surrounding Yuan trilled and dashed at it, knocking the phone out of her hand. And then it was a free for all as more of the magpies forgot about building the bridge and rushed after the shiny bauble. Even when charged with a magical mission, birds were still just birds.

Or maybe even the birds have realized we're not such a special pair after all, Yuan thought, *and the charm is more interesting.*

She gazed after her phone anxiously. If Se woke up from a nightmare, she might try to call her. And if her mom got home before her, she might wonder where she was. She needed that phone back. She hoped the birds would bounce the phone closer to her so she could snatch it.

Then those worries were pushed out of her mind as the magpies that had supported Yuan dropped off to join the chase after the charm, and no new magpies replaced them. Her weight overwhelmed the few magpies that remained on task, and she began to fall. She didn't even have time to cry out.

But then a strong hand caught her right wrist and arrested her descent. Yuan looked up into Jing's face. She was lying down on the bridge of magpies, and she strained as she reached out and held onto Yuan with one hand while fumbling in her purse with the other.

"Let go!" shouted Yuan. "You'll fall, too!" Her world seemed to shrink down to her hands as they clasped around Jing's hand, around her warm, pale skin. She willed herself to let go, but she could not.

"Don't be ridiculous," said Jing, panting.

The magpies continued to fight each other for the shiny charm, causing Yuan's phone to bob up and down over the flock like a stone skipping over water. They had stopped extending the living bridge over the water.

Jing finally managed to free her own phone from her purse. She paid no attention as her purse almost tumbled over the side of the bridge, where it would have disappeared into the roiling waves below. By feel, she pressed the first button on the dial pad.

Yuan's phone came to life and began to vibrate and buzz. The shocked magpies backed off in a panic, and the phone stayed still in the air for a second before falling, faster and faster, and finally disappeared into the Silver River without a trace.

Yuan felt her heart sink. *That cat charm, the first gift Jing had ever given her, now gone forever.*

"Good thing I have you on speed dial," Jing said.

"How do we still have reception here?"

"After all that, *that*'s what you are worried about?" Jing laughed, and after a moment, Yuan joined her.

The magpies seemed to have awakened from a bad dream, and they rushed over and lifted Yuan up onto the bridge. Once the girls were safe, the magpies continued to extend their bridge to the other side of the Silver River, leaving the pair at the middle of the bridge, suspended over the endless water and mist.

"We almost caused the magpies to fail to build the bridge," Yuan said. "It would be so sad if Niulang and Zhinü don't get to meet this year."

Jing nodded. "It's almost midnight." She saw the look on Yuan's face. "Don't worry about not being home. Nothing bad can happen on the night of Qixi."

"I thought you weren't into Qixi."

"Well, maybe just a little bit."

They sat down on the bridge together, watching the moon rise over the Silver River. This time, Yuan did not let go of Jing's hand.

"She's coming," said Yuan. She jumped up and pointed down the bridge towards the eastern shore. Now that she had spent some time on the bridge of magpies, she was getting pretty good at keeping her footing over the fluttering wings.

In the distance, through the mist that wafted over the bridge from time to time, they could see a small, solitary figure making its way towards them.

"So is he," said Jing. She pointed the other way. Through the mist they could see another tiny figure slowly creep towards them.

The girls stood up and waited, side by side, looking first one way and then the other. Being in the presence of the annual reunion of this pair of legendary lovers was exciting, maybe even better than meeting TV stars.

The two figures from the opposite ends of the bridge came close enough for Yuan and Jing to see them clearly.

Out of the east, an old woman approached. Yuan thought she looked as old as, maybe even older than, her grandmother. Her back bent, she walked with a cane. But her wrinkled face glowed healthily with the exertion of having traveled all the way here. Wearing a Tang Dynasty dress, she looked splendid to Yuan. Her breath puffed out visibly in the cold air.

Out of the west, an old man emerged from the mist: straight back, long legs, wiry arms swinging freely. His full head of silvery white hair matched the old woman's, but his face was even more wrinkled than hers. As soon as he saw the old woman, his eyes lit up in a bright smile.

"They're not—" Jing started to say in a whisper.

"—quite what we expected?" finished Yuan.

"I guess I always pictured immortals as being … well, I guess there's no reason to think they wouldn't grow old."

A wispy tendril of sorrow brushed across Yuan's heart. She tried to imagine Jing as an old woman, and the tenderness made her almost tear up again. She squeezed Jing's hand, and Jing squeezed back, turning to smile at her.

The old man and the old woman met in the middle of the bridge, a few paces away from where the girls stood. They nodded at Jing and Yuan politely and then turned their full attention to each other.

"Glad to see you looking so well," said Zhinü. "Da Lang told me that you were having some trouble with your back the last time he visited with his family. I wasn't sure you were going to make it here this year."

"Da Lang always exaggerates," said Niulang. "When he visits I don't dare to sneeze or cough, lest he insist that I go to the moon to visit Chang'E for some Osmanthus herbs. This old bag of bones can't really take any more medicine. I think he's more upset than you or I that his brother didn't want to be a doctor."

They laughed and chatted on, talking about children and friends.

"Why don't they kiss?" Jing whispered to Yuan.

"That's a Western thing," Yuan whispered back. "Niulang and Zhinü are old school."

"I'm not sure that's true. I've seen internet posts arguing people in ancient China used to kiss—but anyway, they're standing so far apart!"

"It's like they're friends, not lovers."

"It seems that we have some curious guests," said Zhinü as she turned around to look at the girls. She didn't sound angry—more like amused.

"We're sorry," said Yuan, feeling her face grow hot. "We didn't mean to be rude." She hesitated. It didn't seem right at all to call this old woman "Big Sister Seven". So she added, "Grandma Zhinü and Grandpa Niulang."

"We just thought," Jing said, "that … um … you'd be more … passionate."

"You mean less laughing, and more tears and recitation of love poems," said Niulang, a gentle smile in his eyes.

"Yes," said Jing. "No," said Yuan, simultaneously.

Zhinü and Niulang laughed out loud. Niulang said, "It's okay. The magpies have been building this bridge for thousands of years, and they sometimes bring guests. We're used to questions."

Zhinü looked from Yuan to Jing and back again. "You two are together?"

"Yes," said Jing. "No," said Yuan, simultaneously. They looked at each other, embarrassed.

"Now *that* sounds like a story," said Zhinü.

"We *were* together," said Yuan.

"But I'm leaving," said Jing. "We'll be parted by the Pacific Ocean." And they told their story to Niulang and Zhinü. It seemed perfectly right to pour their hearts out to the legendary lovers.

"I understand," said Zhinü, nodding sympathetically. "Oh, do I understand."

At first I was inconsolable. I stood on the shore of the Silver River day after day, pining for a glance of my husband and children. I thought the pain in my heart would never go away. I refused to touch my loom. If my grandfather was angry, then let him find someone else to weave the sunsets. I was done.

The first time we met over the bridge of magpies, Niulang and I could not stop crying the whole time. My children were growing up so fast, and I felt so guilty. So, when we had to part again, Niulang came up with a stratagem: he asked the magpies to retrieve two large rocks that were about the weight of my babies and carried them home in two baskets on the ends of a pole over his shoulder, the same way he had carried the boys onto the bridge. And everyone thought they had gone home with him. But unbeknownst to anyone else, I carried the boys home with me on my back.

And after that, every year, as we met on the bridge, we passed the boys back and forth. They'd spend one year with me, one year with Niulang. They would not have their parents together, but they would have both of them.

Each time we met, I told him again and again of the solitude of my hut, the desultory squeak of my loom. And he told me of how he took his herd to the same pastures that we had gone to as a family, to relive the happiness we shared. The grass had grown thin and bare from overgrazing, and his animals were just skin and bones.

And then, one year, when the boys were a little older and could walk on their own, Niulang held me and told me that he didn't want to see me sad any more.

"We live a whole year for this one day," he said. "We're letting our lives pass us by. It's not right that you should sit by your loom pining from morning till evening. It's not right that our sons should think our lives are lives of sorrow. It's not right that we should come to believe that yearning for what we can't have is what love is all about."

"What are you saying?" I asked. I was angry, and I didn't know why. Was he saying that he no longer loved me? I had been faithful to him, but had he been to me?

"We know we cannot be together," he said. "We know that sometimes things happen to people that keep them apart. But we have refused to look for new happiness. Are we sad because we're in love? Or are we sad because we feel trapped by the idea of love?"

I thought about what he said, and realized that he was right. I had become so used to the story about us, the idea of us living our whole lives for this once-a-year meeting that I hadn't really thought about what I wanted. I had become my own legend. Sometimes the stories we tell ourselves obscure our truths.

"You're beautiful when you laugh," he said.

"We're beautiful when we seek to make ourselves happy," I said.

And so I went back to my loom and poured my love for Niulang into my weaving. I thought those were some of the most beautiful sunsets I had ever woven.

And then I found that love was not a limited thing, but an endless fount. I found that I loved the laughter of my children, and the chatter of friends new and old. I found that I loved the fresh breeze that brought smells from far away. I found that other young men made my heart beat faster.

And Niulang went and took his herd to new pastures, and he came up with new songs. Young women came and listened to him, and he found that conversation with them gladdened his heart.

We told each other these things the next time we met over the bridge. I was glad for him and he for me. We had been clinging to each other as though we were afraid to drown, but in fact, we had been holding each other back from moving on.

"And so we each went on and had other loves, joys as well as sorrows," said Zhinü.

"We still meet once a year," said Niulang, "to catch up on each other's lives. Old friends are hard to come by." He and Zhinü looked at each other with affection. "They keep you honest."

"Are you disappointed?" asked Zhinü.

Jing and Yuan looked at each other. "Yes," they said together. Then they said "no," also together.

"Then, are you not in love anymore?" asked Yuan.

"You ask that question because you think if we're no longer in love, then that means the love we had was somehow not real." Zhinü turned serious. "But the past does not get rewritten. Niulang was the first man I loved, and that would be true no matter how many times I fell in love after him."

"It's time to go," Niulang said. The magpies under them were getting restless. The eastern sky was brightening.

"You were together, and you're together now," said Niulang to the girls. "Whatever comes, *that* remains a fact."

"You look lovely together, dears," said Zhinü.

Niulang and Zhinü embraced lightly and wished each other well. Then they turned and began to walk in opposite directions.

"Look!" said Jing, and gripped Yuan's hand.

Where the old Niulang and Zhinü had been, there was now a pair of ghostly figures: a young man and a young woman. They embraced tightly, as if Yuan and Jing were not there at all.

"They were such a handsome couple," said Yuan.

"They still are," said Jing.

And as the bridge of magpies broke up, carrying the girls down to earth, they looked back at the pair of ghost lovers dissolving gradually in the moonlight.

Miraculously, Yuan found her bike where she'd left it.

The sidewalks were still relatively empty. The first breakfast shops were just getting ready for the day, and the smell of warm soy milk and freshly fried *youtiao* filled the air.

"Better rush home," said Yuan. "Don't miss your flight."

"And you need to go, too. Your mom will be worried sick!"

Jing pulled her in, wrapping her arms around her. Yuan tried to pull back. "People will see."

"I don't care," Jing said. "I lied that day at Emerald Lake. I told you I had kissed other girls before. But you were the first. I want you to know that."

They held each other and cried, and some of the passers-by gave them curious looks, but no one stopped.

"I'll call you every day," Jing said. "I'll text you whenever I get a chance."

Yuan pulled back. "No. I don't want you to think of it as a chore. Do it if you want to. And if you don't, I'll understand. Let whatever will happen, happen."

A quick kiss, and Yuan pushed Jing away. "Go, go!"

She watched as Jing ran down the street to catch the bus. She watched as the bus pulled into the stream of traffic, a mighty river of steel like the Silver River, and disappeared around the corner.

"I love you," Yuan whispered. And no matter how the stream of time flowed on, that moment would be true forever.

The Legend Trap

by Sean Williams

Three teenagers step into a booth.

It's the oldest story in the world. Some dumb kid *always* wants to put it to the test. "It" could be any number of things. Jumping when the d-mat process starts to see if it makes you taller. Spinning in a circle anticlockwise in the hope of being switched from left to right. Squeezing thirteen people in at once *just in case* the one with the guiltiest secret disappears.

Or, in this case, the Bashert Ostension.

"It's never going to work," said Damon. The tallest of the three, he also thought he was the smartest, but that distinction probably went to Lydia, Jude's girlfriend. Lydia was skinny like Damon, but with angular hips and long hair in a braid down her back. She was cloud-pale and gray-eyed, and the opposite in almost every respect to Jude. Jude was short, muscular, and dark. She had a tattoo of a small, gray mouse above her left breast. That was how she thought of Lydia, she said: permanently close to her heart. But really it was more about the mouse. Jude liked to dominate.

"Scared?" she said.

"Not at all," said Damon, running a hand through his thin, brown hair. It needed a wash. It usually did, but particularly today. Maybe he was a *little* on edge. "Just being practical. What you're talking about is magic. D-mat isn't *magic*. It's a machine. Urban myths are fun and all, but they're not *real*."

"Who says? Maybe this one is."

"Rituals are real," said Lydia. Her voice was soft. Generally her friends stopped to listen. "We're on a legend trip—you know, checking out a graveyard or a spooky old house? That's what it's called. On the way we tell stories and prove our bravery and bond, and ... oh! We should've brought beer."

Jude produced a small silver flask from her back pocket. "Way ahead of you, babe." She took a swig and passed some of the burning liquor to Lydia through a messy, wet kiss.

Damon sniffed. "I don't need to prove anything. And you two do enough *bonding* as is."

Lydia laughed, pressing a hand to her sternum, where warmth was spreading outward in waves.

"Chicken," she said.

"Yeah, chicken out if you want, Lame-o Dame-o," said Jude. "We're going anyway."

He reached for the flask. She gave it to him. He wiped the neck on his sleeve and deliberately took too much—an asshole tax, he thought of it, not realizing that made him the asshole. For a second he thought he might cough, which would have been devastating.

"So let's do it," he said in a thin, tight voice.

Jude looked at Lydia, who nodded and took her hand.

"Ready?"

"Steady."

"Take us to the Bashert Ostension," Jude said in a clear, loud voice.

The booth doors slid shut. Mirrored walls enclosed them, throwing reflections to infinity in all directions. Light flashed. The three of them held their breaths and were silent.

There are lots of different versions of this particular urban myth, but they all boil down to the same thing.

> *Sometimes you jump somewhere by d-mat but don't arrive where you're supposed to. It looks like the right place, but it's not. There are small differences buried down deep in the details. At first you think you're going crazy, but it's actually the world around you that's crazy—because it's not your world anymore. You've gone sideways, into the universe next door.*

Sometimes there's a sting in the tale.

Look around you. Look CLOSELY. Maybe it's already happened to you, and you just haven't noticed yet.

You can usually write off such tales as older kids messing with younger ones. It's a tradition that dates right back to the first hominids, to whoever or whatever first discovered that language is a powerful tool to mess with those around you, for fun or profit. Some people have argued that the fun-or-profit motive actually drove the evolution of language. Either way, the urban myth predates religion and science and will probably outlast both of them.

The version of the story Jude, Lydia and Damon knew possessed one critical extension.

You can make it happen by asking for a specific destination.

The name of that destination was the Bashert Ostension.

The lights went down. The doors slid open. All three teens peered out.

Their reflections parted to reveal a forest of spindly pine trees painted warm yellows and oranges by sunset. Damon noted the crescent moon in the sky above. Jude sniffed at a faint tang of deer musk. Lydia heard a swallow call and saw a flash of white through the branches that might have been the bird responsible. She had read that swallows were albino here, sometimes.

"Are we having fun yet?" asked Damon.

"Be real, dumbass," said Jude. "Give it a moment."

They stepped out into the dusk to examine their flourishes.

This was part of the ritual that Damon had devised. If the myth was true, the booth wouldn't take them somewhere else in their world, like d-mat normally did; it would take them somewhere that looked the same as their world, except for some tiny details. So each of them had brought a trove of things they could tell quickly had changed—because who could remember if a leaf had fallen or changed color or whatever?

If they were going to do this they were going to do it right, he said, and that meant testing the hypothesis in a methodical way.

Doing it right to Lydia also meant finding exactly the right place to do it. They needed somewhere atmospheric, to enhance the ritual, yet at the same time somewhere away from other people. After a lot of research she settled on Pripyat, an abandoned town in the Ukraine. It was near an old nuclear reactor that had blown up a century or so ago, long before d-mat. She had never heard of it, but radioactive isotopes have a long memory, and people still couldn't live there. The booth was for scientists studying the wildlife. There were more interesting critters out there than just albino sparrows.

Doing it right to Jude meant being with Lydia and winding up Damon until he snapped. They had been friends from an early age. She knew how to have fun with him. He must be getting something out of it too, she reasoned, otherwise why was he still hanging around?

"I read that they call it the Red Forest because of all the blood of the workers who died here," she said, crossing to where her backpack lay on its side in the leaf litter.

Damon didn't bother correcting her. Jude privileged stories over facts, and he could only fight misinformation one factoid at a time, armed in this case with a small but fiendishly complicated three-dimensional jigsaw puzzle that he had first solved at the age of five. By now he knew the sequence by heart. Moving swiftly, ignoring the others, he took the pieces one by one from their tin and assembled them with familiar, deft movements.

When it was done, he rocked back on his heels, feeling something less than complete satisfaction, even though there were no pieces missing; the crystal skull was as it always was.

A sharp tug and he pulled the puzzle to pieces again. The crystal skull was as good a litmus test as any other, but just because it hadn't changed didn't mean they weren't in another universe. And even if it had... What if it had been a crystal dolphin in his home universe and his memories had changed along with it? He would never know the difference.

While Damon considered the deeper ramifications of his experiment, Jude was scanning swatches of translucent cotton fabric for pulled threads and changed patterns. They were family heirlooms her grandmother had left her, mementoes of affluent times buried in a time capsule to preserve them from the Water Wars and retrieved when things got better. There was no material value to such mementoes from the past; nowadays, anything could be scanned and copied in moments. But these swatches had never been scanned, and never would be. They were perfectly imperfect, right down to the grubby fingerprints Jude had left on them as a child—a crime for which she had been soundly beaten.

The fabric was unchanged.

That just left Lydia's collection of rare moths, unaltered in number, shade and sex. Nor was the suitcase altered, or its position, which she had marked out carefully on the ground, or the twigs she had arranged in a rough square around it, or the stones she had placed at each corner of the square. Testing the urban myth may have been Damon's idea, but Lydia was the most meticulous in pursuing that idea to the limit. She liked following other people because it absolved her from having to make moral, or at least practical, judgments, but she was in her own way very competitive.

They compared results.

"Well, that was a bust," said Damon.

"Not necessarily," said Jude. "We might not have found it yet, the thing that separates this world from ours."

"Don't tell me we're going to go look for it. I've got better things to do with my life."

"It could be anywhere," said Lydia, neither agreeing nor disagreeing. She wanted to keep every option open, even as she packed up her moths in preparation for going home.

"Perhaps we should try it again," said Jude. She didn't feel disappointed. If anything, she felt a heightened sense of anticipation. Rising to the challenge.

"No skin off my nose," said Damon. "It's still not going to work."

"Guys," said Lydia. She was facing the booth, the doors of which had shut behind them. "Was that graffiti on there … *before?*"

"I think so." Damon remembered it because he had taken a photo of Jude and Lydia after they'd laid out their flourishes, with their backs against the booth. He had noted the Cyrillic alphabet, which he couldn't understand.

The word traced out in thick but hasty white lines in a diagonal across the booth's front was лох.

"It means *stupid*," said Jude. "I looked it up."

"Just then?" said Lydia.

Jude nodded. "The Air works here. So that's another strike against having gone anywhere."

"Oh." Lydia couldn't help but feel a little deflated. She had been sure the graffiti would be the critical difference. If the Air worked and Damon remembered seeing the graffiti, then maybe this universe really was home after all.

"Uh … wait," said Damon. He had called up the photo in his lenses, and he sent it to the others now.

There, behind the girls, in identical white lines was a single word in Cyrillic, only instead of лох it was хуёвый, which meant worthless.

"The words are different," said Damon, staring from the booth in front of him to the one in his lenses. His mind fizzed a little, as though he was a Coke and reality had just given him a bit of a shake. "The words are definitely different."

Jude stared at Lydia with her mouth wide open, then let out a loud whoop and swept her up in a whirlwind dance around the clearing. Her enthusiasm was infectious. Even Damon grinned a little, as he stared down at the grinning skull and wondered, *So how do we get back?*

Jude had it all figured out. First they would explore the clearing as long as they dared (the radiation wasn't going to kill them any time soon, but the thought of it was still scary) in the hope of finding any more differences (they didn't), then they would get back into the booth and she would do her thing.

"Take us to the Bashert Ostension," she said just as loudly and as confidently as before. The Bashert Ostension wasn't a place, she had reasoned. It was a code, like Improvement or Togetherness or any of the numerous memes circulating at any given time. Jude and Lydia had tried Togetherness once, but they hadn't ended up physically blended into one. Of course. Such things were impossible, or at least utterly illegal and therefore improbable. The fun lay in the imagining and in the attempt, and the reminder that all skin is special, like friendship.

So, saying the code words should take them back. That was Jude's assumption, and it seemed reasonable to Damon. Inasmuch as a situation like this could *be* reasonable. D-mat still wasn't magic. There had to be an explanation that made sense, if only he could think of it.

Lydia watched him rubbing his thumb and forefingers together, over and over. She knew what he was thinking, and maybe a little of what he was feeling too, but figured it would all be okay when they got back. Then he could pretend it hadn't happened, as he always did with problems he couldn't solve.

The doors of the booth didn't close.

"Take us to the Bashert Ostension," Jude said again. Still the doors stayed open.

"Is that what you said last time?" Damon asked.

"Exactly."

"So why isn't working now?"

"I don't know. I don't know. Let me think."

She began to pace. Lydia stepped back to give her room. The booth was a bit more crowded than before, now the flourishes were back in with them too.

"Maybe that's something else that's changed here," Lydia said. "Maybe the code is different."

Jude snapped her fingers. "Right. Let's look it up."

The Air told them the term didn't exist.

"So we can't get back?" said Damon, his eyes wide and a little white around the outsides. "We're trapped here?"

"Unlikely," said Lydia soothingly. "The urban myth will be here too, just like the trees and the leaves and the moon are here too. All that's different, apart from the graffiti, is the code." *I hope,* she added silently to herself.

Jude had a wild idea. "Do you think we could call ourselves?"

"Why would you want to?" asked Damon.

"I'm going to try it," Jude said, and received an immediate error, of course: it's not possible to call yourself through the Air. So instead she sent a chat request to her little sister.

Xena answered immediately. "Get back here, you midget dike bitch. Mum's going to kill you if you don't—"

Jude ended the call. No changes there. "Seems I'm not at home."

"No, you're here," said Damon. "But not *here* here. You're *there* here."

"What?"

"We've swapped places with our other selves," he explained. "They're exactly the same as us, which means they tried the urban myth too. They're back where we came from looking for our code words, while we're where *they* came from, looking for theirs."

Jude could accommodate this new development if she concentrated hard enough. It was better than thinking about her screwed-up family. Apart from two minor details—the graffiti and the code—everything in this universe was the same as her other self's, which meant she wasn't going to run into herself any time soon. Unless the other Jude was trying to jump back right now...?

The booth was still and silent. No one was going anywhere.

She took out the flask and had a solid swig, then passed it around to the others. Lydia allowed herself a taste. Damon waved it away. His lenses were scrolling light right up into his irises.

"I'm searching the urban myths," he said. "Help me out, will you? Nothing fits so far."

All three of them searched, Damon immobile in the booth, Jude pacing in circles around it, and Lydia sitting on a tree stump outside.

Eventually he said, "I think I've found something. Look."

He bumped them a link to an urban myth that initially seemed nothing like theirs.

> *When you use d-mat to go from A to B, you don't go in a straight line. You don't even go in one piece. Your pattern is broken up into tiny packets and each packet follows a different path through the Air, along cables, by satellite or via whatever means are available. Normally it doesn't matter which means it takes. The booth at the other end assembles all your packets the same way. But a system this big is like a maze. There are lots of places where things can go wrong. Dead ends and loops and crossed wires and knots ... and holes.*
>
> *Holes are a particular problem when you're dealing with quantum computers that access the computational power of parallel universes. Engineers call them quantum leaks. There's one particular quantum leak that you can use to get to a world that looks just like ours, but isn't. Not quite. Some people go there to steal stuff. You get there by asking for Wodhams' Gate. Be careful, though: there's no guarantee you'll ever get back. Curiosity killed the cat, remember?*

"Quantum leaks," Damon said. "That almost makes sense."

"Gee, I bet the universe is relieved," said Jude.

"Yeah, yeah," he said. "Are you going to do it or what?"

"Take us to Wodhams' Gate," Jude told the booth.

The doors closed. The light flared.

Lydia nursed a small worry, like a kitten too new and fragile to uncover. It was too late to raise now: they were going *somewhere*. And she knew that she was the fragile one in the kitten metaphor, and that some worries grow roots like oaks when exposed to the light.

For the second time that day they peered out at the Red Forest, only now it was dark and they could see barely anything beyond the white light spilling from the booth. The sun had fully set while they were searching the Air and the new moon was on its way. A faint tang of deer musk still pricked Jude's nose, which was a good sign.

"How do we know for sure?" asked Damon, sweeping in long strides from one side of the clearing to the other. There were their footprints in the leaf litter. There was the rectangular outline of Lydia's suitcase.

"I can think of one way," she said. "Search on Wodhams' Gate."

That produced nothing. There were no references to that term anywhere.

"So we're home?" said Jude.

"Not necessarily," Lydia said, braving the fear. "We have to search on the Bashert Ostension to be sure."

Again, nothing.

Damon sank down on his haunches and put his head in his hands. "Fuck. Seriously?"

"Is this possible?" asked Jude. "We're in *another* universe?"

"There are an infinite number of them," said Lydia. "If two are connected, why not three?"

"We shouldn't have done the second search," said Damon. "We might never have noticed, otherwise."

"And when the versions of us who live here turned up?" asked Jude. "What then?"

"Maybe they wouldn't have. Maybe they would have been happy where they ended up too."

"It still wouldn't be right," said Lydia. "We'd always wonder. Or *I* would."

"What's so special about our universe anyway?" Damon grumbled, but he let up and joined them in the search for another way out.

Lydia was getting the hang of it now. Here there was neither a Bashert Ostension nor Wodham's Gate. Instead there was a Junction 666 that sounded promising.

"It's a joke," said Damon, "but I'll go with it if it takes me home."

They held hands in the middle of the booth with their flourishes on the floor between them as Jude made the request. The doors shut. The light flared. The doors opened.

Pine forest. Nighttime. Deer musk and leaf litter.

But there was no point checking the Air.

There, in the middle of the clearing were another set of flourishes, left behind by someone else.

"Damon's right," said Jude. "This is a joke. It has to be."

She held two swatches of identical fabric, one in her left hand, one in her right. They had the same chocolatey fingerprints, front and back. The same tiny hands that had held them, years earlier, had tried in vain to ward off her mother's blows. Different hands and a different mother in a different universe—that was what they were being asked to believe. But there was another explanation.

"Someone's messing with us," she said. "They're editing the Air while we're in transit, so it looks like the memes have changed, but they haven't really. They changed the graffiti, too. And now they've fabbed copies of our flourishes. We're not going anywhere at all. We never left. It's all one big art-prank, and the joke is on us."

"How do we prove it?" asked Damon. He was juggling two crystal skulls, kind of hoping he would drop them so they would shatter and the pieces would get mixed up. *That* was a challenge he had never attempted before.

"One of us stays behind," Jude said. "That's how we prove it."

Lydia stared at her with wide eyes. "Who?"

Nobody said anything for a long moment.

"Do we *really* need to test it?" said Damon. "Can't we just accept that you're right and leave it at that? Yeah, yeah, yeah—you would always wonder, Lyd, but *I wouldn't*. Near enough is good enough for me. What's stopping me from going home right now and staying there—if it *is* there?"

"Nothing," said Lydia.

"So why don't I?"

"You tell us," said Jude.

He gripped the skulls tightly in his fists. Veins stood out of his forehead.

"I'll stay behind," said Lydia. "You two go. I'll wait and make sure the meme doesn't change. That way we'll know for sure. Then we can all go home together. The legend trip will be over. We can get that beer … okay?"

Slowly the tension left Damon's face and posture. He put the second skull back where he had found it, and nodded. "All right."

Jude was less sure.

"Are you certain you want to do this?" she asked Lydia.

"Yes." Lydia didn't look at the second suitcase. The temptation to send it off with the others was strong, but there was probably a limit to how many moths one should have. "Don't worry. I'll be here when you come back. I'm not going anywhere … because neither are you, remember?"

They hugged. Damon retreated to the booth, already searching for the next meme. It was called the Fistula, which made him think of unfortunate medical conditions and bodily fluids, and his father, and the creeping disease that had killed him. Damon's stepfather John had called it The Ague. When Dad died, John had wept for five minutes, then walked out the room and never come back.

Lydia outside the booth. Jude and Damon inside. The mirrored space seemed empty with only two people.

Lydia gave Jude a tiny wave as Jude called out the name of their destination and the doors slid shut on her friends, leaving her alone in the clearing. It was suddenly dark. She wrung her hands in front of her, imagining radioactive ghosts crowding in all around. That was what she had expected of the legend trip, not this weird existential crisis. Ghosts and other supernatural beings. Aliens, maybe.

The booth whirred and clicked to itself. Maybe it was aliens, she thought, tinkering away in the background and tittering to themselves as their subjects began to show signs of stress. She swore she wouldn't give them the satisfaction. Tucking her long legs up to her chest, she sat on the suitcase and hugged her knees, and waited for her friend and her lover to return.

Two minutes later, the doors opened and Lydia was exactly where she had been, except sitting down now. She looked up when the light fell over her, then stood up, then lit up when Jude emerged, her darkest fears unrealized. Jude had half expected to find the clearing empty and Lydia gone—vanished into another dimension or kidnapped by unknown tormentors. That she hadn't gone anywhere restored her confidence greatly.

They embraced. "Anything weird happen?" Jude asked her.

"Something rustled in the bushes, that's all."

"A Pripyat rat with two heads and four glowing eyes?"

They had joked about this before coming to the Red Forest. Mutant rodents to match the mutant swallows. "Almost certainly."

"What about changes?" Damon asked, coming out of the booth and looking around suspiciously. "Is the Air still the same?"

"Exactly the same." She had been watching it as closely as she had been watching the undergrowth. "The meme hasn't altered one bit. Which means—"

"Which means…" He took over the sentence, then deflated suddenly, collapsing down into himself as though his bones had suddenly d-matted away. It was relief making him weak, and a sense that drama was required. "We didn't go anywhere. We're safe. We can go home. It's over."

"Hoo-frigging-ray," said Jude.

She raised the flask in one final toast and passed it around to the others. Damon took an extra half-swig to cover a slight tremble in his hands.

"Back to my place?" he said. "I'll fab some pizza while we work out how to track the people who did this to us."

"You really want to do that?" asked Jude. "Track them, I mean. Not pizza. Pizza would be awesome." Her stomach rumbled at the thought.

"Credit where credit is due," Lydia said. "This was a great stunt. We were totally taken in."

"Until the end," said Damon with satisfaction. He was wondering what to do with the extra flourishes. "I'd kinda like to rub it in their faces that we worked it out before the big reveal."

"They were reaching a bit with the last name, I thought," said Jude. "Was that a dig at us, do you think?"

Lydia frowned. "What do you mean?"

"The *Fistula*." She made a lewd gesture when Lydia still looked puzzled. "You know? Or are you pretending for Dame-o's benefit that we haven't done that?"

"I, uh, don't know you're talking about," Lydia said. "The last name wasn't the Fistula. It was Addison's Adit. The Fistula was the one before."

"Are you sure?"

"Of course. We used it to get here, and I've been staring at it for five minutes solid. It hasn't changed a bit ... but...

She pulled away from Jude, who looked hurt.

"But *you* have changed," Lydia said.

"Or *you* have!" said Damon. "We're exactly the same as before."

"I don't understand," said Jude. "What's going on?"

"They're still screwing with us," said Damon with a definite snap to his voice. "They changed her while we were in the booth just like they changed the Air and copied that crap we brought with us. That has to be what happened."

"It's not like that at all," said Lydia, amazed by his willingness to jump to that conclusion. "I stayed behind. You two came here. But you aren't the same two *I* came here with. They've gone on to the next world—where another me is waiting, just like the me you left behind. We've got all split up!"

"So what do we do now?" asked Jude, staring at a Lydia who said she wasn't *her* Lydia, even though she looked exactly the same. Perhaps there were subtle differences she would only discover on a close examination—which wasn't as thrilling a thought as she might once have wanted it to be. "Do Damon and I stay here while you go forward? Will that bring us back together?"

"I don't know," said Lydia. "I don't know!"

"Don't listen to her," said Damon. He looked wild-eyed and feverish. His thumb and forefinger were working again. "She's part of it. They've changed her. They're in her head now. She's one of them."

"That's not possible," Lydia said, certain of that much. "You can't just reach into someone's head and change the way they think. You're crazy."

"They'd want us to think that," he said. "Don't listen to her, Judy. She's lying. We know where we are. We know we haven't gone anywhere. Don't play their games anymore. They're laughing at us, and they have been all along."

"Calm down, Dame-o," said Jude, reaching out to touch his shoulder. "You're getting a bit worked up."

"Yes? And why not? I'm tired of this. I'm tired of being patronized by you two. I'm tired of being the third wheel. I'm going home to get pizza. You can come with me if you want, or you can stay here. I don't care."

That he did care was made very evident by the way he hesitated. He was waiting for one of them to side with him. But neither of them did. They looked at each other, and once it was clear that Jude wasn't going anywhere, Lydia decided to stay too. The precise nature of their relationship had yet to be determined, but parting was not an option this time.

"I want to figure this out," said Lydia. "There has to be an explanation."

"Fine," said Damon, stomping in a huff through the booth's open doors, crystal skull held tightly in one hand. "Seeya, then."

"Oh, don't be such a big baby," said Jude, but it was too late. He had said "Home" and the doors were already closing. The booth knew the address, which was evidence in its own right, but tantalizingly inconclusive.

Lydia and Jude waited in silence, unmoving, for the booth to finish working. When the doors opened, the interior was empty. Damon had run from another unsolvable problem.

"Shit," said Jude. "Now what?"

"We keep going," said Lydia. "We see this through without him."

"How? I mean, what address do we use now? I'm confused."

"Addison's Adit," she said. She wondered if *her* Jude looked this lost in the next universe along. Perhaps if they left quickly enough, they'd catch up. "Come on. Let's get out of here."

Jude nodded miserably and followed her inside.

⋇

On the other side of Addison's Adit, there was no sign of anyone else, apart from the flourishes, still abandoned in the clearing. The meme in that universe was called The Long Way Home, and they took it without hesitation, and the one after, and the one after that. Lydia and Jude stayed at opposite sides of the booth, not talking, barely even looking at each other. Damon's absence cast a long shadow across their moods. Every time they arrived at another Red Forest, Jude half expected to see him or receive a message from him, but there was ever only silence, which disconcerted her even though it didn't surprise her. It was as though he had dropped off the face of the earth.

The Shortcut led to The Ultimate Escape led to Intersection 391, where the deer musk was mysteriously absent. They took Intersection 391 to God's Gateway, and there, without warning, the flourishes also vanished. It was as though part of Jude vanished with them, and she fell to her knees in the clearing, not knowing if she wanted to scream or weep.

"Why won't they show themselves?" she asked Lydia, staring out at the trees. "Why are they still messing with us like this?"

"I don't think this sapling was here before." Lydia had been taking snapshots with her lenses and comparing the image with the reality of their next location. There were changes, but they were subtle. It wasn't just the Air and the graffiti and the flourishes. She was convinced now that the worlds weren't the same. They were still being messed with, but not in any simple art-prank way.

Jude pushed past her, ripped the sapling out of the ground and threw it into the bushes. "There. Is that better?"

Lydia knew not to say anything.

God's Gateway led to the first screaming match in the entire three months of their relationship. There was no inciting incident. It just happened. They were suddenly going in circles around the inside of the booth, Jude pressing, Lydia retreating, both shouting passionate, vindictive things they had stored up for weeks. Jude's reactivity. Lydia's passivity. Jude's bossiness. Lydia's stubbornness. Both of them wanted it to stop but neither of them knew how. Being in love with someone took practice, Lydia told herself, trying to see the positive. It was just like sex in that regard, so why not arguing as well? This was their first time. Of course they were doing it badly. They would be better next time they tried it, if they got through this time.

Jude just wanted it to stop. All of it.

"Damon was right," she said. "We're not stuck here. We're not prisoners. No one's making us do this. It's us, all us, and we can end it any time we like."

"Don't go, please," said Lydia. She clutched at Jude's arm, afraid of being alone.

"Why not? I'm tired. I'm thirsty. I'm sick of the view. But not sick of you," she conceded, although she did pull away, feeling slightly guilty. Lydia wasn't *her* Lydia, after all. Was this cheating? "It just has to stop."

"It will soon, I'm sure of it."

Jude didn't know how Lydia could be sure of anything. And by this point, Jude really *had* to be sure. The legend trip was poisoning them. Whoever or whatever was behind it, she needed them to give up now.

Silently, while Lydia searched the Air for the next link in the chain, Jude called the peacekeepers. She told them she was in trouble and she told them where. She didn't look too closely at the interface in her lenses. She didn't wonder why it was black rather than blue. She didn't ask why the PK had never heard of Pripyat and wanted GPS coordinates instead. She just got it done.

"Ready," said Lydia. The name was the Frehling Aperture. She held out her hand. "Shall we?"

Jude hesitated, then nodded stiffly but ignored the hand.

"It won't change anything," Jude said.

Lydia took what looked like fatalism as an affirmative, and took them onward.

The doors opened. White flashlight beams were dancing through the trees. They both could hear shouting in the distance. To Lydia it was a complete mystery. Jude understood that the PKs were coming to rescue her through the Red Forest, since their booth was in use.

"Wait here," said Jude. She didn't want Lydia to know that she had called them.

"No, don't go out there."

Lydia didn't like this. She was already searching the Air for the next step, the next name.

"It's okay," Jude said. "Don't worry."

She stepped out into the clearing and stood up on tiptoes to see through the scrub. The PKs were almost upon them. She waved her hands over her head, although surely they could see the light of the open d-mat booth. There was nothing else for miles.

Angry voices barked in a language she didn't know. She had just enough time to think *Why angry?* when they burst out of the trees and were on her, six men and women in black light armor and face masks, wielding automatic weapons. They physically threw her to the ground, and when she resisted, clubbed her with a rifle butt to stun her, then splayed her out on the ground, face down. Jude blinked rapidly in fright, not knowing what was going on. She could see Lydia through the door of the booth, mouth open in shock. Such delicate lips. They were the first thing about Lydia that Jude had noticed. They were bloodless now.

Jude felt something cold and hard tap the back of her skull. It felt like the barrel of a gun.

The sound made Lydia physically recoil as violently as though she herself had been shot. She fell back into the booth, away from the sight of Jude's ruined face, and somehow the booth heard her words through the hands pressed tight against her mouth. "Shut the door!"

They had killed Jude. Whoever the people in black were, they had really killed her, and they were going to kill Lydia too if she didn't move quickly. Already the weapons were turning her way, dark visors gleaming expressionlessly in the reflected light of the booth.

"The Infinite Intersection—and don't open the door at the other end!"

Light flashed. Engines of transformation worked, turning her from matter into energy, then from energy into information, and then back again. Lights dimmed. The doors stayed shut.

Through them she heard voices, then the hammering of fists against the metal. She pressed hard against the back of the booth and searched for her only way out.

"Sam's Passage!"

She jumped and jumped again, tears pouring down her face, legs shaking, but mind working, searching, questioning, hoping. Maybe in one of the worlds there would be no banging at the door, no shouting foreign tongues, and Jude would be alive. Maybe even *her* Jude, if she could ever be so lucky. If she never gave up.

Another jump. Another. It was silent outside the booth. She sat inside for five minutes without going anywhere, gnawing her fingernails and thinking, thinking. What if it was a trap? What if this universe's equivalent of the people in black were lying in wait for her? What if she opened the doors and they leapt in, dragged her out into the clearing and shot her too?

Who they were and where they had come from were lesser mysteries. Even why they had done what they did. Different universes, different rules. It wasn't just little things that changed, obviously.

"The Bridge Beyond," she said, certain that if Jude had been out there she would have said something, and certain also that she didn't want to die.

Three more jumps and she was ready to brave the silence.

The trees were black but the sky was pink. Sunrise. Had she been really in the booth that long? Maybe, if the jumps took longer than usual—which wasn't an unreasonable hypothesis given she was universe-hopping by means unknown.

There was blood in the clearing from a carcass rendered unidentifiable by the gnawing and tearing of sharp teeth. Standing over the body was a gray wolf with bloody jowls. Calmly, it looked up at Lydia for no less than five seconds, as though considering whether or not to eat her as well—maybe it had cubs somewhere, or pack mates, or was just greedy, Lydia thought, trembling with fright—but then it looked back down at its meal and resumed crunching and chewing through something that might once have been Jude but could be anything Lydia wanted it to be.

Not Jude, she decided as the wolf ate on. So hope remained.

⁎

Alone with an infinite army of reflections, Lydia pressed on. Why? Because she couldn't go back, and she couldn't stay still. Onward was the only option.

The sun rose higher in fits and starts, depending on how long each jump lasted. The entire morning passed in less than an hour from her perspective, and that perspective contained nine different versions of the Red Forest. The clearing shrank and grew larger, contained animals and nothing at all. The trees around it changed from pine to birch to palm to bamboo.

Into the afternoon and the weather began to change too. Sometimes it was hot, other times cold. Once it was snowing, and she spent several minutes in icy melt water to replenish her thirsty tissues. She emptied the suitcase and filled it with snow in case it was a while before she saw water again, then shivered through ten more frigid Pripyats until the Sneak's Retreat brought her to a desert.

She never changed but the scenery constantly did. It began to feel like a dream, and she wondered whether the entire legend trip was some kind of hyper-real simulation. Was she going to wake up in a couch somewhere with wires coming out of her head? Were her friends laughing at her, the last to give up and leave the simulation? She didn't think so. They would cheer her on, she was sure of it. They would want her to break the game.

Civilizations ebbed and flowed outside the booth. Once she found herself in the centre of standing stones that looked thousands of years old. Another time she was surrounded by planes of brilliant glass and metal populated by people so beautiful they looked like machines. The booth was the *other* constant, she realized, apart from herself. She could only leave one universe and enter another one through a booth just like the booth she was in.

Several times the Air failed to respond to her commands. When that happened she had to chase down people outside, if there *were* people nearby and if they spoke her language and if they weren't trying to shoot her. Sometimes they gave her food, clothes, access to a toilet. Sometimes they just shrugged, unable to communicate. But there was always a way to keep going. There was always *onward*, even when it *seemed* that she had reached the end of the line. She could count on that—so in that sense there were actually *three* constants. Herself, the booth, and the quantum leaks. Everything else was in flux.

As the bedrock rose and fell and the skies turned from blue to green to a garish yellow from horizon to horizon, she became more and more certain that she was getting somewhere. Or maybe something was getting nearer to her. Either way, proximity was in the air. It could be Jude, or it could be home. Or something else entirely. But when she found it, she was positive that she would know what it meant. This couldn't be for nothing, all this effort, all these strange journeys nowhere.

Nowhere, and yet *everywhere*. She gazed out at infinite possibilities with a sense of wonder no less authentic than when she had first stepped into a d-mat booth and seen images of *her* radiating outward in all directions. There was both wonder and horror in confronting the unending universe, just as there is both wonder and horror in reaching the end.

Lydia had long lost count by the time the doors opened on an earth with a poisonous atmosphere. Two breaths saw her pitching forward to the ground, trying from long habit to find the way out in time. The words were there—The Long Delay—but she could no longer speak them clearly, just gasp and gurgle and cough. She didn't know if there was just one jump left to go, or a million, or what the booth heard her say, ultimately. But she tried. The last thing she saw as the booth closed for the last time was herself staring up at the mirrored ceiling, her head pillowed by the bag that had once contained Jude's precious swatches. She had traded them long ago for a loaf of bread.

There was blood on her lips, she saw. Her skin was so pale. Not constant after all, she thought. Not constant at all.

Three teenagers enter a booth. One dies, one disappears … and the last one?

By the time Damon comes back to the clearing in Pripyat, it's all over. The clearing is empty. There's no sign of anyone. He's reconciled to the fact that his room in this universe is the wrong color and his father died a year earlier than he should have. What he can't stand is the thought that he's being used. It's occurred to him that the most important thing about urban legends and legend trips—the thing that separates them from horror stories and tragedies—is that if everyone dies, the legend *dies with them*. Someone *has* to survive to propagate the meme.

And it seems that in this case that someone is him, which is an intractable position to be in. He can't tell anyone or they'll think he's crazy. But this isn't a secret he can keep forever, either. Jude and Lydia are going to be missed. He has to tell the peacekeepers something, and what else if not the truth? Does the third one always have to be the lunatic no one believes but whose story everyone remembers?

The meme propagates. The meme wins. All it needs is someone to pass it on.

But what if he doesn't do that? What if he kills himself right here and now? What if he runs into the forest and lets the radiation that turned the trees red eat him too, pull at his cancer-riddled body until it sinks down into the dirt, devoured before its time?

Beside him, the booth doors close and the machines start working.

He sags and laughs in despair. Who is he kidding? The meme spans every possible universe. It's covered against every possible outcome.

When the doors open, Jude leans out to smack him on the back of the head.

"I knew you weren't going anywhere, you big baby," she says. "What would you do without us?"

Tell stories, he thinks. *Or die.* It isn't much of a choice—but is this worse or better? These friends aren't the same ones he knew. They're just identical. Sure, the three of them can pick up where they left off for now, but the odds of none of them ever leaving is zero, right?

"Chicken," adds Lydia with a knowing twinkle in her eye, and as he steps through the doors Damon thinks, *Dead right.*

⋇

(Author's note: The idea of a "Togetherness" meme first appeared in Jack Wodham's story "There is a Crooked Man" in Analog, *1967.)*

End of Service

by Gabriela Lee

My mother's final trip back to Manila was in a box.

Sudden cardiac arrest, said the nice lady from the Department of Foreign Affairs who had made the call. She met us personally in her office, and handed over a sheaf of official-looking papers stamped with the seal of the Philippine government. Dad barely said anything as he signed them. He had interviews with more people from the DFA and the Philippine Overseas Employment Agency. They gave me water and biscuits that tasted like cardboard while I waited.

The POEA had a child psychologist on their staff to help the children of overseas Filipino workers process the loss of their parents. He was mid-forties by the look of his beer belly and the smell of old cologne. "Do you want to talk about it, Aya?" he asked me in a gravelly voice. I stared at him while tucking my earphones into my ears. The whole world disappeared behind a drum and bass intro. He wrote down something on his pad, but I didn't bother reading his upside-down handwriting. I didn't have anything to say. What do you say to people you've never met about a mother you barely knew?

Even before she died, I think I had already lost her. She left for Jeddah as a housekeeper for a wealthy expat family when I was three, and, except for a handful of Christmas visits, I never saw her after that. I remember her as someone who tried to be stylish. She was always wearing lipstick and perfume even when we were just going to the corner store. She smelled of apricots and olives, sun and sand and heat, her warmth enveloping me whenever she came home.

The days when she had to leave again were terrible, as if someone had sucked all the light out of the room. She would go early in the morning, when the streets were empty and dark except for the occasional roar of a distant tricycle. We'd wait for a cab, all three of us. I hated standing in front of the gate, bundled up in a jacket and cardigan, with her and her luggage and three boxes of *pasalubongs* for her wards in Jeddah. They were kids who loved dried mangoes and durian candy and the salty dried fish in vacuum-packed plastic bags that was a staple in every Filipino home. Kids who got to have her full time instead of just for a few days. She would kiss Dad on the cheek and he would smile and tell her that he was proud of her and that he missed her every day, and then she would come over and hug me and I'd be squished against her, surrounded with her perfume. I really didn't want to let go.

But I always had to.

Mama told me that she was doing this because she didn't want me to be like her. She was fifteen, the same age as me, when she dropped out of high school and took her place in the wet market, along with her mother, who couldn't even write her own name, selling fish and vegetables. The only reason she was able to leave was because of my dad, who helped her go back to school and earn a diploma, who helped her find work in Manila. It was her decision to go abroad, because overseas Filipino workers made more money—double, triple, quadruple what she was making as an over-worked and underpaid nurse in a city hospital.

This was the only life I knew: we lived in a small two-storey townhouse in Quezon City, in a compound with nine other two-storey houses that looked exactly like ours. My dad worked in a government office as an accountant. Mama sent money every seventh of the month, and a new phone for me every year.

Sometimes, she sent me emails or Facebook messages, asking me when I wanted to talk to her on Skype. I always told her that I was busy, that I had schoolwork or group work or that the internet connection was weak and unreliable.

But really, I didn't know how to talk to her. How do you talk to someone you barely know? How do you bridge that gap of years and oceans and time? She was my mother because that was her name on the birth certificate, and that was her face, pale and smiling and sweaty, in that photo of when I was born.

She wasn't my mother in all the other ways that my friends had mothers, though.

We held a wake for her for nine days, as tradition required. The family Mama worked for paid for the funeral arrangements, but even though they were super rich, we were given the smallest chapel at the funeral home. There were people from the DFA and POEA crawling all over the place, ignoring the open casket and the trickle of people that had come to pay their respects to my mom, people who were bearing gifts of food and drink and flowers and story.

My dad sat at the pew closest to the casket, his hands folded over his lap as the government people inspected everything from the funeral wreaths to the cookie cutter crucifix that hung behind the coffin. The Christ figure looked benevolently at us even though his face was covered in painted blood dripping from a molded crown of thorns. I wrinkled my nose. I didn't like crosses that depicted the pain that Jesus must've experienced. Who could feel peaceful and holy if they were staring back at someone who always seemed on the brink of dying in the most horrible way possible?

I didn't go to school that entire week. Normally, taking a break would be a treat, but as the days went on, I was actually looking forward to schoolwork and seeing my friends again. Some of them did visit with their parents, and my homeroom teacher, Mr. Alcoreza, came with a giant card that all my classmates designed and signed, but I just wished everything would go back to normal.

Mama's parents came all the way from Abuyog, a small town in Leyte. They were so old they looked like they had tree bark for skin, and they curled into themselves, almost like snails carrying invisible shells. Cradling their hands in mine, I performed the *mano*, lifting one after the other, to my face and touching the backs to my forehead. They were so delicate, I worried I might break them. After my greeting, they hobbled their way to the casket, supporting each other, bony hands wrapped around one another's wrists.

"She looks beautiful," Lola mumbled as she stared at the open casket. There was an arrangement of flowers on top of the clear plastic sheet that protected the body from the outside world. Lola brushed the leaves aside to take a closer look at her face. I hadn't even looked at it yet; that wasn't my mother inside the casket, I was sure of it.

"She looks so young," said Lolo, draping a bony arm over Lola's bony shoulder. "I'm happy they got her like this."

"Her term of service wasn't over yet when it happened, right?"

"No. She has seven more years on her contract."

"That explains it."

This didn't make sense at all. Weren't they supposed to be hugging each other, weeping and sobbing, and wondering what happened to their daughter?

I wanted to ask them what they meant, but before I could find the words, they stepped down from the platform and hugged me. They smelled of Tiger Balm and baby powder. "You are so lucky," Lola said, cradling my cheek in her wrinkly hands. She kissed me twice on each cheek. Lolo simply winked at me, like we were in on a joke that he totally got and that I was still trying to figure out.

Because it was expected for relatives to stay and watch over the dead body all through the night, every night of the wake, the funeral home provided each chapel with a room containing a narrow cot, a fridge and sink, and a tiny bathroom. Auntie Delia took charge of our entire routine, making sure we had enough snacks to feed a small army, and that everyone was taken care of. At the end of each evening, when the priest had finished the Mass, she told my father to go home. He refused, though, so they would end up taking shifts, napping on the cot or sitting with the stragglers outside, reminiscing about my mother.

People told me what a brave girl I was, that I was such a good daughter, helping my dad and Auntie Delia, offering *ensaymada* and *mamon* and Styrofoam cups of instant coffee to visitors. But I didn't feel like such a good daughter—all I really wanted was to lock myself in my room and scroll through stupid webpages that told me how to dye my hair fifteen shades of purple or to read stories about how Iron Man and Captain America were totally in love. And I didn't feel brave either—I didn't want to stay in the room when it was almost empty, knowing that I was in a building filled with open caskets in chapels, with dead people in dead people's clothes.

I couldn't even bring myself to step forward and look inside the casket that held Mama.

Would she still be wearing her favorite shade of lipstick? Did they put perfume on her? Did she look like those corpses on TV and in the movies, so lifelike that they seemed like they were still breathing? What if she *was* breathing inside and we never noticed and it turned out that she wasn't really dead and we ended up killing her ourselves?

On the last night of the wake, while we were having our *pagpag* at the twenty-four-hour Jollibee near our house, my dad leaned over the minuscule Formica table and asked me, "Have you spoken to your mother yet?"

"I'm not really in the habit of talking to dead people, Dad," I said, opening my burger to remove the offending slices of pickle inside the sandwich and discarding them on the tray.

"Don't be rude, Aya Katrina Villanueva. You're not too old yet to be spanked."

I looked out the window that bordered the fast food restaurant, watching the early morning traffic speed past us. A line of cabs stretched haphazardly in front of Jollibee parking lot, the drivers smoking, or napping, rags and old T-shirts shielding their eyes from the glare of the industrial-sized street lamps.

"She'll be cremated tomorrow, and then we'll bring her to the memorial park. You need to say goodbye to her before she goes," Dad said, chewing on his French fries.

"Why is it so important that I talk to her? It's not like she's going to talk back."

Dad sighed and rubbed a hand over his eyes, which were red-rimmed and tired.

I focused on chewing my food. I didn't want to deal with that familiar look of disappointment he got when I did something he didn't approve of. He was a pretty lenient dad, all things considered: I could decide when to sleep, as long as I was awake in time to go to school; there were no restrictions on TV or the internet or my cell phone; I could stay over at my friends' houses during weekends. The list of things he didn't approve of was actually pretty short.

"Your mother loved you very much," Dad said, resting his elbows on the table and steepling his fingers together. "She was happy to give you everything you asked for, even though I told her that she was spoiling you already. She always said that you were the best thing she's ever had, and that someday, when she came home for good—"

"But she's not coming home anymore, is she?" I was surprised at how loud my voice was, how much anger colored my tone. "She's dead, she's not coming back, and even if I wanted to talk to her, I can't."

Dad looked at me for a very long time, as if I was a complicated math problem that he was trying to solve in his head. "You should still say goodbye. This might be your last chance to talk to her."

We didn't talk to each other at all on the way home. The cab driver had his radio tuned to an AM station, and the drone of the newscaster's voice lulled me to sleep. Dad shook my shoulder slightly to wake me up when we arrived.

I'd never felt this exhausted, even when I pulled an all-nighter to cram for my economics exam.

Without even taking off my dress, the seventh black one of the week, I slumped in front of my laptop and flicked it open. There was something comfortably mindless about scrolling through social networks, checking on how my friends were doing. My Facebook page was full of people leaving messages of condolence. I was scrolling through and clicking "Like" on each one when the Skype notification came. It was from my mother's account. I clicked "Accept", wondering if I was going to talk to one of the rich expats she worked for, but when the video screen came up, the image was a familiar face—a face that I thought I would never see again.

"Hi Aya," said the woman on the screen. "I'm so glad you have time to talk to your old mom."

I stared at the screen for an endless moment. Then I closed the Skype window, and for good measure, I turned off the wi-fi signal, and closed my laptop, too.

Then my smartphone rang.

My heart raced and my whole body trembled. I ran into Dad's room, and showed him the phone, too freaked out to even talk.

"That's not your mom," Dad said, without even blinking. It was like he'd been expecting this.

"Then who is it? Was that a ghost? You said as long as we performed the *pagpag* there wouldn't be any ghosts following us home!" I flapped my arms uselessly, trying to expend the extra energy. My heart was still hammering in my chest.

"Aya. *Anak*. Listen to me." He sat at the edge of the bed, hands resting gently on his thighs. "That was not your mom, but a sort of echo. She's fulfilling the end of her service."

"What do you mean?" I demanded. "Dead people can't finish contracts. That's impossible."

Dad took my hands in his. "Aya, I've been trying to find the right way to tell you. Because she wasn't done with her contract yet, they made another version of her to finish the job. The copy has her same set of memories. She's the same in all the ways that Maricar Villanueva was Maricar Villanueva, but she's not her."

"I don't understand," I said. "Mama's still alive?"

Dad sighed. "No, *anak*. Your mom really did die of a bad heart, but according to the Bagong Bayani Treaty, copies of dead workers can be deployed when a sanctioned, recorded, serialized OFW is unable to finish his or her contract. Your mom signed up for twenty years, and her employers want the same caretaker for the whole term. That's why they paid for the funeral, and why we can still have Mama's income."

"So that was why the DFA and the POEA were at the funeral?" I asked.

"And why they asked me sign off on so many contracts. We'll still receive the same amount from your mother, even the pension, as long as she finishes her service." He reached out and patted me on the knee. "It was what she wanted."

"So does she know? The one in Jeddah, I mean. Does she know she's Mom 2.0?"

Dad shook his head sadly. "We can't tell her, Aya. She has to think that everything's exactly the same. To make her aware of her condition as a copy would destroy her. Literally."

Our house was quiet except for the ambient sounds of the outside world filtering through the windows. The city is never really silent, I realized: the hum of the electricity surging through the street lamps, the quiet fall of early morning rain, the buzz of nocturnal insects that moved through our small front garden.

I switched on the TV to distract myself from the thoughts running round and round my head. A late-night cooking show was on, and I left it there, watching a British chef demonstrate the finer points of deboning a chicken.

At the commercial break, the bright yellow intro of a government ad filled the screen. Animated characters jumped up and down, showing different jobs around the world: an engineer in Tokyo, a nurse in Singapore, a doctor in Canada, a sailor in South Africa, a domestic helper in the Middle East. All of the animated characters were dressed in the uniforms of their trades, their animated smiles stretching from ear to ear. Then there was the classic *ka-ching* sound of money as the animation showed the salary difference between working in the Philippines and working abroad. *You can send your children to school! Pay your parents' hospital bills! Pay for a car, a condo, a house! Your problems will be solved forever!*

This was followed by a pre-taped spiel from the president, his hair styled from two years ago, his eyes obviously looking past the camera and focusing on a teleprompter. "Filipinos can be found in almost every part of the world, from down under in Australia to the icy glaciers of Reykjavik. Do your country proud and be one of the new heroes of the republic! Be an overseas Filipino worker and show the world what the Filipino spirit is made of!" The ad ended with the hotline numbers for the POEA and the helpline for the DFA's application process.

Was a commercial like this what made my mother leave? Was this what allowed my dad to let her go into the arms of the government and leave the country, to take care of another man's children and live on another man's land? I had classmates whose parents were also OFWs, who also worked in Tokyo and Toronto and Kuala Lumpur. Did they also know that their parents might not actually be their parents anymore? On the TV screen, the British chef chopped up the chicken on his cutting board, cleanly severing the wing from the breast from the thigh. One stroke of his butcher's knife, and the chicken was no longer a chicken, just the sum of its parts.

I had seven missed Skype calls while I was asleep, all from Mama's account. I cleared the notifications and then headed to the shower to get ready.

Today was the day that my mom would be cremated. There would be the last Mass, conducted at the funeral home's chapel, and then Dad and I and our relatives would head to the crematorium to watch her body turn into ash. Dad had already selected an urn: a coral-blue affair, the gradations of color moving from sand to sky.

The priest talked about life after death. Ashes to ashes, dust to dust, and all that stuff. My mom was dead. There wasn't anything he could say to bring her, the real her, back.

"Many people would say that talking to the dead is the act of a crazy man," the priest said to a rapt crowd of family and friends. I thought of the missed Skype calls. Did the priest even know that there was another woman who bore my mother's face, running around right now, alive and well?

"But I say, talk to the dead," the priest continued. "Remember them in life and in death. Tell others what you remember about them, what you remember of them. Pass on their stories." I looked around. My mother's sisters and brother had stories to tell about her. My grandparents could trace her back to the day she was born. Her friends had their tales of school and friendship and growing old. My dad could find the deepest truth of her. But I had nothing.

When the Mass ended and everyone gathered around my dad and grandparents, I slipped between the well-wishers and made my way to the raised platform. There was nobody near her now.

I stepped towards the head of the casket and peered inside. She *was* wearing her favorite lipstick, and a stylish forest-green dress that reached to her knees. Her eyes were closed and her lips were pulled up in a small smile, as though she had a delicious secret that she wanted to share.

My phone vibrated, so I pulled it out of my dress pocket and looked at the screen.

It was her again.

I swiped my thumb across the screen and lifted the phone to my ear. "Hello?"

"Aya!" My mother's voice was cheerful on the other end of the line. It was the voice of a dead woman. It was the voice of a woman who was still alive.

I kissed the tips of my fingers, and then pressed them against the hard plastic surface that separated the world of the living from the dead. "I love you, Mama," I said.

"Oh, *anak*, I love you too."

"I know."

"Where are you, anyway? It sounds noisy over there."

I looked over my shoulder as I walked away from the casket, the people that surrounded us, the pale funeral wreaths and the sad Jesus, and Auntie Delia distributing the last of the pastries. I pressed my phone against my ear. Copy or not, the woman on the other end of the line, pressing her phone to *her* ear was still my mother.

"Oh, it's nothing, Mama," I said . "Sorry, the reception's just bad. Can I call you again?"

Chupacabra's Song

By Jim C. Hines

Nicola Pallas ripped three paper towels from the roll and wiped down the stainless steel table of exam room two. The fat, gray-chinned Rottweiler who had come in to get his remaining teeth cleaned had left an impressive mess.

In her father's words, the dog was a butt-wagger. When he was happy, his whole body showed it. When he was afraid, he showed that, too. The poor thing had probably begun peeing the moment his paws touched the cold table.

Nicola didn't blame him. Her father ran one of the busiest veterinary offices in southern Illinois, which created a constant flow of people and animals through the waiting room, all barking and yowling and hissing at the strange smells and sounds. Nicola avoided the main office as much as possible, preferring the relative calm of the small animal room in back.

Sopping up the warm urine didn't bother her, but if she didn't take precautions, the sharp eucalyptus tang of the disinfectant would make her vomit as soon as she pulled the trigger on the plastic bottle. She turned up the volume of her music, fitted a latex nose clip over her nostrils, grabbed two more paper towels, and sprayed the table and floor.

Her nose clip was attached to a strap like an oversized rubber band that rubbed unpleasantly at her neck. For the sixth time that afternoon, she moved it back behind her collar and away from her skin.

With one of Haydn's symphonies pounding through the earphones, she didn't hear the door open, but she felt the thud of her father's hard-soled boots on the floor. She finished cleaning the linoleum, then stood up and pulled off her earphones, leaving the nose clip in place. Even after she washed, it would take at least ten minutes for the smell to dissipate from the air and her hands.

"We have one more patient tonight. Is the room ready?" Doctor Sergio Pallas was a soft-spoken man, strong enough to lift a mastiff without straining. A pair of plastic-framed glasses balanced at the tip of his nose. The lenses distorted the lines of his face, as if someone had scooped a chunk out of each cheek.

Nicola threw out the paper towels and set the bottle back into the cabinet, letting her actions answer the question. Her father was wearing his heavy leather gloves, which meant the next animal might be a biter, but it could also be something interesting like a porcupine. She retreated toward the rear door of the exam room and waited.

"You can stay, but keep your nose plug on, and stand back." He ducked out, returning with what looked like an unconscious, mange-ridden Labrador Retriever in his arms. The animal had a flattened head, leathery skin, and a stripe of thick, matted fur down the neck and back.

Only this couldn't be a Lab. Her head was too narrow, and her teeth were too long and sharp. Thick muscles belied the impression of disease. An old nylon leash circled her neck, and blood darkened a ragged bandage on her ribs. The left foreleg leg was wrapped and bloody as well.

Excitement sped her pulse. The soundtrack in her head switched to Prokofiev's "Piano Concerto #3" to keep pace. Nicola's music never stopped. She heard it even in her dreams. The only difference between this and the music she played through her earphones was that the latter allowed her to block out the rest of the world.

She hummed to herself as she crept toward the table.

"I'm not sure what it is," her father said to her unspoken question. Doctor Pallas was known for treating any animal that fit through the door, and some that wouldn't. In the past three months, he had removed a tumor from a pet boa constrictor, splinted a gerbil's leg with paperclips, and amputated two injured legs from a pet tarantula who had escaped and lost a brawl with the family's Maine Coon.

"I found it alongside the road," said Louise Boucher, standing in the doorway. Nicola hadn't noticed her until she spoke. She had an unusual voice, deep and scratchy like an old record. "I couldn't just leave it there."

The animal's teeth and jowls were stained with blood. Possibly her own, if she had been chewing at her wounds. Brown, hairless lids drooped like half-lowered blinds over bloodshot eyes.

"The leg is destroyed, and someone shot it twice in the side." Anger edged her father's words as he cut away the bandage. "Louise, you should have called animal control."

What Nicola had thought to be fur was actually a ridge of spines. They were shorter and thicker than porcupine quills, like a Mohawk of hawthorn spikes.

Her father prepared a syringe of xylazine and injected it with smooth, well-practiced movements. Nicola stepped to one side. Xylazine could cause vomiting, and she didn't want to be in the way.

"It looks like the bullets passed all the way through," her father said. "One rib is broken. I don't feel much internal bleeding. Overall, I'd say this thing got lucky."

"It's the ugliest dog I've ever seen."

"She's not," Nicola said. Anger made her hum louder, her hands twitching in time to the music. Whatever this creature was, she certainly wasn't ugly. She was powerful. *Efficient*. Most animals who came through the office were shadows of what they had once been: proud beasts whittled down to toys. Pets who had been inbred until their hips were ruined or their eyes bulged so much they could pop right out of the sockets, and even that wasn't enough for their owners. They demanded that her father cut off the pups' tails and mutilate their ears to make them stand up straight, though he had stopped cropping ears when he realized how much it upset Nicola.

This animal was an unapologetic hunter, lean and strong. Those spines would destroy the jaw of anything that tried to bite her neck or back. Even sedated, her breathing was unusually quick. Nicola reached out to touch the rough skin.

"Be careful," Mrs. Boucher said sternly. "Those spines are sharp."

The skin was feverishly hot. The heart pounded hard and fast.

"What do I owe you?" asked Mrs. Boucher.

"Don't worry about it."

The rhythm of the animal's breathing shifted, and the music in Nicola's head changed again, becoming wilder. Angry. Like a fire crackling through the woods. Nicola backed away, hands dancing as she searched for words. "The xylazine. It's not working."

"Quiet, dear," said Mrs. Boucher.

That just aggravated Nicola further. She was fourteen, but Mrs. Boucher's words held the same chiding tone you'd use with a four-year-old. She waved her hands at the table.

"What's wrong, Nicola?" asked her father.

The animal jumped to its feet as if electrocuted. Her spines rose, and she staggered toward the end of the table, snapping first at Mrs. Boucher, then at Nicola's father. She held her foreleg close to her body.

"Stand back," her father bellowed. He tried to grab the leash, but the animal jumped away, falling to the floor on Nicola's side of the table. "Don't make any sudden moves. You're safe."

Why was he lying to her? She wasn't safe. She was prey.

"Stop waving your hands like that," Mrs. Boucher yelled. "Do you want it to attack you? Hold still!"

Nicola crossed her arms and squeezed her hands into her armpits. Years of constant reminders from her classmates, her teachers, and other adults had taught her tricks to mimic stillness, at least on the outside. But the more she tried to fight what her father called her hand-dancing, the louder her internal music grew, like Beethoven performed by a grunge music garage band.

The animal stepped closer.

Her father lunged. His fingers clamped around the leash. With a snarl, the animal spun and attacked, teeth tearing into his forearm. He grunted in pain, started to reach for the scruff of the neck, then caught himself. He moved forward instead, forcing his arm deeper into the jaws to try to gag the animal so it would release him.

Nicola began to hum. The opening lines of "Twinkle, Twinkle, Little Star" filled the room. Her father had sung it to her every night for as long as she could remember. Even when he was away and she was alone with the babysitter, he called to sing to her, or else she couldn't settle down to sleep.

It took all of her concentration to keep her fear and anxiety from polluting the lullaby. Slowly, the animal released her hold. She lowered her bloody chin onto her crossed paws, reminding

Nicola of kindergarten, when everyone had to put their heads down on their desks for quiet time.

"What did you do?" Mrs. Boucher whispered.

Nicola kept humming. Her father would be furious. She wasn't supposed to sing *those* songs, especially not where others would hear, but this was an emergency. Her father snatched a roll of gauze and pressed it to his bloody arm.

"She saved your lives." The speaker was a strong, confident-sounding man in the doorway. A boy about Nicola's age stood behind him. "Chupacabras don't usually attack human beings, but they can be vicious when trapped or injured. Where did you find this one?"

"A half-mile south of our farm." Mrs. Boucher sounded like a child, confused and overwhelmed. "Chupacabra? Is that Spanish?"

"It means 'goat-sucker'." The man drew a glass rod from his pocket, and a new song filled Nicola's mind, harmonizing with her own. She felt the music pressing in on her thoughts, tilting the room around her. Her father sagged against the wall. The gauze fell away from his arm, and his eyes closed. Mrs. Boucher was already snoring on the floor.

The man lowered the rod and pulled a roll of duct tape from his pocket. "Martin, tie that thing up so it doesn't escape this time." Then he turned to Nicola. "So tell me, girl, how long have you been able to do magic?"

Nicola tried to answer their questions, but the words were too jumbled. As the man's frustration grew, so did Nicola's anxiety. She needed to retreat to the back room, to turn up her music and let her hands and arms dance, to escape the sight of her father unconscious on the floor, the chupacabra's blood oozing over the linoleum, the strange man with his glass wand and his magic.

Instead, she rocked and hummed to the angry pounding of Nirvana while doing her best to wrap her father's arm with a bandage. Blood darkened his sleeve, but his breathing was steady, and his color was good.

The strangers hauled the chupacabra away. Nicola taped the bandage in place, then climbed to her feet and followed them to the parking lot, her hands dancing to the beat of her steps. She stopped out front, standing in the circle of the porch light. They were shoving the chupacabra into a cage in the back of a blue SUV.

The boy, Martin, spotted Nicola standing on the front steps. "What's your name?" He had a pleasant-sounding voice, friendly and cheerful, but subdued.

"Shut up and get in the car," the man snapped. He strode toward Nicola, one hand in the pocket that held his wand. "What's wrong with you?"

She tugged the clip from her nose, then crossed the parking lot to look in the back window of the SUV. The chupacabra lay on a dirty green tarp in the cage. There was no food or water, no blankets to ease the pressure of the bars.

"Can you talk?"

She nodded hard. The man frightened her. He was like a symphony where half the orchestra was playing a different key, but he could do *magic*.

Nicola had first sung a spell two years ago, while trying to help a squirrel who had been brought in after a fight with a dog. She had tried to save it. The bones had knitted together, but the nerves were severed. Her father had been forced to put it down.

He hadn't understood. Nobody did, and words were inadequate to explain. The world wasn't words, it was smell and feel and sound, it was music, sometimes soft and soothing, other times loud and atonal and overwhelming. How could you teach someone to sing when they couldn't hear the notes? Until tonight, she had never met anyone else who could do magic.

"Chupacabras are pack animals," the man said. "We need to gather the rest. I'd prefer not to have to shoot them, but my wand only works at close range. How powerful is that song of yours?"

She nodded again to show she understood. If he could stop talking long enough for her to put the words together—

He snorted, then gestured toward the SUV. "Get in back with Martin."

Nicola hesitated. For as long as she could remember, her father had made her memorize a long list of safety rules. Avoiding strangers was at the top of that list. But what about the chupacabras? How many times had her father gone out on emergency calls to treat wounded animals? If she could prevent the other chupacabras from being shot, didn't that qualify as an emergency?

She climbed into the back seat. The car smelled like old animal fur mixed with the scent of stale French fries. The latter made her queasy, but wasn't quite bad enough for her to need her nose plug.

"Just do what he says," Martin whispered. "You'll be fine as long as you don't make him angry."

Nicola fastened her seat belt and locked the door. By the time they drove away, she had put her question together. "What will he do with them?"

"Sell them, probably." Martin kept his voice low. "Black market magic is big business. You've got to be careful, but Frank has powerful customers. They use the animals as guard dogs, or as ingredients for various spells. Chupacabra blood is magical and so are those spines."

Martin seemed eager to talk, though he kept looking at Frank, like prey checking for predators. "I do a little book magic but nothing like you. That spell you did back there was awesome. What's your name?"

"Nicola." She blushed, her thoughts singing. Martin was impressed with her magic. And he seemed to like her.

Perhaps she could find a way to save the chupacabras and Martin both.

They parked on the side of the road, a short distance from the Bouchers' farm. Frank took a Maglite and a black handgun from the glove box. He tossed the light to Martin and pulled out his wand. The glass reflected the moonlight, stretching its image into a ridiculously elongated and skinny crescent that made Nicola smile.

"They like to feed on livestock," Martin explained. "Goats, chickens, sheep, even barn cats."

"Stay here," Frank ordered. "I don't want the family interrupting us." He set off toward the house, leaving Nicola and Martin standing at the edge of the cornfield.

Nicola shoved her hands into her pockets, another trick she had learned to help conceal her hand-dancing. The pockets squeezed her hands tightly when she flexed her thighs.

Martin twisted an ear of corn from the stalk and began tugging at the tassel. "For a long time, I thought I was the only one, but there's a whole other world out there, one the mundanes don't know about. Chupacabras are nothing. Wait until you see a wild phoenix. Most folks mistake them for meteorites."

She nodded eagerly, entranced by the excitement in his voice. Her internal soundtrack bridged gracefully into Wagner's "Ride of the Valkyries" as her fears faded. "How many others are there?"

"Oh, there are hundreds of folks like us. Most spend their time trying to hide magic from the rest of the world. Mundanes would probably burn us both if they knew what we could do."

Frank's footsteps crunched the gravel as he approached. "Come on. We'll start at the barn."

The corn was as tall as Nicola. The leaves batted at her arms with every step, no matter how carefully she tried to weave between them. They stopped in the dirt drive in front of the barn. The door was open, but the interior was too dark to see what was within. She smelled dust and hay and manure.

Frank raised his gun. "Go on."

Martin shone his light inside. "Nothing but cows."

Of course they weren't here. The chupacabra was a predator, but many predators were potential prey as well. They might sneak into a barn to hunt, but they wouldn't stay in a place that smelled so strongly of humans and their tools and animals.

"Kill one of the cows," said Frank. "The blood will draw them out."

"No." Nicola shook her head. The cows didn't deserve to die like that.

"The prodigy speaks." Frank turned to study her. "Do you have a better plan?"

Nicola thought back to the chupacabra in the office, the low hum of her growl, and the drumbeat of her heart. Rocking her body in time to the music, she began to sing. She did her best to ignore Frank's gun, concentrating instead on a wordless melody of claws digging into the dirt and spines rattling as you ran with your pack. The rest of the world faded, giving her the solitude she needed as she flung her song outward. The vibrations played through her bones.

A chupacabra howled in the distance, a harsh, rasping sound. Nicola shifted keys, harmonizing instinctively. Music stretched like rubber bands, pulling the animals closer. Six of them approached from the woods beyond the field. They stepped into the light and circled toward Nicola.

She had called them from a meal. Blood painted their muzzles and legs. If they were always this messy, it might explain why they lacked fur. All that blood would make a horrible mess, clumping and tangling their coat. Many species of vulture had evolved along similar lines, their featherless heads making it easier to get clean after feeding.

"Outstanding." Frank stepped forward, wand in one hand, gun in the other.

This was her chance. If she was going to save the chupacabras, to save Martin, it had to be now. She spliced a new theme into her song, a Christmas carol.

Nicola disliked most carols. Each year she heard them at school and at church, dozens of discordant voices butchering one song after another. But "Do You Hear What I Hear" had the chorus she needed. If she could show them, make them see and hear these animals the way she did—

"What are you doing?" Frank snapped.

She tried harder. She had so rarely worked magic, and now she needed to keep the chupacabras calm while simultaneously persuading Frank to leave them in peace. The animals were growling. She shifted her attention to keep them from attacking. Frank pointed his wand, and the closest chupacabra dropped.

Her song faltered. She tried to stop Frank, and one of the chupacabras bounded forward. Martin shouted. Frank grabbed Nicola's shoulder, pulled her back, and moved his wand. The chupacabra fell, then a third followed.

The remaining chupacabras charged, too fast for Frank to use his wand. He aimed his gun with his left hand and pulled the trigger.

Thunder shattered Nicola's music. The metal smell of gunpowder stabbed her nostrils, burning her sinuses. She curled into a ball and fumbled with her nose plug, trying to shut out the sounds and smells as Frank fired again. A chupacabra wailed, a sharp, piercing cry of pain. How had everything gone wrong so quickly?

By the time the noise stopped, five animals were piled on the ground unconscious. A sixth whimpered weakly, bleeding from a hole through his neck and another in his side.

"Leave that one." Frank gasped for breath between words. "It'll be dead before we can get it back."

Martin stepped closer. "Nicola, are you—"

"Leave her too," Frank snapped. "That little retard nearly got us all killed. A broken spellcaster's worse than none at all."

Nicola covered her ears, but she couldn't block out the sound of his disgust, nor the injured animal's whimpers. The chupacabra tried to snap at Martin, but his jaw wouldn't work properly.

Frank scooped up the closest animal. The whimpers grew louder. The bleeding chupacabra let out a low moan and tried to crawl after his packmate. His spines shivered.

Nicola realized she was moaning along with him. Words jumbled together like debris in a river after a flood. There was too much. The gunshots, the dying chupacabra, Martin's attempt to show her kindness, Frank's cruelty … it all tangled together, damming the river of her speech.

"Knock that noise off, girl," Frank snapped.

She shook her head. She couldn't stop. She wouldn't. She needed to save the chupacabra. She needed to *sing*.

Music exploded through the dam, slamming into Frank and Martin both. Frank reached for his wand, but the glass shattered under Nicola's assault. Each note was a syringe piercing their veins, anesthetizing their bodies until they crumpled into the dirt.

Blood oozed from the chupacabra's wounds. He was breathing but not for much longer. Her hands danced furiously as she scooted closer. A low growl warned when she got too close.

Her father could help the chupacabra. He could remove the bullet and suture the wounds. She sat back, imagining his strong fingers pulling the curved needle through the skin. He sometimes sang while he worked, mostly Greek songs from his childhood.

Nicola swallowed hard, then whispered the opening words of "As Eicha tin Ygeia Mou" by Stelios Kazantzidis. It was one of her father's favorites. She channeled him through her words, until she could hear his voice with hers.

The bleeding slowed, but it wasn't enough. She hurried to Frank's SUV and pulled out a blanket, which she wrapped around the wounded chupacabra to protect herself from the spines. She carried him back to the SUV, setting him on the floor beside the caged animal her father had tried to help.

Nicola had learned to drive when she was twelve. She began with the riding mower, but within six months her father had let her plow the parking lot. The next year, she took the truck to the neighbors' houses, plowing their drives while he supervised from the passenger seat. She wasn't allowed to drive more than twenty-five miles per hour, but she could get where she needed to go.

She adjusted the mirrors, fastened her seat belt, and drove.

Her father and Mrs. Boucher hadn't moved. Nicola could hear the magic keeping them asleep. In time, she could probably counter it, but the chupacabra didn't have time. He would be dead before she could wake her father. She would have to do this herself.

She set the animal on the table. He whined and nipped her hand, but she hardly noticed the blood dripping from her palm.

She sang "As Eicha tin Ygeia Mou" again, over and over. Skin and muscle pulled together, one invisible stitch at a time, but he had lost too much blood. Nicola had seen her father operate more times than she could count, but her song couldn't duplicate his skill.

Claws clicked on the linoleum, and she realized she had forgotten to close the front door.

Of course the other chupacabras had followed her here. They were pack animals. They weren't meant to live or die alone. She wondered if they had followed the SUV's scent, or if they had used magic to track their packmate.

Growls and the rattle of spines filled the room. Two of the chupacabras were sniffing at Mrs. Boucher. Another nosed her father. Shrill barks filled the air from the back room as the caged dogs there heard and reacted to the newcomers.

Nicola stepped slowly toward the cabinet and grabbed the disinfectant bottle. Her hands were sticky with blood. Fumbling her nose clip into place, she sprayed both her father and Mrs. Boucher. The chupacabras jumped back as if they had been burnt.

She set the bottle on the corner of the table and turned back to the injured animal, but it was too late. He shivered once, coughed blood, and died.

"I'm sorry." The words sounded flat and were utterly inadequate. The chupacabras moved further into the room, sniffing her and the table. She reached for the disinfectant, but they didn't attack. Maybe they understood that she had tried to help, or maybe the blood of their packmate kept them from thinking of her as prey.

She sat down next to her father and tried to dissect the magic keeping him asleep. The song was a simple one with a repeating four-tone melody. She sang along, letting her voice merge with the spell, then pulling it in a more lively direction.

The chupacabras growled. One collapsed as a new spell filled the air. Nicola started to rise, but Frank rushed through the doorway. His hand clamped around her mouth. The other enveloped her body, lifting her into the air and holding her as a shield to protect him from the animals. She kicked and squirmed, but Frank was too strong. He dragged her out of the room. "Martin, if you can knock the rest of those things out, do it quickly. Otherwise, we'll settle for selling the pelts."

"I'm *trying*," Martin said.

Nicola couldn't breathe. She shook her head and tried to bite. Frank's fingers dug painfully into her cheeks. One of the chupacabras crept toward the doorway. Frank shifted his grip and drew the gun, muttering under his breath.

Nicola wasn't strong enough to pull his arm from her mouth, but she could rip her nose plug away.

The smell of disinfectant assaulted her nose, and she gagged. Her entire torso convulsed, and vomit burst from her mouth.

Frank yelled and flung her to the ground. She coughed and choked as her stomach emptied itself onto the floor. Curled in a ball, her face covered in sweat and puke, she tried to sing.

Dry heaves fractured her song. She plugged her nose with one hand, concentrating her magic on Frank, easing the muscles in his body until the gun lowered.

"Stop it." Martin held a book in his hand. His magic crammed into her mouth, trying to gag her. It tasted like aluminum foil.

She shook her head hard. With shaking hands, she pushed her nose clip back into place.

"I'm sorry, Nicola. Frank's all I've got." His magic reached out from his book, weaker than her own, but enough to dull her song.

She held her dancing hands close to her chest. "Please," she said hoarsely, squeezing the words past his spell. "The chupacabras are like us."

"Don't kid yourself," Frank said hoarsely. "They'd rip out your throat and drink you dry, along with every other animal in this place."

Of course they would. That was their nature. "They're special."

"They're just animals," said Martin.

Disappointment crushed her. He was supposed to understand. He was supposed to *hear*.

"Don't move," Martin said. "I don't want to hurt you."

He wouldn't hesitate to hurt the chupacabras. Or her father, or Mrs. Boucher. His cruelty was quieter than Frank's, but she could hear it now. His inability to truly see the chupacabras. His disdain when he talked about "mundanes".

Nicola imagined a jazz theme harmonizing with Martin's spell. Her hum was barely audible at first, but grew louder as it blended with Martin's, crumpling his magic into an atonal knot.

Frank started toward her. She reached for the memory of her own nausea and hurled it into her song, twining it with the tune of Martin's magic. Of *all* magic. Tears fell down her cheeks, and she squeezed her eyes shut to try to fight the *wrongness* of her song.

"What are you doing?" Martin broke off his spell and clutched his stomach.

She couldn't stop. Not now. As broken and chaotic as her spell was, it still needed an ending, a crescendo that built into a throat-rending scream as she pushed her song through both Martin and Frank.

They retched loudly. She heard the weak tune of Martin's magic, but before he could cast another spell, he threw up again.

"What the hell did you do?" Frank shouted.

Nicola hugged herself tightly. "Magic. Makes you sick." It was the same reaction she had to the disinfectant. They would never cast another spell, nor would either of them be able to get within ten feet of magic.

She sang again, this time to the chupacabras. Just as she had done to Frank and Martin, she reached into the animals and twined the scent of humans to the bite of the disinfectant. They would live and hunt, but would leave people in peace.

They bounded away, and as they passed through the hall, Frank and Martin threw up again. Chupacabras were magical creatures, after all. The animals' mere presence was enough to make them vomit.

Frank and Martin stumbled out of the building, trying to reach a strange car in the parking lot. They must have stolen it to follow her back.

They barely made it down the front steps before Nicola sang them into unconsciousness.

"I don't know if this is a good idea, Nicola."

Nicola didn't say anything. She was watching the lone chupacabra in its kennel. She had freed it from the cage in Frank's SUV, but the animal's foreleg was too damaged to save, so her father had amputated it below the shoulder.

The chupacabra lapped at the bowl of pig's blood Nicola had put in her cage. Nicola had named her Hildegard, after a twelfth century composer.

Her father shook his head. He hadn't remembered anything about the night before, nor had Mrs. Boucher. "Are you sure you know how to take care of a crippled … what did you call it?"

"Chupacabra. She's magical. Like me." She hummed to her friend, and laughed when the chupacabra's tail began to wag, drumming weakly against the floor of the cage. "And she's not crippled. She's beautiful."

The Day the God Died

by Alena McNamara

This isn't a story—or if it is, it certainly isn't mine. It's a memory, one I can't look away from.

I'd tired myself out running, that evening. I was leaning on the rail of the lake path just where it curves near the island, pain singing through my lungs and my quadriceps femoris. The pale November sunset had finished half an hour ago and it was so cold I could feel the cartilage in my ears, but as long as I stayed out I could pretend there wasn't school tomorrow.

A whisper of motion brought my head up. Then I laughed softly, my breath billowing white. It must have been a breeze rattling the last clinging leaves.

A furry, sharp voice in my head said, *Not quite.*

I spun to face the path: empty. As I turned back, headlights swept along the lake road—and over the island. They caught the dome of a broad furry head shiny as an oil spill and flickered in a pair of cat-golden eyes.

Light lingered in those eyes for a long moment after the car had passed. *Come to stare?*

"N-no," I said. I'd thought that shadow a particularly large tree stump. "I didn't know anyone was here."

Hah. It sounded the way I felt when somebody told me I was young or that this was just a phase or that things would get better.

A jogger passed, iPod hooked into her ears. Her glance summed me up as probably harmless. She didn't even look at the island.

My calves had twisted into cramps. There was no way I could run; I'd have to trust that whatever it was, it wasn't going to attack. "Wha—who are you?"

A god.

A god, like a wolf caught in an industrial accident, lurking on a tiny island in one of the urban lakes? I opened my mouth, and then shut it again. If it was telling the truth, it maybe didn't need any more problems, including a smart-mouthed kid. If it wasn't, well, there wasn't much I could do about it.

And you? Who are you?

"I'm—" The name my parents had given me, the names I tried out on myself, the usernames I went by on the internet, all ran through my head. "I'm a human," I finally said.

The god just laughed at me.

I pushed myself to go further before stopping each time I ran. I kept going past the little island like the jogger had, without a glance, and after it snowed and they only plowed the bike path it was easier to avoid looking. Sometimes I felt the god watching me anyway.

That year I was trying not to skip classes. If I wanted to get into a good college and do biology, I couldn't ditch school to read plays in the public library and sketch out dialogue in my notebooks. I threw myself into studying, and stayed up after my homework was done to reward myself with reading just one more scene. It worked, too well. One day in the middle of January there I was, two lakes north of my high school, pounding through the snowbanks drifted halfway up the railing, out of everything but fear and self-hatred.

One of my boots caught in the icy crust. I went down, palms skidding for a grip, and lay there on the hard snow. The last of my adrenaline drained out of me, leaving me shivering and useless.

Human, a voice said in my brain.

"Go the hell away," I said. My eyes throbbed against the cold; I wished for my gloves, a scarf, the tissues I'd had in my backpack.

Human. What happened to you?

"Nothing happened to me." I pushed myself up to sit, dragging my foot out from the hole it had made. The ragged ends of dead plants trailed out of the banked snow behind me. "I fell."

The god laughed. Its laughter was breathier than before. I frowned and shifted sideways to look through the railing supports. I'd been growing my hair out, and my snot and tears tangled the ends—I had to brush it out of my face before I could see.

The daylight faded out the shimmer of colors on its fur. If you ignored the jumble of wolf, coyote, lion, and tiger traits—plus the fact that it stood as tall as my dad at the shoulder—maybe you wouldn't think it was out of the ordinary.

Especially now. It paced its island like a caged animal, angular and nervous. The land was just ten of its steps wide, but it paused every turn and a half to pant white mist.

"What happened to you?" I asked.

Pacing away from me, the god said, *What happens to all of us, in the end.*

"You're dying?" What could kill a god? "Why?"

Who can say why some gods die and others live, the god said, dryly. *Why do they do that to you?*

I said, "No one did this to me. I—I did it to myself." I'd been up too late too many nights; I'd fallen asleep on the light-board during rehearsal. The theater teacher hadn't even yelled at me. He'd just looked disappointed. It had still been worse than getting changed for gym in a room full of guys who were good at being guys, who wanted to be guys in the first place. That, at least, was a daily horror. Theater was supposed to be outside of my life.

The god gazed at me a moment longer, and then started pacing again. If it had had the energy, it might have laughed at me.

"Whose god are you?"

A hiss of breath echoed over the icy lake. *No one's any more. My own.*

I worked a hand between the bars. "You don't have to stay there, you know."

The god stopped. It turned its eyes on me, lit from inside. *Stay here?*

"On the island. The ice, it's solid. You could go somewhere else." Somewhere warm. Somewhere soft. "That island isn't the whole world, you know."

Do you wish to know just how small your galaxy is?

"Right." I took my hand back, stuffed both in my pockets. Did gods even feel cold? "I should go," I said, "before I get frostbite."

The god examined me. I stood up, hair falling back over my face. *You are not sufficiently warm?*

"I'm not stupid," I said. "I know how to dress for winter. I just, I just forgot my gloves." And my scarf. And left my backpack sitting in my locker. My homework—I wouldn't have anything done for tomorrow, unless I went back for it. I'd be late for dinner.

Go, then. I would not wish you to die as well. Snow showered from a tree branch, frosting the god's fur. It didn't move.

"Will you be okay?" It sounded like an idiotic question the second it was out of my mouth.

No. But then no one will be, in the end. The god shook itself off. *Go.*

By the time I saw the god again, the new year had dragged on halfway through March. It was a muddy one, with the crusts of ice still hanging off the curbs and the salt stains on the roads and sides of cars like the scars of winter.

My stop at the railing was only cursory; my body felt more wrong than ever, these days, and I had stopped even glancing in the mirror when I brushed my teeth. I didn't know what to do about it. I'd thrown myself into working out with weights for a couple of weeks, until it was clear that reducing the flab on my body meant less in the chest area, too, so I went back to running as soon as I could ignore the cold.

Before I could get my breath back and move on the god said, *Hello again.* It lay flat, head resting on paws. I hadn't seen it against the mud.

"Hello," I said, drawing closer to the railing. It didn't seem polite to say, I assumed you were dead. "How ... are you?"

Alive. For now. It yawned, showing sharp teeth browned with age and use. *And yourself?*

"The same, I guess." It was kind of a minimum qualification. "Look—is there anything that I can do? To help?" It must have been beautiful once, running free.

What can you do?

"I—I could buy you food, if you needed it, or get you medicine..." My inventiveness petered out. "I don't know."

Those are of no use to me.

"What do you need?" I opened my hands, ignoring the sweat

drying to a chill on the palms. "I can try to do it, whatever it is."

Its eyes opened, glittering. *Get me the sun, that I may eat it. Get me the moon, that I may bathe in its waters. Give me godlings to devour.* It stopped, shook its muzzle, and laid its head down again. *But I am old. They are young, and perhaps it is their time.*

I knew that it knew I couldn't get it any of those things. I stayed quiet until it sighed.

I need my youth again, it said. *But no one can give me that.*

"I'm sorry."

You had little to do with any of it.

"I know." I shrugged. "I feel bad anyway."

The god tipped its head. *Do they leave you alone now?*

I shifted, tugging at the Spandex over my elbow. "Mostly."

What will you give up to get out of the rest of it? The god's eyes held only curiosity.

"Nothing," I snapped, and then said, "I didn't give anything up." I had traded it. I had dropped the show and cut my hair shorter in exchange for no double-takes from substitute teachers and no disappointed looks. It was my choice.

Theater was a crapshoot anyway. Biology was a safer choice, better money. Maybe someday I'd find something that explained how my body ticked, and how I could change it. "I'll go off to college in a couple of years. Then I can be whoever I want."

The god said, *And what if, by then, you do not want to be yourself?*

"I've never wanted to be myself," I said.

The god waited, I think for me to realize what I had just said, but I knew exactly what had come out of my mouth so I waited too.

I see, it said at last.

I said, "I'd better be going. Good luck with—good luck." I didn't look back to see if it watched me leave.

I knew it was dying. That's what I worry at in my brain like a sore tooth. I knew it was dying, and I didn't do anything—though to be fair, I couldn't do what it had asked me to do, and I'm not sure it really wanted me to do that anyway. I could say that when I wasn't near the god its existence seemed vague and uncertain, or that I was busy avoiding my old theater friends, not getting beaten up, and learning how to breed fruit flies, but those are all excuses.

I did stop by in June, after the class above me had walked across a stage and out into whatever the rest of their lives would be, but the god wasn't there—or didn't show itself to me—so it was July before I saw it again. The evenings were cool after the long sticky days, so I ran in the dusk with a little flickering LED on my hip.

I don't think it would have let me know it was there, if it had had a choice. But it didn't. It was mewling like a kitten, the noise going on and on through the air and the ground too. It curled around its stomach and then stretched out, pushing into the dirt. Sapling trees cracked under the weight of those paws.

I vaulted the rail. The lake water reached my knees, splashed up to my thighs. Five steps, and I was stepping up on rattling stones and brushing past the sign that said this was a wildlife preserve.

"I'm here," I said, putting out a hand. The god's fur was bristly and soft at the same time against my fingers and then the god turned on me, snarling, baring its teeth.

I held perfectly still. If it wanted to bite me, it would. There was nothing I could do to stop it. In that suspended moment, I thought I'd almost welcome the pain.

Instead it laughed, muscles twitching. *Here you are again. Can't I get rid of you?*

"No," I said, and I leaned forward to wrap my arms around as much of the god as I could reach.

I'm still going to die, you know, the god said, through what would have been gritted teeth if it'd been speaking out loud.

"I know," I said, and hugged the god tighter to my chest.

I noticed I was crying when the first tear fell onto the god's fur. I hadn't cried in months—not since that day in the theater. I'd swallowed the tears up, somehow, pushed them deep inside me, but now they were welling up without me even asking for them.

When it stopped moving I let my head rest on its quiet flank. I tried to keep myself from sobbing—I hadn't even known it, not really, maybe it had killed millions of people, it had probably been older than I could imagine—but it didn't do any good. Eventually the tears stopped falling and I laid the god down and backed off, half expecting the god's body to vanish into mist, or turn into a baby god, or something. But it just lay there, dead, and after a while I slogged back to the shore and trudged home.

I wish I had something else to put here. I could say that the god had told me its name, that I carry that name still, but I would be lying. I could say I joined a play and stopped worrying so much about my grades, after. Or I could say I got some kind of wacky superpower from proximity. (Do I even have to say it?)

But like I said at the beginning, this isn't a story. It doesn't have some neat ending tying everything up with a bow. Sure, I think about it sometimes. I wonder where gods go when they die. But mostly I'm glad I was there—even if all I could do was hold it as it died.

Signature

by Faith Mudge

Priya Gowda had never met a book she wouldn't read, and she'd met a lot of them. She was born to sell books, or at least that was what Rieke told her.

"I don't know how you do it," he confessed one Friday morning, while they were unpacking a delivery: six boxes of a new thriller that had the author's name in bigger type than the title. "I feel like a dietician selling chips."

"I like chips," Priya said, slitting the tape on the last box and gathering up an armful of books. "What's wrong with chips?"

"They're the twenty-first century's cigarettes. They have no nutritional benefit whatsoever, and they increase the burden on an already dysfunctional medical system. What's right with chips?"

"They taste nice." Priya shrugged. "Life's not all soul searching any more than it's all salad."

She straightened up, books stacked on her lap, and maneuvered her wheelchair out of the storeroom. Behind her, Rieke paused to check the shelving of the children's section. He hated books being misplaced and took every opportunity to reshuffle them into their proper order.

"Doesn't it drive you mad, though?" he asked. "When you see the classics passed over for an empty fad?"

"The classics are still there if I want them," Priya pointed out. "In the meantime, I'm going to read the heck out of sexy super spies."

Priya had worked with Rieke at Nightingale and Priest for just over two years, and she knew he meant well. He was a fully accredited hipster, a bony young man in his mid twenties with ice blonde hair and thick black-rimmed bifocals, and his favorite authors were all ill-fated poets or nineteenth century social activists. He accepted his duty to sell people what they wanted to buy the way a clergyman might tolerate wayward members of the flock, in the hope of converting unwary customers to greater things.

The bookshop was inner city, between a sushi bar and a bakery, with displays of paper art in the windows and a blackboard by the door listing new releases and discounts. Inside, the floor was glossy black, the walls papered in the design of a seventeenth century map. Sleek red lamps hung from the ceiling at key points, radiating warm light.

A landmark compromise between caffeine-junkie computer programmer Cassandra Nightingale and her indie publisher girlfriend Emilia Priest, the shop was a fusion of their passions. Shiny black shelving overlooked a cluster of red-topped tables, with barstools arrayed along the counter, and there was even a shelf of free books—an eclectic, eternally changing collection, pages dog-eared and margins full of other people's thoughts. Added to wi-fi and Saturday night author talks, it really wasn't surprising that Nightingale and Priest had gained a devoted community.

Cassandra was rarely in the shop, providing funds rather than presence. When she dropped by it was like receiving a visiting dignitary, sending her employees into a delighted panic. Emilia came in more regularly. She liked to arrange impromptu poetry readings and was currently editing an anthology of modern verse, including several original poems by Rieke. He adored her.

Priya loved bookshops on principle, and Nightingale and Priest had always been her favorite. In her last workplace she had been the brown disabled girl. Here, Emilia wanted her marketing suggestions and Rieke was supportive to the point of being overprotective. Later that day when a customer asked Priya where she was from—rather, where she was *really* from—he came barreling out of the aisles like a very tall, thin tank, and Priya had to talk fast to get in first.

"Woodridge," she said brightly, pushing the woman's bagged book across the counter. "How about you?"

"The racism in this country!" Rieke fumed afterwards. "She took one look at your skin and assumed you'd just set foot on Australian soil. How do you put up with people like that?"

Priya sighed. "If I were an ambassador for immigration, I'd have a big fancy car with flags on it. My job isn't to explain myself, it's to sell them books."

"You were born to do this," Rieke said, and Priya tucked the words away in a corner of her memory to savor later on the way home.

Her brother Kabir met her at Central Station, as usual, because her mother worried about her on public transport alone at night. He was not much of a bodyguard, slender rather than toned, boyishly scruffy with his rumpled black hair and electric blue shoelaces, but he worked in the city too, taking calls for the ambulance service. On the way home he told her about the stupid pranks that had wasted his time that day, and she told him about Rieke's latest protest against populism.

"He's got a point," Kabir said. "I mean, maybe the classics need some defending."

"You only say that because you fancy him." Priya glanced at her brother slyly. "Has he made you read Keats yet?"

Kabir went pink. "How did you know?"

Priya settled back contentedly. "I'm your inside woman on this. Trust me, it's a good sign."

In Queensland, August could be the golden month on the cusp between unnatural cold and unbearable heat. Priya's family spent a lot of time outside in weather like this. Their four-bedroom house was not really designed to accommodate seven people, let alone

one with a wheelchair—sometimes the only place to get some quiet was in the street outside. The best space they had was the back deck, where everyone could gather around the same table. After dinner they lingered to talk while the younger kids chased each other around the lawn, but as the others began to drift away, Priya stayed, watching the dusk fall.

"Come inside," her mother called from the kitchen window. "Why must you work out there? You'll be devoured by mosquitoes."

Priya held up a textbook, inviolate armor to her parents. "I'll be in soon."

When she was sure she wasn't being watched, she reached into the book bag at her feet, bringing out a notepad and a sleek white cell phone. She kept an eye on it as she worked. It had been in her possession for well over a year, but it wasn't hers. Every time she wondered whether she was being tricked, all she had to do was look at the phone. It never needed credit, or even signal.

It was dark when the call came, later than usual. Priya answered at the first ring and the voice on the other end purred against her ear like a chilly breeze.

"What have you been up to, my dear?"

"Keeping busy!" Priya said, forcibly bright. "How about you?"

"Don't be facetious, child." The voice sharpened, from a purr to a growl. "I know everything you do. It would not hurt, I think, for you to remember that."

"A good night to you too." Priya opened the notepad to a list of names. "Let's get on with it, shall we?"

The bargain had been a bad idea. Priya had known that from the moment she found the phone and heard her name at the other end, but she had made it anyway. Fate had reached out a helping hand when she needed it most.

The bargain had brought her to the bookshop.

Emilia was there when Priya arrived the next morning, sitting at one of the barstools and spinning a spoon dejectedly in her empty cup. She was a slight, elegant woman in her late thirties, wearing a pearly chiffon scarf to complement her black and white polka dot dress. It was only close up that Priya realized one spot was spilt coffee.

"Good morning," she said tentatively. "Is everything okay?"

"No," Emilia said. Her voice, still crisply British after eight years living in Australia, was terse with exhaustion. "Things are anything but okay."

"What's happened?"

Instead of answering, Emilia got up and made herself more coffee. She made a cappuccino for Priya too, nudging aside a chair to make space for her to roll up.

"So what's wrong?" Priya asked, breathing in the aroma rising from her cup.

Emilia sighed. "Look. You're a smart girl, Priya, and you know me pretty well, so if I tell you something weird, you'll know I mean it. Yes?"

Priya nodded.

"We're about to be evicted. By a Fate."

Priya opened her mouth at the first sentence. The second froze her in place.

"By Fate," Emilia added, "I mean an actual manifestation of destiny. Go look it up in the mythology section if you like. I have. It doesn't help much."

Priya put down her cup with inordinate care. "Oh," she said. "No." Her voice sounded hollow. *What have I done?*

"It's all my own stupid fault," Emilia sighed. "I'm a stone cold bibliophile, you know that. My press means the world, but you would not *believe* the bad luck ... I only kept in the black by working around the clock. Eventually Cass gave me a deadline: find a new job or a new girlfriend."

Emilia smiled tiredly. "A bookshop seemed the best balance—that way I could keep up my press on the side—but bookshops aren't exactly hot stuff right now. I couldn't get the money I needed from a bank. Then I met *her*. Imagine a female Rumpelstiltskin in a nice business suit who lends out all the golden straw and makes you sign a contract as long as your arm."

Priya choked. "You've seen her?"

"She gave me three years to figure out her name," Emilia continued, as if she hadn't heard. "It seemed such a long time. I mean, there are books, online databases, census records. I thought I could do it. Three years, and it's up on Monday. I was so *stupid*."

She lifted her head. "You're taking this well. You must think I've gone crazy."

"I don't," Priya whispered. "I still have a year and a half left."

The bookshop had never been so silent.

"What," Emilia said, at last, very carefully, "did you ask for?"

"I needed a job." Priya looked at her hands while she spoke. "It was—I couldn't afford to keep studying. Either I had to ask my parents for a loan or give up my degree, and they don't have the money to spare. Somehow, she knew."

"She brought you here?"

Priya nodded. Emilia stood up abruptly. "I need more coffee."

One of the glass doors swung suddenly open and both women jumped, but it was only Rieke. He unwound several yards of thin sage green scarf and came over to their table, slowing down as he took in their expressions.

"What's wrong?" he demanded.

"It's complicated," Emilia sighed. "What do you know about Fates?"

Rieke dropped his scarf. He stared at Emilia, panic-stricken. "I didn't have a choice! I had nowhere to go, and she found me—"

Emilia braced herself against the table. "Dear God."

Priya had been grateful at first. If she could guess the Fate's name within three years, she would be left in peace; if she could not, her degree and all results therein would be forfeit. Like Emilia, she had been sure she could find the name in the allotted time. Like Emilia, she was no closer now than she had been on the day she'd signed the contract.

Emilia paced back and forth, listening as Rieke told the same story. When the old-fashioned station clock above the counter struck nine, though, she pulled herself together.

"We are unspeakably screwed," she said fiercely, "but we can still sell books. Priya, open the doors!"

Saturdays were the busiest day of the week at Nightingale and Priest and this was no exception—the tables were full all morning, and Priya kept busy behind the counter bagging books. Occupied with the familiar pattern of the day, she didn't notice anything was wrong until Emilia suddenly stiffened and leaned over to hiss, "*She's here.*"

Priya followed her glare to an elderly woman in a crisp white business suit with a crocodile skin handbag hooked over her arm. Her white hair was twisted into a complicated knot at the back of her head. She met Emilia's glare and smiled sweetly, like someone's executive granny.

"I am *not* serving her," Emilia muttered. "I just *won't*."

They couldn't kick her out, though, not in front of a whole café of oblivious onlookers. Priya might not know much about magic, but customer service, she understood.

"You go," she said. "I'll do it."

By the time the old lady, or Fate, or whatever she was reached the counter, Emilia had fled to the furthest reaches of the history section. Priya dredged up a smile.

"Hello, ma'am, how can I help you today?" she reeled off. She had said the same words so often that they sounded permanently strung together, like a hackneyed song lyric. The old lady smiled too, her lips pastel pink, her teeth very white.

"Well, I'm not sure yet," she said. "What can you offer?"

"We have coffee, tea, hot chocolate, iced chocolate, fruit juice or mineral water."

The old lady looked at the laminated menu propped up in front of the coffee machine. "A pomegranate juice would hit the spot."

Priya smiled. Maybe she would be losing the best job of her life tomorrow because of this woman, but if it came to a contest, she could out-smile her. She wheeled to the glass-fronted fridge, bringing her legs into full view. Their distorted shape was visible under Priya's skirt; she didn't dress to hide it. When she turned around with the juice in her hand, the Fate looked vaguely horrified, the very picture of a sweet old lady feeling embarrassed for her.

"Oh *my*," she said. "I'm so sorry."

"It's no trouble," Priya replied, placing the chilled bottle on the counter. "That's four fifty, thank you."

The Fate opened her crocodile skin handbag. "How did it happen, dear? Your ... impairment, I mean. It must be so hard."

"Well, it would be nice if more trains connected to platforms properly," Priya agreed. "Do you happen to work for Queensland Rail?"

The Fate gave her a hard look. Priya kept smiling. Her "benefactor" had been more frightening anonymous at the other end of a phone. Priya knew how to deal with people like this, the ones who felt better by trying to make her feel worse. It made sense that the Fate would be one of those. What was the use of people who were content with their lives if you made your living out of desperate souls?

"Thank you, dear," the Fate said, no longer smiling.

"Have a nice day." Priya beamed.

Priya didn't go home when the shop closed that evening. She called her mother to say she was out with friends and repeated the message to Kabir, assuring him she'd take a taxi later. Then she joined Emilia and Rieke at their table.

Emilia had popped out briefly to fetch supplies from the bakery next door, so there was a bag of cheese croissants amidst the coffee cups. Priya was the only one who had any appetite. She was on her second croissant when the sharp click of Cass's footsteps sounded on the pavement outside.

Cass was not much taller than Emilia, but looked like she should be. Her hair was a dynamic bottle green, cut in a sharp bob, and her sweeping black eyebrows gave all her facial expressions extra drama, making her look annoyed even when she wasn't—though tonight she probably *was* annoyed. She shrugged out of her black brocade jacket and grabbed Emilia's cup of coffee, draining it in one gulp.

"Right," she said. Her Irish accent was much stronger than usual, a sure sign she was angry. "Solutions would be good any time now."

Rieke hunched unhappily in his seat, as though her words had been personally directed at him.

"Do you know anything about creatures like this?" Priya asked, not hopefully.

"What, because I'm from Ireland?" Cass laughed sharply. "When I was little my nan told me not to wear green or the fairies would take me away. That's the sum total of my paranormal knowledge." She glared at Emilia. "I can't believe you didn't even *ask me* before you went and signed your life away."

"Excuse me, you cared? That's news," Emilia snapped. "What happened to, 'it's your mess, sort it out'? You thought the shop was a terrible idea from the start. Why would I ask you for advice when I knew you'd tell me not to even try?"

Cass flinched, color bursting across her cheeks as if Emilia had slapped her. "That's what this is about? Tell me, when was the last time you let me help you with *anything*?"

Rieke looked on in a state of horrified stupefaction. Priya thought about dead crocodiles and eyes that were complacent and hungry at the same time. Maybe the Fate would have called in Emilia's contract anyway, but why come in person?

She slammed her hands down on the table, startling her employers into silence. "Why does she want to close down the bookshop? It's making money, and from the look of things, she likes money. Why does hearing someone else figure out her own name matter more than repaying the loan?"

"I—" Emilia hesitated. "I thought it was just malice."

"This is the supernatural," Cass scoffed. "Why would it make sense?"

Priya chose to ignore that. "The way I see it, she has other plans for this place. Malice doesn't pay for crocodile skin bags."

"She'll probably sell it off to some other idiot," Emilia muttered. Cass twitched her hand, as though she was going to reach out, but didn't.

"Oh, what's the use," Emilia said bitterly, pushing back her chair. "I've gone through millions of names, literally millions, without ever getting the right one. I'm not going to guess it now. I'm sorry, Priya, Rieke. However you got here, you've been fantastic employees. I may not be able to keep the shop open, but maybe the references and experience will help you get a job somewhere else."

She stood up stiffly. "I'm going home."

Rieke unfolded himself abruptly, and gave her a brief, awkward hug. Priya came over to hug her too, then Cass, who looked startled at being included.

"Whatever happens," Priya said, "we'll be okay. Right?"

They all nodded, but none of them believed it.

Getting home was a pain. Priya called a taxi just like she'd promised, but despite her specifications the first one that showed up was a regular cab and she had to wait another two hours for a maxi-taxi that could take her wheelchair. Rieke waited with her, slumped gloomily against a wall, not talking.

All the way home, she turned the same question over like it was a kind of Rubik's cube and if she just looked at it from the right angle she could make the colors align. *Why?* Priya closed her eyes, trying not to cry.

"What's wrong?" were her mother's first words as Priya bumped through the door. The rest of the family was already in bed, but Priya's mother was waiting up in the kitchen with a cup of tea and the radio turned down low. All Priya wanted was to fall into bed and forget that tomorrow she might not have a job.

"I'm fine," she said. "Really, Mum, I'm fine."

"Nonsense. Come here and I'll make more tea."

Reluctantly, Priya edged into the kitchen, which, with its elderly four-seater table and enormous fridge, was a bit too crowded to maneuver through easily. As she pulled up on one side of the table, Priya's eyes went automatically to the two framed quotes that hung above the sink. *They cannot take away our self-respect if we do not give it to them*, Mahatma Gandhi said in neat calligraphy, and *If you're going through hell, keep going*, Winston Churchill added. They were the sentiments by which Priya's mother had lived much of her life.

"Did you have a nice evening?" her mother asked, watching her narrowly.

"No," Priya admitted. Her mother pushed a mug across the table and she took it with a sigh. "Cass and Emilia are in trouble."

"What kind of trouble?"

"Their lender is a crook. They might lose everything. It's so unfair. Emilia put her heart and soul into that shop."

"What about *you*?" her mother demanded. "Is there any trouble with the law?"

"No. They've done nothing illegal."

"Can they still pay you?"

Priya shrugged. "I'll be fine. It's them I'm worried about. And Rieke." She remembered what Emilia had said about malice and looked at the quotes again. "Do you believe in fate, Mum? That things can't be changed?"

Her mother looked surprised. "Never," she said, without hesitation. "We always have choices. Not all of them will be good, but they are ours to make."

"Yes," Priya said thoughtfully. "I think so too."

Sunday was not one of Priya's days at the bookshop. She slipped the white phone under her mattress and spent the morning at a nearby internet cafe, trying to define the nebulous shape of an idea. She needed more data.

When she came home, she heard the soft buzz of the phone and pulled it out. She looked at it for a long time, letting it ring in her hand. Then she fetched her father's hammer and smashed the phone into tiny pieces.

On Monday she arrived early to find Rieke compulsively straightening the shelves as though a precise alignment of spines could prevent anything bad from happening. When Priya called out "good morning!" he turned around and stared.

"Good?" he echoed disbelievingly.

"The shop's still open," Priya told him. "That's a start."

Emilia came out from the aisles. Her eyes were very red. "If you say so," she said. "I've made a sign explaining things—well, what I can—I'll post it on the door."

"Don't," Priya said hastily. "Please, not today."

"Today is the last day," Emilia said tiredly. "Our regulars deserve to know."

"Please, Emilia. Let's go about business as usual. The Fate is bound to come back, she'll want to see the effect this is having on us. So let's show her."

"A brave face?" Emilia smiled grimly. "Well, pride I do have. Or so I'm told. All right, we'll hold it together for one last day. Rieke! Open up. We have books to sell."

Priya was on alert all morning, waiting for a glimpse of crocodile skin or pastel lipstick. Emilia, her smile so determined it looked slightly dangerous, organized an impromptu poetry recital and for the first time ever Rieke did a reading. Priya applauded from behind the till. The crowd of customers clapped too, pleased but bemused by the strangely defiant atmosphere. At the back, clapping thin, beautifully manicured hands, was the Fate.

Finally, Priya thought.

The Fate was smiling, but she wasn't pleased. Priya rolled carefully between the tables until one of her wheels bumped gently against the crocodile skin handbag.

"Back again!" she said, before the Fate could speak. "How *can* we help you?"

The Fate looked, for the briefest moment, unnerved. Then a deeply unpleasant smile spread across her face.

"You can watch," she said, in a low but clear voice, her eyes fixed on Priya's, "as this little enclave is shut and its patrons are cut adrift in the world. You can watch me drink down its dreams and eat up its hopes. And I will watch *you*, my dear. You'll drift from job to job, never quite fitting in, taken out of pity and pushed out the door when indulging your ... misfortune ... becomes too much of a bother. Without my favor, you will become nothing."

Her words hit Priya like venom. She spun quickly to retreat behind the till, but not before she'd caught a glimpse of the Fate's satisfied face. Her cheeks were flushed a healthy pink.

"You see, my dear?" Priya heard her say. "You can help me."

All day long, the Fate sat in that corner. At closing time, when other customers had made their final purchases and vacated their tables, she remained. Emilia was locking up when Cass arrived. They looked at each other with a taut uncertainty, then Emilia yanked down the shutter and turned on the Fate.

"Well," she said, "you want the shop? You'll have to take it from me."

The Fate stood up, carefully brushing down her jacket. She was smiling indulgently, as if Emilia was a recalcitrant granddaughter.

"I did so hope you would say that. Invitations make it so much easier. These silly rules!" She gave a light, almost girlish laugh. "You painted dreams into the walls, dear. All those things you've wanted for so long and been told you couldn't have. They smell *delicious*. You will chase chance all your life but never taste them again. They're already gone." The Fate's voice dropped to a stage whisper. "After all, what do you love that you have left to lose?"

Cass looked at Emilia urgently, as though waiting to hear that refuted, but Emilia didn't look at her. She had her hands over her mouth and tears welling up in her eyes. Emilia, who never gave up.

Cass rounded on the Fate instead. "Fuck you," she spat, disgustedly. "What are you going to do? Use your great and terrible powers to throw us out? All I've seen are cheap tricks and mind games."

"The best tricks are the ones you don't see coming," the Fate said confidingly. "And you never do, do you! Always blindsided, always left behind. You pretend you *want* to be different, but that's not true, is it?"

"How can you live with yourself?" Rieke stepped forward, his fists balled. The Fate looked at Cass for a moment longer, with the air of someone licking the last dregs of cream off a spoon, before turning her pastel smile in his direction.

"A rhetorical question!" she cried jovially, as if Rieke had made a good joke. "Perhaps what you're really wondering is how it's done? *You've* never been very good at living with yourself, have you, Frederik? Not even your own name! You know that everyone you meet is only ever putting *up* with you, don't you? And when they get tired of tolerating those awful little quirks of yours, it's your own fault. That nice young lad—Kabir, isn't it? He's been so polite, putting up with those strange tics that you think pass for flirting, but you know that won't last."

Rieke's face had gone grey. The Fate, by contrast, was practically glowing with health as she watched him, her skin visibly smoother. Inside Priya's head, the last squares of the Rubik's cube slotted into place.

"Actually," she said, "that's not true."

The Fate began to say something about misery and cripples but Priya talked over her, raising her voice. "My brother has had a crush on Rieke from the day they met. You're not a Fate at all, are you? You're a sort of vampire. And those silly rules count for something. That's why you made Emilia sign the contract. You can lie about everything else, but not—"

The Fate brought up a finger and leveled it like a gun at Priya's head. "You," she said, sweet as poison, "shall. Be. Silent. This is *my* ground. It was where my maker drank my soul and where I woke, immortal. I was here when carriages rolled in the streets, not pathetic little girls. There have always been broken souls like you, looking for a place to call their own, and there always will be. You know, they say your appetite wanes as you get older, but I am so *hungry*."

She turned back to Emilia, smiling again.

"Who would have thought I would find such a feast?"

Priya shrank back instinctively from those teeth. Her hands tightened on the arms of her wheelchair, but the fight or flight instinct was one she was used to overriding. She chose a third option: think.

"We all signed your contracts," she repeated, doggedly. "Which means they matter. So I *name* you. I name you..." Priya hesitated, then shrugged. It was already too late to help herself if she was wrong—she might as well enjoy the moment. "I name you Spot."

The color drained from the woman's face, her skin collapsing into wrinkles as if unseen hands were crumpling her up. She looked stunned.

"You have no power over this place," Priya said firmly. "Or anyone here." She raised her hands in dismissal. "Begone, foul Spot!"

The woman whined, a wordless sound of entreaty, while her eyes blazed with rage. Priya wanted to look away but didn't dare. The creature *crumbled*, drifting apart like burnt paper until all that was left was dust on the floor.

There was a long silence. Emilia was the first to move, nudging the sad pile with her toe. "How did you do that?" she breathed.

"I didn't expect *that* to happen," Priya confessed. She realized her hands were shaking and squeezed the arms of her chair tightly. She felt horrified and elated at the same time, and rather sick.

"It's like Cass said," she added, "that ... whatever that was, was all about mind games. If she was really a Fate, she'd know how Kabir felt—and instead, all she had were lies. Saying those awful things was feeding her somehow. She was feeding off all of us. Particularly you, Emilia. This was your dream, and she wanted to eat it whole."

Emilia jerked back from the dust. "She almost did. She almost took everything." She looked at Cass uncertainly. "I suppose that's my fault for not asking for help."

Instead of agreeing, Cass seized Emilia's hands and pulled her into a ferocious hug. "Fuck," she half-wailed. "Did that really happen?"

Emilia hugged her back hard, burying her face in Cass's jacket. "I'm sorry, I'm sorry, I'm sorry," she chanted, her voice muffled. "I dragged you into all this—" She twisted briefly to look over her shoulder. "Priya, consider yourself employed for life, okay?"

Priya laughed shakily. "Is it too soon to ask for a contract?"

Emilia shuddered. "Way too soon."

Priya heard a door open and jumped nervously, but it was only Rieke, returning from the storeroom with a vacuum. They all watched in silence as he ran the nozzle repeatedly over the same patch of floor until long after every speck of dust had to be gone. Then he stripped out the bag, threw it in the sink behind the counter and pulled a box of matches from his pocket, setting the thing on fire.

"Vampires have to be burnt," he said flatly.

Emilia walked over to stand beside him and turned on a tap to wash the ashes down the drain. "And drowned," she agreed.

Later that night, meeting her at the station, Kabir told Priya she looked tired.

"Are you okay?" he asked.

"I'm fine," she said, smiling at how the words sounded in her mouth. "Just fine. Call Rieke and ask him out tonight."

Kabir blinked. "What?"

"I'm your inside woman on this," Priya reminded him. "Tonight's a good time."

Kabir pulled his phone from his pocket and dithered over it for a moment with his finger on a speed dial he'd never used. "Are you sure about this? Won't he think it's weird, me just calling out of the blue?"

"Maybe," Priya said. "Then he'll say yes."

Kabir hit the number.

The train was pulling in. The platform streamed with people who didn't know about a Fate who was a vampire in disguise, who didn't know there was a bookshop called Nightingale and Priest with dreams painted into the walls. Who had no idea how big the world really was.

It wasn't Priya's job to tell them. Her job was to sell them books.

The Lovely Duckling

By Tim Susman

MT. HOOD SPECIAL ABILITIES SCHOOL APPLICATION

[office use only]

[NUMBER: 2133/13]

[ASSIGNED: ~~MK~~ BSW

[Billie—assigned this to you after reading. Let me know if you have any questions —Maureen]

NAME: Mara Pachacutec

ADDRESS: 81 Ocala Drive, West Cypress, FL

EMAIL ADDRESS: mpacha@fmail.com

PHONE NUMBER: 850-555-9398 (but please don't call in the evening because I am at home then and my family doesn't like me to be on the phone when I'm home)

Middle School/Junior High (grades): St. Agatha's Catholic School (5-8)

[X] **Academic transcripts available through EDUSA**

[ ] **School will send transcripts separately**

I affirm that I, student, and I, parent or guardian, have read the accompanying page detailing the risks in attending the Mt. Hood Special Abilities School.

Student: Mara Pachacutec

Parent: E. Pachacutec

Please state, in your own words, why you think you would be an exceptional student at Mt. Hood Special Abilities School:

I have had dreams of flying, and sometimes I feel like feathers are ready to burst out of my skin. The first time I heard about shifters was three years ago when I snuck out of the house to see the movie *The Dream War*. All my friends were talking about Bryce Warner who played the glamourist, but I couldn't stop thinking about Matt Martin, who played a wolf-shifter. Even though I'm a condor, not a wolf, I knew exactly how he felt, and when he changed, it was the most thrilling moment of my life.

Ever since then, I have been looking up shifters and your school on the internet. When I went to Richmond last year with the band, I faked being sick to go visit Monument Special Abilities School. They said I have a great affinity for the Other Side. Mr. Deveraux promised to give you a full report if you write him. He wanted me to go to Monument, but that's best for foxes and snakes and horses. And elephants, I guess. I'm a condor. I want to go to school on a mountain.

Please write a free-form essay that you think is relevant to your application:

The Lovely Duckling

A fairytale by Mara Pachacutec

Once upon a time, there was a duckling who looked like all the other ducklings. She had a yellow bill and webbed feet like all the other ducklings had, and soft brown feathers and brown eyes that everyone said were very pretty.

But the duckling also had a secret that none of the other ducklings had. She knew that she wasn't really a duckling.

She lived with her father, who was a duck, and when she was growing up she thought that maybe her mother had been an eagle or a condor, and that was why she wanted to spread her wings and soar, to fly for miles and miles. But then she found out her mother was a duck, too. So whatever was inside her had come from somewhere else. When she asked her father about it, he told her there was an evil spirit who cursed some people, but he told her that she shouldn't worry because she was a lovely duckling. The little duckling did not feel better.

She was popular in the pond, but the duckling felt that her "friends" only liked who she was pretending to be, and if they could see what the evil spirit had put inside her, they would turn on her and drive her out of the pond. So every time someone said they thought the duckling's feathers were beautiful, or told her she would grow up to be a lovely duck, she made her bill smile even though she wanted to hide it under her wing.

One day the duckling's pond was visited by a majestic stork, and he had a magical glass eye. He told the ducks that he could see their future, and he told them they would lay many eggs and have charming families. But when he spotted the little duckling, his eye fixed her so sharply that she knew he could see inside her to the darkness there, and she ran away from him.

The stork found her hiding in the rushes and told her that she had nothing to fear from him. He said he could see how different she was and that it was nothing to be ashamed of. She asked him to take her away, but he said that all he could do was to teach her a word that would let her inner spirit out.

"But then," she said, "everyone will see it!"

"Yes," he told her, "they will."

"Teach me the word," she said, because she wanted to know it, even if she didn't ever say it.

The little duckling knew that her father would be very disappointed if she said the word, because he wanted very much for her to grow up to be a lovely duck, to have many eggs and a charming family. But the spirit inside her would not go away, and so one night, she stood at the edge of her pond and spoke the word.

The duckling was no longer lovely on the outside. The other ducks would have called the hard, hooked beak a terror, the wide wingspan excessive, and the taloned feet dangerous. But the condor's long, sleek body was beautiful to him.

Without a word to another duck, the condor launched himself from the edge of the pond and flew off to find his people.

[office use only]

[RECOMMENDATION: Proceed to interview. –BSW]

FROM: pachacutec@rdmdesign.com

TO: info@mthoodsaschool.edu

SUBJECT: Mara Pachacutec application

To whom it may concern. I have just learned that my daughter Mara forged my signature on a check and most likely on an application to your school. Please do not cash the check, or if you have cashed it, please refund the money. You may send it to the address on the check. You can throw the application away.

Yours,

E. Pachacutec

FROM: billie@mthoodsaschool.edu
TO: pachacutec@rdmdesign.com
SUBJECT: Re: Mara Pachacutec application
Dear Mr. Pachacutec,

I am sorry to hear that your daughter forged your signature. However, I believe that Mara could have a bright future at Mt. Hood, and so I would be glad to return your check but waive her application fee. We are always in need of talented students and I would appreciate the chance to talk to Mara about her future plans.

Blessed be,
Billie Seven Winds
Assistant to the Director of Admissions
Mt. Hood Special Abilities School

FROM: billie@mthoodsaschool.edu
TO: mpacha@fmail.com
SUBJECT: Your application to the Mt. Hood Special Abilities School

Dear Mara,

My name is Billie Seven Winds, and I'm the assistant to the Director of Admissions at Mt. Hood Special Abilities School. Before I write anything else, I have to tell you that under Mt. Hood's policy, this email is being sent through an independent legal authority to verify that I am not writing anything improper.

This authority may release the transcripts in case of a police investigation; otherwise they remain sealed in the school's files.

I have just heard from your father, who says you forged his name on the check. Mara, I would like to talk to you further about your admission to this school, but without parental consent, we simply cannot go ahead with the admissions process.

You indicated that we should not call in the evenings. If you would prefer to call me, my direct line is (501) 555-1009, and all conversations on that phone are also recorded and transcribed at the same legal authority. This time of year I am in the office quite late, so go ahead and call whenever you want. I hope we can work something out.

Blessed be,

Billie Seven Winds

Assistant to the Director of Admissions

Mt. Hood Special Abilities School

PHONE TRANSCRIPT

ORIGINATING NUMBER: 850-555-9398

DESTINATION NUMBER: 501-555-1009 B. SevenWinds

SevenWinds: Hello, this is Billie Seven Winds.

850-555-9398: Billie, this is Mara Pachacutec.

SevenWinds: Mara, it's good to hear from you.

850-555-9398: If my mother would sign a consent form, would that be okay?

SevenWinds: That would probably work. Did she agree to sign it?

850-555-9398: I haven't asked. She lives in Alabama and I haven't talked to her in a year. She wants to see me but she's afraid of Papa. But if I can get away, I can get her to sign the form.

SevenWinds: Why is she afraid of your father? Is he abusive? I mean, are you all right?

850-555-9398: He just threatens my friends and doesn't let me watch shifter movies. And he keeps buying me cheap perfume and spraying it around my room until I get sick from the smell, and he took down the nest I built and he doesn't like sports! What kind of father doesn't like sports? Anyway, I'll get in trouble for the application but I don't care. He'll just ground me and make me cook dinner and it'll be horrible like it always is.

SevenWinds: You're sure?

850-555-9398: If I can get away from here, I'll be fine. But I need your help.

SevenWinds: Mt. Hood Special Abilities School can't help you with that, I'm sorry. If you've already gone through the official channels and your father isn't abusive … I can email you the parental consent form to bring to your mother, that's all.

850-555-9398: I just don't know how to get to her. I walked to the bus last year once, but the bus driver knows my father. He wouldn't pick me up.

SevenWinds: Is everybody afraid of your father?

850-555-9398: No boy would ask me to the eighth grade dance because they were scared of him, not even my friend Tomas.

SevenWinds: Mara, like I said, the Mt. Hood school can't help you get away from your father. As much as I sympathize—

850-555-9398: Teach me how to take the condor shape over the phone.

SevenWinds: What?

850-555-9398: Because then I could just fly to Mama, get her to sign the form, and then fly to your school. I would only do it once. I know untrained shifting is dangerous, but…

SevenWinds: Oh, Mara, I can't do that.

850-555-9398: Is it because this is being recorded? You can call me back from a cell phone. I won't tell, I promise!

SevenWinds: No, Mara, I can't. But besides that, I mean—the reason you come to shifter school to learn shapes is because you have to know them from being close to them, and getting close is very dangerous without supervision. I know you love those shifter movies, but what the movies don't show is that people without training can get seriously injured.

850-555-9398: I'm not afraid. I know condors. I've watched them on video like every day.

SevenWinds: I know, Mara. But first of all, the condors you see in this world aren't quite the same as the condors you would shift into. And second, just watching them on video isn't enough. The programs here prepare you for the Other Side for a full year before you even start studying your shape—

850-555-9398: I've already shifted.

850-555-9398: Hello?

SevenWinds: Mara, do you mean you've taken a condor shape?

850-555-9398: Well … no. I changed my … hair color. Everyone thought I dyed it.

SevenWinds: Thank the Goddess. Hair color is fine. I changed my skin color, and—well, yes. That's all right. You can do that because you know exactly what your hair looks like and it's still part of you.

850-555-9398: Oh. I thought that meant I could unlock the shape if I knew the right words.

SevenWinds: Shifting isn't a video game. No, you're doing very well to be able to change your hair color. Most of the students who enroll here can't do that much. It means you really are in tune with your abilities. But I'm afraid you still can't change to a condor. Part of the instruction here is learning how to match the shape to what's inside you, what's part of your spirit, and you can't just turn it on with a cheat code. You'll have to find some other way.

850-555-9398: I don't know what else I can do. I have to fly away! I can't … do anything else.

SevenWinds: Is there a teacher at school you can talk to?

850-555-9398: I can barely talk to anyone. Tomas's mother might drive me to Tallahassee. I have a key to Tomas's house, but Papa knows he's my best friend. He's really my only friend. Papa would hurt Tomas or get his mother fired or—he's home. I have to go!

SevenWinds: Don't give up, Mara.

[CALL TERMINATED]

FROM: pachacutec@rdmdesign.com

TO: billie@mthoodsaschool.edu

SUBJECT: Re: Mara Pachacutec application

Miss Seven Winds,

In case my previous letter was not clear, I don't want any further contact between Mara and your school.

E. Pachacutec

FROM: billie@mthoodsaschool.edu

TO: pachacutec@rdmdesign.com

SUBJECT: Re: Mara Pachacutec application

Dear Mr. Pachacutec,

May I ask why you are so opposed? If you are worried about the dangers of Mara becoming a shifter, the attached brochure has a thorough explanation of the safety measures we employ and it also explains the many spiritual reasons to have your child put in touch with her inner form as well as the financial security most shifters enjoy.

Children who express a strong affinity for a shape and are not allowed to learn that shape in a controlled, informed environment often grow into unhappy adults. There are few who show as strong an affinity as Mara. I hope you will read the above documents and reconsider your position.

Blessed be,

Billie Seven Winds

Assistant to the Director of Admissions

Mt. Hood Special Abilities School

FROM: billie@mthoodsaschool.edu
TO: maureen@mthhoodsaschool.edu

Hi, Maureen,

See attached email from Mara Pachacutec's father. If he doesn't respond, is there any way we can invoke discrimination laws? What about the Johnson kid in Kansas City a couple years ago? Can we use that?

Blessed be,

Billie

FROM: maureen@mthoodsaschool.edu
TO: billie@mthoodsaschool.ed

Billie,

The Johnson kid was beaten; the Crossover laws were applied because it was already a felony and the Bakegamaa School presented itself as a viable legal guardian. I will review the emails again and see what we can do. Do not contact her again. I know it hurts leaving her alone, but if we get sued, they will drag out the case long enough to make it impossible for her to enroll.

Maureen

PHONE TRANSCRIPT
ORIGINATING NUMBER: 850-555-9398
DESTINATION NUMBER: 501-555-1009 B. SevenWinds

SevenWinds: Hello, Mara?

850-555-9398: This is Eric Pachacutec. Who is this?

SevenWinds: Mr. Pachacutec. This is Billie Seven Winds. I—

850-555-9398: I thought so. You sound like a hippie. What have you done with my daughter?

SevenWinds: Mr. Pachacutec, I can assure you, I have had no contact with your daughter since your email.

850-555-9398: I thought she might have been calling you people. Sure enough, I found your number in her cell phone. But now she's not in her room. You want to tell me one more time what you've done, or do I have to call the FBI?

SevenWinds: I promise you, we have not—

850-555-9398: I can snap my fingers and have a dozen agents looking up your asses. They'd just love an excuse to come down on you people. Trying to turn our kids into animals—by God, I wish Robertson had won. He'd have kicked you all out.

SevenWinds: Mr. Pachacutec, your daughter is very confused, and if she doesn't come to our school—

850-555-9398: Ha! If she doesn't come to your school, she'll live a normal life, marry a good man, have kids. She's just going through what all teenagers do—rebellion against her family.

SevenWinds: I think it's more than that.

850-555-9398: You talked to my daughter once. I've known her all her life. So shut up and keep away from her.

[CALL TERMINATED]

CALHOUN COUNTY SHERIFF'S OFFICE EVENT REPORT
CC03-13-00043
ENT: 20:39 DSP: 20:44 ARR: 20:53
ADDR: 91 N. Palm Dr. CITY: West Cypress
TYPE: [85] RUNAWAY CHILD PRI: 1
CALLER'S NAME: Eric Pachacutec
CALLER'S ADDR: 81 Ocala Dr. West Cypress
CALLER'S PHONE: xxx-xxx-xxxx

COMMENTS:
20:39 CALLER'S DAUGHTER MARA MISSING 1 HR...REF PREV ATTEMPTS TO RUN AWAY...SUSPECTED DAUGHTER AT FRIEND MARTINEZ HOUSE 91 PALM DRIVE...REQ POLICE ASST

OFFICER: 11/914 S. DAVIDSON
NARRATIVE:
I responded to a call from Mr. Pachacutec and spoke to him while en route to Palm Dr. address to clarify initial report. Mr. P. said his daughter had tried to run away three times over previous year and he suspected that her friend Tomas Martinez and his mother Inez Martinez were assisting her. He did not have cordial relations with Mrs. M. and requested police assistance because he was worried about Mrs. M.'s actions if he entered her house under Florida's "stand your ground" law (Florida Statute 776.013).

I secured a description of Mara Pachacutec and upon arrival at Palm Drive found Mrs. Martinez leaving in a white Toyota Corolla with two children in the back seat. She stopped upon my request and I identified the two children as Tomas Martinez and Mara Pachacutec. Mrs. M. did not contest my identification, neither did either child. I informed her that I was required to bring Mara Pachacutec to police station and she surrendered the child to my custody.

While transporting Mara to the police station, I attempted to engage her in conversation but she remained silent. At the station, she requested a private room, so I put her in Sheriff's office and locked the door, then called Mr. P.

At 21:18, Mr. P arrived and I accompanied him to the Sheriff's office. Upon unlocking the door we found Tomas Martinez in the office. Mara Pachacutec was not present. I checked the window and found it secure, and Mrs. Ward affirmed that the door had not been opened since I locked it.

Mr. P. assumed that glamours had been cast on the children prior to my arrival at Palm Drive and asked why we did not check for them. I reminded him that no glamour detection personnel have been assigned to Calhoun County since the tax cuts in 2002. He grew abusive toward me and demanded that we track down Mrs. M. and arrest her and recover his daughter.

Officer Jensen was dispatched to pursue Mrs. Martinez [incident report CC03-13-00046]. Along with Officer Cruz, I questioned Tomas as to how he had come to be in the police station. Transcript attached below.

DAVIDSON: Tomas, I know I brought Mara Pachacutec out of your mother's car and left you in the back seat. How did you get into the office? Where did Mara go?

MARTINEZ: You brought me here and told me to wait there until Mr. Pachacutec arrived.

DAVIDSON: Were you disguised as Mara Pachacutec at the time?

MARTINEZ: Yes.

DAVIDSON: How did you make this glamour?

MARTINEZ: I didn't cast a glamour.

DAVIDSON: Did Mara Pachacutec cast the glamour?

MARTINEZ: No.

DAVIDSON: Is Mara Pachacutec still disguised as Tomas Martinez?

MARTINEZ: Maybe. Maybe she's in her real shape now.

DAVIDSON: Did the people from the Mt. Hood School help her at all?

MARTINEZ: Mara talked to them. But her father told them to stop talking to her and she hasn't heard from them since then.

DAVIDSON: Do you know where she and your mother were going?

MARTINEZ: I don't know. Mara just wanted me to sit in the car until the police came. Can I have another candy bar?

CRUZ: Here.

DAVIDSON: Did Mara cast the glamour or did someone else?

MARTINEZ: I didn't see anyone cast anything.

DAVIDSON: All right. I guess that's all.

Officer Cruz observed the conversation. Based on her experience with juveniles, she believed that Tomas Martinez looked relaxed and his answers appeared to be truthful. Without arresting him, we could not administer a lie detector, and Captain Yin did not see sufficient grounds for arrest.

I offered to allow Tomas Martinez to wait at the police station until his mother was located, but he elected to return home. I brought him to his residence in a patrol car, waited while he unlocked the door, and ensured he was safely inside before returning to the station.

PHONE TRANSCRIPT

ORIGINATING NUMBER: 251-555-8719

DESTINATION NUMBER: 501-555-1009 B. SevenWinds

SevenWinds: Hello, this is Billie SevenWinds.

251-555-8719: Hi, Billie. It's Mark Pachacutec.

SevenWinds: Mark?

251-555-8719: Last time we talked, I was Mara. I'm Mark now. I looked like my friend Tomas at first, but then I shifted to look more like Mara used to look, only if Mara was a boy.

SevenWinds: You ... shifted?

251-555-8719: Uh-huh. It wasn't easy. I know how I feel, and I know how Tomas *looks*, like, I see him almost every day, but I couldn't get it right until I was in Tomas's room and I could hear him and get the boy smell of his room. You know how boys smell, how *we* smell, it's great, it's all like sweat and dirt and stuff. Well, I still didn't completely get it. But all the parts people can see, anyway. It was hard in the police station, because Tomas wasn't there, but he gave me his phone with his voice recorded on it, and the police station kinda smells like boys too—

SevenWinds: Police station...?

251-555-8719: Don't worry about it. They're looking for Mara. She's gone now. I wish I could be there when they pull over Mrs. Martinez and find Tomas in the back seat.

SevenWinds: Mark...

251-555-8719: They'll probably take him to a glamourist.

SevenWinds: I shouldn't be talking to you—

251-555-8719: My father told you not to talk to Mara, right? Like I said, she's gone. It's okay.

SevenWinds: I appreciate that, although legally—anyway, I was going to say, I shouldn't be talking to you, but if you want, I can give you some phone numbers to call of people who can. They're local Florida authorities, people you could look up in any library with an internet terminal—wait, are you still in Florida?

251-555-8719: I'm on my way to my mother's place and I just wanted to tell you I'm okay. The bus driver likes the Tide and I like the Seminoles and we talked football for hours. It's awesome.

SevenWinds: The bus driver? Mark, be very careful.

251-555-8719: That's why I'm calling you. He's a Greyhound driver named Roger Jefferson. They put him in charge of me because I'm an unaccompanied minor but I just wanted to be sure, and I know you're recording this, so I'm telling you his name in case

I disappear or something. But it's cool. He's really nice, and I told him my mom's expecting me, so I don't think he'd do anything even if he was a creeper. Oh, he's into shifter movies too. Uh-oh, I gotta go, my bus is boarding.

SevenWinds: Call me from your mother's.

251-555-8719: Thanks, Billie! Bye.

[CALL TERMINATED]

Report of the Federal Bureau of Investigation

To: FBI, Portland, Oregon

FBI File no. 24-50203-122

Complaint Filed

Eric Pachacutec of Calhoun County, FL, alleged misconduct by Mt. Hood Special Abilities School with his daughter Mara prior to her disappearance.

Action

Subpoena issued to Mt. Hood Special Abilities School for all contact with Mara Pachacutec (documents attached Q01-8). Documents verified valid and complete by Portman, Schultz, & Markinson.

Calhoun County Sheriff's report referenced (document attached Q09).

Result of Examination

Unfortunately, the FBI was unable to allocate "a dozen agents" to this case, but the investigation proceeded regardless. Documents demonstrate that Mt. Hood Special Abilities School conducted themselves in accordance with all federal laws. No wrongdoing was found. This office reported to Mr. Pachacutec that his complaint had no basis. Mr. Pachacutec demanded any information that might lead to the location of his daughter Mara, and this office regrettably was unable to provide such. Mr. Pachacutec did not inquire about his son Mark, and so no information was offered about him.

Kiss and Kiss and Kiss and Tell

By E.C. Myers

Everyone leaned forward to watch the animated beer bottle spin on the iPad in the center of their circle. Everyone but Rene. She tilted back slightly, as though that would help the bottle pass her by.

She wrapped her hands around a warm can of PBR, open but still as full as when Cedric had handed it to her at the door. Dad had insisted she take her medication before she left the house; he'd even watched her swallow the white and yellow capsule. If he'd known there would be alcohol—and worse—at this party, she wouldn't be here at all. She was beginning to think that might have been for the best; thanks to her medication, she didn't really feel like part of the group anyway.

Braden reached around Yasi's waist and pulled her into a tipsy kiss. Whatever they'd seen together during their turn in the closet must have been good because they had been all over each other since.

"Hey, you two. Save it," Cedric said. "Respect the bottle."

The animated bottle slowed, wobbled, and settled on Rene. The iPad emitted a tinny chorus of "Oooohhhh!"

"Finally," Jenny said. "You're up, Rene." She reached across the circle and handed Rene a battered Altoids tin. Jenny's peach lipstick was smeared suggestively on the right side of her mouth after her turn with Kell two spins ago.

Rene wondered what it would be like to kiss Jenny Trinh—not in a dark closet in Braden's basement rec room, but after they had enjoyed dinner at Norton's and seen a romantic movie, when they were saying good night to each other in Jenny's Prius.

Rene put down her beer and opened the creaky lid of the tin. There were two tiny blue pills inside.

She closed the tin. "Actually, I have to get going. It's late."

"It'll only take seven minutes," Braden said. "Or less." He smirked at Cedric, who had spun the bottle that had chosen Rene.

"We've all gone except you," Yasi said. "More than once."

"That's not my fault. It's totally random." Rene gestured at the iPad.

"Rules are rules," Kell said. Her eyes were closed and her voice slurred.

Rene stood. "I'll go first next time."

"Don't be that way," Braden said. He kept grinning, but his voice was hard.

Rene faltered. *Don't be that way*. Don't be a freak, he meant.

What happened to you? Where did you go?

Everyone had wondered where she'd been for the month following winter break, when she hadn't returned to school. After she refused to answer enough times, people stopped asking. Then they stopped talking to her altogether. She thought by coming here tonight, she'd be able to reclaim some of her popularity. Maybe remind herself of what it had been like to be part of the in-crowd and get straight As and be the perfect daughter with a promising future. Recapture some of what she had been like before ... *Before.*

But she clearly wasn't ready for all this. She didn't feel comfortable with her old friends anymore, and she wondered if she ever had. Maybe what she remembered, what she missed, had just been another symptom of what was wrong with her.

"Come on. It'll be all right. I promise." Cedric smiled. Once upon a time, a smile from Cedric Collins had been a major turn on for Rene. She would have jumped at the chance to kiss those lips. She didn't feel that anymore either, but when he offered his hand, she took it and followed him into the closet.

"Hi," he said.

"Hi," Rene said.

"I'm glad you came tonight. We missed you." He sat down across from her on the carpet, pushing aside a pile of board games. Risk.

Life. Sorry! "I missed you. I was hoping the bottle would land on you." He brushed his tousled brown hair away from his eyes.

Rene blushed.

"This is your first time taking Nemo, isn't it? It's understandable to be nervous, but there's nothing to worry about. It's completely safe."

"Nothing is completely safe," she said.

She flipped open the lid again and studied the two pills inside. They looked harmless enough, but she knew now that most drugs were anything but. Even good ones, like the kind that kept her from hearing the voices, usually had side effects. She was slower in school these days, her emotions were numb. She was much less horny, which actually worked well since she didn't feel very social any more. Even colors seemed muted.

But these pills were a brilliant blue, standing out from her sepia-toned world.

Nemo had started circulating in the school while she was away. She'd heard the resident bad boy Samson Baum was dealing the pills, and that they only worked on teenagers. Unlike some of the other popular designer drugs making the rounds, the media hadn't caught on to Nemo yet.

"But what is it? What does it do?" She touched one with the tip of her index finger.

"It takes you a little into the future with the person you're kissing," he said. "It's incredible. Sometimes you're even having sex, but it's better somehow. It's still just a kiss, but it feels so real."

"Imagined sex is better than actual sex?" Rene asked.

"It isn't fake. It just hasn't happened yet. And if it isn't good, it doesn't have to happen."

Rene wanted to ask what Cedric saw when he had taken a turn with Matt earlier. Rules are rules, after all. Both boys had been silent when they emerged from the closet, and they had avoided looking at each other for the rest of the night.

"What about side effects? What happens if you mix it with other drugs?"

"Alcohol only makes it more potent, if that's what you're worried about."

It wasn't, but she couldn't tell him about the other pill she'd already taken, and he wouldn't know how the drugs would interact anyway. She knew she shouldn't risk it.

But there could have been something between her and Cedric once. She'd wanted him. And when she'd returned to school, he'd been more concerned about her than anyone, until she had finally pushed him away too. This moment could bring them back together, back on the track they were on before.

Before her brain had betrayed her.

"The easiest way is just to show you." Cedric smiled again. That smile.

It was just one pill. It was just one kiss.

He picked up one of the pills between his thumb and index finger.

"It works pretty fast, but it doesn't last long. About seven minutes," he said. "Just put it under your tongue, like this, and hold it there until it's gone." He demonstrated.

Rene took the second pill and placed it delicately under her tongue, eyes on Cedric.

"Now what?" she asked. She could feel the pill dissolving, but she didn't feel any different yet. It tasted like gym class.

"It activates when we kiss," he said.

He demonstrated.

Rene watches Cedric pull his pants on and tuck in his rumpled shirt. He looks older. She notices his hair is thinning on top when he leans over to tie his shoelaces.

"What?" Rene says.

"It was great to see you again, Rene," Cedric says, not looking at her.

She sits up, then realizes that she's naked and pulls the bedspread up to cover herself. His lips widen in a familiar smile.

"You're ... leaving?" she asks.

She wants to ask him what he's doing there. She wants to ask what they did... Last night? But that seems obvious. Morning sunlight streams through the window of an apartment she doesn't recognize, but she sees a picture of her and her dad on the dresser beside it, so she guesses this is her bedroom.

"I'm glad I came to the reunion after all," he says. "I wasn't going to."

He has a wedding ring.

"You're married," she says. She doesn't want to look around her room anymore. She closes her eyes. She doesn't want to look at him anymore. She can't remember what happened, how they got to this place. This ... time? What happened to the last ten years? The last thing she remembers is...

Blue. A blue pill.

Is she back in the hospital? Is this really happening?

"Don't make this a thing," he says.

"What is going on?" she says. "You said it was harmless."

"Don't be that way," Cedric says.

"Get out," she says.

"Rene? Where did you go?" he asks.

She opens her eyes.

Cedric waved his hand in front of her face. "Where did you go?"

Cedric hasn't changed. He's still seventeen, still stunningly handsome, still single.

"What was that?" she asked. "Did that really happen?"

"It might," he said. "I hope it does."

She frowned. "What did you see?"

"It was prom," he says. "We were having an epic makeout session in the limo. We were kissing, but we were about to do more than that. Too bad the drug doesn't last longer. To be continued."

Rene's hands started shaking. She tucked them under her legs.

"Rene? Isn't that what you saw?" he asked.

"Yeah," she lied. She didn't know why it had shown her something else, obviously much farther in their future. For all she knew, it was all in her head. She listened, afraid she would hear them again.

"So how about it?" he asked. "Wanna go to prom?"

"What color was my dress?" she asked. "I was too distracted to notice."

"Purple," he said. "Kind of shimmery fabric. Really nice up top." He glanced at her chest as if he'd never really looked at it before.

"I hate purple," she said.

Tomorrow she was going to take that dress back to the store. She'd picked it out just before she went to the psych ward, back when the only thing she had to worry about was who she was going to prom with and what she was going to wear. It probably didn't even fit her anymore, she'd lost so much weight.

The scary thing was she really didn't like purple anymore. How could a drug change something like that? What else was it changing about her?

The closet door opened. Trish lowered a cell phone she'd been pointing at them, clearly disappointed.

"They're just *talking*," she called over her shoulder toward the group.

"Samson Baum?" Rene said.

The boy slammed his locker shut and spun his wheelchair around to face her. His eyes traveled from her waist up to her face, lingering midway just long enough to show appreciation without being pervy. The former track star was cute enough to get away with it.

"Call me Sam," he said. "Are you looking for someone?"

She replied with the password: "No one in particular."

Braden had told her how to get her own supply of Nemo, in the afterglow of whatever he'd imagined doing with Rene while they were on the drug. Rene had been agitated over the future she saw with him: she'd been crashing on his couch, temporarily homeless. He'd told her she needed to leave, to get psychiatric help.

Sam looked around. The hallway was empty. School had just let out, and everyone was heading to the soccer game. Rene was glad to find him alone, though he always seemed to be by himself. Ever since his accident.

Sam jerked his head down the hall and she followed him into an empty classroom, hurrying to keep up. She closed the door and saw they were in one of the chemistry labs. That seemed appropriate.

"Is this where you make it?" she asked.

He snorted. "Make what?"

"Nemo."

"Do I look like Walter White? I'm planning to be a voice-over actor," he said. "I don't know the first thing about making drugs."

"So you have a supplier."

"Sort of," he said. "Do you want some or not?"

"I want to ask you some questions," she said. She pulled out her notebook.

"Sorry, but I don't do interviews. I'm sure you understand." He guided his wheelchair around her. She put a hand on its arm, to stop him from leaving, but then she yanked it away as if it had burned her.

"I'm sorry," she said.

He narrowed his eyes. "Everyone is." He nodded at the door. "I can't open that with you standing in the way."

She stepped aside, but she didn't open the door for him.

"I need to know how this drug works. I've seen some disturbing things," she said.

He paused, his hand on the door knob. "Like what?"

"Like my future," she said.

He smiled. "That's how Nemo works. Did you see yourself doing something you never thought you would? That's why people like it, because they can fool around with lots of different people without any consequences. Sex with no fuss and no muss. It's okay. It's all in your head, unless you decide to make that future happen."

"I've kissed dozens of people—"

"You going for a world record or something?" His expression softened. "That isn't like you, Rene. You don't need this stuff."

"How do you know what I'm like?" she snapped. "How do you know what I need?"

His eyes widened.

"I guess I don't," he said.

"That makes two of us. I haven't for a while."

"But what are you up to?" he asked. "Why the kissing spree?"

She'd made a point of going to all the Nemo parties after school, what one paper had referred to as kissing orgies in a shocking exposé on teen behavior that didn't mention Nemo at all. Rene could kiss a handful of people on a single dose.

"I'm not a nympho or anything. It's for science," she said.

The problem was, even though things never went beyond a kiss, everyone claimed she was hooking up with them in their Nemo-induced visions of the future. She couldn't even dispute what they'd seen because she was seeing something else. Which left her with a new reputation as the new class slut, despite the fact that she had only ever had sex with a total of two people, and she hadn't gotten laid in months.

"Science. And I'm sure you don't enjoy it at all," Sam said.

"Well, sometimes, sure. Depends on who I'm kissing." She wasn't being all that picky. "But that's beside the point. I'm doing research, recording everyone's Nemo experiences with me. Most of our classmates aren't seeing past the next seven minutes, let alone next Thursday. They're just fantasizing about rounding all the bases."

"And what are you seeing?"

"The *future*. Ten weeks from now, or ten years. Twenty years."

"That's interesting," Sam said. "I'd assumed we didn't see that far into the future because Nemo works differently on adults."

"What do you see when you take it?"

Sam broke eye contact and half-turned his chair away.

"Nothing."

Rene studies Jenny while she sleeps in her bed—in *their* bed. Since she opened her eyes, she's had a chance to look around, and it's clear that they live together and have for a while.

She fights the urge to stroke Jenny's back, just to feel her warmth and the touch of her skin. Rene's oddly impressed with herself for scoring Jenny, because she's always had a little crush on her. But by now she knows that this will be when it all ends.

Jenny stirs and stretches and looks up at Rene sleepily. Rene smiles, but Jenny's face closes up.

"What?" she snaps.

She gets out of bed and Rene watches her move. This is probably the only time she'll ever see this glorious body naked. Jenny must be in her thirties, but she still looks amazing. She has two Chinese characters tattooed over her left shoulder that would be a cliché on anyone but her.

Rene has avoided the floor-length mirror in the bathroom, but she feels heavy, physically and emotionally. She caught a quick glimpse of her face as she opened the medicine cabinet. Her hair is short in this now, dyed blonde, like she always wanted/threatened to do.

There's no sign of Advantic or any other kind of psychiatric medication in the bathroom or anywhere else in their sprawling

New York City apartment overlooking Central Park. There's no sign of bright blue pills either. What would happen if she took Nemo now, and kissed Jenny in the midst of this vision? But no, they're adults, and the drug isn't supposed to work on them anymore.

Jenny shrugs into a silk robe, her motions jerky, harsh. She moves differently from the high school girl currently kissing Rene in the closet. She's more confident. In control, like the successful businesswoman she must be.

"You came home drunk again last night," Jenny says.

That explains the dull pounding in Rene's head. A hangover. She's never had a hangover before. She isn't supposed to mix drinks with her medication. She isn't supposed to mix drugs either, but she still took Nemo.

"I'm sorry?" Rene says. Nothing she says now will make a difference. This is the moment it ends, the way it ends/will end with all the others she's been with for a seven-minute glimpse into their futures together: Cedric, Braden, Yasi, Javier, Kell, even Trish. And dozens more.

It doesn't matter, because this moment will never happen.

"You *are* sorry," Jenny says.

Rene closes her eyes.

Rene opened her eyes at the same time Jenny did. They looked at each other for a moment. Jenny's eyes were soft and gentle, like her lips. It's the way she might look at Rene if they kept along this path together.

To be continued.

"I think I'm in love," Jenny said. She leaned forward eagerly for another kiss, but Rene jerked back. She wasn't interested in returning to that future any time soon. Whenever she kisses the same person twice, the vision picks up right where it left off. Some of them are too horrible for her to even think about. She wondered if there was any future in which she could be happy.

"What did you see?" Rene asked.

"See? Not much. It was dark and I was drunk. *So* drunk! But oh God, it felt…" Jenny shivered.

Rene pulled out the little notepad she carried everywhere and a pen. She turned to a fresh page at the back and quickly drew Jenny's tattoo from memory.

"What does this say?" Rene asked. She showed Jenny the page.

"That's my name," Jenny said. "You learned how to write my name in Chinese?"

"Do you have a tattoo?"

"No way. I'd never do that." Jenny put a hand on Rene's. "I can't believe how real it all was, like it was really happening."

"It didn't happen," Rene said. "It won't happen."

Rene pulled her hand away then flipped to a new page, pen poised. "Tell me everything you remember."

Sam unlocked the top right-hand drawer of his desk and retrieved a flimsy cardboard box marked Mnemozyne IX. He shook it and it sounded nearly empty. He flipped the lid open and pulled out a small paper packet between his index and middle fingers, flicked it to Rene.

She caught it and sat on the edge of his bed to read the tiny print on the envelope. It looked like one of those single servings of "Unaspirin" the school nurse gave you when you complained about a headache. Under the brand name, the drug was identified as amygdamine "instant action tablets". She smiled, considering what they were used for.

"That's Nemo," he said. "All I do to 'make it' is I file off the name stamped on the side of the tablets."

"What is it for?" she asked.

"It's a new Alzheimer's medication. Side effects include headache, diarrhea, confusion, dizziness, and unusual urges."

"'Unusual urges.' What does that mean?"

"You aren't much of a scientist if you haven't figured that out already."

She rolled her eyes. "Where are you getting these? This doesn't look over-the-counter."

"My mom. She's a pharma rep, so she gets plenty of free samples. More than she can keep track of."

"So you decided to start selling them yourself?"

He wheeled himself over to the side of the bed. "We've been struggling with medical bills, so I thought I'd help out.

And I'm saving for prosthetic legs. Mom thinks I've been tutoring."

Rene was all too familiar with medical bills and medication they couldn't afford. But the alternative would cost her much more, if she'd learned anything from her glimpses of futures spent off her meds, in which every relationship crumbles or implodes.

Rene shook the drug envelope. "If it's Alzheimer's medicine, what's it *supposed* to do?"

"Reverse memory loss and minimize the effects of dementia. At least, in adults. For kids our age, it does something very different."

"Precall," Rene said.

He raised an eyebrow. "What's that?"

"Like… Remembering the future." She blushed.

"Oh, I see. Cute portmanteau." He grinned. "You're more of a dork than I expected, Rene."

"This coming from a guy who uses words like portmanteau."

"I just meant that I thought you were interesting when you were Miss Popularity at Briar Woods," he said. "But I think I like you even more now."

"Thanks, I think," she said. "You never showed any interest."

"You just weren't paying attention. All the guys were into you. And plenty of girls."

"As I recall, you could have had any girl in school."

"Not you. You were different."

Rene squeezed the envelope. "Because I like girls too?"

"No! Do you also remember I used to be kind of a dick?"

"I remember."

"Oh. Good. Well, maybe I never had much trouble getting dates and action, but that's all it ever was. I don't think I was ever with one girl for more than a week. If you'd said yes to me, I would have wanted more than that. Or maybe I wasn't ready, and I would have thrown away that chance. But it's a good thing we weren't going out, because then *this* happened." He punched his thigh angrily.

She considered the drug in her palm. "Like that would have changed anything."

"It changed *everything*."

"So what happened, anyway? I've only heard rumors." The most popular was that he'd been hit by a drunk driver while running along the side of the road. The most outrageous suggested he'd been in a freak snow plow accident.

"I turned left when I should have turned right."

Rene winced.

"I was jogging along the side of the road, grooving to 'The Final Countdown.' I just wasn't paying attention to traffic. I still can't listen to that track. Your turn," he said.

"What?"

"What happened to *you*? I've heard rumors. You look really good for someone who just had a baby."

Rene hadn't done anything about the rumors, because they were obviously unfounded, and the truth was much more embarrassing. The one about her being in rehab was closest to the mark, and she'd rather everyone explained her erratic behavior and babbling outbursts on a bad drug trip than mental illness. One, at least, could be cured.

"Nothing happened to me," she said. "I just needed some time off."

He studied her for a moment. Then he turned away. "Okay. Then why don't you give me more details about what you've been seeing when you take this drug?"

She told him about Cedric. She told him about Jenny. She told him about Matt, their two kids, and the morning he would walk out of their suburban home in Westchester, N.Y. with a suitcase. How she and Yasi would part ways the week before Rene gave her valedictorian speech, when she told her she was two months pregnant and didn't know who the father was. How Kell would get too attached after a summer fling before they left for college. She told him about Kimi. Alex. Simon.

"All in the future," Sam said.

"How can they all be true?" she asked.

"They aren't. What you're experiencing is very elaborate, but these visions are no more real than all those hookups everyone else experiences under Nemo."

"How can you be sure they aren't possible futures? And I'm somehow changing them?"

He laughed. "You're just imagining things."

She chewed her lip.

"These aren't possible futures," he said. "They're pretend ones. That's what the drugs do. What else are you going to imagine while you're kissing someone, right? You're going to take things a little farther, maybe. Maybe make things a little weirder than you're usually comfortable with. Nemo lets you experiment without experimenting—play out different parts with different people.

"But it's just a kiss, Nemo interacting with hormones and neurochemicals and sometimes a bit of alcohol. You just have an overactive, and admittedly freakish imagination."

"But how can people remember the same thing?" Rene riffled the pages of her notepad. "I've documented so many cases in which couples report that they've shared the same … hallucinations."

"You did it yourself. Whenever someone asks you if you saw the same thing, you've been lying. Sometimes people start to believe the lie. And like I said, it isn't a stretch that they'd be imagining the same situation. And when they compare notes, they blend their stories into one shared experience. It's like a dream that you can't quite remember that changes as you tell it to other people."

"But I remember my Nemo experiences perfectly," Rene said. "And Cedric knew what my prom dress looked like in his vision."

"Just because you're seeing different things, that doesn't mean you're seeing an actual future. What, you think the drug is triggering some kind of latent psychic ability or something? Why would it happen to you and not anyone else?"

Rene slapped her notebook shut and stood up.

"I'm just trying to understand what's going on," Rene said. "We could be onto something incredible here. A way to see our futures before we live them. Before we're stuck with them."

"There's one big flaw in your theory," Sam said.

"What's that?"

"Every one of your future fantasies involves someone from our high school. Whomever you happen to be kissing at that moment. I mean, when I graduate, I'll be happy if I never see any of you ever again. Although, now that I think about it, maybe that proves your argument; if it isn't real, then your imagination is somewhat limited."

"*My* imagination is limited? You said you don't see anything when you take Nemo."

Sam fell silent. "That's because I know there's no way I can have any kind of future with the person I'm kissing. You can keep that." He nodded at the packet of Nemo in her hand. "A going away gift. Good luck with your groundbreaking research."

Sam turned away to place the box of drugs carefully back into his desk. Rene let herself out of his room.

He had made some good points. She needed more data.

Rene locked her bedroom door and sat at her desk. After her talk with Sam, she reasoned that perhaps whatever was happening to her, whatever Nemo was doing to her, or allowing her to do, didn't even require a partner.

She tore open the packet and tipped the pill onto her desk. She turned it over so she could see the name Mnemozyne on one side. She picked it up. She placed it under her tongue and got ready for some instant action.

Nothing happened. By now, it would normally have kicked in. By now, she would normally be kissing someone.

Hormones and neurochemicals, Sam had said. It didn't activate until you were kissing a partner. All right then.

Rene opened her laptop and opened her hidden folder of porn she'd copied from her dad's computer; he really had no clue how to setup a home wireless network without sharing all his files.

She started a favorite. It usually took her a little while to get into the video. As the two women pirates began making out, she unbuttoned her jeans. When the swashbucklers unbuckled, she lowered the zipper. Rene slipped her hand into the waistband of her bright blue panties and closed her eyes.

Rene opens her eyes and stares down at her hands. They're red, bright red. She's sitting on a toilet, naked in a bathroom. Water plips in the tank at her back. Harsh fluorescent light. Cold tiles beneath her bare feet. Tiles splattered with crimson drops leading to the closed door, back out of the bathroom.

She screams.

Her voice reverberates hollowly in the small space, but no one rushes to the bathroom door to check on her. She's hyperventilating, and she struggles to control her breath, to control her body. She squeezes her shaking hands into fists and presses them against her thighs until they're steady. She opens her hands.

The blood isn't hers.

She stands up, unsteadily, and lurches over to the sink. She grabs onto the cold porcelain. Her grip slips, she starts to fall, but she catches herself. She pulls herself up and looks into the medicine cabinet mirror.

Her eyes are wild, panicked. But otherwise she looks the same, seventeen years old. Her hair is the same, down to her shoulders the way she wears it now. This could be tomorrow. This could be *today*.

When was the last time she took her pills? Not Nemo, not Mnemozyne, but Advantic? She opens the medicine cabinet, but her medication isn't there among the aspirin bottles and allergy pills and vitamins, the Band-Aids and dental floss.

There's a razor in the sink, the blade removed. The blade missing.

Rene turns and stares at the bathroom door. It takes her a few attempts to open it, though the slick blood is turning tacky on her skin.

She stumbles out into a dark bedroom. The room smells like sex and blood. Someone is in the bed. Someone familiar, though she only looks at him from behind, admiring his tousled dark hair and the tone of his muscles. One leg sticks out from under the rumpled sheet tangled over him.

Rene can't see his face, but she refuses to try to wake him in case he doesn't stir. She refuses to look for the source of all that blood.

She picks up her cell phone, the same one she uses now. She scrolls through the list of contacts, leaving a pink streak on the screen. She settles on the last number she dialed.

Samson.

None of this is real, he said. She doesn't have his number in her cell phone in real life, so this isn't actually happening. Maybe if she talks to him now, in this vision, he can tell her that again. Maybe he'll know what's happening to her, and can tell her what to do.

She should call 911, but instead she calls Sam.

She presses her cell phone to her ear so hard she can hear her heart pounding until the line connects and rings. A moment later, "The Final Countdown" starts playing, accompanied by the sound of a phone vibrating.

She looks up, and on the night table beyond the boy in the bed, a cell phone screen lights up and displays her picture.

She closes her eyes.

Rene opened her eyes and grabbed her cell phone. Before the numbers slide from her memory, she dials them and listens to the line ring. Finally he answers.

"Samson?" she said.

"Rene? Who gave you this number?"

She told him what she saw.

"Calm down," he said. "It's okay. None of that happened, remember. None of it is going to happen. Now tell me, what are you *on*?"

"Are you trying to be funny?" she asked.

"This dark, dark moment could use a little light, I thought," he said. "But I'm serious: is there something you aren't telling me?"

"I'm coming over," she said.

He drew in a quick breath.

"Okay," he said.

Sam opened the door before she knocked. His bedroom had its own entrance behind the house, with a ramp leading up to an enclosed porch.

"Are you psychic?" she asked.

"Now who's trying to be funny?" he asked. "I heard your car pull in."

He moved his chair aside so she could come in. He closed the door behind her and rolled around to face her in one fluid motion. She stared at his legs. Where his legs should be. They ended just before the knees, and the denim of his jeans were folded over the stumps and held in place with safety pins.

"What?" Sam asked in a tight voice.

"I'm sorry, but … I just remembered. In the vision or whatever I just saw, you were… You still had legs. Well, at least one, that I could see."

Sam paled. "I did?"

"Yeah." She sighed and sat down on his bed. "So that means I did imagine it after all."

"I'm not so sure," he said.

"It wasn't your bedroom either." She looked around. "Shouldn't I have pictured it here, if it was just my subconscious running rampant? Maybe I was picturing us in the future, like a dorm room or something."

"I want you to look at something," he said. "Go upstairs, go to your right, and open the door on the far end of the hall."

"What's up there?"

"Just go look, and come back and tell me what you see."

When Rene opened the door at the top of the stairs, she gasped.

It was the bedroom from her vision. And there, through another door on her right, the bathroom she'd huddled in, cold and naked and covered in his blood. Only this bathroom was empty. No drugs or razors in the medicine cabinet.

She lifted the lid of the toilet and threw up.

She flushed and washed, then went back down to Sam's room.

"That's my bedroom up there," Sam said. "Before I lost my legs. I moved down here to the guest room because it was too much trouble to rig up an elevator for my chair. My parents have been great about setting up ramps and rearranging the house so I can get around, but I haven't been upstairs in two years."

Rene dragged the dusty desk chair from the corner of the room and collapsed into it. She sat on her trembling hands. "I'd never seen that room before, so how did I imagine it?"

"I think what you've been seeing is some other life that we could have been living. Think about it: maybe you're seeing things that could have happened if I hadn't been in that accident."

Rene shivered. "Which means it's possible that I could kill you."

"It's possible that that Rene could. But if I'm that different, who knows what the other you was like? Who knows what kind of drugs we might have been on? I have a hard time believing you would do something like that. That isn't you. Why would you want to kill me?"

"It stands to reason that if you still had your legs, then you would still be a dick," Rene said. "But you're right. That girl wasn't me. She was crazy." She shook her head. "Only that *is* me. I'm crazy."

"Don't be so hard on yourself for something you didn't do. You're no more a killer than you are a slut."

"The difference between me and her is she didn't get help when she needed it."

"What do you mean?"

"I missed school because I was in the hospital. In the psych ward. Being treated for schizophrenia. Before, I was hearing things that weren't there. Imagining things that aren't possible. Without my meds, I get paranoid delusions and think everyone's against me, running experiments on me."

"What are you taking for that?" Sam asked.

"Advantic."

Sam nodded. "Well, that's it. That's the variable."

"Variable?"

"You're a scientist. That drug is the one thing that you're taking that no one else is. Somehow, your meds and the Mnemozyne are combining with your unique brain chemistry—"

"That's a nice way of putting it."

"—and giving you these glimpses into other paths you might have taken. Or might yet take."

"So in some of those lives I imagined, I'm not sick," she said. "Or I am, and it's damaging my relationships, or I'm not taking my medication."

"Or you're taking your medication, but you're also taking other things—things more harmful than Nemo," Sam said. "I had a second medication too, right after the accident. Zearex. It's an anti-depressant."

"They gave me that in the hospital too," she said.

"When I took it and Nemo together and kissed Kell, I saw myself with legs." He spread his hands on his thighs, fingers spread.

"What else did you see?"

"We were just ... walking. Walking along a beach, holding hands with a woman. It was perfect."

"So... You're into Kell?" Rene asked.

He laughed. "I was just showing her what Nemo can do. Drug dealers are supposed to give the first one away free, right? She said she saw us having sex, but I could tell she didn't like it much. I saw myself with someone else entirely. She didn't like that much either. I gave her a discount."

Rene stood up and went to Sam's desk. She turned the key in the drawer and took out two packets of Mnemozyne.

"You told me you didn't see anything when you took these," she said.

"I don't anymore. I used it once more, when I wasn't on Zearex. I kissed Jenny and that time I didn't see anything. For me, it was just a kiss, and not even a good one. It was interesting to observe her reactions to whatever steamy scene she was imagining for the two of us, even though I was still in the chair.

"It was kind of a relief. It was painful to see a life I can never have. I haven't taken Nemo since. The drug doesn't affect adults this way, so I figured it had already stopped working for me," he said.

"There's one way to find out," Rene said. She tossed one of the drug envelopes onto Sam's lap. He didn't touch it.

"Hell no," he said. "I'm not taking that, and certainly not while kissing *you*."

"Thanks," she said.

She tore the envelope open and slid the pill under her tongue.

"I'm starting to worry that you might be addicted. Oh, and that'll be thirty dollars," Sam said.

"Thirty? Is that how much you charged Jenny?"

Rene crawled into Sam's bed and lay on her back.

"Um. What are you doing?" Sam asked.

"I'm concentrating on something erotic." She closed her eyes. "If you aren't going to help, then keep quiet."

Rene smells the ocean.

She opens her eyes and sees she's in a small cabin, lying in a narrow bed, pressed against the cold metal wall by a snoring man. She twists around and doesn't recognize him, but she's relieved that this one isn't dead. It doesn't matter who he is, because if her future history is any indication, this will be the end of whatever relationship they will have had.

He doesn't even notice when she wriggles out of bed, though he stretches out to take up the full bed. She pauses for a moment to appreciate the view. Another future, another life, whatever, she seems to be enjoying it and she has decent taste.

She pulls on a black T-shirt she finds on the floor, maybe his, and turns to appreciate a different kind of view: the open sea outside of the porthole. She catches her reflection in the glass. Short hair, and she's a little bit older. In fact, she knows exactly when this is: she'd been trying to decide whether to do Semester at Sea in college, and it looks like she will.

She settles down at her desk and picks up a chic magenta purse, admiring her taste once again. She'll have to keep an eye out for it on some future shopping trip. She rummages around inside and comes up with a bottle of pills. It isn't Advantic, but from the label it seems to be another type of antipsychotic medication. So far so good. She's supposed to take one of them in the morning, so she pops one of the pills, just in case. She wonders if it will somehow interact with the Advantic and the Nemo she took earlier.

Rene glances back at the dark-haired stranger in her bed. He's a heavy sleeper. She opens her laptop and calls up her free internet phone service; she doubts her cell phone would work on the ocean. From memory, she dials Sam. The number comes up in her favorites on her computer before the call connects.

"Sam?" she says.

"Do you know what time it is?" He sounds groggy.

"No. It's about nine in the morning where I am."

"Ungh." He rustles around. "3AM here. Where the hell are you?"

"I don't know. Open sea somewhere."

"Nice life," he said.

"Sam. It's me. Rene."

"I know. Are you drunk?"

She cups her hand over her nose and mouth and exhales. "I don't think so."

"Did you take your pill?"

"I did. Do you think it'll affect the Nemo in my system?"

"Why did you take Nemo?"

"Try to keep up, Sam. It's me. Rene. Right now, while we're talking, I'm actually in your bed. I've just taken a dose of Mnemozyne. Do you remember that day?"

He's quiet. "You're drunk."

"Sam, I'm not drunk! I'm on Nemo. Right now. Do you remember that day?"

"Yeah."

"And we're friends? In this life?"

"We are," he said.

Rene smiled. "Good. Finally a future I can look forward to."

She stops herself from asking the next logical question: *Are we more than friends?* The man in her bunk suggests otherwise. She doesn't want this moment to be about the end of her relationship with Sam, whatever it is. Even if it's all just a hallucination.

"Why are you calling me, Rene? You have to admit, this is bizarre."

"If you remember what we were talking about that day, you know that we were trying to come up with proof that what we see under the influence of Nemo is real. I thought if you told me something that the Rene of then couldn't know, that I could prove to the Sam of then that I was just in the future."

"I think *I* need a drink," Sam said.

"Samson!"

"I mean this in the most loving way possible, Rene, but you're nuts."

"Tell me something I don't know. Look, I only have another couple minutes before I come out of this."

"Okay, then. Rene, I love you. Tell my handsome younger self that."

"Shut up, Sam. I'm being serious."

He sighs. "I always promised I would never admit this to anyone, and the only reason I'm sharing it now is because you're halfway around the world, and I've moved on, and none of this is real."

"Get on with it."

"My accident wasn't an accident," he says.

"Oh my God." Rene closes her eyes.

Rene didn't open her eyes. Sam's chair squeaked as he rolled it back and forth across his room nervously.

"What do you mean your accident wasn't an accident?" she asked, eyes still closed.

The squeaking stopped.

"Excuse me?"

"I was just in our future, and you told me that."

"Why would I say something like that?" he asked.

"Because I needed something that could convince you that I was in the future."

She opened her eyes and sat up to look at him. Sam's eyes were closed.

"Okay," he said. "I was running, like I said. But it wasn't the driver's fault. *I* was on something. A few things. I don't even remember what anymore, which isn't surprising. Not my mom's samples, thank goodness.

"The pills made me fast, Rene. Made me *feel* fast, anyway, almost like I was flying. I think I actually jumped into an intersection. There was no way the car could have stopped in time."

"That's awful," Rene said.

"At least the drugs were so strong, I didn't feel any pain. Not until much later. And it hasn't stopped yet."

"Why didn't you say anything?"

"I was ashamed," he said. "It was such a stupid thing. We were lucky the woman driving the car didn't press charges against *us*. But that's why insurance won't cover my bills."

He covered his face with a hand. "I can't believe I just told you all that."

"We all screw up sometimes," Rene said. "And we have to live with the consequences."

"Not anymore," Sam said. "With Nemo, we can see the consequences before we make mistakes."

"Speaking of potential mistakes... What's it going to take to get you to kiss me?"

"No," Sam said. "No, no, no."

"Am I so horrible?"

"I don't want this to be something else I regret," he said. "Other people fantasize about what happens *after* the kiss, but me ... I fantasize about the kiss. That moment can tell you everything you need to know about who you're with. Every possibility exists in that one sweet moment. You could take Nemo to see if things are going to work out later on, but that's cheating. And I think you risk missing out on some beautiful moments in between."

"So you like to focus on the beginning of the relationship."

"And you focus on the end," he said.

"If I take Nemo, it will always interact with my other medication," she said.

"Have you considered not taking Advantic?"

"Have you considered not using your wheelchair?" she snapped.

"Point taken. I'm sorry."

"Everyone is. Forget it. If you can accept that I'm mentally unbalanced, I can accept that you're an idiot."

"The solution to our problem is clear," Sam said.

He went back to his desk. His chair blocked her view, but she saw him drop something inside the drawer and heard him lock it.

"My supply's almost out, and I'm not going to steal any more. We can resist temptation until it stops working for us, right?"

"I've never been good with that," Rene said. "But I suppose I can learn."

He rolled his wheelchair closer to the bed.

"Was I still a paraplegic in the future you just saw?" he asked.

"I don't know. We spoke over the phone."

"Oh."

"But it doesn't matter," she said.

"Why's that?"

"The only thing knowing your future can change is your future. You're still on your own in the present."

"But that doesn't mean you have to face it alone," Sam said.

They leaned toward each other. She closed her eyes. Their lips brushed against each other. They both pulled away. Then they kissed.

The ocean again, only this time, she's on a beach, her bare toes burrowing into the soft, wet sand. Someone is standing next to her. A hand takes hers, a strong hand, but she resists the urge to look at him. They gaze out at the sea together as the sun dips closer to the water and a white cruise ship glides past miles away, so small in the distance it looks like a toy boat.

But Rene was also still aware of every moment of the kiss in the now. She felt Sam's stubble graze against her chin and his hand as it caressed her arm.

After a long moment, with the future dimming and fading toward the present, Rene opened her eyes at the same time Sam did.

"You tasted like Nemo," she said accusingly.

"I have trouble resisting temptation too." He grinned.

"Sam! What did you see?" she asked.

"Nothing." He stared off into the distance like he was watching something move across the horizon.

"Come on. Spill," Rene said.

"You first, Rene. What did *you* see?"

"That some things have to end so something else can begin."

Vanilla

by Dirk Flinthart

23 January

This is my new journal.

Miss Carpenter says I should keep one because she's worried about my father. She's concerned that he wants me to be a proper Australian, not a Somali. She says that Australia is a country of diversity, and Somali-Australians are just as much proper Australians as anybody else. She says she's concerned about my "developing sense of identity".

Isn't that a nice phrase?

That's not the real truth, though. Actually, Miss Carpenter is just uncomfortable with me the way I am. She wants me to *join in*. She wants me to have friends. She wants me to be *her* idea of a proper Australian.

Now you're wondering why I'm not called Amina, or Jamina, or Fatima or something similar. Don't be ashamed. Everybody wonders, but almost nobody ever dares to ask me. Maybe they think it would make them racist. Is it racist to expect someone with Somali parents to have a Somali name?

My father is named Hakim, and he is from Somalia. My mother was called Falis, and she too was from Somalia. They met here in Australia, where my father had already abandoned his second name for that of the Prime Minister. I, their first and only child – my mother died in childbirth—he named for a popular actress and singer. I am Kylie Howard, born in Australia.

Falis is a beautiful name. I wish there had been an Australian singer named Falis.

6 February

Let's talk about friends. I said Miss Carpenter wants me to have friends. That's not right. What she wants is for me to have the *right* friends. Hkund Ar, Fen My, and the other Hairies are not the right friends.

We're not supposed to call them Hairies. They are !gontok, and Walton Hill Church Grammar was the first private school in Australia to accept !gontok students.

Principal Reyes made a speech when they came. You can still find it on YouTube. "Our new students will learn of our proud tradition of tolerance and integration," he said. "The !gontok people have a great and proud culture and history of their own, and Walton Hill Church Grammar is delighted to welcome these students. We will learn from them, just as they learn from us, and one day we will all be Australians, and citizens of Earth."

Then the school band played the National Anthem, and Hkund Ar and the others entered the assembly hall. One of their Elders made a speech while Hkund Ar and the rest shuffled, and sniffed at the air with their long, flexible snouts.

I couldn't hear properly because Adra and Malu were giggling. Adra and Malu both have Indian parents, and their names come from India. They giggle a lot. They giggled when they first learned my name, but they don't talk to me because my skin is too dark. That's important in India. My father says it isn't important in Australia.

I think it was Adra who first used the word "Hairies" in front of me.

I don't see the problem, really. Fen My tells me the !gontok don't find it offensive, and hardly anybody here knows how to make the funny clicking sound that we write with an exclamation point. At least we can pronounce "Hairies".

When I asked Fen My what name the Hairies used for humankind in private, he took a long time to answer, and his ears drooped. Back then, I didn't know that meant he was embarrassed, so I pressed him, and he said, "Sometimes when one of us gets very sick, the hair comes off. It is not a good thing. For some, the hair will not return. We have a word for them. In your language, it might be hairless?"

"Bald," I said. "Old humans, especially men, lose their hair too. They are bald. Sometimes, people use the word 'baldy'. It's a little rude, but 'baldies' is a word for people with no hair."

"Baldies," said Fen My, and his ears flicked back and forth. I knew even then it meant he was laughing. "Yes. We call you people Baldies."

His ears flicked again, and I laughed too. Maybe that's when I first thought we might be friends.

17 February

Sometimes I wonder why Principal Reyes can't remember the names of the Hairy students. He remembers Adra. He remembers Malu. He even remembers all eleven syllables of Balamugunthan Wickremayanake's name, especially when Balam is in trouble. Yet he always confuses names like Bar Han, Doko Pring, La! Banak.

Some people say Hairies all look the same. But I've heard people say that about the Chinese, too. Principal Reyes never forgets Lily Wing, or James Pang. So how can he forget that Doko Pring has wide, low-set purple eyes? How can he confuse Tay Hu!ok, whose fur is short and dark, with Fen My, whose fur is long, and almost golden?

Principal Reyes isn't the only one. Some of the students invent names for them, stupid, childish names like Whap Dick, Dog Suck, and Butt Roast. They make a game of it, interrupting the Hairies at their play during lunch to call out these names, and snigger.

The Hairies almost never forget our names, although it is hard for them to make the "ess" sound.

Miss Carpenter doesn't confuse the Hairies, or call out stupid, made-up names. But when they eat, her mouth thins. She narrows her eyes and looks away.

Miss Carpenter is a vegan. The Hairies are predators. They eat their meat uncooked, and enjoy snapping up live rats.

Is that so bad? People in Africa eat rats. Guinea pigs are commonly eaten in some parts of South America. I've even heard that in the southern states of the USA, people shoot and eat squirrels. Is it so important that we cook our meat, and the Hairies do not?

I tried Somali food once, at a street market. My father didn't know. I ate *canjeero*, and *hilab ari*: a kind of bread, with goat meat. The woman who ran the food stall told me what the words meant, and I wrote them down so I wouldn't forget. The goat meat was very spicy. Pizza is better. But I suppose I would eat goat meat if it was common here, in Melbourne.

I would probably even eat rats or guinea pigs. But I would like them to be cooked.

1 March

Some of the students raised a petition today. They want a separate eating area from the Hairies. They say that rats and raw meat are unhygienic, and we shouldn't eat in the same place. Of course, the rats are tame and I know people who keep them as pets. And if raw meat is unhygienic, then the French and the Italians with their *tartare* and their *carpaccio* must also be unhygienic.

I admit that I don't like it when the rats squeal. But mostly, Fen My and the others finish them in one bite. Fen My says that the fur and the bones are important to Hairy digestion, that a diet of simple raw meat, fat and organs will make them sick.

Of course, they must also have their supplements. There are some chemicals which don't occur much on Earth that the Hairies need. I looked up "amino acids" on the internet, but I'm not really sure I understood everything. The Hairies need two amino acids that are rare in nature here on Earth. They only need a little, but if they don't get their supplements, they get sick.

That's another reason they eat rats. Their food animals don't do very well here yet. Their Elders are working with our scientists, but until it's all sorted out, the Hairies eat rats and raw chicken, and they take supplements.

When the petition was started, students put copies up on the notice boards. Adra and Malu carried clipboard folders, and went around at lunchtime asking people to sign them. They didn't ask me, and when I saw what they were doing, I picked up my lunch and sat next to Fen My.

Fen My lowered his ears and looked sideways at me, his snout wrinkling.

"What's wrong?" I said.

He moved a little farther along the bench, making space between us, but his ears flipped forward again. “We don’t eat close together,” he said. “Do you see?”

I looked around. It was true. I hadn’t noticed. I suppose my attention was fixed on their food. But when Fen My showed me, I felt stupid. The Hairies don’t cluster together shoulder to shoulder the way humans do. They leave almost an arm’s-length between themselves. And if there isn’t enough room at the tables, they wait until someone else finishes.

“I’m sorry,” I said, and then I waited because Malu was hovering near us, pretending not to listen. When she moved on, I said, “Eating together is something Baldies do. Friends do this.”

Fen My flipped his ears just once, and flicked a gobbet of meat into his mouth. “Baldies are omnivores,” he said. “You eat everything, and you forage together. Hairies are meat-eaters. We divide the kill, and eat separately.”

I looked at my Vegemite sandwiches. I hate Vegemite, but my father says it’s healthy and good for me. He always puts Vegemite sandwiches in my lunch. Sometimes I can trade them, especially with Robert Grey, who doesn’t like it when his mother gives him curried egg. I like curried egg.

“What do Hairies do to be friends?”

Fen My flipped his ears again. “Run together. Play together. We make games. Sometimes we hunt together.”

“That isn’t really very different,” I said. “Except the hunting. Although I know there are people who do that. And fishing, too. Do you have any Baldy friends?”

This time Fen My looked at me directly, and his ears flicked forward. "I didn't think so," he said. "Now I'm not sure."

I smiled at him. But then I remembered something I had read, about predators and showing teeth, and I wondered if Fen My understood. Maybe I should try something different?

I put my fists on either side of my head, touching my ears. Then I put up two fingers on each side, and flicked them back and forth very quickly. Fen My blinked. Then his ears flicked back and forth very quickly.

I think that's how Hairies laugh.

5 March

My father doesn't like most of the Somalis here in Melbourne. "Bloody refugees," he calls them. "Boat people!"

Father says he's not a refugee. He came here in a Qantas aeroplane, as a sponsored migrant. He has built up a business around mud bricks. He knew a lot about them from Somalia where they are common. Here in Australia mud bricks are still a new thing. Dad says they're better than concrete or regular brick for the environment. He says mud bricks make houses cooler in summer, warmer in winter, and easier to maintain.

He makes the bricks out of mud and straw and a little concrete. He also knows how to lay them properly, and mortar them in place. He teaches other people about mud bricks when he's not building houses and walls and sheds with his mud bricks. Dad works hard, and he is very proud of his work.

The refugee Somalis, Dad says, are trash. They don't want to work. They are too afraid to stay in Somalia and fight the al-Shabaab, so they flee to another country and demand to be supported. Dad often says we must "stop the boats", like the Prime Minister used to say before he got elected and stopped saying anything at all.

Of course, hardly anybody talks about "stopping the boats" anymore. When the Hairies came in their huge ship, it was like the whole world stopped. I remember the news headlines, all the fear and the hope. All the crazy religious people demanding that the Hairies be destroyed. All the Lefties and Greenies demanding that we give them a land of their own.

Dad doesn't like the Hairies. He thinks they should have stayed behind, using their technology to survive until the effects of the comet that smashed into their planet wore off, and they could rebuild.

When I was small, I believed what my father said about the Somalis. I believed what the man who is now the Prime Minister said. When people asked me if I was Somali, I said Somalis were trash. I said I was Kylie Howard, born in Australia.

Australia has accepted Somali refugees in the past because of treaty obligations. Because the Somalis have nowhere left to go. Because Somalia is a "failed state", full of warlords with guns, full of pirates, and Islamic extremists.

Australia accepted some of the Hairies as part of a deal with the United Nations. The Hairies sold their super-efficient solar energy technology and their nuclear fusion technology to Earth in exchange for the right to live here, among us.

They paid us. Their home planet is lifeless now, and their ship of two hundred years is too old and frail to find another planet orbiting another star, but still: they paid us. Dad calls them refugees, but they paid to come here, just like him.

He says he's a migrant. He says he's Australian, and he works hard to prove it.

I don't know what the !gontok Elders do. I feel it is likely that they work hard also. Perhaps Fen My will tell me, if I ask.

12 March

Today I learned to play a game of the !gontok. I have often watched them at play, dashing here and there, running and leaping, ignoring the onlookers. I know it's wrong to assume I can read their body language. I know that even though they have silky-soft hair and warm blood pushed around their bodies by two hearts, my Hairy friends aren't really mammals.

It doesn't matter. Their games looked like fun.

When Hkund Ar took a break, throwing himself down on his side in the warm sun and panting, I sat near him. "This is a game," I said, and pointed at the other Hairies, running about on the field.

"A game," he agreed. "You're curious?"

"I'm curious," I said. "We have games too."

"I know," he said. "I'm interested in your *cricket*. I had not imagined a game of striking at a ball with a stick. That is very strange. Our games are more like your football, I think."

I put my hands by my head and flip-flopped laughter with my fingers. "You're not the only one who thinks cricket is strange," I said. "I don't understand the rules at all."

Hkund Ar looked at me with his dark grey eyes, and flip-flopped his laughter. "With your hands," he said. "I've seen you do this with Fen My. You know what it means?"

"I think so," I said. "The same as this." I laughed for him.

"I think so too," he said, and sat up. "Shall I tell you the rules of our game?"

I looked at the field. All the Hairies were out there, running back and forth. One of them had a rubber ball in his teeth. Two had plastic flying discs, like Frisbees, and they threw them at others on the field. I knew that when you were hit by one of the Frisbees you had to stop and pick it up, and throw it at someone else. But that was all I knew.

"Yes," I said. "If you can explain it to me."

He tried, but the rules were complicated, and I couldn't keep track because I kept watching the others at play. At last I stopped him. "Maybe if I could play, I could learn as I went."

Hkund Ar sat very still. His round, mobile ears trembled ever so slightly. "Yes," he said at last. "If you want."

"I do want to learn," I said.

"Our homeworld had more gravity," he said. "Our ship was spun to match it. We are stronger than you."

"I don't mind," I said.

Still he hesitated. "Our ancestors were hunters. We ran down our prey. We are faster than you."

"My ancestors hunted too," I said. "We weren't the fastest, but we could run a very long time, and tire our prey. You Hairies play in short bursts, with a lot of resting. I think I can keep up."

Hkund Ar's ears flip-flapped madly. "You can try, Baldy," he said, and dashed back out onto the field.

I went after him. He was right. The Hairies were stronger than me, and faster. But by the time they were tired, I knew the rules. I had the ball and one of the discs as well.

The game is called Po!ak Mor. I don't know what that means, but it's a lot of fun.

16 March

Of course, the Hairies aren't my only friends. But it's difficult.

I think I like boys more than girls, for example. (I'm not talking about sex and romance, by the way.) I like the games boys play, and the easy way they laugh together. I like how they boast and posture without holding grudges.

I'm less comfortable with most of the girls. Maybe it's because I had no mother in my life. I don't always understand the rules that the girls use.

Adra and Malu understand those secret rules very well. They are always giggling, whispering behind their hands, part of a group of girls I don't like very much. Maybe if my mother hadn't died, I might have learned more about how to be a girl. Or maybe not. How would I know?

It doesn't matter anyway. I'm not allowed to spend more time with the boys, even if I'd like to. Dad doesn't want me to do that.

Dad says I'm not Somali. He says I'm an Australian girl, and he wants me to act like one. He says we aren't Muslim anymore. He left behind even his religion when he left his country. (I don't mind. I think religion is silly. I should ask Fen My what the Hairies think about that.)

The problem is that even though Dad says he wants me to act like an Australian girl, he gets angry when I do. I'm not allowed makeup. There's a Somali word he uses for women who wear makeup. He won't tell me what it means, but I can guess. I'm not allowed two-piece swimming costumes. I'm not to wear the wrong shoes. I'm not to have my hair done provocatively.

Is that even possible? How do you make something that looks like a brown dandelion provocative?

I've tried to argue. I've showed him what the Australian girls wear at school, and on the television. I told him that if he wanted me to be a proper Australian girl, I have to dress the part.

He only says, "Not like that!"

You don't want to know what my father thinks of boys. I can't imagine having a real boyfriend. I do like boys, though. (And yes, this time I'm talking about sex.) I often sit with Robert at school, and we trade sandwiches and talk about boys. Robert likes them too.

20 March

Even if I did have more friends at school, I would probably still hang out with Fen My and the others. Why wouldn't I?

I know some people are frightened of them, but what for? There's seven billion of us. There's only two hundred and fifty thousand of them, and by the terms of the agreement, they have been separated into communities of a few thousand, scattered around the countries which agreed to host them.

I asked Hkund Ar if he minded being separated that way, and he flapped his ears in laughter. "Not at all," he said. "The great ship was crowded. I didn't know how crowded it was until I came here. Running and playing under a wide sky is so good! The Elders say that on the homeworld we lived in wide-spread packs with large territories. They say the custom arose from times before we learned to manage tame food animals. We just naturally like plenty of room."

"Don't you feel crowded in the city?" I said. "Melbourne has more than three million people. That's more than all the Hairies in your ship."

"Melbourne has more than three million Baldies," said Hkund Ar. "There are only four thousand of us !gontok here. It isn't crowded at all."

That made me feel a little nervous. It seemed as though he didn't think of us Baldies as people. I remembered the rats and the raw meat. If we aren't people, maybe one day we might be prey?

Hkund Ar told me they can't eat anything intelligent. They won't even eat pork, because they say pigs are too smart.

Muslims and Jews won't eat pork either, though, and that doesn't stop them killing each other. I'd like to be sure that Hkund Ar and the others know we're people.

31 March

I think I've worked out why the Hairies don't feel crowded by us. I think it's about *scent*.

I can't really smell Fen My or Hkund Ar unless they're wet. But Fen My says that smell is a primary sense for his people. They can't see color the way we do, though their eyes can see farther into the infrared because their star was older and cooler than ours. Their hearing isn't as good as ours either. The Elders say that our atmosphere isn't dense enough, so things don't sound right. But scent is important to them. Fen My says that it's the easiest way to tell us Baldies apart.

I asked him how I smelled. He told me I smelled with my nose, and flapped his ears. Then he told me he had been watching an old movie with some people called the Marx Brothers, and I hit him on the shoulder, and he flapped his ears even faster.

That's how I found out that Hairies tell jokes too.

"You smell … *interesting*," Fen My said eventually. "Not bad. There are some of you who smell very bad. Then there are some who smell all right, but use those terrible sprays. The smell is so powerful!"

"I know," I told him. "The school banned those spray-on deodorants, but a lot of people still carry them."

"Why are they called deodorants?" he said. "I know that de- is a prefix, and it means to remove, or take away. But deodorants don't take away a smell! They just cover it up with something worse. I went into a shop in the middle of the city, once. You know the place? The Myer place?"

I nodded. I knew where he was going, but I let him finish.

"There is a part of that Myer place where they sell smells in little bottles," said Fen My, and his ears lay flat alongside his head. "I thought I would choke. I thought I would die!"

"I've been there," I said. "It's terrible."

Fen My looked at me, and his ears came up again. "I am glad you don't try to cover your smell," he said.

"You can thank my dad," I told him. "He won't let me."

After that, just for fun I tried to disguise my scent. I rubbed myself with peppermint essence. I left chili peppers in olive oil for a week, and rubbed the oil into my skin. I traced a fresh-cut root of ginger over myself one day. The next, I did the same thing with a piece of garlic. I chewed cloves. I ate fresh coriander.

I never fooled Fen My. Sometimes he laughed. Sometimes his snout curled, and he drew away. Garlic, he told me, smelled like medicine. Ginger made him sneeze. Chili peppers he did not like at all. They smelled like an enemy, he told me, and I saw that his fine, soft hair lay close and flat, next to his skin.

No more chili peppers, I promised him.

5 April

I like the soft, silky fur of the Hairies. I like the way that they touch each other so often, bumping, rubbing against each other, sometimes nipping at one another playfully. To me it seems they are always sending messages with their skin and their fur.

I wish human people were more like that. When I was small, my father would pick me up, and tickle me, and swing me around. Sometimes he would lie on the couch and watch TV, and I would lie in front of him, curled up against the curve of his belly. He was so warm, so strong at my back. There were times he would fall asleep that way, tired after a day of mud bricks, and I would lie there listening to him breathe until I, too, fell asleep.

My father doesn't do that any more. He hasn't done anything like that since I started wearing a bra. Now, if he touches me at all, it's only my hand or my face. For important moments he has a kind of clumsy hug that ends in him patting me on the back.

With Fen My, it's easy. I know now not to sit close when he eats, but at other times I can bump into him deliberately, press against his soft fur. The !gontok, with their beautiful, silky fur, aren't concerned by being naked. Sometimes they wear clothes, but it's always for a reason. At school, they wear smocks in the school colors, smocks with pockets for carrying things like pens and notebooks. But the smocks are loose and open, because it's hard for the Hairies to cool down with all that fur and it gets really hot in Melbourne.

Fen My bumps into me as well, and sometimes even nips softly at my arms as he does to the other Hairies. His teeth are sharp, but he never hurts me and my skin rises up in goosebumps afterwards. He is not the only one, either. My Hairy friends touch me as lightly and easily as they touch each other. When I join their games, we wrestle and struggle, and when we grow tired we stretch out in the sun together.

Principal Reyes came over today as we lay on the grass, my head supported by Hkund Ar's broad back, my fingers buried in Fen My's soft fur. (When they took to the great ship, the !gontok were careful to leave behind all the little parasite creatures that used to hide in their fur. But they still groom each other, and enjoy being touched that way. It's like scratching a big cat, except that Fen My and the others can't purr.) Principal Reyes stood over us, his shadow blotting out the sun. He licked his lips and took a breath, then he paused as though he couldn't figure out what to say.

"Good afternoon, sir," I said. "Can I help you?"

Hkund Ar and Fen My ignored us both, except that Fen My shifted a little to bring my fingertips to the place on his back between his shoulders where it's hard for him to reach. Principal Reyes licked his lips again, and shifted his weight from one foot to the other.

"It's good to see you're reaching out to our k-gontok students, Miss Howard," he said. (He never even tries to click their name. He just says a kind of sharp -k sound in the back of his throat.) He shifted his attention to Fen My. "Is she—is this..."

"She has long fingernails, Principal Reyes," said Fen My, without looking up. "I like the way Kylie scratches my back. This planet is very warm, and I often feel an itch. Kylie is very kind."

Principal Reyes reached up with one hand and adjusted his glasses, then smoothed his hair back though it wasn't out of place. "Good," he said finally. "That's all right, then." He took one last look at the three of us, then glanced at his wristwatch and walked off in a straight line towards his office.

I wonder what he was thinking.

12 April

Tonight was the social dance. We have them every year, and I attend because it's easier than not attending. Walton Hill Church Grammar prides itself on its "thoroughly rounded" education, and that includes proper social interaction. Supposedly you don't have to show up at the dances, but if you don't it will be noticed, and soon you will find yourself being pushed into other events and gatherings.

Father doesn't mind the dances. He came to the first two, back when I was in year seven, and saw the awkward boys and the giggling girls staying in separate groups. He saw the teachers watching over everything, and he must have felt it was safe, harmless fun. Now I am allowed to attend the dances on my own, and since I turned sixteen, I am even allowed to catch the local tram home afterwards.

Did I mention the Hairies don't hear as well as we do? Yes, I think I did. Well, it shouldn't surprise you to find that they don't appreciate our music. They can follow the rhythms quite well, though, and I spent half an hour with Fen My and Hkund Ar making up dance moves that didn't look too stupid. Hairies don't have dances, and with their skeletons, they can't just copy our moves.

We tried stuff: jumping, spinning, kicking, shuffling back and forth. Fen My made up a sort of shimmy that only the Hairies could manage with their long and flexible bodies, and tried to lip-synch a song by Tame Impala. Hkund Ar curled into a ball and rolled back and forth. It was so funny that even some of the other students joined us, rolling about like little kids and laughing.

Of course, Fen My and Hkund Ar tired before I did. The night was very warm, so we went outside to lie on the oval and look up at the stars. The grass hadn't been cut in a few days. It was soft, and smelled very sweet, and that mingled nicely with the vanilla I'd put on in another failed attempt to disguise my scent. We sprawled together, but Fen My and Hkund Ar couldn't seem to get comfortable. They moved restlessly, pressing against me, drawing away, turning, twisting.

It took me longer than it should have to realise that my two best friends were... umm.

You know.

I know that the !gontok don't have the same shyness we do about doing these things near others. But I'm human, and when I understood what they were doing I felt the blood rush to my face, and I scrambled to my knees.

Without looking at me, Fen My reached out. I took his long, slender hand in mine, and he squeezed. "Don't go," he said. "Stay with us."

I stayed.

7 May

Who gets to set the rules? The !gontok aren't human. They live here now, though. There's no choice for either of us, unless we want to kill them all. We don't want that. I don't want that. They're people, if not people just like us. They laugh and they play, they have art and sport and science and stories. Every day, the newspapers and the internet run stories about new discoveries that have come about from cooperation between the !gontok Elders and our scientists. They say we may even be able to build a new kind of engine—one that warps space, for real starships.

One day, we might be able to help the !gontok to a home of their very own.

Is that what we want? Is it what they want? I don't know.

It isn't what I want.

I explained to Fen My and Hkund Ar the human taboo about

sex where others can see. They were confused. It was especially difficult to explain the amount of sex on TV, in the movies and on the internet. The idea of wanting to watch what we're not supposed to see puzzled them. I did some research, and learned that higher primates often send visual signals to initiate sex, like the colored backsides on female chimpanzees. I told them I thought that maybe all the sexual imagery worked a bit like that.

Fen My and Hkund Ar laughed at that. The !gontok use scent cues, they explained. They thought we all knew that already.

It's not our first misunderstanding. It won't be our last.

We've been spending a lot of time together since the dance, even outside of school. My father grumbles, but since I'm not going with human boys he doesn't object. He may not like the !gontok, but they have status. They are rare and important. Our friendship makes my father look good, which is good for his business.

It's the same with Walton Hill Church Grammar, too. Photos of us show up in the newspapers and the magazines. We are minor celebrities, an example of the great Australian traditions of tolerance and integration.

Are we *integrated?* Is that what I am? I know this much: it is good to have people who care for me, and for one another. It is good to have people to share things with. Fen My and Hkund Ar don't care if I'm Somali or Australian, so long as we're together.

What more can I ask?

⁎

17 June

Miss Carpenter, you said this journal could be private, and I didn't plan to show it to you, but I've changed my mind. I guess this was a better idea than I first thought. All this putting my feelings into words and exploring my opinions—it's been helpful during a difficult time. I don't think you meant things to turn out this way, but that's okay.

I've learned a lot about !gontok reproduction. Not just about the affection and the social stuff. I've learned some hard facts about the mechanics of how the Hairies make babies.

You'll find this interesting: there is a chemical in the commercial extract of the vanilla orchid which mimics one of the most important pheromones in the !gontok biochemistry. Hairies of the right stage of development who are exposed to vanilla in the right way will react physically. Their bodies respond. They become ready to mate.

Of course, they have to be with someone they want, but the vanilla gets them really … *frisky*.

I've always liked the smell of vanilla. Since the night of the dance, I've been wearing it more often.

Here's something else that's interesting: reproduction among the Hairies requires not two, but *three* participants. The !gontok aren't male, or female. If anything, they're all both. Any adult Hairy can be implanted, if they're old enough. And any two adult Hairies can do the implanting. The two contribute their genes to the offspring. The third, the implanted one … let's call her the mother, shall we? To make things easier. Her body supports the developing young ones. (Yes. The !gontok usually have two to three offspring at once. Fortunately they are small, and they become independent quite quickly after birth.)

Do you know about epigenetics? It's new science. I looked it up. It seems that the environment and conditions that affect the mother can change how the genes of the babies work out. I should have said that this is new science to us, to humankind. The !gontok have known about this for a long time. In a breeding three, the two contributing parents look after the mother very carefully, trying to ensure the best epigenetics for the offspring.

You can probably see where this is going, but I didn't. Hkund Ar and Fen My didn't either. No one thought it would happen with us. We all assumed humans and Hairies were too different to be able to breed.

My father is going to be very angry with me, Miss Carpenter. I'm going to need all the help I can get. Hkund Ar and Fen My are doing their best, but I am afraid of what will happen if someone decides we must be separated. Do you think you could get some of those amino acid supplements for me? I want the little ones to be as healthy as they can be.

You said you were concerned about my identity. I don't know who I'm supposed to be. My parents were Somali, but I was born in Australia, on the planet Earth, and my two best friends and lovers are soft-furred, beautiful monsters from a dead world.

Do you think I will be a good mother?

Careful Magic

by Karen Healey

It's 7:04AM on Tuesday, and being late is making me crazy. Today will not be a good day.

Invisible spiders are walking up and down my spine. I run my thumbs over my clenched fingers, and tap the knuckles of the pinkies three times. Then I tap the knuckles of my pointer fingers. I'm allowed to yell now.

So I do, right through the open door of the house. "Mum! It's 7:05!"

"It's fine, Helen," she yells back.

It is not fine. My stomach is knotting. Before I can walk through the main school doors, I have to walk around the big building widdershins, then cast Shadow of the Sun on the third tree without a single mistake. Shadow of the Sun is my favorite cantrip, but the pronunciation is very difficult. If someone interrupts me—

which might happen, if we're late—I have to start over. And if I'm late for home class coven, I have to apologise to every person individually, even though Ms Apllyn says a group apology will be fine.

My mother blows out the door, her black skirts tangling around her legs like a storm cloud. There are three pixies in her hair, tying off the last of her braids, and she flaps them away. Gruffyth is in his carry basket, howling the protection charms to keep the house safe while we're gone. When her red-booted foot hits the fifth cobblestone, I put my seat belt on.

When she hits the seventh cobblestone, she stops.

That's not how it's supposed to happen. My breathing halts.

Mum looks at the door, then into my face. I stare back at her, willing her with everything in me to take that next step.

She sighs, and steps onto the eighth cobblestone. My fingers splay and curl.

She puts on her belt and starts the car. Gruffyth flicks his ears at me, and settles down to sleep. "I forgot my lunch," she says.

Mine is in my bag. One tuna and mayonnaise on white, one roast beef and cheddar cheese on wheat, three slices of apple. I never forget my lunch. I don't say this; I stare at the dashboard and will time to slow down.

"Honestly, Helen, we're only five minutes late."

"Six."

"Thirty seconds to go back for my lunch; does it really matter?"

This is a question to the air; she knows I won't answer. On some level she knows it does matter. Dad has told her, the counselor has told her. But she won't fully believe them.

I tell myself that it's okay. Mum is helping me anyway; she's taking me to school early so that I can start my day on time and don't have to listen to my classmates giggle and whisper when I apologize to them all, one by one.

It's not so important that my mother doesn't understand what matters to me.

What counts is that she didn't go back.

We arrive at 7:23, one skin-tensing minute late. I think Mum used a working on the traffic lights. She'll probably be fined for improper magic; traffic signals work with Order, and even a Chaos queen might not be able to slip around all the border marks undetected. I'm grateful all the same; only the teachers are at school, and the boys practicing basketball in the gym. They won't bother me.

I begin Shadow of the Sun, and my tongue curls easily around every syllable. I nudge the tree towards growing. It used to be a sickly thing, until I began to care for it. Now its branches stretch wider than any other tree within the school's wards.

Halfway through, the pattern changes. There is someone at my back.

Male, I think, and tall, and not a stranger; this much I can glean from the world's warp and weft, open to me now in all their intricate detail. I could learn more, if I plucked at that thread, if he spoke or moved. But I keep going, my lips sure around the phrases, even with my mind half gone. My watcher waits, silent, until the cantrip is done.

So, turning, I am the first to speak: "Thank you."

It's Gilbert Hill, who has burnished brown skin and long lashes. He's my age, in none of my classes, and yet I know his name and face. "Thank you for what?"

"For waiting. Thank you for waiting."

"You were working," he says, faintly baffled, as if no one would ever interrupt, or pick a thread out of my work for their own use, or think it fun to "help" and throw their bright, senseless workings into my careful magic.

Gilbert Hill is fifteen years old and already a duke of Chaos. They say he'll be a king before he's thirty. I hope his courtesy doesn't fade as he ascends.

He puts his palm on the tree's rough trunk and I can feel its dumb vegetable pleasure in the skin-warmth. I'm still attuned to the tree. I should pull myself back.

I don't.

"I thought growing things was Chaos-work only," he says. "I've never heard that cantrip before."

"Shadow of the Sun. It's old."

Gilbert smiles. My skin tingles. "From back when we thought the world was Ordered?"

Back then, before the mathematicians played with uncertainty, and the physicists discovered the observer effect, and the witches realized how much power they could glean from unpatterned workings.

Back then, when at least my magic would have been normal.

Gilbert's smile fades when I don't answer. His shoulders stiffen. "You're the only Order worker in school," he says.

"The only declared," I remind him. There are others that I think might be more kin to Order, when they're older and don't mind being known. But most people our age tend to Chaos, even if they're not declared. A talent for Order usually surfaces well after adolescence.

At our school, where I walk around being visibly strange, other Order workers might be even more reluctant to declare.

Our school is co-ed, and has plenty of dark-skinned kids, so I only stand out for two reasons; for my compulsions, and for my talents. They really aren't connected. There are Chaos workers with needs like mine in the forums I read, and most Order workers don't have the same compulsive drives that I do. But it's easy for people to equate the two and draw lines straight from one discredited way of being to another.

So when Gilbert points out that I am the only Order declared, my mouth goes sour. I am braced for well-meaning kindness, or confusion, or disdain, or any of the other ways my peers ordinarily point out how very different I am.

But Gilbert Hill refuses to be ordinary. "My sister is bespelled," he says. "She needs you. Please. Please help."

"We were just joking," Rosalind says.

Rosalind Hill is darker than her younger brother and more beautiful. Her dark hair is cropped close to her elegant head, so that nothing spoils the line of her slender neck. Her eyes are enormous, framed by long lashes and the sharp wings of her eyebrows. She is symmetrical, architectural, untouchable, exact.

She clings to my hand, and her fingers are damp with sweat.

"It was a joke. A stupid dare. It was never meant to happen. But you can fix it, right? I don't want this."

I pry myself free of her grip. I can't remember ever being this furious. "Love magic is illegal."

This is an understatement. Only death curses and obedience spells attract higher penalties for malignant magic. But Rosalind thought nothing of this when she dared Kinai Hayashi to make her fall in love with him. And Kinai didn't consider what might happen when he tried.

Neither of them expected him to succeed.

"You don't need me. You need certified curse-breakers." I frown. "Maybe even the police."

"But we'll be expelled," Kinai says. Even in the stark lighting of this tiny room, he is too pale. He keeps as far from Rosalind as he can, bracketed from her by her brother's wide shoulders.

"Kinai might go to *jail*," Rosalind adds. Her hand, now free, reaches towards Kinai. Gilbert captures the hand, returns it to her custody.

Rosalind stares at her wayward limb and shudders.

I have never been in the gymnastics storage room before. It stinks of rotting rubber and moldy feet. And there's too much feeling bound into these old mats and pieces of battered equipment: sour victory and shocked defeat; resignation and despair; the odd bright spark of a fragile joy.

And Rosalind's love for Kinai, smothering everything else with sickly tenacity.

The problem with love spells is that they're biological—which is also why they're very difficult to get right. Any reasonably practiced Order worker could undo an illusion worked through air and light. I've been known to destabilize a movie projector by walking into the theatre. But Kinai's spell is rooted in Rosalind's body. Her brain is high on dopamine and low on serotonin. Endorphins are flinging themselves happily around her veins.

She is genuinely in love, and Kinai made her that way.

Two years older than me, with all their brains and Chaotic talent, and these two idiots broke one of our oldest laws in the most careless possible way.

"It was a mistake," Kinai says. He looks like he's trying to crawl into the wall. "But you can fix it, Helen. You're a declared Order worker. Everyone says you're good."

"Everyone says I'm *strange*," I snap back. "Do you think I can't hear you, when you whisper in the halls?"

Kinai flinches. "I didn't know—I didn't think—"

"Clearly. Do you ever?"

"Don't take that tone with him!" Rosalind tells me, suddenly fierce. "It's all my fault anyway!"

"Oh, hell," Kinai says. "No, it's not, Rose. That's the spell."

When she looks at him, her entire body changes. The tension flows from her like storm water down a hill. "But I dared you to do it."

"And I made the choice to try," Kinai says. "The real mistake was mine."

I think a little better of him for admitting it.

He must sense my softening, because he refocuses on me, eyes bright. "I'm sorry about, you know, that stuff. I wouldn't have said anything if I'd known you could hear me."

I'm not sure what he wants.

But my silence means he keeps talking. "You have to admit, Helen, the things you do are pretty weird. The finger-tapping, the old cantrips. You circle the school, you eat the same lunch every day. You twirl your pen three times before you write anything. You—"

"You've been watching Helen very closely," Gilbert says. His voice burrs with something that might be anger.

"Yes," Rosalind says, and she doesn't bother to hide her dismay. "Why have you been paying so much attention to a second-year?"

Kinai looks at her, then his feet, then at my left shoulder, where the thick weight of my braids lies.

"You're kidding me," Rosalind says blankly. "*Her?*"

"Shut up, Rose," Gilbert says. "Helen, don't—"

But I am already leaving, stumbling my way up the rough stairs, keeping the count automatically. My cheeks are burning, my throat is dry. I don't want anything to do with Hayashi Kinai, or his reckless ideas of romance. He and Rosalind can deal with their own sordid affairs.

On the last step, my foot angles oddly. My weight shifts, overcorrects, and my balance is gone. Wild, I claw at the air.

Behind me, Gilbert shouts.

My palm skids and breaks along the concrete wall and my power surges through the contact, seeking out the patterns, the connections. Concrete is composed of ancient granite and fine sand, calcium carbonate and clay, water and silicone and traces of iron. There is water in my belly, calcium in my bones, and iron in my blood. The stones are my bones and the bones of the earth, and they will hold me, strong and stable, on my two steady feet, *now*.

I land, upright and calm, on the eighth step.

Gilbert's shout is still echoing off the wall. His voice has become wind, soft and pliable, a buffeting force that was meant to mold to my body and cushion my fall.

I caught myself. I didn't need him.

But it's nice that he tried.

"You're not just Order declared," he says behind me, soft. "You're an Order king."

The only king in our school; the only one with that much power. The third reason for people to talk about me, if anyone knew.

I turn to face him. My hair is wild with static electricity, the bleed out of the energy I created. That's the problem with instant magic. Spells and cantrips carefully build in places to put that energy. Chaos workers can usually draw on the energy itself and push it into another, smaller spell. But Order workers can't work with something so random and so it comes back to us; our own bodies, our own environment. There has to be a balance.

Gilbert hasn't bothered to draw on the energy backlash from his own spell and I'm glad. The energy bleeds out as light. Every line of his body is blazing.

I look into the heart of the sun, and do not flinch.

"I'll help your sister," I say.

He exhales. His breath ghosts across my skin. "Thank you."

"You three meet me back here after school. I'll tell you my conditions then."

I don't listen to his hesitant questions as I walk back up the stairs, tapping my thumbs along my knuckles. It's 8:07, and I'm late for home coven. I'll say sorry to every member of my class and watch them react with well-meaning kindness, or confusion, or disdain.

Because I *am* different. And I know exactly what I'm going to do.

It's not a good school day. In Physics, it's weather patterns, and I get by. In Biology, it's genetics, and I'm fine. But in English, it's *Ulysses*. Everyone else loves this stupid book; it's supposed to be the first great Chaotic literature. I can't handle it. Every time I think the author is going to stick to a thought, he leaps into something else. He can't sustain a single notion for longer than a sentence, and even the sentences break all the rules.

We get our essays back. I have a circled F and a See Me. Behind me, Celia Nakamura is showing her A- to her girlfriend. I put my head down and don't cry.

When we break into groups for discussion, I gather all my courage in both hands. "Celia, do you still tutor?" I ask.

She tilts her head at me. "No. I work at the library after school, now. Why, are you having trouble?" The question is kindly meant, but it falls into one of those sudden silences, the random blanking out of noise that happens when every other person in the room has momentarily fallen silent.

"Always having trouble," some idiot mutters from the back.

Laurel Spildren giggles behind her notebook. Celia nudges her into silence.

Ms Apllyn clears her throat. "Ten minutes until gather-and-share," she reminds us, and the class hum starts up again.

We have six discussion questions. Celia and Laurel do the talking. I twirl my pen three times and write it all down.

When I go back to the gym storage room, they're all waiting. Rosalind leaps across the room to wrap her arms around my torso.

People don't usually touch me. It's okay if they do, but I'm not sure how to react.

"Thank you, thank you, thank you so much. I am *miserable*. I mean, I'm kind of really happy? But I don't *want* to be."

I pat her shoulder twice before I step back. "I have conditions."

"Gil said. I'll do anything."

"Do you drive to school?"

"Yes," she says. "I mean … I share the car with Gil. But I do most of the driving."

"From now on, you pick me up. You'll be ready and waiting by 6:50AM. Every school day, for the rest of the year."

I watch that sink in. People will talk, because people always do. She won't be able to explain it away without revealing what she and Kinai did. They might even think we're together, the Order-declared weirdo and the most beautiful girl in school. Maybe they'll bother me less; maybe more. But I'll be on time every day, and I'm very good at ignoring whatever they say.

Rosalind isn't. She swallows, hard. "That's … are you *punishing* me?"

I blink at her. "You need a love spell undone. I need a ride."

"I could give you a ride," Kinai says. Rosalind giggles at the phrasing, but I scowl. Curiously, so does Gilbert.

Kinai actually flinches from my glare. I want to say, *what did you expect?* You can't say mean things about a girl and expect her to realize that it means you like her, much less expect her to love you for it. That's three-year-old logic; it's barely logic at all.

I had half thought that I might make Kinai tutor me in English. But I don't want to be near his heavy silence and awkward glances. Now that I recognize the desire in his eyes, I don't want to see it again. "The other condition is that you'll stay away from me," I say. And, just to make certain he understands: "I don't like you."

Gilbert chews the inside of his cheek, but I see the smile struggling at the corner of his lips.

Stomach fluttering, I turn back to Rosalind. "There are two ways to undo a spell like this. The gradual method will be easiest. We can sit in the parking lot for ten minutes every morning, and that will give me time to suppress the chemical responses and draw out a little of the spell root. You'll feel fine in a week. You'll *be* fine in three months—right before you graduate."

"What's the other way?" Gilbert asks.

"I'd go in and uproot the spell at one time. It would create a great deal of energy and the bleed out would be extreme. Any spell would have to be extensively adapted to ground that safely."

Gilbert is nodding. "And it'd still be dangerous."

"I don't mind the risk," Rosalind says. "It would be better to get it over with."

"Haven't you learned a damn thing?" Gilbert demands. "Rose, you have to be careful."

She laughs. "I'm a Chaos queen!"

"That's an excuse for being impulsive, not a reason! Helen's mother is a Chaos queen, and she handles the school administration. Do you think she gets to do whatever she feels like with no thought for the consequences?"

Rose's elegant cheekbones flush dark with blood. "Hey, watch it, brat. I'm still your big sister."

"So why am I always the one covering up for *your* mistakes?" Gilbert shakes his head and shuts his mouth firmly. "I'm done," he says after a minute. "This is the last time I help, Rose. Next time you pull a stunt like this I'm telling Mum and Dad." He looks at me. "Sorry. We'll see you tomorrow."

Rosalind chases him up the stairs. I watch them go.

The weight of the room changes, and I realize I am alone in it with Kinai.

"I just wanted—" he begins, and I cut him off, slicing my hand through the air like a blade.

"You don't talk to me," I say. "That's the condition."

I don't wait to see him acquiesce before I leave.

Later, I know this was a mistake.

It's 6:33AM on Wednesday, and a silver car is waiting outside. I take my pills and position the water glass in the right place on the windowsill. I twist my braids into a French roll and secure it with my grandmother's blue pin.

It takes me four tries to get through my bedroom door, but I grit my teeth until I can stop tapping the door knob and instead turn it.

"My friend is picking me up," I call towards the bathroom. "See you after school."

I knew this wouldn't pass without comment, but I didn't expect

Mum to run from the shower into the hallway.

"Your friend?" she says. "Helen, are you—what's—"

"You're wet! You're naked!"

She waves these trivialities aside. "A boyfriend?" she asks hopefully. "Girlfriend?"

"I am not talking to you while you're naked!"

Mum picks up Gruffyth and holds him where he just barely covers everything vital. "There."

Gruffyth surveys me with stern inquiry. I can tell I'm not going to get out of this conversation unscathed.

"Just a friend. Rosalind Hill."

Mum blinks. "The fourth year? I wouldn't have thought she'd—" she floats her hand in the air.

"—want anything to do with me?"

Mum rolls her eyes. "I was going to say, interest you. She was kicked off the cheerleading squad for skipping practices. She's racked up at least twenty tardies this year."

"Well, she's early now," I say. "I should go."

"We'll discuss this later!" she yells after me. Gruffyth mews.

Rosalind is sitting in the driver's seat, smiling widely. Gilbert is nowhere to be seen, and I am so busy trying to keep my disappointment off my face that I don't notice Kinai is hiding in the back until he sits up at the first traffic lights.

They're red, so I go for the door handle at once.

"Nope," Kinai says. The doors make that heavy chunking sound. I flick the lock up again. Nothing happens.

"Kinai thought you could take the spell off me all at once," Rosalind says helpfully.

"This is kidnapping," I say, very clearly, and reach for my phone.

Kinai takes my bag off my shoulder. "Be reasonable," he says.

"Be reasonable," Rosalind repeats. Her eyes are too bright. I meet Kinai's gaze in the rearview mirror.

He doesn't look abashed now. He looks triumphant. I lose all hope of talking some sense into him. He knows exactly what he's doing.

"Obedience spell," I say.

He laughs. "You're so smart, Helen. I love that about you."

"You're disgusting. As soon as I escape, I'm calling the police."

He shakes his head, still smiling. "No. You won't escape, and you won't call the police. You'll love me too much for that."

My heart stutters.

Most of the time, I need calm to work my magic. Failing that, I need a connection to something real, something with an Order I can recognize. There's metal in the car frame, but it's moving too fast, and Rosalind's erratic driving is making it impossible to sketch out a pattern. I can just barely make out the electric fuzz of her confused thought processes.

But even the most reprehensible, irresponsible person can't be stupid enough to try something as complicated as a love spell on an unwilling subject in a moving vehicle. At some point, there will be an opportunity for me to get help.

I tap my knuckles, and count the telephone poles, and wait.

Rosalind drives us to school. Kinai winks at me. "I don't want you to be late to class," he says. I was hoping he wouldn't be smart enough to know that people will notice if I change my routine. But he's been watching me for too long.

"Park on the gym side, Rose," Kinai says.

I have no idea how he thinks he can successfully move me into that little storage room. The parking lot is almost empty of cars, but there are lights on in some of the buildings. A teacher could look out the window; one of the weightlifting squad might be in the free weights room. I have never been so happy to know that there are people around.

Because I do not intend to go quietly.

"Helen, when we get out, Rose is going to walk in front, then you, then me. You won't make a noise, or beckon anyone over, or do anything stupid."

I am not good at concealing my emotions. Kinai smiles at my expression. "Rose, cut your hand."

The little pocket knife in Rosalind's hand is small and sharp, and it draws a red line through the pink flesh of her palm before I can do more than inhale sharply. She winces—the obedience can't disguise the pain—but she looks at Kinai for approval.

"Is that clear?" Kinai asks me.

I nod. It's very clear. I will have to rescue us myself.

"Let's go, then." Kinai releases the door locks. I get out, moving as slowly as I dare. My brain is going very fast. A few minutes' walk to the gym, then sixteen steps down to the fetid storage room.

Then the spell. I'd like to think love wouldn't make me stupid; that I wouldn't instantly forgive Kinai all his malice. But I remember Rosalind's defense of him and I wonder whether she actually dared him to try to make her love him. That Gilbert believed it too doesn't make me feel any better about my own prejudices.

The closer we get to the gym, the harder it is to breathe. I tap my knuckles as fast as possible, but I mess up the pattern and have to start again.

"Stop doing that," Kinai hisses behind me.

"You know I can't," I say, as calmly as I can. I really hope he won't try to physically stop me. If he does that, I'll start shouting, and that will draw a lot of attention. I think about Gilbert, and that helps a little. Warm eyes, a quiet manner, the way he was ready to catch me when I hauled myself to a stop—

My breathing hiccups. On the eighth step.

Will it work? Twice isn't much of a pattern, but I'll have to make do.

I'm too quiet. "Why do you even want me?" I say.

"I'm not sure," Kinai says. "You're sort of weird, and you're not that pretty."

"I'm pretty," Rosalind says.

"You're very pretty," he agrees. "But Helen doesn't care what anyone thinks. I respect that."

His hand lands on my shoulder. I want to turn my head and bite him, hard. This isn't what respect looks like.

Rosalind leads us through the gym and to the top of the stairs. I put my foot on the same step I stumbled on yesterday, and plough directly into Rosalind's back. It's not a controlled descent this time. Rosalind and I tumble inelegantly, all tangled limbs and scrapes. Desperation lends me enough strength to keep us mostly upright as we hit the eighth step.

Kinai might not know exactly what I'm doing, but his defenses slam into place all the same; I'd have no hope of reaching his mind, even if I wanted to taint myself with the same kind of spells he'd used. If he were my target, I'd be done for.

I grab Rosalind's bleeding hand and scrape it across the concrete wall, where yesterday my blood was spilt.

And just like that, we're connected. I yank power from every orderly pattern I can find: from the stone, from the timing, from the biological programming locked in our cells. We must have a shared ancestor or two, some six or seven generations back; that's something. We're both O positive; that's something else. Thanks to vaccination, we have whole battalions of memory B cells dedicated to the same diseases. I am Rose and she is me and I am free from forced obedience and unwanted, unwarranted love and so is she, *now*.

The bleed out snaps back through me, static electricity lifting every hair on my body. Electrons are dizzily moving from one atom to another in intricate, chaotic dances—not entirely random, but not patterned enough for me.

My skin vibrates. The sickly scent of ozone pricks my nostrils.

Rose's eyes snap into brilliant, terrible focus. She drags every bit of that wild power from my stinging skin and points at Kinai.

He has just enough time to recognize she's free before the lightning strikes.

The police show up five minutes later.

I am concentrating on my breath. Rose has stopped asking me questions, and Kinai's groans are so much empty noise to me now. I go deep, follow my breath as it travels down, through windpipe, and down each bronchial tube, past the tiny, filtering cilia and down, down, to inflate my alveoli. Breath to blood to brain, keeping me alive and whole.

A police officer asks me something, but it's static. I shake my head, eyes screwed shut.

"She can't answer right now," Rose says. Her hand is on my shoulder and our connection is still strong; I can feel the deliberate attention that forces her shoulders down and her head high.

"Helen? Rose?" a new voice says, and I open my eyes. Gilbert is there. Kinai is gone.

"Miss, I really need to speak to you," the cop says. He's young and white, with pale blonde wisps slipping out from under his uniform cap. I shake my head again.

"Our father represents my sister and Ms. Adebayo, and will need to be in attendance before any questions are put to either of them," Gilbert says, very polite, very firm. "He's on his way now. I'm Gilbert Hill; I called you."

The cop flips his notebook. "You said you thought your sister had been kidnapped. How is it that Mr. Hayashi is the one with electrical burns?"

Rose smiles, and the cop actually goes a little bit pink. "Our father is on his way," she says sweetly. "We'll be happy to talk to you then."

For a moment, I think he's going to press the issue. We are three dark-skinned teenagers, and he is a white adult. But Rose is beautiful, and I am small, and we're both bleeding. It might help that Gilbert's father is a lawyer. It might help that the cop is only a few years older than Rose. Whatever the reason, he retreats, to consult with his partner, and talk to the EMTs.

Gilbert crouches beside me. "Thank you," he whispers.

"You called the police," I say.

"Desperate measures. It'll be fine. Do you want me to call your mother?"

"No." I uncross my legs and stand, pushing myself up with my shaking hands. The breathing helped a little, but I'm still unsteady, a queasy knot of spent adrenaline curling through my gut.

"Why don't we go into the office to wait for her?"

I twist my hair back into my twist. "I need to do Shadow of the Sun first."

"Are you sure? Aren't you tired?"

I want to scream into his face. "I *need* to do Shadow of the Sun," I repeat, and shake my head at his stare. "Do you think I want to? Do you think I wouldn't stop if I could? It doesn't matter that I'm tired! I do not get to choose. I have to do Shadow of the Sun before I can walk through the main doors." My cheeks are wet. I refuse to wipe them. "I have to."

"Sure," he says, and lurches out of my way. And then, behind me: "Helen, I'm really sorry."

I ignore him. Trailed by Rose and the young policeman, I start my widdershins trek around the big building. It's not going to be a good day.

It's 6:50AM on Friday, and Mum is still in the shower.

Standing in the front hall, I run my thumbs over my clenched fingers and tap the knuckles of my pinkies three times.

"Mum! We're late!"

"Don't you want to stay at home another day?"

"No! I'll be in the car!"

Two days off school were more than enough, with the police questions I had to answer and the media Mr. Hill kept firmly away from me. But "sources inside the station" talked, and now everyone knows what I can do.

Last night I hid under my blanket and clicked through links. There are lots of articles and interviews. There's a fan page. There's a Tiny Order King meme.

Most people seem to be impressed. I'm the hero, who took down a criminal with nothing more than a blood tie and a concrete wall. Rosalind is the damsel in distress, breathlessly grateful for my intervention. I'm annoyed that these roles are incomplete and inaccurate, but at least they mean Kinai is indisputably cast as the villain.

And everyone wants to be close to the hero. Half the kids in my classes are jumping at the chance to talk about how modest and restrained I am.

It's a new way to be talked about. I'm not sure what to do with it yet.

When I haul the front door open, Gilbert Hill is on the other side, fist raised to knock. He lowers it.

"Um," he says.

I raise my eyebrows.

"Sorry, again," he says. "I didn't get it. That's not your fault."

I nod. "Okay."

"Um, I just, I shouldn't have said that. I should have listened to you. But what you did was so cool, and you saved my sister, and I thought that you should get a chance to rest some."

"It doesn't work like that." There is a smile tugging at the corner of my lips. Gil thinks I'm cool.

"I know. I'm sorry."

"Okay. Apology accepted."

He exhales. "Would you like a ride?" he asks. Rose waves at me from the car's passenger seat.

I glance down the hall. "Yes," I decide.

"Laurel Spildren declared herself an Order worker yesterday," he adds. "Says she's inspired by your example."

I snort, and haul my bag over my shoulder. "Maybe they'll stop saying all Order workers are like me."

"We could do with more people like you," he says. It'd be corny, but he twitches after he says it, and carries on, fast, as if he's worried I'll think it's a line. "She also said you're not fond of *Ulysses*."

"I'm not," I say, and study his face. I'm free to do it—he's looking at my feet.

"We studied it last semester. So I was wondering," he says. "I mean, only if you want to. I'm not saying that you need my help. Or any help. I'm okay at English, that's all. You probably don't want to spend more time with us. Rose thought that maybe—"

I laugh and touch his shoulder. Just a light brush, but I think I can be brave enough to do it again some time. "Gil, I'm terrible at English. Will you please tutor me?"

"Yes," he says, and meets my eyes. "I'd love that."

"Me too," I say, and check the time. "But we have to go now."

"Right, of course. Shadow of the Sun."

I still have to be careful. He could hurt me so easily, without meaning to at all. I am beginning to suspect that I could hurt him too.

But today might be a good day.

And Gil's smile is warm, like light on the bark of a growing thing.

Walkdog

by Sofia Samatar

This paper is in response to the assignment "Know Your Environment". In this paper I will discuss an animal called Walkdog which is native to my local environment which is South Orange, New Jersey. First I will describe the animal ("Brief Description"), then I will write about it's origin and habits ("Research"), then I will conclude with why I chose to write about this animal and why its important ("Conclusion"). Thesis statement: <u>Even though not much has been written about it, Walkdog is an important part of North American wildlife</u>.

1. Brief Description

What is Walkdog? Well Mrs. Patterson you probably know better than me. However, I am writing this paper and not you, because I need the grade as you know very well, so here is what I know.

Walkdog contrary to it's name is not a dog. It is more like a beaver or large rat. It lives mostly in sewers but also creeks and rivers. It is nocturnel and believed to eat fish and also, excuse me, excrament.[1] Walkdog when walking is said to be about 5 feet long, including the tail, but when it stands up it looks taller than a man. Its fur is black and oily. Its a great swimmer and can stay underwater for 3 days without coming up for air.

Other names for Walkdog: Grimdog, Grimwolf, The Dog that Walks Men, The Dog that Walks Hisself, Jumpy Leg, Conjure Dog, Canewolf.

Some people also call it Growldog, but this is stupid because Walkdog doesn't growl. It has no voicebox.[2]

---

1 The reason Walkdog is supposed to eat excrament is simply common sense, because what kind of fish is it eating in the sewer? Also we can assume that Walkdog has a seriously powerful gut and high-level immune system because eating random fish out of Jersey creeks will kill you. If Walkdog can eat bugged-out radioactive fish it would probably consider excrament a healthy snack.

2 Marjorie Wilson, "Sounds of the Jersey Night", in Voices of Nature, ed. Steven Wilkins, Rutgers University Press, 1980, p. 115. "Then there is the Walkdog, a creature without a voicebox, known only by its footstep and its splash."

2. Research

One thing you will notice when you start researching Walkdog is that not much has been written about it at all. It gets mentioned in a sentence here and there but you won't find a book about it or even a Wikipedia page which is weird, don't you think? Its like its hiding from everything with some kind of magic. Probably the person who knows most about Walkdog is your nephew, Andrew Bookman, the most hopeless dork in this school you'll excuse me for saying, because you know its a fact and facts as you say are the Building Blocks of Research.[3]

From Andy I learned that the origins of Walkdog are, as he put it, "obscure". There are three main theories on the origins of Walkdog:

a) indigenous animal related to otter

b) came over from Europe or Asia with immigrants

c) came over from Africa on slave ship[4]

---

3 Facts about Andrew: fat (nickname: "Bubble-Butt"), glasses, always reading (and his last name is Bookman!), started calling himself "Andy" when he started highschool, which anybody should of known that was a stupid thing to do, he should of just stuck with Andrew, even Drew would be cooler, but no, he had to be Andy. Also, his aunt is a teacher (you) which does not help anybody I am sorry to tell you. The cloud of nerd gas surrounding Andy is so strong it could make your eyes water. People only go near him to mess with him. As a teacher you probably know this unless you are unbelieveably clueless.

4 Source: private conversation with Andrew Bookman. Andy's personal favorite of these theories was #3. Mostly because of the name "Canewolf" which must mean sugarcane which is something we don't have a lot of here in Jersey. Andy's grandmother, who I guess was possibly a relative of yours, died and left him what he says is a mat made of Walkdog hair. His grandma called it her "conjure mat". This mat supposedly came from the Caribbean somewhere which Andy also says supports his theory. He kind of lost me at that point—he talks really fast when he gets going, and his face, which is already oily, starts getting oilier than ever, I mean really impossibly shiny, which is distracting—but it was something about slave routes and stopping points and getting from Angola

In other words, the origins of Walkdog are the origins of just about everybody. This is why I describe it as a native animal. I mean I consider myself a New Jersey native, what else would I be, even though I'm African and German and Spanish and God knows what else.[5]

Now for the habits of Walkdog. These habits are not what you would call nice. Walkdog steals kids (another name for it is The Child Thief). It does not steal them to eat, as stated above, it eats fish and excrement mainly, but it steals them at night and then *it takes them for walks*.

It takes them for walks. It just takes them around with it. I want you to think about what that's like. Imagine your a normal kid asleep in your normal bed. Don't imagine yourself as Andy Bookman, because that kid is not normal *at all*, but imagine you're somebody regular like me. Me, Yolanda Price. I would say I'm pretty normal. I'm not popular, in fact I generally have to keep my head down, just smile at the right times and keep my mouth shut, because I am almost on the edge of nerd, I only manage to

---

or somewhere to Charleston. I don't know. Poor Andy. He had on a white button-down shirt. Big sweat stains under the arms. It was like he didn't *want* to be normal.

5 This note is not exactly related to the above, I just want to clarify the previous note in which I named my source as a private conversation with Andrew Bookman, but I also said earlier that people only go near him to mess with him. I want to be clear that I myself never messed with your nephew in any way, also I did not go near him at school because to be frank I did not want to get contaminated by his nerd gas. I went to Union Market on the weekend because as you must know that is where Andy goes every Saturday to run a coin swap booth with his parents.

Andy's parents are also terrible nerds, his dad in combat boots, his mom in a red wig, both of them obsessed with antique coins. Their super nice which just makes it worse. I guess you know that though. You certainly didn't stop by their booth while I was there.

do all right because I can sing. If you have a cool talent like that and are not stupid you'll be okay. I'm not saying that singing could of saved Andrew Bookman. Your nephew I am sorry to say was a grade-A world class nerd and singing probably would of just made things worse for him. Do you know he told everybody that after graduation he was going to go eat strawberries in Denmark? Who *says* that? Strawberries and new potatoes and the grave of Hans Christian Andersen. People called him The Little Mermaid for weeks. Bubble-Butt, your too ugly to get into another country. Did you notice? Were you afraid that defending him would make things worse? If so you were probably right. It was best to just ignore it. There are places that once you step in, you can't get out.

So, you're me, Yolanda, lying in bed. There's a tap at the window. Tap tap tap. Annoying. You think its a tree branch on the glass. You get up and open the window, even if its winter you would open it to break off the branch and get rid of that awful tapping. So you open the window, lets say its winter like now, February, the worst time of year, with no holidays in sight except Valentines Day a.k.a. National Torture Day, and not being able to sleep is just the last straw, so you open the window and theres a small black shape looking at you from the yard. You stand there, because what is it? Too big for a cat or even a racoon. And then it rears up. It hauls itself up and its tall, its snuffling at the window, and its eyes are small red lights and it says in this voice that comes from no voicebox, this voice in your head, it says Come on girl lets get walking.

Where are we going?

Down to the creek.

I don't want to.

It laughs: Eee, eee, eee.[6]

I don't want to. But your already putting your knee on the sill. Walkdog reaches its paws up and catches you as you fall out. It smells like drains. It puts you down on the ground and crouches on all fours. Bam, just like that, its small again. It sets off walking over the snow, and you follow. Your sliding down the slope at the end of the yard. Now you're on Varsity Ave. It's all dark out. I don't know if you're crying. Would you cry? Some of the stars are gold, the same color as the streetlights.

Now you are going to walk for a long time.

You might walk as far as the Wolf-Boy, Carlton O'Neill. Just trying to get back home again. I know for a fact you could walk to Indiana easy, like in the song "Indiana Morning" by Blueswoman Maisie Oates.[7]

---

6 This is the sound of the Walkdog laugh as you hear it in your head. Carlton O'Neill who was abducted by Walkdog when he was nine years old and let go again for some reason when he was thirty-six described the sound for the Star Ledger. "It sounded like a kid locked up and crying or a train whistle far away." "'Wolf-Boy' Found in Livingston Reservation", The Star Ledger, August 14 2005, p. 1. Carlton O'Neill was skinny and a mess when he was found. He said he'd been to Canada and the farthest tip of Argentina. All on foot. They gave him a pen to write down who he was and when he remembered how to write his name he fainted.

Andy who was a Walkdog fanatic had this newspaper article tacked to his bulletin board. He also had Carlton O'Neill's signature on an index card. He had actually tracked the guy down and gotten his autograph. Carlton lived with his mother in East Orange at that point. I don't know where he is now.

7 Indiana morning, I'm as low as I can be.
Indiana morning, I'm as low as I can be.

Walking and walking. You'd see a lot. Maybe you'd like it since you are such a fan of Research. You could do all the Research you wanted, walking up and down the country. I think you'd be cold though. You'd sleep in ditches and drains. Curled up against Walkdog for warmth. Walkdog's voice in you murmuring, Time to get up.

3. Conclusion

In this conclusion I will write about why I chose Walkdog for this assignment and why its important.

I chose Walkdog because I heard about it from Andy. What happened is two boys who you definitely know so I won't repeat their names slammed into Andy in the hall and sent his papers flying. This happened on a daily basis. *Every day*. You have to ask yourself why Andy was always carrying stuff in his arms when he also wore a backpack. Why not keep everything in the backpack and then when people banged into him he would fall but his stuff would not be all over the hallway. Theres a sign above your desk

---

Went to walk my hound dog, but now he's walking me.

This song is from the album *Indiana Morning* by Blueswoman Maisie Oates. I heard it at Andy's house which is also where I read the article about Carlton O'Neill, and also I may as well say since its part of my Research that I saw and touched the "conjure mat" Andy inherited from his grandma. I am wondering if you know anything about this mat? Have you ever seen it? Its gray and hairy and about as big around as those things you put on the table under hot dishes. I said I thought it would be black and Andy said he doesn't know why its gray, he thinks maybe since its cut off the Walkdog its lacking essential oils. That was in his room which is like Nerd Heaven, full of action figures and model planes. You can't touch anything or Andy starts freaking out. Obviously I would not be caught dead going in the front door at Andy's house. I went in the back. He opened a window.

that says "Nobody is Unteachable", but Mrs. Patterson I beg to disagree. In this matter Andy was 100% Unteachable. So there his papers went as usual and these two boys enjoyed kicking them and leaving footprints on them. One of the papers slid over to me and almost touched my foot. I didn't pick it up, because unlike Andy I am Teachable, but I glanced down at it. There was a drawing of something black and blobby with red eyes and underneath it it said Walkdog.

You could say that that was when I got the idea for this assignment even though you had not given it to us yet. I got curious about Walkdog. It seemed like such a weird thing to draw, even for Andy. I asked my parents about it at dinner and they'd never heard of it. Sounds like an urban legend, my mom said later, when I told her about my Research. Mm-hm, said Dad. Mom did remember when Carlton O'Neill got found in the reservation. That poor man, she said, God bless him. She said that's probably where Walkdog got started, and poor wandering Carlton is the only Walkdog there ever was. I asked how she would explain the song "Indiana Morning" which was recorded back in 1955. Oh that's just a metaphor she said, and I said, a metaphor for what? She looked uncertain. Alcoholism?[8]

---

8 This is Mom's explanation for most bad things. It is based on personal experience because my grandfather (her dad) drank himself to death. In my opinion this is the reason she married a security guard (my dad) who works at the same bank where Mom is a teller. Security is her thing. This is my parent's week: Bank, Bank, Bank, Bank, Bank, Groceries, Church. After graduation I am going to Rutgers and my mom assumes I will major in Accounting. Accounting is a good secure choice. I want to major in Music. The only person I have told this to (besides you) is Andy Bookman. It was after we listened to "Indiana Morning". He said I should do Music if I want,

When you gave us this assignment I went to the Union Market and found Andy at his parent's booth and asked him about his picture that said Walkdog, and whether it was something that would be good for a paper on "Know Your Environment", and he said it would be awesome. Andy was always saying things were awesome, and he meant it. He beamed at me from under the leaves of a plant being sold in the stall next to his. He didn't even think that I might of come out there to mess with him or make fun of him even though that was the most likely scenario. Mrs. Patterson, Andy was special. I know you know that. I know you saw him getting picked on every day. When he raised his hand in class all it took was for somebody to shout *Bookman!* and the whole class would burst out in these awful little giggles. They didn't even have to use his nasty nickname. Imagine how it would feel if just your name made other people laugh. You never batted an eye, you just said Yes, Andy? like it was all normal and like I said before it was probably the right thing to do. And then Andy would say whatever he was going to say, always something smart, while people made fart noises and snickered or whatever. You know Mrs. Patterson, this school is actually hell. I don't know why everyone acted shocked when Andy got beat up the way he did. Special assembly and Principal Reed on the stage with his voice all wobbly. He said we must realize we are becoming men and women.

---

maybe I should even go to an arts school instead of Rutgers. I never thought of that, I said. I felt like such an idiot. But Andy didn't laugh. He looked calm and thoughtful. Its hard to get started, he said. Its hard to get going by yourself. He was looking at my boots, which I'd left by the window. Snow melting off them on the floor.

He's right about that. But that doesn't mean we're changing. It just means we're bigger now, big enough to put somebody in the hospital.[9]

It's true. People act like highschool students are kids and need to be taken care of all the time but we are actually adults. If this was the Middle Ages we'd all be married or in wars and you, Mrs. Patterson, you'd be considered a very old lady. And the truth is, you are a very old lady. The day after Andy got beat you looked so frail. You had that old lady's look of being lost in the world. The truth is, Mrs. Patterson, that a lot of us kids are married and a lot of us are in wars. Andy was both.[10]

Now when I think about why I chose Walkdog, I think I really chose Andy. I think I chose him even before I knew it. That black, bulky shape on the paper was just an excuse. I wish I could end

---

9 They cornered him down by the creek. Behind the fucking police station. I am sorry, I don't care that I'm swearing in my paper. Why did he have to walk that way? Why couldn't he have gone down South Orange Ave. like everyone else? Why didn't I invite him to my house? Do you think Andy Bookman has gotten invited anywhere since seventh grade? They cornered him down by the creek. They yanked off his backpack and threw it in the water. They broke his nose. They broke three of his ribs. They stepped on his wrist and broke that too. They kicked him all over, those same two boys that I won't repear their names. Nice boys that everybody knows. All they got was suspended because they're sorry. Right behind the police station. Where were the police? Where was fucking Walkdog when Andy needed him? I went to the hospital after and Andy's father was crying in the hall.

10 His bed was so saggy. He'd probably slept there since he was six years old. It seemed too small. He had the best smile, a perfect dimple on either side. Long eyelashes that brushed my cheek. I don't want to ruin anything, I said, and he said what? and I said I don't want to mess up your trip to Denmark. I was already hoping he'd cancel and stay with me because even if I had my own money my parents would never let me to go Europe with a boy, not even a boy like Andy who was so sweet, its not secure, even though there is no place more secure than Andy's arms. He laughed and kissed me. Your not ruining anything. I love you. Model plane wings turning, shadows on the wall. Snow outside and the windows all blue. He hugged me and I just sank. There are places that once you step in, you can't get out.

my paper there and say that getting to know Andy was getting to know my environment. You might give me an A for a paper like that, or you might give me an F, but I wouldn't care because I would be going over to Andy's after school, or I would have invited him over to my house, and on National Torture Day we would have watched dumb horror movies in my basement and laughed. My head on his shoulder oh God Mrs. Patterson where do you think he is? Is he still alive? Is he with Walkdog? Is that it? Is he walking around? Is he going to appear in thirtysome years in the forest like Carlton O'Neill and are people going to start calling him another Wolf-Boy? I went to look for Carlton, you know, after Andy disappeared, but I couldn't find him, he's not at his mother's house anymore. I found his mother and she blew a ton of cigarette smoke in my face and said He gone for a walk and shut the door on me. Is that where Andy is? Just gone for a walk? If I'd known I never would have gone back to his house for the conjure mat like he asked me. Yes, I went back for it. He told me where to find the spare key and I went into his house and got the mat from his room. His stupid action figures staring at me in their creepy way. The mat was on top of the filing cabinet. It felt prickly and weird in my hand. I put it in a plastic bag that used to have my lunch in it and stuck it in my purse and went back to the hospital. Maybe I should of known something was wrong, but I just wanted to make Andy happy for once, and I could tell the flowers I'd brought him weren't doing anything. He just sat in the bed and stared at nothing. White bandages over his nose, white light everywhere. He looked really drained there, drained and small. I didn't know how to touch him, he looked so hurt. I was crying but he didn't seem to notice. He just said in this muffled voice: Get me the conjure mat. Okay, I said, still crying. Andy's parents were outside. Are you a friend? his mom asked, and I said, I'm his girlfriend.

Some girlfriend, right?

I never went anywhere with him. Never went in his front door. Never, ever walked home with him from school.

I should have walked home with him. I should have. *I should have walked him home.*

So now you know why I couldn't finish my solo at the service they held in his honor. Praying for news of the missing Andrew Bookman. The choir kept going and I just stopped. I saw you out there in a pew, looking at me, so sad. I couldn't keep going. My voice was just gone, cut off, there was nothing but air, like I was all full of dust, like I didn't have a voicebox.

Mrs. Patterson this is my thesis statement: Even though not much has been written about it, Walkdog is an important part of North American wildlife. I hope you can see why Walkdog is important. I hope you can help me. The fact is I think your nephew conjured up Walkdog using the conjure mat. I think he felt so alone, so abandoned by everybody, including you and me, that he did something drastic, he summoned up Walkdog and Walkdog came. I want you to tell me if I'm right. Did you know that conjuring grandmother? What was she like? Did she leave you anything? Did she tell you the counterspell?

I want you to tell me that yes, you know a spell, or you have your own conjure mat. I want you to tell me how to find Andy. I need him. Mrs. Patterson this hound dog is walking me and he's walking me hard. Everywhere I go I hear his footstep and his splash.

If you can't give me a spell then I want you to tell me that Walkdog is not a devil or anything scary but that its a helper and a friend. I want you to tell me that Andy's not scared right now and not alone. He's just walking. He's doing Research, which is another kind of Nerd Heaven. Maybe he's walked to Indiana by now. Maybe he'll get to Denmark. Maybe he'll swim with Walkdog who can stay underwater for three days. I see this boy in the waves, he's holding onto Walkdog's small black ears and heading out to where its strawberry season. I always see him in his hospital gown, the way he was the last time, the way I imagine he got up one night, his conjure mat in his hand, and walked through the hospital in the ghostly light and opened the doors and there was Walkdog waiting, black and low to the ground. Come on lets get walking. I want you to tell me that Andy's not going to come back all skinny and beat-up like Carlton O'Neill. I want you to tell me that he's not cold. Somebody's always with him. He's got protection. No one will ever hurt him again.[11]

---

11 To complete my Research here is the rest of the song "Indiana Morning".

If you got a dollar, why don't you give me half.
If you got a dollar, come on and give me half.
The stories I could tell you, they'd make a preacher laugh.

When I had a good man, the sun shone every day.
When I had that good man, the sun shone every day.
Now I need this whiskey to take the pain away.

Budworm in the cotton, beetle in the corn.
Budworm in the cotton, beetle in the corn.
Feel like I been walking since the day that I was born.

Hear that hound dog. Day that I was born.

Celebration

by Sean Eads

There wasn't much conversation during our drive to *Celebrate Your Life*, the "healing institute" my parents booked me into for the summer. I knew it was a conversion therapy center, the equivalent of a mental health facility for the clinically gay. I'd learned my fate yesterday, right after the last day of my junior year in high school. You forget to erase your browser history *one little time*, and then you get shipped off for psychotherapy. My slip-up actually happened several months ago, but my parents had played dumb, buying time to research and enroll me into a *Very Special Summer Camp*.

Finally I said, "What about my friends?"

Without looking back, Mom said, "They'll be told you're spending the summer with your Aunt Sally."

I fumed. "Isn't that what parents in the 1950s said when their teen daughters got pregnant?"

"Life was so much simpler then." Mom's tone was wistful.

"Does the fact I'll hate you for the rest of my life mean anything?"

"Jim," Dad said. "You've hated us for the rest of your life since you were three years old."

"Well, now I mean it."

I crossed my arms. My dark mood had already given me a new slogan for my situation: *Celebrate Your Life—End It.*

But I wouldn't be killing myself. A very small part of me was even intrigued about *Celebrate Your Life*. At least I'd finally meet some other gay kids. I savored this exciting prospect and was likely the world's first gay boy to have a chubby when he arrived at a reparative therapy center.

Celebrate Your Life consisted of five buildings. The main facility had steepled roofs and looked like a hastily repurposed church. There was plenty of open space—nice for the brochure pictures. We'd probably be forced to play football. A forest to the east looked promising if I decided to flee. Which of the five buildings kenneled the baying hounds?

Mom read my mind. "Don't even think about running away, Jim."

"Open the damn trunk so I can get this over with," I said, getting out. The trunk popped up and I took my three suitcases. All of my possessions were in them, minus my cell phone and anything else technological.

"You must be the *humanoid* known as Jim," said a man hurrying towards us. He seemed nice enough, and not too old. Maybe thirty. His *Doctor Who* shirt made him look younger. Kind of cute in a geeky way, and he certainly *sounded* geeky. But his pleasantness also put me on edge. *Celebrate Your Life* might operate on an elaborate good cop/bad cop set-up. This was *good cop.*

"I'm Matt and I'm a counselor here." After a handshake with my parents, Matt pushed between my shoulder blades and steered me toward the main building.

Good cop was taking me to jail.

"*Jim*," Mom said. I didn't intend to look back. Why did love, of all things, have to be so damned complicated? Why couldn't it be as basic as an atom? Hell, maybe it was. My family was constantly splitting and there was always fallout.

Matt assured my parents they should go, and they did.

"Glad that's over," he said. "It gets better once the *'rents* leave. You nervous, Jim?"

"I guess."

"First time away from home?"

I started to say, "Yeah," and realized I was buying into his act. So I forced myself to return an icy stare.

He smiled. "You'll like it here. We just want to encourage you."

"To celebrate my life?"

"Yes."

"With the opposite sex?"

"Keep an open mind, okay?"

"What happens if I don't?"

Matt shrugged. "Then I guess your parents wasted a lot of money."

I smiled and he frowned.

"That makes you glad, Jim? Having your parents go broke trying to make you happier?"

"It's a hobby."

He grunted. A little bit of tarnish was showing on his *good cop* badge.

At the receptionist's desk, Matt presented me to a woman in her late sixties. She stared off into space, her mouth unhinged.

"Miss Billings?" Matt said. "Miss Billings, this is—are you *okay*, Miss Billings?"

She made an alarming gargling sound that made us both flinch. Then she snapped to attention, her face tightening as a bright smile drew her skin taut.

Matt raised his eyebrows, then clapped a hand on my shoulder, saying, "Miss Billings, this is our latest arrival, Jim Wilde."

She looked at Matt, squinting, and said, "*Well go on you old bitch, say hello to the little faggot.*"

Matt gasped. "Miss Billings, I don't—"

Then she looked at me and said: "Hello, little faggot."

Matt practically picked me up and put me behind him. "What's going on here?"

She blinked at him and shook her head. "That greeting was incorrect?"

"Hell—I mean *heck* yes. How could Jim here trust us if we hold him in contempt? How about an apology?"

I swelled with dopey pride at how Matt defended me and fought to regain my cynicism. The whole point of this place was Psy Ops, right? Old woman uses a slur, the hip younger therapist berates her, and the gay rube bonds with his captor.

Brilliant.

Except Miss Billings sort of looked like she'd fallen victim of a con herself.

"It's okay," I said. "Can I just go to my room?"

"It's *not* okay. You're a wonderful person, Jim."

The old lady was slack-jawed again. If she were a computer, she'd be rebooting.

"Is she having a stroke or something?"

Matt waved a hand in front of her face and got no reaction. "Look, how about I take you to the cafeteria? It's also the rec room. You can meet the other guys."

"I'm all about meeting other guys," I said. Matt frowned and motioned me onward. I looked back just once to see Miss Billings' entire body twitch. Then she became animated and gave me an enthusiastic wave. I gave her the one finger salute and thought, *Celebrate this!*

"Celebrate this!" she said, and her voice was very cheerful.

⁎

I was still shaken by Miss Billings as we entered the cafeteria. There were just eight tables, each with four chairs.

"So is this place really so small or do the inmates eat in shifts?"

Matt was confused for a moment, and then chuckled. "You're an observant guy, Jim. *Celebrate Your Life* is very exclusive. It's easier to give individual attention to smaller groups."

"Easier to watch them as well, right?"

"Like I said," he said coolly, "you're an observant guy."

I observed our recreational activities were limited indeed. A foosball table occupied the far right corner while an air hockey station took up the left. There was also a bookcase filled with black bibles. I sighed. You can count on a long summer when *Leviticus* is your beach read.

Two boys huddled together at the table furthest back. One stared at me; the other found the tabletop more interesting.

"Go make friends," Matt said. "I'll see about Miss Billings."

Glad to ditch Matt, I walked over to them. They seemed my age.

"Hey," I said.

"I'm Nathan," the first kid said, his voice pleasant and deep. He'd looked good from far away. Up close he was a god. He had shaggy blond hair and blue eyes and a strong chin that was perfect even with a big red pimple. He was also one of those dudes who just really knows how to wear a T-shirt. It was like when people talk about art—they can't explain it but they know when they like it.

This guy was art.

"I'm Jim," I said, maybe speaking a little deeper than usual.

We shook hands like we were businessmen at a conference and I sat down. The other guy at the table rocked back and forth, his mouth slightly open, his eyes downcast. He seemed totally spaced.

"Is there something in the water?"

"What do you mean?"

I told them about Miss Billings and what she'd said to me.

"Weird," Nathan said. "She seemed nice before. Figures she'd be a homophobe too. This is Vinnie."

"Hey, Vinnie."

"Dude's not talking. He was fine two days ago. I didn't see him at all yesterday. Guess he got his first treatment."

I swallowed and leaned closer. "*Treatment?*"

Nathan nodded. "My guess is electric shock. Like when they shove a rag in your throat to keep you from swallowing your tongue."

"Jesus! They can't do something like that, not without—"

"Parental permission? We're here, aren't we?"

Vinnie twitched and moaned. It was easy to imagine he'd spent an hour hooked up to a car battery.

"So how long have you guys been here?"

"Four days for me. Vinnie was already here by himself."

The cafeteria suddenly seemed a lot larger. "You mean there are just *three* of us?"

"At least until next week, from what I've been told."

Just then an old man entered. He had the sour look of an embittered gym teacher.

Bad cop.

"That's Mr. Locke. He runs this place. He took Vinnie away yesterday."

Vinnie started rocking harder and saying in a broken voice: "It's not okay to be gay, it's not okay to be gay, it's not okay to be…"

As Mr. Locked turned to us, Vinnie got up and started shouting it.

"What's going on here?"

Mr. Locke was very tall. I was almost six foot and this man still had four inches on me.

He ignored Vinnie and looked at me. "Who are *you*?"

His gruffness scared me, and my fear pissed me off.

"James *Caleb* Wilde," I said.

"James Caleb Wilde." He looked down at his clipboard.

"*Caleb*. You have to pronounce it right. There's an accent over the whole word."

Nathan laughed. He had a surprisingly high-pitched laugh considering the deepness of his voice and I wondered if too many suspicious giggles had punched his ticket to *Celebrate Your Life*.

"It's not okay to be gay! It's not okay to be gay!"

Vinnie's shrieking was terrifying. It was like hearing Dorothy chanting, "There's no place like home," when *home* meant *heterosexuality.*

Mr. Locke tilted his head and listened for a really uncomfortable amount of time, like he was listening to beautiful music in Vinnie's pain. He probably played tortured screams on his iPod.

"What did you *do* to him?" I said.

"He's just … adjusting."

"You don't have the right to hurt us. We're *normal*, no matter what you think—"

Vinnie interrupted me with a series of strange and shocking noises. At first he sounded like someone trying to hold in an explosive sneeze. Then he seemed to be containing a cough. His cheeks puffed out and—I swear—the side of his *throat* bulged.

"He's having a seizure!"

"No, he's not," said Mr. Locke with impressive certainty and calm. He put a hand on Vinnie's shoulder. I thought there was this flash of blue light, but surely I'd hallucinated it in the chaos of the moment. What mattered was Vinnie, and Vinnie seemed a little calmer.

Mr. Locke said, "Beng nik attu deenan. Beng nik attu. Deenan, Elbaton. *Deenan.*"

The words were creepy. Was Mr. Locke using some kind of hypnosis? They scrambled our minds and then implanted us with some nonsense control words they could repeat whenever we went haywire?

"Now," Mr. Locke said, "isn't that better—*Vincent*?"

Vinnie looked around with unfocused eyes. His face still showed the strain of his shouting, but he now had this odd little smile.

"Come with me now, Vincent."

They walked off hand in hand, a gay teen boy and the mean old man determined to make him straight.

⁎

The place should have been called *Celebrate Your Regimented Life*. Breakfast was always at 7:30; dinner was at 5:30. We took these meals together. Lunches were often solitary since we had our therapy sessions at different times. We did get ninety minutes to hang out in the rec room before a nine o'clock curfew. Then we went to the third building to get locked into individual rooms.

On my third night, I was in bed, curled up in a fetal position and all but sucking my thumb. That morning, Matt took me over to the fourth building, which ended up being a psych ward. There I got my first experience with *aversion therapy*. For an hour, I saw pictures of hot guys paired with images of the most revolting things imaginable. Soft music played the entire time. On paper this seems laughable, but at the end of the session I felt scooped out. They were trying to empty me and fill me with something different. The music probably had subliminal messages. God, could they really change me? It frightened me and I was crying when Matt came to get me. Christ, I'd cried in Matt's arms.

Tap. Tap. Tap.

I sat up, thinking I might be imagining the sound. The door opened and there stood Nathan, fully dressed. His right index finger was pressed to his lips.

He motioned for me to follow. I needed no coaxing and got dressed.

As I got close to him, he kissed me. Not a long kiss, not even a romantic one—though it sure as hell set my heart aflutter. I grinned, tingling all over.

My first kiss!

Nathan opened his hand and showed me a ring of keys. *Freedom.* I followed him out and down the hallway. We passed Vinnie's room. His door was cracked open. I looked in and found it empty. I looked at Nathan, who in turn shook his head and looked very intense.

Afraid to say a word, I kept following Nathan. We exited through a side door. The air outside was really strange. It carried an electrical charge, like when lightning is about to strike. The hair on our heads stood up.

"Crazy, isn't it?"

"What's causing it?"

"I'll show you."

We snuck over to the main building and went around the side. Nathan stopped at a steel security door marked *Mechanical Room.* He found the right key and we walked into pitch-black. The electrical charge ceased, leaving my skin crawling. As I rubbed my arms, Nathan turned on the lights. We were in a room lined with HVAC pipes and electrical fuse boxes.

"We can talk a little louder in here, but keep it kind of low."

"What are we doing?"

"Hang tight with the questions. There's something I got to do first."

Nathan leaned forward and kissed me again. This one was a *lot* more than a peck, and it left me weightless.

"I know what you went through today. Thought I'd give you some counter-therapy."

I touched my mouth. My lips felt fuller, more mature. *Weightier.*

I never thought I'd be thanking my parents and lucky stars for getting shipped off to a homophobic prison. I wanted to celebrate the kiss, but it would have to wait. "Where did you get those keys?"

"On my second night I was in my bunk, and something sharp jabbed me. I discovered a slit in the mattress. I dug into it and found these, as well as a note."

I widened my eyes. "Who wrote it?"

Nathan shrugged. "It was just a scrap of paper that said, *Hope they don't change the locks.* Guess they didn't. I've been out exploring most nights."

"Damn, dude." His bravery awed me and I leaned in for a kiss—my own act of courage. Nathan didn't leave me hanging.

"When I knew I could get out, I really thought about running away. But I didn't want to leave behind Vinnie—or you."

"So where *is* Vinnie?"

Nathan smiled. "The cafeteria."

He wouldn't say any more. We left the Mechanical Room, stepping through into a small business office. The desktop computers had screen savers that showed Jesus leading a mixed flock of children, lambs, tiger cubs and wolf pups. It was pure cheese and

I wondered—*When Jesus is your screen saver, does that make it a screen savior?*

Nathan scowled when my giggle startled him.

"We can use the computer to send an email. Post an SOS on Facebook."

"Already thought of that. They're password protected."

We entered a hallway. The lights were off. The main entrance to the cafeteria was just a few yards away, and bright blue light flooded through the crack.

"I *knew* they'd be meeting again."

"Who?"

"Vinnie and Mr. Locke and Miss Billings."

"*What?* The three of them are in there right now?'

"Yeah, and saying some crazy shit. I discovered them the fourth night out of my cell. The air was weird outside like it is now. I'd decided to steal some food. That's how I discovered them. They were sitting together at one table and holding hands. And—*dude.*"

"What?"

"There was like this blue fire burning in the middle of the table. I think that's what makes the air weird."

"Oh, come on."

"See for yourself!"

I didn't want Nathan mad at me. For once I wished I'd heeded Mom's advice and worked on sounding less sarcastic.

"I believe you, Nate." I hoped he liked being called *Nate.* "It's just all so strange."

"It gets stranger. Listen."

I heard three distinct voices chanting some kind of nonsense. Were they Druids? Satanists? I could have laughed, imagining my parents sending me off to Devil worshippers to get me right with God.

One look. I've got to see.

Pulling away from Nathan, I leaned to peek through the opening—

"What the *hell* are you boys doing? What's going on here?"

I jumped as Matt clamped down on my shoulder. He spun me around but I fell out of his grasp and hit the floor. He still had Nathan by the back of his neck, like a puppy grabbed by his scruff. Nathan winced.

"You're hurting him!"

Matt spoke through gritted teeth: "I. Said. What's. Happening. *Here.*"

The blue light ceased and the chanting stopped. Matt swore under his breath. Suddenly from the dark came Miss Billings' unmistakable voice:

"Christ, why do I have to deal with these stupid little faggots? At least I'll get the pleasure of seeing them *changed.*"

Matt gasped. The ceiling lights flashed on. Miss Billings, Mr. Locke and Vinnie stood in the cafeteria entrance with ramrod straight postures and cold expressions.

Matt opened his mouth but it was Miss Billings who said, "What dumb faggot shit is going on now?"

Matt's eyes widened. He took one step back, and then another, dragging Nathan with him. "You—you know what I'm—"

"Thinking," Miss Billings said.

Mr. Locke stared at Matt. "Release the boy."

"Sure, Larry," Matt said, stammering. As soon as he did, Nathan rushed over to me. He shivered violently.

"Miss Billings," said Mr. Locke, "what are the boy's thoughts?"

The old woman's gaze fixed on Nathan. His shivers seemed to transfer over to her as she said, "Just let me go home. Why can't I be good? Why can't Mom and Dad love me?"

"Enough," Mr. Locke said, now pointing to me. "And this one?"

What the hell is happening?

"What the hell is happening?"

I kicked away from her in a renewed burst of fear. She'd read my thoughts almost before they occurred.

Matt meanwhile was slowly backpedaling down the hallway. Mr. Locke raised his right hand and said, "Stop."

Matt froze. Mr. Locke walked toward him. His index finger flared with blue energy.

"Don't," Matt said, blubbering. "*Don't—*"

Mr. Locke touched him in the middle of his forehead.

"Forget everything. You are dreaming of a new type of therapy."

"*A new type of therapy.*"

Matt sounded robotic.

"To change these poor, lost, hopeless humans."

"*To change these poor, lost, hopeless … humans.*"

"Now go and revel in your success."

Matt left, smiling.

Mr. Locke turned back to us. He brought his glowing fingertip to Nathan's forehead and started talking. Like Matt, Nathan repeated the words. Mr. Locke told him he was to forget everything and return to bed to have a pleasant dream.

"No!" I said.

Vinnie said, "Is a pleasant dream so bad a fate?"

"I want him to remember our—"

"Kiss," Miss Billings said.

It was too late. Mr. Locke had finished. Nathan left, also smiling. Mr. Locke now pointed his finger at me. "This will not hurt you."

I started crying. "Please don't make me forget my first kiss!"

Vinnie stepped between us. "Desist, Moguul."

Miss Billings said, "I agree with Captain Elbaton."

Mr. Locke—or whoever he was—scowled. "We cannot jeopardize the mission!"

Vinnie—or whoever *he* was—laughed. "There is no jeopardy."

"His memory *must* be changed." Mr. Locke looked at me with some sympathy, the expression didn't suited his face. He put his finger to my forehead—only to have Vinnie slap it away.

"My decision is made, Moguul."

Mr. Locke sighed. "Yes, sir."

I did a double take at Vinnie. "*You're* in charge?"

"Captain Elbaton is our commander," Miss Billings said.

Mr. Locke said, "But I am his second in command, and the captain has been unwell."

"I am better now." Vinnie sounded annoyed. He turned to me, as if expecting I'd understand what he said next: "The assimilation process is always difficult, but mine was harder due to the host's broken spirit. It left me very weak."

Mr. Locke began pleading. "Elbaton, I *implore* you to reconsider this breach of protocol."

Vinnie raised his right hand. Mr. Locke fell silent. He gave a rigid bow and left, followed by Miss Billings. They were like obedient soldiers.

But in what army?

We sat at the same table where I'd first met Vinnie. Now he drummed his fingers a moment and looked me in the eyes.

"The humans known as Vincent, Miss Billings and Mr. Locke are currently hosting an alien species."

I just stared.

"Their identities were assimilated a few days ago, shortly before you came. Assimilation requires an adjustment period. During this time, the hosts may act strangely to the native race. Lieutenant Moguul came first and was well-assimilated by the time I and Nosswana arrived."

"What are you here for?"

"We're simply gathering routine data to assess whether or not your planet will be invaded."

I jumped up, stunned as much by his words as his casual attitude.

"You're *spies*? What kind of information could you get here? Why didn't you go to the White House or the Pentagon or something?"

"The data we seek is cultural, not military. Your tanks and planes will mean nothing when the invasion comes."

"Wait, you mean you've already decided?"

"The invasion will happen beyond your lifetime. You've no reason to worry."

"No reason? You're talking about destroying—"

"What? Your own parents consigned you to this awful place. Celebrate my revelation. In my experience, the oppressed enjoy the destruction of their oppressors."

"I'm not defending *this*! But it doesn't mean we deserve to be invaded."

Vinnie responded with a yawn.

I gaped at him. "Does our moral right to exist bore you?"

"The mission is complete. Tomorrow we depart."

I hit the table with my fist. "You said you've only been here a few days. That's not enough time to judge the whole world. There are tons of cultures on Earth. At least visit Canada, they're friendly."

Now Vinnie looked grim. "Chance brought us to this—*institute*. Chance further made me assimilate a child crippled with fear and hurt. I saw clearly the cruelty and hatred of your people in the echoes of his pain. I have more than enough information, human, and have communicated it all to the High Command. Sixteen years of this boy's experiences are the foundation of my opinion."

I stared at my feet, wondering if my own childhood would also convince him the whole human race should fry.

"What happens now? What happens to us?"

"Live your life. You have time for that. The question is what do you want to do with the knowledge I have imparted. It will burden all of your days. Isn't ignorance better?"

He raised his glowing finger. I stared at it.

"*No.*"

"Very well," he said.

We walked back to the dormitory.

The next morning, it was clear Nathan remembered nothing. Vinnie was even more withdrawn. Miss Billings greeted us, but I knew it wasn't her. Or rather, it *was* her, the original Miss Billings—the one who *couldn't* read minds.

So that's it, then. The aliens have left. And Earth is screwed.

We also now experienced the real Mr. Locke's personality, which was worse than Moguul's. Before breakfast, he preached. We were sick but he knew we could get better.

"Isn't that right, Vincent?"

Vinnie stared at the floor.

I was numb to Mr. Locke's sermon. I touched my lips. What good was a first kiss when Nathan didn't know it happened?

But there wasn't much opportunity to ponder this. The real Mr. Locke ran a nasty ship. The individual therapy sessions became longer and more aggressive. They were like grueling math classes where we learned to subtract love from our lives. God help me, I started to wish the invasion could happen *right now.*

By the start of the third week, I couldn't visualize an existence beyond *Celebrate Your Life*. Ten more teens had arrived, mirrors of my earlier self—defiant, naïve. They didn't like me. They saw their future in my face and were frightened. But I knew of a future far more terrifying.

The only kid doing worse than me was Vinnie. He showed no signs of remembering his assimilation but he reeked of loss, as if a part of him had been ripped away when Elbaton left. I felt the anguish that had overwhelmed Elbaton and pushed him to his decision. I actually thought Vinnie would kill himself if he could. He never talked. He barely ate. Matt and Mr. Locke seemed to consider him a rousing success.

Then came the night, around midnight, when Nathan opened my door.

He was fully dressed and steadily defiant.

"We get one chance," he said.

I rushed into my clothes.

"What about Vinnie?"

Nathan shook his head. I felt awful, but I accepted reality. We were going it alone.

Sneaking out seemed as easy as the last time. I was even amused, faking shock when Nathan showed me the keys. But there were a lot more kids at *Celebrate Your Life* now, and more staff too. We got caught before we even reached the woods.

They hauled us into the fifth building. Rumor had it the shock treatment therapy was done there.

Rumor proved right.

We were detained in the treatment room about thirty minutes before Mr. Locke arrived with Matt. We'd both been frisked. Nathan's confiscated keys were now in Mr. Locke's right palm.

"This is a very serious infraction," he said.

I looked to Matt, desperate for a trace of the *good cop*. Matt didn't bother hiding his contempt.

"I knew these two would need the juice," he said

My rage exploded. "You can't *shock* us as punishment. That's not therapy, that's—"

Torture.

They hauled me onto the table and strapped me down. I fought back but they were stronger. I couldn't see Nathan from all my thrashing, but I heard Mr. Locke yell, "Go after him!"

Run, Nathan. Run as hard as you can and have a great life.

I was alone with Mr. Locke. My struggles against the restraints made him chuckle.

"The bark's worse than the bite," he said, putting electrodes on my temples. I thrashed my head, trying to shake them off, and started pleading.

"Please, don't do this. I'm sorry."

"Why are you sorry?"

"Because—because I ran away."

"Isn't there *another* reason?"

I knew what he wanted to hear. My breath hitched as I made my decision. Better to swallow my pride than swallow my tongue.

"I'm sorry I'm gay," I said.

He patted my chest and smiled. "That's a great first step toward getting better. Now let's take the second."

He started readying the equipment. I shouted at him, but he ignored me. He ignored me until he flipped the switch to turn on the current.

A blue bolt of electricity surged from the machine and dropped him to the floor. I writhed, convinced I was being electrocuted.

Then I realized I wasn't.

In the doorway stood Vinnie, with Matt and Nathan behind him. Matt seemed lobotomized.

Nathan rushed forward and undid the straps. "When I got outside, Vinnie was waiting. I've got my memories back. *All* of them."

He helped me off the table. We contemplated Mr. Locke's body. He was dead. Wrong as it was, I didn't feel sad.

Vinnie stepped forward.

"*Elbaton*? You returned?"

"I never left. I dismissed my subordinates, but I opted to stay and observe further."

Clinging to Nathan, I said, "Guess you haven't changed your mind."

"I'm more interested in whether subsequent events caused you to change *your* mind?"

I sighed. "The human race has its share of jerks. But there are people like us, too. Don't we matter?"

"Perhaps," Elbaton said. "The forces aligned against this world are vast. I will not change my report but Earth might benefit from a few ambassadors making its case directly."

I looked at Nathan, considering.

"How many ambassadors do you need, Elbaton?"

He allowed himself a smile. "Three will suffice. This host, Vincent, has already agreed to come. It will mean leaving your families behind. But in my experience, new families are formed with every journey. Therefore departures are cause for celebration rather than sorrow. Do you choose to celebrate?"

Nathan held me close and nodded.

"We do," I said.

The Truth About Owls

by Amal El-Mohtar

Owls have eyes that match the skies they hunt through. Amber-eyed owls hunt at dawn or dusk; golden-eyed owls hunt during the day; black-eyed owls hunt at night.

No one knows why this is.

Anisa's eyes are black, and she no longer hates them. She used to wish for eyes the color of her father's, the beautiful pale green-blue that people were always startled to see in a brown face. But she likes, now, having eyes and hair of a color those same people find frightening.

Even her teachers are disconcerted, she's found—they don't try to herd her as they do the other students. She sees them casting uncertain glances towards her before ushering their group from one owl exhibit to another, following the guide. She turns to go in the opposite direction.

"Annie-sa! Annie, this way!"

She turns, teeth clenching. Mrs. Roberts, whose pale powdered face, upswept yellow hair, and bright red lips make Anisa think of Victoria sponge, is smiling encouragingly.

"My name is A-NEE-sa, actually," she replies, and feels the power twitching out from her chest and into her arms, which she crosses quickly, and her hands, which she makes into fists, digging nails into her palms. The power recedes, but she can still feel it pouring out from her eyes like a swarm of bees while Mrs. Roberts looks at her in perplexed confusion. Mrs. Roberts' eyes are a delicate, ceramic sort of blue.

Anisa watches another teacher, Ms. Grewar, lean over to murmur something into Mrs. Roberts' ear. Mrs. Roberts only looks more confused, but renews her smile uncertainly, nods, and turns back to her group. Anisa closes her eyes, takes a deep breath, and counts to ten before walking away.

Owls are predators. There are owls that would tear you apart if you gave them half a chance.

The Scottish Owl Centre is a popular destination for school trips: a short bus ride from Glasgow, an educational component, lots of opportunities for photographs to show the parents, and who doesn't like owls nowadays? Anisa has found herself staring, more than once, at owl-print bags and shirts, owl-shaped earrings and belt buckles, plush owl toys and wire statues in bright, friendly colors. She finds it all desperately strange.

Anisa remembers the first time she saw an owl. She was seven years old. She lived in Riyaq with her father and her grandparents, and that morning she had thrown a tantrum about having to feed the chickens, which she hated, because of their smell and the way they pecked at her when she went to gather their eggs, and also because of the rooster, who was fierce and sharp-spurred. She hated the chickens, she shouted, why didn't they just make them into soup.

She was given more chores to do, which she did, fumingly, stomping her feet and banging cupboard doors and sometimes crying about how unfair it was. "Are you brooding over the chickens," her father would joke, trying to get her to laugh, which only made her more furious, because she *did* want to laugh but she didn't want him to think she wasn't still mad, because she was.

She had calmed down by lunch, and forgotten about it by supper. But while helping her grandmother with the washing up she heard a scream from the yard. Her grandmother darted out, and Anisa followed, her hands dripping soap.

An owl—enormous, tall as a lamb, taller than any bird she had ever seen—perched in the orange tree, the rooster a tangle of blood and feathers in its talons. As Anisa stared, the owl bent its head to the rooster's throat and tore out a long strip of flesh.

When Anisa thinks about this—and she does, often, whenever her hands are wet and soapy in just the right way, fingertips on the brink of wrinkling—she remembers the guilt. She remembers listening to her grandmother cross herself and speak her words of protection against harm, warding them against death in the family, against troubled times. She remembers the fear, staring at the red and pink and green of the rooster, its broken, dangling head.

But she can't remember—though she often tries—whether she felt, for the first time, the awful electric prickle of the power in her chest, flooding out to her palms.

There are owls that sail through the air like great ships. There are owls that flit like finches from branch to branch. There are owls that look at you with disdain and owls that sway on the perch of your arm like a reed in the wind.

Anisa is not afraid of owls. She thinks they're interesting enough, when people aren't cooing over them or embroidering them onto cushions. From walking around the sanctuary she thinks the owl she saw as a child was probably a Eurasian Eagle Owl.

She wanders from cage to cage, environment to environment, looking at owls that bear no resemblance to the pretty patterns lining the hems of skirts and dresses—owls that lack a facial disk, owls with bulging eyes and fuzzy heads, owls the size of her palm.

Some of the owls have names distinct from their species: Hosking, Broo, Sarabi. Anisa pauses in front of a barn owl and frowns at the name. Blodeuwedd?

"Blow-due-wed," she sounds out beneath her breath, while the owl watches her.

"It's Bloh-DA-weth, actually," says a friendly voice behind her. Anisa turns to see one of the owl handlers from the flying display, a black woman named Izzy, hair wrapped up in a brightly colored scarf, moving into one of the aviaries, gloved hands clutching a feed bucket. "It means 'flower-face' in Welsh."

Anisa flushes. She looks at the owl again. She has never seen a barn owl up close, and does not think it looks like flowers; she thinks, all at the same time, that the heart-shaped face is alien and eerie and beautiful and like when you can see the moon while the sun is setting, and that there should be a single word for the color of the wings that's like the sheen of a pearl but not the pearl itself.

She asks, "Is it a boy or a girl?"

"Do you not know the story of Blodeuwedd?" Izzy smiles. "She was a beautiful woman, made of flowers, who was turned into an owl."

Anisa frowns. "That doesn't make sense."

"It's from a book of fairytales called *The Mabinogion*—not big on sense-making." Izzy chuckles. "I don't think she likes it either, to be honest. She's one of our most difficult birds. But she came to us from Wales, so we gave her a Welsh name."

Anisa looks into Blodeuwedd's eyes. They are blacker than her own.

"I like her," she declares.

⁎

A group of owls is called a Parliament.

Owls are bad luck.

The summer Anisa saw the owl kill the rooster was the summer Israel bombed the country. She always thinks of it that way, not as a war—she doesn't remember a war. She never saw anyone fighting. She remembers a sound she felt more than heard, a *thud* that shook the earth and rattled up through her bones—then another—then a smell like chalk—before being swept into her father's arms and taken down into shelter.

She remembers feeling cold; she remembers, afterwards, anger, weeping, conversations half-heard from her bed, her mother's voice reaching them in sobs from London, robotic and strangled over a poor internet connection, a mixing of English and Arabic, accents swapping places. Her father's voice always calm, measured, but with a tension running through it like when her cousin put a wire through a dead frog's leg to make it twitch.

She remembers asking her grandmother if Israel attacked because of the owl. Her grandmother laughed in a way that made Anisa feel hollow and lost.

"Shh, shh, don't tell Israel! An owl killed a rooster—that's more reason to attack! An owl killed a rooster in Lebanon and the government let it happen! Quick, get off the bridges!"

The whole family laughed. Anisa was terrified, and told no one.

⁎

Why did the owl not go courting in the rain? Because it was too wet to woo.

"What makes her 'difficult'?" asks Anisa, watching Blodeuwedd sway on her perch. Izzy looks fondly at the owl.

"Well, we acquired her as a potential display bird, but she just doesn't take well to training—she hisses at most of the handlers when they pass by, tries to bite. She's also very territorial, and won't tolerate the presence of male birds, so we can't use her for breeding." Izzy offers Blodeuwedd a strip of raw chicken, which she gulps down serenely.

"But she likes you," Anisa observes. Izzy smiles ruefully.

"I'm not one of her trainers. It's easy to like people who ask nothing of you." Izzy pauses, eyes Blodeuwedd with exaggerated care. "Or at least, it's easy to not hate them."

Before Anisa leaves with the rest of her class, Izzy writes down *Mabinogion* for her on a piece of paper, a rather deft doodle of an owl's face inside a five-petaled flower, and an invitation to come again.

Most owls are sexually dimorphic: the female is usually larger, stronger, and more brightly colored than the male.

Anisa's mother is tall, and fair, and Anisa looks nothing like her. Her mother's brown hair is light and thin and straight; her mother's skin is pale. Anisa is used to people making assumptions—*are you adopted? Is that your stepmother?*—when they see them together, but her mother's new job at the university has made outings together rare. In fact, since moving to Glasgow, Anisa hardly sees her at home anymore, since she has evening classes and departmental responsibilities.

"What are you reading?" asks her mother, shrugging on her coat after a hurried dinner together.

Anisa, legs folded up underneath her on the couch, holds up a library copy of *The Mabinogion*. Her mother looks confused, but nods, wishes her a good night, and leaves.

Anisa reads about how Math, son of Mathonwy, gathered the blossoms of oak, of broom, of meadowsweet, and shaped them into a woman. She wonders, idly, what kind of flowers could be combined to make her.

There are owls on every continent in the world except Antarctica. The so-called war lasted just over a month; Anisa learned the word "ceasefire" in August. Her father put her on a plane to London the moment the airports were repaired.

Before she started going to school, Anisa's mother took her aside. "When people ask you where you're from," she told her, "you say 'England', all right? You were born here. You have every bit as much right to be here as anyone else."

"Baba wasn't born here." She felt a stinging in her throat and eyes, a pain of *unfair*. "Is that why he's not here? Is he not allowed to come?"

Anisa doesn't remember what her mother said. She must have said something. Whatever it was, it was certainly not that she wouldn't see her father in person for three years.

The Welsh word for owl once meant "flower-face".

When Izzy said Blodeuwedd was made of flowers, Anisa had imagined roses and lilies, flowers she was forced to read about over and over in books of English literature. But as she reads, she finds that even Blodeuwedd's flower names are strange to her—what kind of a flower is "broom"?—and she likes that, likes that no part of Blodeuwedd is familiar or expected.

Anisa has started teaching herself Welsh, mostly because she wants to know how all the names in the *Mabinogion* are pronounced. She likes that there is a language that looks like English but sounds like Arabic; she likes that there is no one teaching it to her, or commenting on her accent, or asking her how to speak it for their amusement. She likes that a single "f" is pronounced "v", that "w" is a vowel—likes that it's an alphabet of secrets hidden in plain sight.

She starts visiting the owl centre every weekend, feeling like she's done her homework if she can share a new bit of *Mabinogion* trivia with Izzy and Blodeuwedd in exchange for a fact about owls.

Owls are birds of the order Strigiformes, *a word derived from the Latin for witch.*

During Anisa's first year of school in England a girl with freckles and yellow hair leaned over to her while the teacher's back was turned, and asked if her father was dead.

"No!" Anisa stared at her.

"My mum said your dad could be dead. Because of the war. Because there's always war where you're from."

"That's not true."

The freckled girl narrowed her eyes. "My mum *said* so."

Anisa felt her pulse quicken, her hands tremble. She felt she had never hated anyone in her whole life so much as this idiot pastry of a girl. She watched as the girl shrugged and turned away.

"Maybe you just don't understand English."

She felt something uncoil inside her. Anisa stood up from her chair and *shoved* the girl out of hers, and felt, in the moment of skin touching skin, a startling shock of static electricity; the girl's freckles vanished into the pink of her cheeks, and instead of protesting the push, she shouted "Ugh, she *shocked* me!"

In her memory, the teacher's reprimand, the consequences, the rest of that year all melt away to one viciously satisfying image: the freckled girl's blue eyes looking at her, terrified, out of a pretty pink face.

She learned to cultivate an appearance of danger, of threat; she learned that with an economy of look, of gesture, of insinuation, she could be feared and left alone. She was the Girl Who Came

From War, the Girl Whose Father Was Dead, the Girl With Powers. One day a boy tried to kiss her; she pushed him away, looked him in the eye, and flung a fistful of nothing at him, a spray of air. He was absent from school for two days; when the boy came back claiming to have had a cold, everyone acknowledged Anisa as the cause. When some students asked her to make them sick on purpose, to miss an exam or assignment, she smirked, said nothing, and walked away.

Owls have a narrow field of binocular vision; they compensate for this by rotating their heads up to two hundred and seventy degrees. Carefully, Izzy lowers her arm to Anisa's gloved wrist, hooks her tether to the ring dangling from it, and watches as Blodeuwedd hops casually down on to her forearm. Anisa exhales, then grins. Izzy grins back.

"I can't believe how much she's mellowed out. She's really surprisingly comfortable with you."

"Maybe," Anisa says, mischievous, "it's because I'm really good at not asking anything of her."

"Sure," says Izzy, "or maybe it's because you keep talking about how much you hate Math, son of Mathonwy."

"Augh, that *prick*!"

Izzy laughs, and Anisa loves to hear her, to see how she tosses her head back when she does. She loves how thick and wiry Izzy's hair is, and the different things she does with it—today it's half-wrapped in a white and purple scarf, fluffed out at the back like a bouquet.

"He's the worst," she continues. "He takes flowers and tells them to be a woman; as soon as she acts in a way he doesn't like, he turns her into an owl. It's like—he needs to keep being in charge of her story, and the way to do that is to change her shape."

"Well. To be fair. She did try to kill his adopted son."

"He forced her into marriage with him! And he was a jerk too!"

"You're well into this, you are."

"It's just—" Anisa bites her lip, looking at Blodeuwedd, raising her slightly to shift the weight on her forearm, watching her spread her magnificent wings, then settle, "—sometimes—I feel like I'm just a collection of bits of things that someone brought together at random and called *girl*, and then *Anisa*, and then—" she shrugs. "Whatever."

Izzy is quiet for a moment. Then she says, thoughtfully, "You know, there's another word for that."

"For what?"

"What you just described—an aggregation of disparate things. An anthology. That's what *The Mabinogion* is, after all."

Anisa is unconvinced. "Blodeuwedd's just one part of someone else's story, she's not an anthology herself."

Izzy smiles, gently, in a way that always makes Anisa feel she's thinking of someone or something else, but allowing Anisa a window's worth of view into her world. "You can look at it that way. But there's another word for anthology, one we don't really use any more: *florilegium*. Do you know what it means?"

Anisa shakes her head, and blinks, startled, as Blodeuwedd does a side-wise walk up her arm to lean, gently, against her shoulder. Izzy smiles, a little more brightly, more for her, and says: "A gathering of flowers."

Owls fly more silently than any other bird.

When her father joined them in London three years later, he found Anisa grown several inches taller and several sentences shorter. Her mother's insistence on speaking Arabic together at all times—pushing her abilities as a heritage speaker to their limits—meant that Anisa often chose not to speak at all. This was to her advantage in the school yard, where her eyes, her looks, and rumors of her dark powers held her fellow students in awe; it did her no good with her father, who hugged her and held her until words and tears gushed out of her in gasps.

The next few years were better; they moved to a different part of the city, and Anisa was able to make friends in a new school, to open up, to speak. She sometimes told stories about how afraid of her people used to be, how she'd convinced them of her powers like it was a joke on them, and not something she had ever believed herself.

Owls purge from themselves the matter they cannot absorb: bones, fur, claws, teeth, feathers.

"Is that for school?"

Anisa looks up from her notebook to her mother, and shakes her head. "No. It's Welsh stuff."

"Oh." Her mother pauses, and Anisa can see her mentally donning the gloves with which to handle her. "Why Welsh?"

She shrugs. "I like it." Then, seeing her mother unsatisfied, adds, "I like the stories. I'd like to read them in the original language eventually."

Her mother hesitates. "You know, there's a rich tradition of Arabic storytelling—"

The power flexes inside her like a whip snapping, takes her by surprise, and she bites the inside of her lip until it bleeds to stop it, stop it.

"—and I know I can't share much myself but I'm sure your grandmother or your aunts would love to talk to you about it—"

Anisa grabs her books and runs to her room as if she could outrun the power, locks the door, and buries her fingernails in the skin of her arms, dragging long, painful scratches down them, because the only way to let the power out is through pain, because if she doesn't hurt herself she knows with absolute certainty that she will hurt someone else.

Illness in owls is difficult to detect and diagnose until it is dangerously advanced.

Anisa knows something is wrong before she sees the empty cage, from the way Izzy is pacing in front of it, as if waiting for her.

"Blodeuwedd's sick," she says , and Anisa feels a rush of gravity inside her stomach. "She hasn't eaten in a few days. I'm sorry, but you won't be able to see her today—"

"What's wrong with her?" Anisa begins counting back the days to the last flare, to what she thought, and it wasn't this, it was never anything like this, but she'd held *The Mabinogion* in her hands—

"We don't know yet. I'm so sorry you came out all this way—" Izzy hesitates while Anisa stands, frozen, feeling herself vanishing into misery, into a day one year and four hundred miles away.

Owls do not mate for life, though death sometimes parts them.

The memory is like a trap, a steel cage that falls over her head and severs her from reality. When the memory descends she can do nothing but see her father's face, over and over, aghast, more hurt than she has ever seen him, and her own words like a bludgeon to beat in her own head: "Fine, go back and *die*, I don't care, just *stop coming back.*"

She feels, again, the power lashing out, confused, attempting both to tether and to push away; she remembers the shape of the door knob in her hand as she bolts out of the flat, down the stairs, out the building, into the night. She feels incandescent, too burnt up to cry, thinking of her father going back to a country every day in the news, every day a patchwork of explosions and body counts, every day a matter of someone else's opinions.

She thinks of how he wouldn't take her with him.

And she feels, irrevocably, as if she is breathing a stone when she sees him later that evening in hospital, eyes closed, ashen, and the words reaching her from a faraway dimness saying he has suffered a stroke, and died.

"Anisa—A*ni*sa!" Izzy has taken her hands, is holding them, and when Anisa focuses again she feels as if they're submerged in water, and she wants to snatch them away because what if she hurts Izzy but she is disoriented and before she knows what she is doing she is crying while Izzy holds her hands and sinks down to the rain-wet floor with her. She feels gravel beneath her knees and grinds them further into it, to punish herself for this, this thing, the power, and she is trying to make Izzy understand and she is trying to say she is sorry but all that comes out is this violent, wrecking weeping.

"It's me," she manages, "I made her sick, it's my fault, I don't mean to do it but I make bad things happen just by wanting them even a little, wanting them the wrong way, and I don't want it anymore, I never wanted *this* but it keeps happening and now she'll die—"

Izzy looks at her, squeezes her hands, and says, calm and even, "Bullshit."

"It's true—"

"Anisa—if it's true it should work both ways. Can you make good things happen by wanting them?"

She looks into Izzy's warm dark eyes, at a loss, and can't frame a reply to such a ridiculous question.

"Think, pet—what *good* things do you want to happen?"

"I want—" she closes her eyes, and bites her lip, looking for pain to quash the power but feels it differently—feels, with Izzy holding her hands, Izzy facing her, grounded, as if draining something out into the gravel and the earth beneath it and leaving something else in its wake, something shining and slick as sunlight on wet streets. "I want Blodeuwedd to get better. I want her to have a good life, to … be whatever she wants to be and do whatever she wants to do. I want to learn Welsh. I want to—" Izzy's face shimmers through her tears. "I want to be friends with you. I want—"

She swallows them down, all of her good wants, how much she misses her father and how much she misses just talking, in any language, with her mother, and how she misses the light in Riyaq and the dry dusty air, the sheep and the goats and the warmth, always, of her grandmother and uncles and aunts and cousins all around, and she makes an anthology of them. She gathers the flowers of her wants all together in her throat, her heart, her belly, and trusts that they are good.

⋇

The truth about owls—

Anisa and her mother stand at the owl centre's entrance, both casually studying a nearby freezer full of ice lollies while waiting for their tickets. Their eyes meet, and they grin at each other. Her mother is rummaging about for caramel cornettos when the sales attendant, Rachel, waves Anisa over.

"Is that your mother, Anisa?" whispers Rachel. Anisa goes very still for a moment as she nods, and Rachel beams. "I thought so. You have precisely the same smile."

Anisa blushes, and looks down, suddenly shy. Her mother pays for their tickets and ice cream, and together they move towards the exit and the picnic area.

Anisa pauses on her way through the gift-shop; she waves her mother on, says she'll catch her up. Alone, she buys a twee notebook covered in shiny metallic owls and starts writing in it with an owl-topped pen.

She writes "The truth about owls—" but pauses. She looks at the words, their shape, the taken-for-granted ease of their spilling from her. She frowns, bites her lip, and after a moment's careful thought writes "Y gwir am tylluanod—"

But she has run out of vocabulary, and this is not something she wants to look up. There is a warmth blossoming in her, a rightness, pushing up out of her chest where the power used to crouch, where something lives now that is different, better, and she wants to pour that out on the page. She rolls the pen between her thumb and forefinger, then shifts the journal's weight against her palm.

She writes "ان الحقيقة عن البوم معقّدة", and smiles.

Krishna Blue

by Shveta Thakrar

For Anita Allen

Basmati rice seasoned with cinnamon and cloves, green beans and potatoes flecked with cumin and cayenne pepper, and thick, spicy lentils mixed with homemade yogurt—all Neha's favorites hooked her by the nose and held her fast. Maybe she'd have two helpings of everything. Or three.

Across the table, her sister Sarita rubbed her temples and grimaced. Neha winced in sympathy. Another headache?

"How was school?" Her father smiled, making the crow's feet crinkle around his odd ice-blue eyes, the same ones he'd passed on to her. She liked the way they blazed against her brown skin, taking people off guard.

"Honestly? It sucked." Neha stuffed a piece of chapati into her mouth. Warm, fluffy, and slathered with ghee, it only made her hungrier. "Like always."

"It's hard coming into a new school," her father said. "You're only a freshman. Look at Sarita; she's found her place."

Neha crushed green beans between her teeth. Yeah, yeah, soon-to-be-valedictorian Sarita, with her glossy hair and her future aerospace engineering degree and absolutely no concept of being lonely. If only Neha could try on her life. "I guess. I started a new painting, at least."

"See, Neha's doing just fine," Sarita said, looking up. Neha shot her a grateful glance.

"People come and go, Neha," her father said sternly. "In time you'll see the most important part of school is what you learn."

"And what you do with it afterward," her mother put in. "That will determine your whole life. Have you given it any more thought?"

The old despair enveloped Neha, choking off her appetite. She searched the room for distractions. "Yeah, art."

Her mother sighed. "You need to be realistic, dikra. You can't—"

"Hey, Mom, guess what?" Sarita interrupted. "I got an early acceptance from Arizona State!"

"That's wonderful!"

"Well done," her father said. He turned to Neha. "If your sister can do that, so can you. Why not try chemistry? Smart brains need constant stimulation."

Neha's gaze settled on her mother's velvet shrine under the windowsill. Perfect. She squinted, and everything else faded into the background.

Sarita nudged her under the table and rushed on. "So I just have to get a couple more letters of recommendation, and then I'll be done. I might need your help with some of the questions, Dad."

On the shrine, a picture portrayed the divine lovers Radha and Krishna nestled together on a swing. Neha began breaking them down into component colors. Radha's skin was ivory, her sari alizarin crimson and quinacridone violet, and her jewelry a gleaming mix of gold and yellow-orange. Radha was easy.

But her flute-playing paramour—he was the real challenge.

"Did Arizona State mention anything about a scholarship?" her mother asked.

Krishna's dhoti could go a couple ways, but Neha decided on canary yellow and cadmium green. His hair was even simpler, lamp black with streaks of German earth. The tone of his skin, though, a deep, dark, unfathomable blue, continued to elude her, slippery as the butter he loved to steal as a child.

"The more choices you have to pick from, the better," her father said.

She'd capture Krishna eventually. Oh, that blue. So rich, so frustrating. Did it change when she wasn't looking?

Azure? Too dark. Ultramarine? Not vibrant enough. What if she combined the two? No, that wasn't right, either.

Paint hues insinuated themselves into her mind like the words of a spell: cobalt, King's blue deep, manganese.

Her food flared to life, as if each mustard seed and grain of rice were a tiny lantern. Sweat broke out over her suddenly flushed skin. Neha blinked twice, but the incandescence only spread until the decorative plates, the family photographs, the walls themselves all glowed so vividly, they pulsed.

"Neha!" her mother snapped. "Are you even listening? This is your sister's future!"

Everyone was staring, their luminous eyes just too much.

"I—I don't feel good," Neha blurted, and fled to her room.

Standing at her easel in advanced art, Neha considered her self-portrait. All she had to show for the seven aborted sketches by her bag was a vague undercoat, round and empty as a mirror. She could be anyone. No one. A faceless entity in a crowd of faceless entities.

Paint, she told herself. *Just paint.*

Tuning everything else out, she wrung huge lumps of terra rosa, Naples yellow, and yellowish zinc buff out of their tubes and blended them into something like her skin tone.

On her right, Chris squinted at his canvas. Neha sneaked a glance at his T-shirt, trying to make out the caption beneath the angry rooster. *Go cluck yourself.*

She groaned a little too loudly, and Chris raised his eyebrows.

God, she was a moron. Neha darted her gaze away—just in time to see a stubby finger jab at her canvas.

"What are you trying to say, Ms. Shah?" Mr. Stone glowered, his bushy eyebrows at odds with his thinning ponytail. "I moved you into this class because I saw real potential. You have a fine grasp of technique, but where's your *spark*?"

"My spark?" Neha parroted. She hated how her teacher prowled through the room, ready to attack. Chris must have felt the same way, because he kept his head down.

Mr. Stone grabbed her stack of sketches. "Let's take this piece, for example. None of these tell me anything about who you are." He leaned closer. "You know, you're fortunate to have such a rich heritage to draw on. India, with its long and celebrated history of art—miniature paintings, the Taj Mahal, even Bollywood—but I'm not seeing it in your work. Why?"

"Mr. Stone—"

Mr. Stone held up a hand. "Let your work answer the question."

Neha's nerves throbbed, exposed, but she wouldn't cry. She'd paint. Her brush swirled in strange, wild patterns over the canvas, hypnotic and compelling. No more holding back.

A minute later, an hour later, the bell rang.

Neha shuddered. She'd given herself fangs. And why the hideous slash for a mouth? She didn't want to eat anybody. She started to cover her mistakes with smooth, even strokes.

"No, leave that," Chris said, tucking a lock of scraggly brown hair behind his ear. "It's interesting."

Neha nearly dropped her brush. He never talked to her.

"Don't forget those pretty eyes of yours." Chris snapped his portfolio shut.

Neha's stomach, already nervous, grew tighter. *Pretty eyes.* That was flirting, right? The blank-eyed, lipless face on her canvas stared back, hopeful.

She squeezed Sevres blue onto her palette. Her hand flitted over the painting, crafting irises, adding depth and sheen. Those were pretty eyes.

When she turned to show Chris, he'd already left. Even Mr. Stone was gone.

Mr. Stone.

Neha blinked back her tears. That ignorant jerk wanted to see her heritage in her work. Which to him meant melodramatic imagery from the kind of red-sari literature she couldn't stand. And instead of refusing, she'd frozen.

A thought unfolded. Her heritage, huh? Her palette with its bold smears of color was the artist's version of her mother's steel spice box, the same way her mother's canvas was the tongue. There, multihued pools of fragrance and flavor joined to create something even more sensual and complex.

In the same way, Neha could blend the paints that would create the shades of turmeric and chilli and garam masala, amchur and cumin and coriander.

She uncapped another tube. Turmeric yellow oozed out, making her gasp. It was so bright, so beautiful. Its golden glow promised to fill her, to illuminate the corridors of her arteries and veins and soothe the dark, lonely chambers of her heart.

Images and ideas slipped through her mind in dreamy golden waves. If turmeric was like paint, then paint was like turmeric…

Stupid. Oil paint was toxic. How many teachers had drilled that into her head? Neha shook her head and reached for a paper towel.

Turmeric, something within her insisted. Somehow, instead of the paper towel, she'd seized the blob of paint. The tip of her index finger glistened yellow.

Neha paused, trapped between possibilities, teetering between potential universes. She might hate her life, but she didn't want to die.

Yet her finger was at her lips now, parting them. She was so sick of everyone knowing better than her. She wanted to do this for herself, to taste turmeric yellow.

At the brush of her lips, the color exploded, bursting over her taste buds and splashing liquid saffron into her bloodstream.

Everywhere Neha looked she saw sunlight. The yellow was hers now, bright and bubbling. She twirled joyfully, radiant with it.

Then she glanced at the smudge on her finger. Horror and wonder fought to leave her breathless.

The paint had turned a lifeless gray.

In the safety of her locked bedroom, Neha tried again and again to recreate the experience with her paints, touching bright, dark, and everything in between. No matter what she did, the colors, though crisp as ever, remained mute.

At dinner, she was too excited to eat. Instead, her stomach cramped, too full of fluttering yellow butterflies to let anything else in. "Neha's in love!" Sarita teased, but under her breath, so only Neha heard. It made her laugh.

Later, she beamed at her reflection in her bedroom mirror, at the strange blue eyes Chris had complimented. She could almost see the yellow shining out her pores, so fresh and cheerful.

Chris must have seen it, too, because when she smiled at him in class the next day, he smiled back. He even asked how she was doing. Flirting, definitely flirting.

The family sat at the table, the way it had every night since Neha was small. But she hadn't felt like eating for the past three days. Nothing tasted as intense as it should, as if the flavors were coming through a filter. What a waste; she loved dal.

Next to her, Sarita wasn't eating much, either. She looked like she'd folded in on herself.

Even the yellow singing inside couldn't numb Neha's concern. She motioned to her sister and got up. "Thanks for cooking, Dad."

"But you barely touched it," her father said. "Can't wait to get back to your homework, huh?"

"Something like that," Neha said, already hurrying off. She paused at the shrine. That shade, that enigmatic, enticing shade!

Not like blue corn or blue potatoes, and definitely not like blueberry pie. Her mouth watered.

In her room, Gujarati mirror-worked hangings and Rajasthani paintings vied with prints by Mucha and Klimt for space on the lavender walls. A Moroccan lantern scattered light over the bookcase crammed with novels and art tomes.

Sarita snagged a sketchpad from the heap on the desk and thumbed through it. "You seem pretty happy. Anything to do with this?"

Seeing all the renditions of Chris laid bare left Neha raw. "Could we maybe not look at that?"

"Why are these all yellow?"

Neha shrugged. "I was trying something. Anyway, what's going on with you? You were so quiet at dinner."

Sarita let the sketchbook fall to the floor and patted the bedspread. "Come here, silly."

Relieved, Neha kicked the sketchbook away, then rested her chin on Sarita's shoulder. "What's up?"

Sarita leaned her head against Neha's. "You know how I've been having those headaches?" Neha nodded. "Well, I'm kind of freaked out. I have to get an MRI."

"Oh, wow." Headaches didn't mean anything. Everyone knew that.

"I'm scared, Nehachu." Sarita picked at her nail polish. "What if…?"

"It'll be okay. I know it will," Neha lied. A tiny, treacherous voice whispered that if things *weren't* okay, well, that was only fair, right?

"The doctor's office is supposed to call on Friday," Sarita said, squeezing Neha's hand.

The appetite Neha hadn't had for dinner surged back, a sudden, aching need strong enough to make her sick. She rubbed her belly. What was *wrong* with her? She had to distract herself, had to distract Sarita. "Hey, what's going on with your yearbook spread?"

A few minutes later, Sarita left, and Neha was alone. She paced the length of her room. Her sister had to be okay. She had to. And Neha could never think like that again. Ever.

She found herself turning the door knob to her closet. A row of hanging silk and satin greeted her, salwaar kameez and chanya choli in red, green, shocking pink, violet, sapphire, and mango. The colors were so bold, so unafraid to be what they were. *Look at us*, they demanded.

She looked. They swirled around her, inviting her to finger the silk, to stroke the satin, to drink them in. She did.

Amethyst and fire opal liquefied under her gaze, their hues streaming from the cloth and soaking into her skin. Hints of grapes and twilight, citrus and sunset, teased her tongue, then slipped away, even as the fabric in her hand dulled to gray.

Neha stood at her easel, admiring her self-portrait. She'd nearly finished the fangs, which jutted Naples yellow from the pyrazolone red scarlet mouth. The image's hair swung in shining black ropes around its face, menacing like Medusa's snakes.

It scared Neha to see herself like this, but it excited her, too. The woman on the page knew secrets, had tasted colors. She didn't just produce; she also consumed. Something shivery raced down Neha's spine, and her brush danced and danced.

When Mr. Stone took his mid-class bathroom break, Juana walked among the easels and distributed folded sheets of paper. "See you at the party," she said, handing the last one to Neha's neighbor. "Everyone'll be there."

Neha smothered the pain in her chest. Who cared about Juana and her parties? Her work was so generic, she should never have placed into advanced art.

Still, the question spilled out. "Don't I get one?"

Juana gawked at her, then hurried to Stephanie's side. "Oh, my God, she just asked for an invitation. Who *does* that?"

Stephanie whispered something, and they both snickered.

Neha elongated the points on her image's fangs, picturing how easily they'd slide into the girls' necks.

"Hey, you okay?" Chris asked.

"Sure. Why not?" Her face hot, Neha concentrated on detailing thick serpents for eyelashes around those pretty blue eyes. Had he heard?

"You're breathing pretty hard. I thought you were having an asthma attack or something."

"Nice, very nice," Mr. Stone commented, saving Neha from

having to explain. He ran a hand through his goatee and stood back to study the canvas. "This is what I wanted to see from you—excitement, passion. You're taking risks, and it's paying off."

Neha flushed again, this time with triumph. Let Juana have her parties. *She* had art.

Sarita wasn't answering her phone. All Neha had gotten was a text message saying she'd be home around midnight. Nothing about the doctor's report.

Neha felt like ants were marching under her skin. Before long, she drifted into the kitchen, where her mother stood chopping vegetables. Large pieces of onion, tomato, and jalapeño created an assemblage, the red so rich, the green so sharp, the yellow of the onion sweet and alluring—to look at.

The thought of actually eating the vegetables, of putting them into her mouth and shredding them into mush, made Neha gag. She moved toward the shrine and asked the first question that came to her. "Hey, Mom, why do people always make Krishna blue if his name means 'black'?"

Her mother set down the knife. "I have no idea, beta. What made you think of that?"

"I read it somewhere." Neha stared at the shrine. Krishna was so blue that soon she could think of nothing but that irritating, soothing, amazing hue—not azurite, not cerulean, not even Prussian blue.

"I have a surprise for you, Neha," her father said. "I arranged to have you come in as an intern this summer to see what a chemist's lab is like. You and me. Won't that be fun?"

Neha jumped. When had he come in?

The smell of cooking erupted in her consciousness then, so pungent she almost swooned. Garlic, ginger, onions, all ingredients she'd loved, now made her cough as they sputtered on the stove.

The only thing she wanted was to sink back into Krishna's riot of color.

"Aren't you pleased?" her mother pressed. "You'll get to spend the summer with Dad."

Pleased to spend the summer helping her father's receptionist file? Hardly. Neha yawned. "I just—I'm tired. I'm going upstairs."

"No, you're going to have dinner with us," her father said, "and we're going to talk. I'm worried about you. Why haven't you been eating?"

"I'm just not hungry, okay? Is that a crime now?"

"But dikra, I made chana and saag," her mother said, sounding wounded. "You love them."

"I know, and that's awesome, but I really just don't feel good." Neha made her face as pathetic as possible.

Her parents frowned. "I'll leave a plate for you in the fridge," her mother offered at last. "And come check on you later."

Neha nodded, already on her way out. As soon as she reached her room, she locked the door. She was so sick of other people telling her what to do. *Be like this, don't be like that. Do this, don't do that.*

Without the shrine to keep them away, the ants returned. Where was Sarita?

Neha opened her box of paint tubes and squeezed each one onto a piece of plastic. She studied the swirls. She sniffed them. She stuck out her tongue and lapped at the air around them. They whispered to her of hunger and satiety, promises of solace etched in Persian rose and iridescent copper and phthalo turquoise…

She closed the box, reached for her colored pencils instead, and hugged them to her chest in the dark.

Neha spent the next morning in bed. Around noon, her mother brought her a plate of khichdi, a gruel made from split mung beans and rice, with a pat of ghee melted on top. Neha choked back her nausea and made herself swallow one bite. Her mother stroked her forehead. "Eat up, beta. You need the nourishment."

Neha forced a smile. "Okay." As soon as her mother left, she sneaked into the bathroom and flushed the khichdi down the toilet. Once a comfort food, now it tasted of nothing.

She vomited right afterward, her head and heart both pounding. Somehow she managed to drag herself back to bed, where she passed out.

A knock woke her. "It's me," called Sarita. The door opened, and she sat down on the corner of Neha's bed. "Hey, sleepyhead."

"Where were you? I waited and waited, but you never called," Neha whispered. "I was so worried."

"I'm sorry, Nehachu," Sarita said contritely, looping her finger around Neha's big toe. "I went to a party and didn't want to wake you when I got in. Some people from your art class were there."

Neha chewed her cheek. "You were at that party?"

"Oh, crap, did you want to go? I should have—"

"Juana gave everyone but me invitations, so I asked for one." Shame reared up in Neha, but the colors numbed it. "They—they laughed at me."

Sarita's brow furrowed. "What a cow. I can't believe she didn't invite you."

"It doesn't matter." Neha waved her arm to show just how much. "So what did the doctor say?"

"Everything's normal! She wants to keep an eye on me, of course, but just as a precaution."

All Neha's anxiety burst like a giant balloon. She fell back against her pillow. "Thank God."

Sarita laughed. "You're so cute. I'm sorry I made you worry, but everything's okay." Her mouth quirked. "Well, maybe not everything. Mom said you're sick?"

Neha couldn't tell her the truth, not after her good news. Even if she'd let Neha worry. "I'm fine."

"If you need anything, just tell me, okay?"

"Thanks." Neha looked at the glow-in-the-dark constellations dotting the ceiling. "I was—I'm glad you're all right."

"Me, too." Sarita got up. "We'll talk more later." She shut the door behind her.

"I'm glad you're okay," Neha told the door. Her thoughts chased one another in circles: Sarita at the party, chatting away with the people who sneered at Neha every day. Ignoring Neha, who was at home, gnawing her fingernails to nubs.

She was so alone. She had to get outside, had to get some air.

Neha threw on old clothes and slipped into the backyard. Birds twittered in the trees, some of her mother's daisies still bloomed, and everywhere she turned, there was green. An entire spectrum of green, ranging from the bluest shade to the yellowest hue. She stared at it, awed. How could she ever have thought yellow or even orange and purple could be enough?

Barefoot, she ran through the soft grass. Pebbles cut into the soles of her feet, and a slug squished its sticky entrails all over, but she didn't care.

Sarita was going to be fine.

Quick and sharp as a bee sting, pure green seeped into her. She saw moss, she tasted cilantro. The hollow place in her claimed it all.

Relief rushed through her arms, then her legs, and she flopped onto her back. Her anger, her hurt, drained away, replaced by compassion. *This* was green, this connection to life. Everything pulsed with it, the plants, their leaves, the golden dandelion heads in the grass. Even the slug she'd stepped on had bled this vital essence.

The green slithered through Neha's body like a snake, easing her hunger. Every atom in her body sang with life, drunk on it. If she cut herself, she might find sap in her veins.

She had to stop feeding, or she would rupture. Woozy, Neha opened her eyes—and forgot to breathe.

The entire space, from the smallest blade of grass to the highest tree branch, had turned shadow gray.

Neha put the final touch on her portrait, a rainbow impaled on the image's extensive fangs. Falling limply back to the palette in the image's clawed hands, the rainbow bled from numerous puncture wounds. Satisfied, she set down her brush.

Mr. Stone applauded. "Excellent work, Ms. Shah. This passion, this *rawness*, that's what I wanted to see. Class, you could learn from this."

Neha's cheeks warmed with pride as the other students gathered around. She'd actually pleased Mr. Stone—without resorting to even a hint of exoticism.

"I love the fangs!" Aarti, one of Stephanie's friends, said, giggling. "Sometimes you just have to bite back." Stephanie and Juana glared at her.

"What's it called?" Mr. Stone asked.

The kaleidoscope of colors twisted within Neha, forming new pictures. Then she had it. "*A Feast of Many Colors.*"

Appreciation lit Chris's pale green eyes as he flipped open a little notebook. "What a great concept. Mind if I borrow it?" Before Neha could answer, he went on. "Yeah, so I've been writing these screenplays, and I think this would make an awesome story."

Neha gaped at him. "You do?"

Chris clicked his pen a few times. "It's, like, picture a color vampire on the screen, sucking the heart out of everything and leaving it black and white. Dead. Ruined. Really powerful stuff, so carnal and tragic."

Bubbles filled Neha's belly, effervescent and gleaming, yellow and purple and orange and green. He liked her idea! A grin stretched over her face, wide enough to hurt.

"Wow, that would be really cool. But listen, if you want to talk about it more—" Her heart banged against her ribs as fast as the words flying from her mouth. *Now or never.* "I mean, do you have time to grab coffee or something after we get out of here?"

Chris jerked his head back. "I don't… Look, I've got a girlfriend."

"Oh." Neha's grin contorted into something else.

"Yeah, I just thought this was a cool idea, that's all. Sorry."

Behind them, Stephanie snorted. "Did she actually think he'd go out with her? Seriously, how is she that clueless?"

"She's a freak," Juana said. "What do you expect?"

What was left of Neha's smile quivered. She couldn't think, couldn't move. She was an animal straining at the bars of her cage, laughed at by everyone in the zoo.

The colors embraced her, reminding her she didn't need anyone. She wasn't an animal but an artist for whom the rainbow danced.

Chris could write all the stupid screenplays he wanted, but he'd never understand colors the way she did.

It almost worked, too.

Neha hurled her supplies into her bag and ran from all the knowing smirks. Somehow her cell phone made its way into her hand. She jammed the buttons to dial Sarita. "I need you. Now. Please."

Sarita had asked for a brownie with raspberry sauce, so Neha bought one, but the cloying stench of melted chocolate made acid rise in her throat. She shoved the plate as far as she could across the table. How could anyone *eat* this stuff?

All around the bakery, people sat enjoying their treats. Everything was too bright, too loud. Neha buried her head in her arms, but she couldn't stop imagining the snickers as word got around school. How they would look at her like the freak Juana had called her.

Damn Chris!

Why had she thought he would like her, anyway? Her own sister had blown her off the other night.

She'd started to float off into a gentle cloud of colors when Sarita called her name. A hand touched her shoulder. "Are you okay?"

Neha sat up and swiped at her face, surprised at the wetness there. "Here," she said, gesturing to the brownie. "I got this for you."

Sarita handed her a tissue. "What happened?"

Humiliation crashed over Neha again as she recounted the story. She'd have to transfer schools. There was no other answer.

"What a loser. He doesn't deserve a second of your time." Sarita took a deep breath. "Hey, is this why you haven't been eating?"

"What? No. Something's wrong with me. I—I can't eat anymore." The haze roiled inside Neha, suffocating. "I don't need to."

"Neha," said Sarita slowly, "whatever's going on, you can't starve yourself. Talk to me. Let me help you."

"You're not listening!" Orange seethed, while purple flooded Neha's memory. Yellow retreated, and green scorched her thoughts. "I'm ... eating the colors out of things. I mean, did you see the lawn?"

Sarita tilted her head. "Wait, are you saying you did that? I thought it was chemicals."

"Look, I know it sounds crazy, but I can eat colors, I swear. I'll prove it to you." Neha scanned the store, hunting for the telltale glow. Where was it? She ran her fingertips over the mosaic tabletop, imploring the teal and violet tiles to wake up. "Honestly, I can!"

"I know you're going through a hard time right now, but..."

Neha stopped rubbing. "But what?"

Sarita moved around the table and put her arms around Neha. She stiffened, then relaxed. It felt so good, so comforting, to be held like this. It felt ... brown. Brown like chocolate.

"I know school can be really awful sometimes, and bullies are the worst." Sarita stroked Neha's hair. "You really are fun and talented and smart, and I wish I could get you to see that."

The hunger rose in Neha, eager to be sated. *No. Not now.* Frightened, she pulled out of her sister's arms.

Irritation flickered in the depths of Sarita's dark brown eyes. "But the thing is, you don't have to make yourself a target."

"What?" Neha felt bruised.

"You don't pay attention to the signals people give you. I think maybe there's a part of you that likes being misunderstood."

Everything shifted and collided, a stained glass window smashed to smithereens. Didn't Sarita know Neha would give anything to fit in?

"I just want to belong," Neha mumbled.

"Oh, Nehachu, I know, I know. I'm so sorry the people in your class suck. But if you don't respect yourself, who else will?"

"So it's okay for Stephanie and Juana to treat me like crap?"

"Of course not! They're awful. But why did you beg her about the party?" Sarita poked at the brownie. "That's what I don't get. Did you really think it would change her mind?"

Neha was sure all the eyes in the shop had turned to her. All the fingers were pointing, all the mouths laughing. Even her sister thought she was a fool.

Sarita pointed with her fork. "You don't have to do things like make up crazy stories to show everyone how special you are."

An invisible clamp gripped Neha's heart. Her vision blurred as she stared at Sarita, then sharpened into perfect relief. "I didn't make it up."

Sarita, Ms. Normal, with her perfect body and her flawless

skin that never scarred, not like Neha's. What did she know about anything?

Flawless brown skin that glowed…

"Neha? Hey, I didn't mean everything was your fault." Sarita took Neha's hand. "I'm just—never mind. I'm just tired of seeing you get hurt."

Just a bite. Just one bite to see what normal tasted like. Why shouldn't Neha get to try it, too?

Suddenly her fingers were sucking on Sarita, drinking the color in violent waves. Something snapped into place, and Neha's head lolled, lost in the delectable scent of rich, velvety chocolate. She could feel the silky taste on her skin, in her veins, on her tongue.

Cushioned in dark brown sheets of satin, she was whole, she was safe, she was full.

A far-off cry pierced a hole in her cocoon. Something juddered—Sarita, trying to break away. "What are you doing? Stop it!"

Neha meant to, but the flavor called her back. She drank and drank and drank the sweet brown bliss. It was so good, so very, very good.

At last the haze dissipated, and Neha could see again. She recoiled. "Ohgodohgodohgodohgod."

That hateful gray of decay. Dead. Dead like the lawn. Gray where her sister should have been brown.

Her sister…

Oh, God.

Neha fled.

Despite the dreary rain that stabbed downward, muting everything, colors shimmered and smoldered for Neha. Sarita's brown nuzzled her like a loving pet, making her want to claw off her own skin.

Home beckoned. Mom and Dad would help her make it all right. They loved her.

Yet when she reached the familiar door, she couldn't go in. She circled around and around the slick concrete, letting the torrent soak through her clothes and drench her hair. Clear and colorless, like her tears.

But there was nowhere else to go. Steeling herself, she finally turned her key in the lock.

The table in the dining room was spread with a steaming banquet. All Neha's old favorites, waiting for her. She retched.

"Neha?" her mother called from the living room. "Is that you?"

An ember flared in Neha long enough for her to force out two words. "Mom. Mom."

The phone chimed in the distance. An eternity passed as Neha waited, trembling.

"One second, beta." Her mother switched into her softer, for-strangers voice. "Hello?"

Neha's heart wept, and she staggered into the kitchen. An offering. She needed an offering. Her hand closed around a stick of butter. She crawled back to the dining room and dumped it onto the shrine.

"Help me." Water trickled from her bowed head to collect on the floor. "Help me, please! I didn't want this. Help me fix it."

When she raised her head, Krishna had changed.

His mysterious blue crackled as she watched, chipping away to reveal something darker underneath, like the lava under magma.

Dizzy, Neha rubbed her eyes. The blue kept cracking open, exposing more and more.

Somewhere across the city, Sarita lay prone, but Neha could see her through the window of blue. Her sister's body was a hollow gray gulf separating Neha's dark from Sarita's light, from her colors, from her love.

Neha braved a glance into Sarita's shadow-soaked gaze. "I just wanted you to believe me."

When her sister didn't react, Neha tried again. "I didn't mean to hurt you, I swear." She waited, but Sarita wouldn't respond. "Answer me!"

The corpse stared back.

Neha crumpled onto the chilly tiles. Her arms cradled her knees as she rocked. She had to find a place where dark and light were one, where they were everything. Where they were the only thing.

Her mother's scream etched itself on Neha's brain, high and haunting like a wooden flute.

Krishna. Krishna was everywhere and everything. He belonged more than anyone. If the stories were true, he *was* everyone.

Neha's stare lingered on that impossible, elusive, tantalizing Krishna blue, the blue that was truly black, the blue that cracked open like an eggshell to spill out the impossible color of the void underlying all things.

Starving to the marrow of her bones, she stood.

She moved closer, one step, then another.

What possible flavors might a god have?

Every Little Thing

By Holly Kench

"Earth to Mandy. Earth to Mandy."

Fingers snapped in front of my face, breaking me from my reverie. I turned toward my friend Natasha who was scowling, a finger pointing meaningfully at my notebook.

"Have you done any work this lesson? You know we have to get this finished by Friday."

I rolled my eyes. I knew that secretly Natasha didn't want me to do any work. Group work, she believed, was institutionalized torture for school children, designed to pull up the "juvenile delinquents" (by which she meant B-grade students) at the expense of "tomorrow's leaders". She preferred me to leave all the work in her perfectionist hands. Definitely.

"I'm pretty sure it isn't due till next Tuesday, Tash," I said, ignoring her question.

"We need to get it done by Friday so we can start on our assignments for science that are due on Wednesday. Seriously, Mandy, how do you even function?"

I assumed this last question was rhetorical but answered all the same. "On Red Bull and M&Ms mostly."

It was Natasha's turn to roll her eyes.

"What were you thinking about anyway?" Natasha looked over to where I'd been staring and let out an exaggerated sigh. "Let me guess: Leah."

I closed my notebook and looked at Natasha. "Nope. I was thinking about the American Civil War and about..." I paused for a moment and looked at the classroom whiteboard, which sadly gave me no clues.

"Mandy, we're studying the American Revolutionary War. You're only a century out but good try."

"Close enough." I grinned at Natasha, daring her to argue. From the corner of my eye I could see Leah flick her hair over her shoulder as she chatted to Brodie next to her. Mr Milne, our teacher, was sitting at the front of the classroom with his legs crossed and reading some history book. With everyone doing group work, he had given up on even the pretense of managing the class.

I wondered whether he was secretly reading a comic book within the folds of the fat book. Probably not, he wasn't cool enough to like comic books. Perhaps some stodgy thriller then. There was no way he could be that engrossed in a book about some war years ago, on the other side of the world.

"I don't know why you like her," Natasha said, watching Leah with a look of suspicion she usually reserved for spiders and Brussels sprouts.

"She's different to what you think. She can be really nice."

Natasha raised her eyebrows as Brodie kicked out one of our classmate's chairs and Leah laughed.

"I think she just acts like that because—"

"Because she's a bitch," Natasha finished.

"Hmmm." I knew how Leah seemed to people. She was the Queen Bee, loved and feared to equal extents by most of the school. But I had seen another side to her and knew that her cold exterior was only a façade. The year before when I'd messed up my meds and passed out in the middle of the lunch hall, it was Leah who had come to my rescue, helping me up and getting me water, even glaring at Brodie when he laughed, while the rest of the school looked on with disinterest. Ever since, I'd been crushing on her like some pathetic princess who falls in love just because she gets rescued. I should have been embarrassed by my crush, but I couldn't bring myself to care. Leah was gorgeous, tall, blonde, and perfect enough to be a cliché. And no matter what Natasha thought, she was a good person. She could be so kind, but she could also be cruel and that was the only side Natasha saw.

I knew what it was like: high school was a battle zone that you had to claw through at whatever cost. Natasha wasn't immune to its effects either. I knew that beneath her pink sweater she was wearing a vintage *Star Wars* T-shirt. Of course, she couldn't hide her nerdy ways when she tried so hard to do well in class, but she still tried to fit in, to be some semblance of what passed for normal around here. And to do that she hid the more geeky side of her persona, the side that I liked best. That was always the way, I thought, everyone kept their best sides hidden.

"Anyway, like you can talk," I said. "You're the one who likes Brodie."

Natasha clamped her hand over my mouth. "Shhh. Not so loud. He'll hear. Besides, the difference between you and me is that I know I *shouldn't* like him. And I would never ever date him." She smiled looking over at Brodie. "I just like to admire him from afar."

Since Natasha had not removed her hand and was now openly "admiring" Brodie, I did what I considered the only reasonable thing to do and stuck my tongue out, effectively sliming her hand.

"Gross!" She wiped her hand on her pants. "So mature."

"I try."

Natasha turned back to her work. I looked down at my closed notebook and thought about opening it. Then I looked at Leah. She was running her hand through her golden hair and laughing, not her cruel, mocking laugh, but the one that sounded like melodic wind chimes.

I smiled and turned back to Natasha to see if she had noticed the difference, if she could see Leah's other side when she laughed like that. But she was concentrating on her history book.

"Tash," I whispered. "Tash, I'm bored."

Natasha pursed her lips in a way that told me she was deliberately ignoring me.

Leaning over my desk, I sheltered my left hand in my right and rubbed my fingers together, watching as sparks flicked off my fingertips. Once I could feel the energy flowing easily through my hand, I leant over and lightly tapped Natasha on the arm. To an outside observer it would have appeared an innocent enough call for attention, but my finger sent a slight electric shock through her.

Natasha looked at me and took one slow blink. “Oh my god, Mandy. Just try to do some work. Plus, no…” she mouthed the word *magic* “...in school! Someone will see.”

She twisted round in her seat, her eyes flicking across the faces of our classmates to check if anyone had noticed.

“Well they will if you keep looking around like that,” I said.

Natasha looked back at her book, prepared to ignore me again but I could tell that being-worn-down-by-Mandy-itis was setting in. She pulled her notebook closer to herself so it was hidden from the view of nearly everyone but me, and drew a small symbol on the corner. She tore the corner off her notebook and leaned over, pressing it onto the top of my hand, whispering faintly as she did. When she lifted her fingers the paper was gone and an image of a small heart appeared on my skin, disappearing nearly straight away, followed by the words “Do some work” in Natasha’s handwriting.

I smiled and mouthed, “Okay,” before opening my notebook again, determined to try if only to make her happy.

I had taught Natasha a few spells over the last year, nothing that someone without innate magical abilities could do, but a few little tricks that were fun. My mum would have been furious if she knew I'd told anyone, but she needn't have worried since Natasha was more conscientious about keeping my secret than I was. I hadn't meant to tell her in the first place, but when I was fifteen, and just coming to terms with my abilities, they had been harder to manage. We'd been sitting and chatting over lunch in the cafeteria when my hands started to shake. They glowed and sparks shot wildly in every direction. Without hesitation, Natasha grasped my wrists and shoved my hands in my pockets. She dragged me from the cafeteria before anyone could see. She didn't question me or seem scared, just asked if I was all right. And when she did, I just knew I could tell her everything. Once I had finished, and my hands had stopped shaking without me even noticing, Natasha had hugged me tight.

"So you'll still be my friend?" I'd asked.

"Of course," she'd said, pulling back from the hug to look me in the eyes. "I always knew you were a freak."

By the time class ended, I had managed to take enough notes to make Natasha happy. The bell rang and, without any acknowledgement from Mr Milne, the class stampeded out the door.

"Catch you next period?" Natasha asked leaning half in and half out the door, while I remained slowly gathering my things.

She was always one of the first up and out of her seat, not because she wanted to get out of class, but because she wanted to get to her next one. When the rest of the school was on lunch break, Natasha was usually doing advanced placement study, ostensibly to give her a better chance of getting into a top university, but I had some concerns that she actually enjoyed studying.

"I think I'm gonna head home. See you tomorrow?" I answered slinging my bag over my shoulder and heading towards the door.

"Okay. I'll take notes in English for you." She smiled and waved, dashing down the hall before I could say thanks.

I stopped by the school office to let them know I was going home and headed to the bus stop at the front of the school.

To my surprise, Leah was perched on a low wall just along from the school bus. She was leaning back and staring absently up into a tree. Streaks of sunlight pierced the branches, leaving a pattern of leaves across her face.

I leant against the wall beside her to wait for the bus. "Hey."

She jumped in surprise at the sound of my voice and looked in my direction. "Oh, hey. I didn't see you there."

"No worries," I said. "Sorry to frighten you."

"Nah, I was just thinking." She waved her hand across the air as though she was brushing off her thoughts.

"Yeah, what about?"

She hopped off the wall to lean against it with me. "Nothing interesting. You ditching this afternoon?"

"I suppose." I didn't really consider it ditching when I had permission to head home if I got too worn out or felt too unwell, but I figured I knew what she meant. "What about you?"

Tilting her head up towards the school, she said, "I didn't think I could handle another minute of that place so I'm going to the movies."

"Oh, right! That new space one is out, isn't it?" I couldn't remember what it was called, but Natasha had been nagging me all week to go see some movie that involved space. She assured me I would love it, and I knew I probably would, but I didn't tend to become quite as excited about sci-fi as she did. Well, no one got quite as excited about it as she did.

Leah laughed and rested her hand on my shoulder. I tensed a little, surprised by the familiarity of the contact.

"You're such a crack up," she said. "We'll probably go to some action one. I don't really care, but the cinema is a good place to hook up. Oh hey, Toby!"

Leah pulled her hand away from my shoulder to wave at a car that was pulling up in front of the bus zone. The shock from the absence of her hand was almost more than the initial surprise from the contact, and I was hyperaware of the feel of my skin where she had touched me.

"Hey babe." A boy who seemed too good looking to actually exist in reality, or at least outside of a men's underwear commercial, leaned out of the car. He must have been a few years older than us, maybe a college student. "Ready to go?"

"Sure am," Leah said, then turned back to me and kissed me on the cheek. "See you tomorrow, gorgeous."

I watched as the two of them drove away, my cheek buzzing along with my mind. Gorgeous? She called me gorgeous, but then she'd hopped in a car with some male model, apparently to go make out with him at the movies.

My hands were shaking and I reached up to brush one through my hair. Before my hand reached my head, however, I realized that it was glowing. Sparks were flying haphazardly, and I saw with horror that the beginnings of flames were extending from the ends of my fingertips. I had to calm down, to stop thinking about Leah. I consciously took long deep breaths, and managed to reduce the fire hazard enough to put my hands in my pockets before the bus arrived. But I still couldn't think straight.

I sat in the bus fuming, more figuratively than literally, I hoped. Why was life so unfair? I'd had a crush on Leah for so long, and I knew she liked me, but it seemed like she would never *like*-like me. She was more interested in college boys than silly high school girls. Then it dawned on me. Maybe I could make her like me. Just for a little bit. Just long enough to make her realize how perfect we'd be together.

As soon as I got home I rushed up the stairs. Adrenaline pushed me along and even though the nagging voice in the back of my head told me I'd pay for it later, I grabbed some painkillers from the bathroom cabinet so I could keep going instead of having a sleep.

It was 1PM and no one was home. Mum must have just headed to work and would be there till late since she had the afternoon/evening shift, so I felt secure in the knowledge that I had the house to myself. Heading up to the attic, I opened the door. It creaked loudly, an alarm system that had formed as the house had aged around my mother's secret space. I paused. I wasn't allowed into the attic without her and she definitely would not approve of my reasons. Then I pictured Leah driving off with that boy. I pushed the door fully open.

The room smelled like rosemary and oranges, and was brightly lit via a skylight and a window that overlooked the bay. Its bright interior reflected my mum's own disposition and made me feel momentarily guilty for breaking her rules. She was the sort of mum who became "disappointed" rather than angry, and sometimes I felt like that was worse. But what she didn't know wouldn't hurt her.

The room was lined with bookshelves and cabinets, and in the center was a small table with a mortar and pestle, mixing bowl, candles, and other useful objects that betrayed the room's purpose as something other than a suburban mother's sewing room. Mum wasn't the sort to have a sewing room; no, this was her spell room.

I wasn't sure where she kept the books containing love spells, but I knew she had them. I remembered her helping another lady to break a love spell a few years ago, and one of the very first things she'd taught me about witchcraft was that you couldn't break a spell without knowing how to make it.

I scoured her bookcases. I knew it wasn't in the first one, which held all the books for my own study in the craft, mostly harmless spells for things like helping plants grow and basic manipulation of molecules. While I could turn water into apple juice, she flat out refused to teach me how to turn water into wine. Totally unfair. Quite a few of them were also about containment of natural powers. Mum said these were essential learning for young witches, and given my sparking hands this afternoon, I figured she was right. But they were also really boring.

The second shelf seemed to be mostly books about healing. I ran my fingers along their spines and sighed. Mum did so much healing work, she could heal a broken leg and stop a virus in its tracks, but she couldn't help me. Some things, she said, just *were*, and witchcraft couldn't change them. I would always huff and roll my eyes, and she would remind me that sometimes the things in our lives that made living so difficult could also be the things that made us who we were. It all seemed like hippy-dippy spiritual nonsense to me, but then again, if I hadn't fainted that day with Leah, perhaps I wouldn't have realized how wonderful she was.

Thinking of Leah, I hurried along to the next bookcase and on the top shelf I found exactly what I was looking for, *Basic Love Spells and Other Charms*. Mum might think that witchcraft couldn't solve everything, and I knew she thought love spells were an abuse of the craft, like any spell that attempted to control someone else's mind, but I was determined. I would show Leah how much she could love me, just for a bit, just until she could see it for herself.

I flipped through the book to a simple spell that looked easy enough even for a beginner like me. It didn't require much. Unlike in movies, there was rarely all that much preparation required for basic spells, and I'd never heard of any real witch with a cauldron. A tad disappointing; a cauldron would be kind of cool. According to the book, all I needed was to combine a few herbs, which I found in Mum's cabinets, a lock of Leah's hair and a small burst of will. I could totally do this.

"Jeez, you look like crap." Natasha slid into the chair next to me in the library. "I mean… Ah, that came out—"

"Accurately." I tried to smile but gave up. I felt hungover from the combination of painkillers and adrenaline from the day before.

"Bad night?"

"Hmmm." I didn't want to lie to Natasha, but I didn't think she'd approve if I admitted I'd made myself sick planning a love spell instead of going straight to bed.

She patted me on the back before placing a can of Red Bull on my desk. "This might help."

"You angel!" I hugged her in exaggerated joy. "Have I mentioned recently how amazing you are?"

"Yeah, pretty much whenever I hand you caffeine based drinks or chocolate… I wonder if I should be offended."

We both laughed and I felt a little better. Natasha had a way of making me smile even on my worst days.

Friday mornings meant free-study period in the library, so Natasha pulled out a book to do some homework. She handed me some pages of notes from the classes I'd missed yesterday and I shoved them in my bag to go through later.

"We have a new assignment for English," she said without taking a pause in her writing. "But it isn't due for two weeks, so we need to keep working on history and then science first." She looked at me, slumping in my chair without any books on my desk, and raised her eyebrows. I took her hint and pulled out my history book, but before I could pick up my pen, Leah walked in.

My hand moved automatically to the little pouch of herbs in my pocket. All I needed was a lock of her hair and the spell would be ready.

Grabbing a pair of small scissors from my bag, I stood up. Next to me, I vaguely heard Natasha ask where I was going, but I was too focused on my task to pay her any attention. Leah walked over to a bank of computers where Brodie and some of her other friends were working. I reached her just as she sat down, and she turned to smile at me.

"Hi, Mandy."

All thoughts of my hangover disappeared as I smiled back. "Hi. How was the movie?"

"It was alright." She shrugged dismissively. "Better than English with Mrs Brown, anyway!"

"Right." As we talked, I wondered how I would get a lock of her hair without her noticing. "Do you need some notes from class? Natasha took some—"

"Nah," Leah interrupted, and I thought that was probably lucky since despite my near-offer, I doubted Natasha would be all that pleased about sharing her notes with Leah. "But, hey, do you want to come round to my place tonight? I'm having a party."

She'd never invited me to one of her parties before and I felt a little breathless. Her parties were epic. Her parents went out of town for work all the time and let her do whatever she wanted in the house. I couldn't imagine my mum being so relaxed. But I also knew I couldn't go. Parties were noisy and crowded and I knew that, for someone sick like me, as much fun as a party sounded, it would end up being exhausting and painful.

I frowned. "I can't but thanks so much for the invite!"

"Damn, why not?" She tugged a strand of her hair, reminding me why I was standing there. "We can totally tell your parentals that you're coming round to study, if they're the problem."

"No, it's not that," I said. "It's just that I'm not well enough to go to a party."

Leah tilted her head sideways as if trying to see some feature of mine she hadn't noticed before. "What do you mean?"

"You know, because I'm sick."

Her quizzical expression didn't change as she looked at me. "But you don't look sick."

I had no idea what to say to that. It was the sort of thing strangers said, or people who didn't know me very well. The sort of thing that made me feel that horrible combination of defensive and angry and just… sad.

Leah knew I was sick. We might not have been close friends but we'd been going to school together for years. She'd seen me leave in the middle of the day and surely must have known there was a reason I was excused from P.E.

And, of course, she had saved me when I'd fainted that time.

I couldn't believe that Leah, my Leah, could be so oblivious.

"Well, yeah," I said, unsure how else to respond.

"Right…" she said, looking away from me, as though she wanted to be anywhere else other than talking to me.

Behind her, I saw Natasha appear. She was hovering only a couple of meters away and I wondered how much she'd heard. She'd probably be annoyed that I'd even consider hanging out with Leah at all.

Instead of getting annoyed, though, Natasha said, "You can't go to a party tonight, Mandy. We already planned to have a *Stargate* marathon."

We hadn't planned any such thing, and she knew it, but she also understood I could never go to a party. I couldn't believe, though, that she'd owned her love of *Stargate* in the middle of the library, in front of all our classmates.

"A *Stargate* marathon?" Leah raised her eyebrows in derision.

"Yeah, that's right." I grinned up at Natasha.

"Your loss." Leah flicked her hair over her shoulder in a way that I'd always found beautiful and that Natasha had always said was obnoxious. Now I realized it was neither of those things. She wasn't perfect, not even close, but she wasn't a bad person either.

She swiveled in her chair, turning her back to me and starting up a conversation with Brodie.

I walked over to Natasha and we returned to our library desks. I put the scissors back into my bag and sat down. The pouch of spell ingredients was still in my pocket and I pulled it out.

"What's that?" Natasha asked.

"Nothing," I said, closing my hand around the pouch. Glancing back over at Leah, I squeezed it tight for a second, the tiny herbs inside digging into my skin through the fabric. Then, looking around to make sure no one was watching, I opened my hand palm upwards and blew across it. At the touch of my breath, the pouch disintegrated, leaving only tiny wisps of dust that spiraled away, combining with the air around us.

I leaned my head on Natasha's shoulder and the two of us watched as my spell vanished before our eyes.

"So, my place around 5 o'clock?" Natasha broke the silence.

"We're not really going to have a *Stargate* marathon, are we?"

"Definitely," she said. "We'll start at the beginning and we can argue about the scientific validity of traveling through wormholes."

I pulled myself up from leaning on her shoulder and shook my head. "You know something, Tash?"

"What?"

"You are such a freak."

"I love you too," she said, and we both laughed.

Happy Go Lucky

Garth Nix

Jean was seventeen so her Luck was the average of her two parents, a very healthy four point five. When she graduated from school in a little less than three month's time, she would test her own Luck, but everyone knew that it would not be less than Dad, the surgeon's, four point nine or Pop, the mathematician's, four point one. Privately, Jean thought it would be at least a five, almost as high as you could get. After all, she was young and pretty and very smart. Surely her Luck must be even better than her parents?

But she did not think about her Luck as she strolled down the street towards her home, the last sunshine of the afternoon lighting her way as if she trod upon a golden road. She didn't pay any attention to the street sweepers, who had just begun to come out as the day faded, ready to work through the night. They wore shabby reflective vests over many-times patched clothes, and each wore an ironic crown of twisted black wire upon their heads, the mark of the Unlucky. The crowns were attached to anyone whose Luck tested below one point two, and could not be removed. No one was ever lucky enough to recover from below one point two.

Both her fathers were already home, Jean saw as she approached the house, which was very unusual. High among the Lucky, they both had the latest model electric runabouts, Dad's bright blue with a yellow stripe, Pop's a more subdued shade of grey. They were parked in the drive, somewhat haphazardly, as if both had sped home in answer to an emergency.

Jean frowned, and quickened her step. The front door, responding to the Lucky golden bracelet shining on her wrist, slid open to admit her.

Inside the house, her fathers were arguing. They were normally very calm and analytical men, who would sit down and talk through any major issue. Now they were up and shouting, and Jean was shocked to see her dad actually tearing at his hair. She'd thought that was something people only did in stories, but there he was, tugging at the hair on either side of his temple as if he might rip some out by the roots.

"What's going on?" asked Jean.

"You tell her," said Dad to Pop. He stopped pulling out his hair and sank into one of the living room chairs, which sensing his tension, immediately began to massage his back. "It's all your doing."

Pop looked at Jean. His face was kind of screwed up and she felt the shock of sudden realization. He had been crying, in fact he had only just managed to stop when Jean came in.

"I … I wrote a paper on probability and chance," he said slowly. "It was purely theoretical, I didn't even *attempt* to publish it—"

"You never should have written it in the first place!" said Dad.

"I don't understand," said Jean. "You write papers all the time about all sorts of things."

"The paper showed what Luck really is," said Dad. "And he left it in his archive."

"It was locked," said Pop. He sat down too, and stared at the wall. "I don't know how it got out."

"How it got out?" asked Dad, incredulous. "It didn't need to get out, you idiot! Every archive is trawled, it's only a matter of time before anything subversive gets noticed!"

"Subversive?" asked Jean. "What are you talking about?"

"Our Luck is going to be re-tested," said Dad grimly.

"Re-tested? You mean mine is going to *be* tested," said Jean. "When I turn eighteen."

"I mean all of us," said Dad. "And it won't be good, I can tell you."

"But … no one gets their Luck retested after they grow up," said Jean. "Do they?"

Dad and Pop looked at each other.

"Not everything is like they teach you in school," said Dad.

"Very little," said Pop. He looked directly at Jean, his face a study in misery. "I'm sorry, darling. I'm very, very sorry."

"What for?" asked Jean. "Why are you sorry?"

"When they retest our Luck, we *will* go under one point zero," said Dad.

Jean stared at her parents, unable to comprehend what her dad was saying.

"But how can you know that?" she asked. "The Luck meter is impartial ... you must be wrong. We're Lucky! I'm going to be a five point zero! I know it!"

Pop bent his head. Dad went to the drinks cabinet, and poured a massive slug of whisky.

"Won't be any of this where we're going," he said.

"You're already drunk!" said Jean with distaste. "I don't know what's wrong with you two, but I'm going to my room."

Retreating to her room was Jean's standard tactic when she didn't get her own way, or was otherwise displeased with her parents. They usually let her go without comment. This time, they didn't.

"Jean, please," said Pop, clutching at her elbow, panic on his face. "This is real. We have to face up to it, talk about what we are going to do."

"You talk about it!" shouted Jean, twisting herself free. "I *know* the Luck meter will test me as a five. Maybe even higher. Good night!"

She stormed upstairs. Pop went after her, but stopped halfway up the steps as Dad called after him.

"Let her go," said Dad. "She won't believe it. She probably *can't* believe it. Not until it happens."

He took a sip of the whisky, but then set it down and slid the glass away. "You're right about facing up to it. They'll be here soon. I heard if you strap your watch to your ankle they sometimes miss it. And don't wear good shoes. They take them."

"I'm sorry, Nathaniel," said Pop wretchedly.

"Maybe it's just our luck," said Dad. "The real kind. We'd better start gathering whatever valuables we can hide."

"Valuables?" asked Pop. "What for? They'll make an example of us … down to Unlucky for sure. Money won't help us—"

"No," said Dad. He looked at the bottle of whisky. "We will be Unlucky. But there's a black market for small luxuries, things we might miss … money might give us some options."

"Options? What options?"

"I don't know," said Dad wearily. "But better to have something just in case. Get everything small and valuable, and old clothes. We have to be ready."

"And Jean?"

"The only thing that will break through twelve years of indoctrination is harsh reality," said Dad. He hesitated, before adding, "We can't protect her from this. We can only…"

He gulped and looked down.

Pop held out his arms, and Dad came into his embrace. They stood tight together for a minute, then slowly moved apart. Pop went to gather their jewelry, while Dad unstrapped his watch.

⁎

The Adjudicator and the Luck testers came at twenty past three that morning. Dad was waiting for them, empty glass in hand, the lounge still massaging his back. There was plenty of stress there, more than any upmarket furniture could massage away. Pop had fallen asleep next to him, his head on Dad's shoulder. He was still unable to believe it was really going to happen.

The first thing Jean knew about it was when her room turned all its lights on at maximum brightness, played her usual wake-up music for ten seconds far louder than usual, and then followed with a bored official voice she'd never head before.

"Get up, Jean. Get up. It is time for your Luck to be tested. Good luck."

Suddenly worried, Jean slid out of bed, her heart thumping. She barely had time to slip on some clothes before the door opened and the two Luck testers came in, their uniforms harsh and red in the bright light. One had a Luck meter in her hand, the other a laser cutter. Without preamble, the one with the meter pointed it at Jean and pressed the button. Heavenly voices sang from the meter, only to stop suddenly and be replaced by a dismal groan.

"Zero point seven," said the meter, in a harsh, croaking voice.

"Unlucky," said the tester. Jean stood uncomprehending, unable to believe what had just happened, her mouth open. It was too fast, too much for her to take in. The first tester put the Luck meter away and took out another tool from the pouch at her belt.

The second tester stepped closer, took Jean's unresisting arm and neatly cut off her Lucky golden bangle.

"No!" cried Jean. She made a lunge for the tester with the meter, who stepped aside. "Test me again! It can't be right."

"Don't make this difficult," warned the tester. She replaced the Luck meter and drew a small, egg-shaped device from a holster on her hip.

"Difficult!" screamed Jean. "I'm Lucky! Test me ag—"

The tester pressed the egg against Jean's reaching arm, above the elbow. There was a bright, actinic spark and a sharp crack. Jean collapsed instantly, crashing to the floor, her muscles in spasm.

The first tester stepped forward with the strange tool and ran it around the young woman's head. She felt a slight discomfort, not quite a pain, and saw in the large mirror by her wardrobe that she now had a crown of twisted black wire around her head.

The mark of the Unlucky.

Jean stared at her reflection, unable to believe what she was seeing. There was her perfect, dark skin without a blemish, her sparkling deep brown eyes, her beautiful tightly-curled hair … and somehow, totally ruining this picture was the twisted wire around her brow.

Frantically, she tried to lift her hands to the crown, but her fingers wouldn't work and deep down she knew that even if they had, the crown could not be removed.

The testers picked her up and dragged her downstairs. Her

parents cried out as they dumped her in a chair, and tried to go to her, but were waved back by the testers.

"You have twenty minutes for her to recover," said the Adjudicator. "Once outside you have an hour to leave Gardenside."

"Leave Gardenside?" mumbled Jean. Her voice was slurred, but still furious. "I'm not leaving Gardenside."

"You can't stay here," said the Adjudicator. "This suburb is zoned four plus. Penalties apply if you are still here within the stated time."

Jean snarled at him, so angry words would not come out of her unresponsive mouth. This could not be happening. She couldn't believe it. She was Lucky, and things like this just didn't happen to the Lucky.

"We'll carry her," said Dad. "Is that allowed?"

The Adjudicator made a dismissive wave of her hand. The testers stood back, though one still held the shock device ready.

Pop and Dad picked Jean up. She tried to struggle, but only succeeded in flopping around a bit more. Her parents clumsily maneuvered themselves and their burden out through the front door, and into the night.

They were Lucky no more.

Two days later, Jean came out of her rage and coolly decided that she simply wasn't going to accept what had happened. She left the room Dad had found for the three of them to share in an Unlucky hostel that occupied the lowest level of a deep parking garage, and walked up the ramps toward the daylight. The black wire crown around her head glinted as she stepped out into the sunshine, the bright sunshine forbidden to the Unlucky.

She crossed the street and began to walk along the broad footpath reserved for the Lucky, striding back towards Gardenside and her former life. But she had only walked a hundred meters before a black and silver runabout whirred silently towards her. There was a loud popping sound and the next thing she knew she was tripping over herself and colliding with the pavement, her legs wrapped in some ropy, sticky substance.

A Luck tester casually climbed out of the runabout and walked over to her, brandishing one of the egg-shaped weapons Jean had been shocked with before.

"No!" protested Jean. "I'm Lucky, this is all a mistake. I'm Lucky—"

This time, the tester put the weapon against her head.

When she regained consciousness, Jean found herself back in the room under the car park. Her Pop was sitting by the bed, but there was no sign of Dad. Pop lifted Jean's head and helped her drink a cup of water. It tasted metallic, another sign of how their life had changed. The Lucky drank filtered water.

Jean drank slowly, her conscious mind slowly reassembling itself into a working whole.

"You mustn't go out in daylight again," said Pop. "They said that was your last warning. They'll kill you next time. You *must* realize that we are Unlucky now."

"I know," croaked Jean. She grimaced as a pain shot through her temples. "But that doesn't mean we can't do anything about it."

"No, no, Jean," said Pop, his voice full of horror. "I just told you! They'll kill you. We have to lie low, learn how to live as the other Unlucky do—"

"No," said Jean, forcefully. "I'm not going to do that. I'll find a way out."

"Out?" asked Pop. "What do you mean *out*? Jean, I know this is all my fault, and I'm desperately sorry, but we have to live within—"

"No," interrupted Jean. She sat up, held her head for a few seconds, then gingerly got to her feet. "I'm going to go and talk to some people. Ask around."

"Ask around about what?" exclaimed Pop, hovering around her as if she might fall over at any second. "Please, Jean. Be sensible. Lie down again. You don't have to start work until tomorrow night, they said that at least, and it's only street-cleaning. I did it last night, it isn't very difficult."

"I'm going to ask about getting out of here," said Jean. "I mean really out."

"What?" asked Pop. His forehead was creased with deep concern. "Jean, you need to lie down. Dad will be back soon, he's helping a patient, you know the Unlucky … we … can't visit the proper clinics, he's doing what he can, if there's some medication you need there's a chance he can get it…"

"I'm okay, Pop," said Jean, giving him a quick hug. "I'm going to ask around about how we can get to Starhaven."

"*Starhaven...*" Pop stopped talking, but looked no less anxious. His mouth worked a bit before he got out another word. "What ... what do you mean?"

"We all know it's up there," said Jean. "I've seen it at night, crossing the sky. Some of my friends talked about it, they said there are people who can smuggle you there. And Starhaven *doesn't* have the Luck system."

"All those things are true," said a voice from the door. Pop jumped in instinctive fear, but relaxed as he recognized Dad.

"Starhaven is up there, as are other orbital habitats," continued Dad. "They don't have the Luck system, though some have other kinds of restrictive societies. And there are ways to get there. If you can pay for it."

"*Can* we pay for it?" asked Jean. She'd seen her parents remove various hidden valuables from their clothing when they'd first arrived, watches and jewelry and some ancient golden coins. Dad had taken them away somewhere the first day.

Dad didn't answer. He sat down on the foam mattress that served as bed and lounge. Pop went and sat next to him.

"Can we pay for it?" asked Jean. "Can we go?"

"I don't know..." said Dad. "We might be Unlucky, but as long as we follow the rules, we'll get basic food, this place to live ... it's nothing compared to what we were used to, but at least we're alive."

Jean looked around the bare grey walls of the room, taking in the pale single light panel, the dirty foam mattress, the plastic crate that contained a little food and a large bottle of water that had been filled from a park fountain.

"It's not enough for me," said Jean. "If I can't get to Starhaven, I'll try to get out some other way. I'm not putting up with being Unlucky."

"I don't know..." said Dad.

"We might get retested in a while," said Pop hopefully.

"Don't talk nonsense," snapped Dad. "No one has ever been retested out of Unlucky. Why would we be different? I've told you that over and over. This is it."

"At least Starhaven would be a chance of something better," said Jean. "Surely a chance is worth ... worth anything."

"Let me think about it," said Dad. "*You* think about what it means to at least be alive. Even if it is as an Unlucky."

"I'm still going to ask around," said Jean. "I mean, how to get to Starhaven."

"Feel free," said Dad. "We'll talk about it later. I need to get ready. We have to go out to work."

"Work," said Pop, the mathematician, as he helped one of the former most-gifted surgeons of the city into his high-visibility coat.

Jean did ask around, talking to the Unlucky around her own age as they went off to work, or as they came back in the grey interval before the dawn. Most would not answer her, fearing some kind of Luck tester trap. The few that did offered nothing beyond the fact that if it were possible to get to Starhaven they would already have gone themselves.

Dad and Pop returned with the last group of Unlucky, too tired and dirty to want to discuss anything but a wash and sleep. When they awoke in the afternoon, Dad hushed Jean as she tried to bring up the subject.

"I've asked a woman who knows someone," he said. "I'll let you know what she tells me, when I hear. Let's leave it until then."

But Jean didn't leave it. She kept asking, in the underground settlement, and out at night among the work gangs. The work was almost pointless, and very easy, simply a bit of sweeping and carrying that could be done in under an hour, though the shift went for a good ten hours of darkness. There was plenty of time to talk.

After a week, Jean found someone who claimed to have a connection to a people smuggler who arranged passage to Starhaven. A man in his twenties who had been born Unlucky told her there was a rendezvous once a month at a landing site outside the city. If you could pay, in precious metal or drugs or something equally transportable and negotiable, the smugglers would take you away. He had never had the chance to steal anything valuable enough to pay his way, but he told Jean he knew someone who had a few months before.

Jean told her parents the next morning. She wanted them all to go to the rendezvous and if possible, fly away to a new life, where they wouldn't have crowns of braided black wire and there would be a chance she could study and become something. Not just a street sweeper confined to the night.

Her parents looked at each other as Jean spoke. Finally Dad interrupted.

"That rendezvous is a scam," he said heavily. "The man you spoke to would be waiting there to rob us."

"How do you know," said Jean. "It's worth a try. Anything is worth a try!"

"I know because I've been asking around as well," said Dad. "There is a real rendezvous for the people smugglers. And...I...we..."

His voice faltered and he wiped angrily at his right eye.

"We've got you a place on a ship, Jean," he said bluntly. "To Starhaven."

Jean jumped up and flung her arms around him, but the hug grew looser as she realized exactly what he'd said.

"You've got me a place..." said Jean in a small voice. Fear had replaced anger, her defenses were broken. "What about you?"

"We can't all go," said Dad gently. "The fact is—"

"We're too old for Starhaven or any of the other orbitals," broke in Pop quickly. He gave a warning look to Dad over Jean's head. He didn't want their daughter to know they had only just scraped together enough money to send her, and there was no prospect of ever earning or gaining any more. They had nothing left to sell. "So we have to stay here."

"Yes," said Dad. "It won't be so bad for us, Jean. The Unlucky need doctors so we'll be looked after, as best as they can. Besides, we've had a long … we've had plenty of good years. And perhaps we should now be paying for the Lucky time we had, not caring about our fellows."

Jean cleared her throat and wiped her eyes.

"Maybe I shouldn't go either then," she said bravely.

"You took your lead from us," said Pop. "You shouldn't feel guilty. And we want you to have a better life."

"But without my parents!" exclaimed Jean. Her face was scrunched up, but no tears came to her dry eyes.

"Do you think you could stay here like this?" asked Dad. "Cleaning streets? Seeing the sun only at dusk and dawn? With nothing to look forward to?"

Jean stared at him.

"That's what it would be," said Pop. "I … we … we have to give you something better than that. We have to."

"We're not going to let you waste your life," said Dad, very firmly. "Besides, we've paid for your place."

Jean didn't answer. She looked at them and then slowly nodded her head.

"I'll go," she said. "But I'm going to come back for you. One day."

Dad smiled, but it was a small smile, the kind you have when you know something is forever beyond your reach. Pop smiled too, with a greater belief.

"We'd better get going then," said Dad. "We have a long way to go to the pickup and no easy way to get there."

There were no electric runabouts for the Unlucky, and they were only allowed on the trams after midnight. The three of them walked out of the city, on one of the roads that had an extra narrow lane for the Unlucky to trudge upon to their work.

It took another three hours at a steady pace to cross the green belt. They were all tired by then, so they stopped under one of the last trees and ate some of the basic fare of the Unlucky that Pop had brought in his backpack: vitamin-laced ration bread and the metallic water from the park fountain.

The desert lay beyond the green belt. They followed the single straight road out, walking through pools of darkness between the stark patches of light from the occasional lamps that hung high above from some invisible filament, anchored every now and then by a slender tower of only slighter thicker material.

Though the road was at least partially lit and the surface kept in good repair, doubtless by Unlucky labor, none of them knew for sure where it went. Geography was not an approved subject for the Lucky, they were taught to believe nowhere else really mattered. It was harder to ignore the orbitals, because they could be seen at night flashing across the sky, but again they were not considered a proper subject to discuss at any length or learn about.

"How far to go?" asked Pop, after they had walked for another hour. Dad still had a watch, but it was a simple extruded prefab now, not the status symbol of gold antiquity.

"Can't be long now. They just said keep walking down the road until we see it," said Dad.

"See what?" asked Jean. Her question was almost automatic, her voice without inflection. She still couldn't believe what was happening.

"That, I think," said Dad, pointing. Up ahead there was another patch of light, the last before a very long stretch of darkness. But it wasn't the harsh, steady white illumination of the overhead lamps. It was blue and red, and flickered.

Closer, they saw that the light came from the idling exhaust of a scramjet, lined up to use the road as a runway, though only Pop knew what it was, and his knowledge was academic. He'd never actually seen one.

A woman, strangely dressed to their eyes, in a coverall with a ring collar for a helmet seal, came to meet them. Up close she was stranger still, for her skin was a pallid white, the color of a wound dressing, so unlike the rich brown of Jean and her parents.

Jean stared at the woman for a full second, unable to look away, only now fully realizing that she was about to leave everything familiar behind her, even the basic appearance of people. She had never seen a pale-skinned person before.

The woman directed them off the road and into the sand to take a wide berth around the back of the scramjet. She had a weapon of some kind in a holster at her side and her hand constantly rested on the butt.

"Okay, I only got one passenger listed," she said. "Unless you got a whole lot of extra currency on you."

"It's just me," said Jean. "To Starhaven."

"Yeah, yeah," said the woman impatiently. "Say your goodbyes, because you two old guys need to get clear before we take off, and that's in fifteen minutes. Make it quick, girl, because I got to get you rigged up."

Jean felt nothing as her fathers hugged her. It was if she were somewhere else, far away, watching all this happen. They both cried, but she had no tears within her. Her anger was long gone. Now she simply had a grim acceptance. She would go to Starhaven, and learn and grow, and then one day she would come back. Come back to rescue her parents, and all the Unlucky, and throw down the whole Luck system to give everyone an equal chance to make their own future.

The woman scowled as the hug continued.

"Hurry up," she said. But it was a perfunctory warning and she didn't try to separate them.

"Don't cry," soothed Dad, though it was him and Pop who were crying. "It'll be good up in Starhaven. You'll make friends up there, find someone, have a better life…"

"You will," muttered Pop, his voice breaking. "We love you. Always."

"I love you too," said Jean automatically. "I love you."

"We got to go," said the woman. She hesitated, then added a grudging, peculiar apology that was more to Dad and Pop than Jean. "Sorry. It's just the … we have to get going."

Last kisses were exchanged. Jean was led away towards the front of the scramjet. Her parents watched for a moment, then started to trudge back through the sand, their heads bowed. After a few paces, their hands went up and clutched tight together.

Jean looked over her shoulder just as they disappeared into the night, blue-tinged shadows absorbed into the darkness. She felt a sudden pain pass through her body and an incredible weariness centred in her heart, on top of the physical ache from their long walk.

She knew then she would never see her parents again.

"Step into this," said the woman, opening up an orange coverall that came with attached boots and gloves. "This is your survival suit. Anything happens, you pull this clear hood up and over, it'll seal automatically when you hold it closed here. Then you got twenty minutes of air and it will set off a beacon. You understand?"

Jean quickly sealed the suit and pulled the hood halfway up a couple of times to see how it worked.

"Sure," she said. This was the beginning of her new life. She had to be keen and sharp and do everything properly. "Uh, what do you mean if something happens? How will we know?"

"Just routine," said the woman, but she didn't look Jean in the eyes. "It's not like driving around your dinky city. Come on."

Jean followed her up the lowered ramp and into the scramjet. She saw several crewmembers through the open cockpit door, but they looked through her or off to the side, as if she wasn't really there, and quickly turned back to their glowing holographic controls.

The woman with the sidearm opened an internal door and gestured for Jean to go through into a sparsely-outfitted cabin.

There were rows of long, couch-like benches with angled backs inside, and already quite a lot of people half-lying on them, maybe forty or fifty, all in orange survival suits.

"Find a place, fit your feet under the restraints on the floor, lie backwards and hold on to the handles at the sides. Don't let go unless instructed. If you have to vomit, there are pouches in the thigh pocket of your suit, seal it up straight afterwards. This is a quick trip, you won't need food, water or a toilet."

Jean nodded and walked into the cabin. A man and a woman who also wore the dark crown of the Unlucky shifted across a bench to make room for her at the end of the second row. Jean sat down, her mind noting that they were both older than her parents, so what Dad had said about being too old was clearly a lie. Inwardly, she had always known the truth, that there simply wasn't enough money to send them all, and that only strengthened her determination to come back.

Jean slotted her feet into the restraints, leaned back and felt for the hand-holds on either side.

"Starhaven?" asked her neighbor.

"Yeah," croaked Jean. It was hard to get the word out without a sob.

"It'll be better there," said the man. "A lot better."

He sounded like he was trying to convince himself.

A crewmember poked her head into the cabin and shouted, "One minute! Hold on and don't let go."

Withdrawing, she shut the door behind her, and the passengers heard the heavy clank of it being manually dogged shut. There was a faint murmur at that, a restless shuffle along the benches.

It didn't feel like a minute before there was a sudden roar of the jet and an acceleration that at first pushed them gently back but then continued, the push increasing until it hurt, at first a little and then a lot as there was a sudden change in engine pitch and the scramjet became nearly vertical. Jean pushed hard to keep her feet in the restraints and hold on, her knuckles went white. She heard screaming and shouting behind her: from the sound of it someone had come loose and crashed against other passengers.

A few minutes later, the acceleration increased even more. Jean felt as if someone was probing her face, pushing fingers into her cheeks hard enough to push through to her jaw, pressing her eyes into their sockets. She cried out, involuntarily, adding to the cacophony of screams and cries in the cabin. Then she passed out.

Jean came to only minutes later. The pressure had abated, and with it the pain. But now she felt an uneasy sensation in her stomach, as if it wanted to rise up through her throat. She gasped and coughed, and willed herself not to be sick.

Slowly the screams and the shouting subsided, but it was replaced by the sound of retching and whimpering. Jean looked around. She could really only see down her row, and no one was being sick there, but there were lots of white faces and screwed-shut eyes.

"Can't be too much longer," whispered Jean's neighbor. He looked very pale and ill, the flesh bruised around his eyes and his lips a little blue. "We must be in orbit now. Free fall."

Jean nodded anxiously. She was trying to be tough, but couldn't help starting to worry about what would happen to her in Starhaven. Everything was happening too quickly—

A deafening alarm klaxon sounded, followed immediately afterwards by an amplified voice.

"Put your hoods on and seal. Put your hoods on and seal."

Jean let go of the handles and began to fumble with her hood, but rose up out of her bench at the same time. She pushed her feet in hard and tried to flex herself backwards, still grappling with her hood. She got it up and over and closed, and heard a hissing noise from somewhere around the back of her neck. She grabbed the handles again and pulled herself back into place, taking a breath that smelt of dust and tainted plastic.

The man next to her was writhing about near the ceiling and still hadn't got his hood over his head. Jean let go with her right hand and reached up to pull him down, but at that moment the ceiling above her suddenly parted down the middle and split apart. The man was jerked from Jean's grasp and she lost her grip with her left hand and went spinning after him, one of fifty orange bundles propelled out into space in a haze of vented atmosphere and ice crystals.

Tumbling end over end, Jean saw the scramjet dwindling away from her, the top cargo doors closing. Already there was no one close to her, she could only just make out a few orange specks disappearing towards the stars or to the brilliant arc of the world below.

Instinctively Jean pulled herself into a ball, not because she thought it would help the spinning. Strangely, she was not terrified. She had known a moment of terror when she had been flung out of the spacecraft, but it was gone now. She was scared, but she forced the fear down and concentrated on trying to slow her breathing. The twenty minutes of air promised by the crewmember was likely as much a lie as the journey to Starhaven.

Whatever air was left to her she would use slowly. There was probably no chance of rescue, but whatever tiny chance there was, Jean thought, she would multiply it. She would count ten between breaths, and breathe shallowly, and think of past happiness.

Her fathers would think her safe, she thought, and that was one small good thing.

She shut her eyes, and thought of sunshine, her breath very low and slow. Her arms and legs trailed out as she relaxed, unintentionally reducing the spin. Another little piece of space debris, drifting out to join the many others waiting in that long, cold sub-orbital graveyard, waiting until the Earth would bring them down for a swift cremation, weeks or even months ahead.

But unbeknownst to Jean, there was a slow reaching arm of a grapple about to pluck her from that graveyard, a grapple from a battered craft that was firing micro bursts from its thrusters to match her velocity and vector.

Her air ran out as the arm brought her aboard. People in proper suits rushed through the airlock procedures, lifting her inside to their waiting medic, who hastily brushed them aside and cut off her hood, clamping on an oxygen mask and a telltale on her ear.

Muzzily, Jean saw her rescuers looking down on her. She saw strange faces, with skins of many different shades, but also with metal and plastic in place of flesh: a glittering steel eye surrounded by scarred flesh, a nose remade in plastic, a mouth refashioned after some terrible injury.

She could hear them too, talking among themselves. Something about refugees and Starhaven refusing responsibility, and the smugglers getting even worse, not even trying to drop their passengers anywhere they'd get picked up, and if they could catch that scramjet they'd vent it, just see if they wouldn't, and there was one more they might be able to pick up, maybe two, but if this one's air was already gone then their suits were useless, there was no point...

Jean tried to talk, but only a bare croak came out. Her throat felt incredibly dry and strange.

"Don't talk," said the woman ... or maybe it was a man ... with the steel eye. "Just rest. You'll be okay."

"You were lucky we were so close," said someone else. There was a little chorus from everyone around.

"Very lucky."

"Amazingly lucky."

"Astonishingly lucky!"

Jean looked at their kind, caring faces, and finally began to cry.

Ordinary Things

By Vylar Kaftan

Katie is performing a ritual now. She fills her plastic cup with water from the office cooler and returns to her desk. As her co-workers make frantic phone calls ("hello ma'am I'm from AT&T and we have a special offer for—"), Katie tilts her head back and drinks her water in eight gulps. One, two, three, four, five, six, seven, eight. She's out of breath by the last swallow, and it's larger than the rest. But she's learned always to drink water in patterns of eight.

There are rules for the ritual. Small glasses of water may be completed in four gulps. Large glasses may be done in ten, but must be re-filled and then finished in another six, for a complete sixteen. Four, eight, sixteen. These are the rules for this ritual.

Katie performs this ritual because her girlfriend Vick has just left a text message on her phone. She performs this ritual every day, every time she drinks water—which is a lot, because Katie likes water. Katie returns for more water, her practiced feet avoiding the dark tiles in the floor pattern. She's extra-conscious of the rituals today because of what Vick's message said.

Vick said: *Left some things at the apartment. Coming back tonight*. This message makes Katie shiver in the air-conditioning.

Katie takes the water to her desk, then goes to the women's restroom, where she has some privacy. She messages her friend Jay: *Jay please be with me tonight*. She waits on the toilet for his reply, pants around her ankles, so that anyone glancing below the stall will think she is peeing. Trouble is here. Chaotic lines circle around her, twisting gray energy with no pattern. She is most afraid when these lines do not pattern. Jay, where is Jay? Finally he replies: *Will be there by seven.*

Katie relaxes. She pulls up her pants and leaves the stall. With her feet, she traces the patterned tiles. The path leads back to her desk and requires her to take slightly larger steps than usual. No one else will notice her ritual. This is critical in learning which patterns are rituals: they must be secret. She walks from tile to tile, taking care to step only on the white ones and not the brown or gold. The energy lines around her align into whorls like fingerprints. Her size-five feet skim the tiles, avoiding the cracks. Katie doesn't fear breaking her mother's back if her foot touches the wrong place. She does not play children's games in the rituals. She fears worse things will happen—things she can't even define without giving them power.

Katie is nineteen, which is a problem. She considers this as she rides the train home from San Francisco to Berkeley. The gray lines stream alongside—neatly in parallel, like the train she rides and its rhythmic hum. She carefully folds her feet beneath her on the seat as the train speeds under the Bay. This is a ritual: to keep her feet off the ground during certain events. The journey under the Bay is one. The cut to commercial is another, when she watches TV. Her feet must not touch the ground when the show switches to advertisements. Katie's changed her habits. She watches a lot of PBS now. She bought an ottoman so she could always keep her feet off the ground, just to be safe. It's cheap wicker, but effective for what she needs. Vick likes the ottoman too, and Katie used to fight her for it. Katie fought by piling stacks of classical CDs on the ottoman. Vick wouldn't touch the music, so Katie could remove the CDs when she sat down and then pile them back on when she left. Vick hated when she did that.

Katie stares out the window at the black tunnel. It's a problem to be nineteen, because it's an odd number. Nineteen doesn't complete a musical phrase, like four or eight or sixteen. In a month she'll be twenty, and while it's not perfect, it'll be better. She wants to be thirty-two. Ever since she was nine, she's been sure that thirty-two was the end of her life.

Her phone beeps as the train leaves the tunnel and stops at West Oakland. Jay has messaged her again. *Delayed but there by eight*. Katie panics. The gray lines knot her wrists. Her breasts ache, purpled with bruises from Vick's lovemaking. Vick likes to bite her and forgets Katie hates it.

Katie reviews her day in her head: has she broken any rituals? She turned the dial all the way cold before hot in today's shower. She stood on a bathroom mat when the toilet fell silent after flushing. She secured the three door locks in the correct order—door knob, deadbolt, deadbolt—and she drank every glass of water in patterns of eight. She must be safe. She has to be safe.

Her phone beeps again as the train is stopping at MacArthur station. Vick has messaged her: *What did you do with my iPod?* Katie stops breathing for a moment. Vick is already there, already in her place. Their place, the one they rented together—that Vick left last night. She glances at her phone. It's 6:45. She must go to the apartment alone. She closes her eyes, imagining Ani's smooth gray fur, and purring under her hand. Katie likes Ani because the cat is safe.

As the train dives underground, Katie wonders if Vick will kill her.

Katie likes math and music. Bach is safety. Bach married numbers to music and let them sing. Katie listens to "Toccata and Fugue in D Minor" on Vick's iPod—*her* iPod, she's sure—as she walks from the Berkeley station to the apartment. This is the piece that most people know from Bach, the one that recalls a wild musician at the pipe organ, or perhaps a mad scientist in a lab. Katie likes it for its subdivision, each note divided into halves, then fourths, then returned to wholeness. Bach is about numbers and time. Time is important to the rituals—time and numbers.

Katie's stomach is a mess of butterflies as she turns the corner to her apartment. She sees her front door open and stops. She's torn. She's blocked from her ritual. Katie doesn't know if Vick unlocked the door in the right order, or whether it even counts if she did. She doesn't know if other people perform these rituals or if they have different ones entirely. But a ritual is broken. Her safety is gone. Her stomach butterflies turn to slugs.

A broken ritual, Katie knows, is not a certain indication of disaster. But each broken ritual is a crack in the stone, a gap in the wall. The gray lines always surround her, spiraling towards her, seeking a weak point. Perhaps nothing will find the hole. Or perhaps something will. With each broken ritual, the chance of disaster increases. And sometimes nothing happens at all, and sometimes disaster happens even when she has completed every ritual. When that happens, Katie must add new rituals to cement those gaps and keep herself safe. Katie stares at the open door. A bee flies in. She realizes she can wait, she can hide until Jay gets here, she doesn't have to face Vick alone. Katie turns to run, but Vick is shooing the bee out the door, and sees her.

"I want my iPod back," Vick says. She comes outside and stands in front of Katie, arms crossed over her T-shirt that says Silence Equals Death. Vick's head is freshly shaved. Katie shrinks away and moves around Vick, ducking into the apartment. *Her* apartment. The one Vick moved into with her. She sets the iPod on the floor and looks at the space where Vick's furniture used to be. Katie's ottoman is missing, and she glances out the window. Vick has loaded it into her truck.

Vick follows her in and stares at Katie darkly. "God, Katie, you never say anything when you're mad. You're such a cold fish. Talk to me. Are you that upset, that you can't speak?"

Katie is, but she can't say that. She finally says, "Where's Ani?" She sees a trail of kitty litter on the floor, and the empty litter box by the door along with Vick's jeans and pajamas.

"Ani's mine," snaps Vick. "She was mine before I moved in. She stays with me."

Katie knows Vick is right, but it still hurts. Ani has no rituals around her. Ani is a ritual herself, and Katie can lie on the futon and pet her, knowing that the smooth gray fur would never let her be hurt. Katie knows not to show where she hurts, not to show how she fears, not to make any noise. She confronts Vick. "Ani's yours, but the iPod is mine."

"I paid for it."

"You gave it to me."

"You took it," says Vick. She lets out an angry breath. "But whatever. I'm done with your mind games."

Katie sees Vick slapping her in the face. Vick has never hit her, except in her imagination a thousand times. The gray lines in the room darken and solidify. She's losing their patterns. Katie steps onto the braided blue rug in the kitchen. This is a ritual: to stand on the rug while Vick is angry. This is how she stays safe.

"Aren't you going to say anything else?" Vick asks angrily. "You won't fight. You never fight. You just bottle shit up and then you leak it everywhere. You resent everything and you never talk."

Katie closes her mouth. Vick smells like baby-powder deodorant and it makes Katie cry. She sits on the rug, wishing she had some water. But it's too late for rituals. Once disaster happens, it's always too late for rituals.

"You are such a head trip," says Vick. "I want to provoke you sometime. I want to see you lose this precious polite crap you've built up. I want to see you break because it'd be good for you. God."

"Leave me alone," says Katie as she lies down. She curls up on the rug, her head resting against the cabinets. She's a small woman, but not small enough to crawl into the cabinets like she wants to.

"Christ!" yells Vick. She grabs Katie's arm and crushes it in her large hand. Katie buries her head under her arm, wanting Jay, just wanting Jay. She's four years old again. The world is too large and dangerous. She's lost in a crowd, looking for her mother, and she's lost all her numbers. She hears music with no beat, no time, and she's buried in an earthquake of people, too many of them, everywhere—

Vick shakes her. "Katie! God, I don't know where you go when you do this. Talk to me. Yell at me. We're done now, I'm not coming back, we're over—so tell me to fuck off. Tell me I'm a bitch, a bulldagger, a goddamn whore, anything—I just want to hear you fight. Let it out. Come on, Katie. Jesus fuck."

Katie's not listening. She's singing numbers in her head, arpeggios and scales of fours and eights. She holds her breath. If she can hold her breath until Vick lets her go, then she wins. That's a ritual. She can drive Vick away. She sees Vick killing her, punching her face, until she has no breath to hold. Katie sees herself in danger. The gray lines pound against her ritual wall, driving into her like a broken musical score. But Katie resists. She is lightheaded with lack of air but holds on.

Vick lets her arm go. Katie expels her breath in a burst, then pants as she tries to regain it. She stares at her knees. Vick's voice moves away. Now she's at the door. "Katie, you are so psycho. God. What the hell ever. I'm leaving."

Vick kicks the door on her way out. Vick's truck sputters and then drives away. Katie remains on the rug. She stays there for a long time, thinking of Vick. She lifts her head and looks at the fridge. There's still the picture of Katie and Vick from last year, held up by letter magnets that spell nothing special. In that picture, Katie's hair is still waist-length. She used to brush it and pretend she was a sun goddess with golden rays of hair streaming to earth. Vick, who is one-quarter Mexican and very proud of it, told her she was too Aryan and she didn't look queer enough. Vick shaved Katie's head for the Pride Parade last year. Now Katie's hair flops loosely around her chin. She thinks to herself that now she can grow it out again. This thought makes her cry. Katie sobs on her kitchen floor, wondering why she misses Vick already.

This is how Jay finds her: crumpled on the blue braided rug that's so ugly but she insists on keeping. He walks through the open front door and kneels next to Katie. Katie knows he's come in, that it's Jay and not the rapists she's sure are lurking around the house, the ones that she has developed rituals to avoid. She knows it's Jay because his sweat smells distinct, like kickboxing gloves.

She hears him set his gym bag down, and she looks up at him with tears streaking her cheeks. "Jay," she says, her voice breaking.

"Oh, hon," says Jay, and wraps his arm around her shoulder. Jay's wiry but strong. His parents are Thai, but he wishes they were Korean. He teaches taekwondo at the Berkeley YMCA. He's applied for an award that would let him study in Korea for three months. Jay has studied five martial arts and mastered two of them. Katie likes this about Jay.

"It's over," says Katie.

"How do you feel?"

"Broken."

Jay takes her shoulders and looks her in the eye. "Katie, you'll be fine. Vick was a bitch. It hurts now, but you'll get through it."

"How?" asks Katie. She doesn't know, she genuinely doesn't know.

"You just go on with regular life. Don't sit home and cry. The past is done—let it go. Keep doing things the way you always do, until it doesn't hurt anymore and you wonder why it ever did. Tuesday night is grocery night, right?"

"Yeah," says Katie, swallowing thickness in her throat. Tuesday night groceries isn't a ritual. It's merely a habit.

"Okay," said Jay. "Let's go. I'm coming with you. We can talk while we get groceries. You'll feel better if you have some food in the house. Last I checked, you only had spaghetti sauce and ramen in here."

Katie stands slowly, with Jay's aid. She gets a glass of water and drinks it—one, two, three, four (deep breath here, she can't drink it all in one breath, but it's okay to break at four as long as she continues to eight) five, six, seven, eight.

"I'm ready," she says. As she walks out the door, she notices Vick has taken her iPod and her Bach. Katie digs her nails into her palms.

Jay's not much taller than Katie, and she likes that about him too. He takes her to the grocery store in his blue Saturn. Jay ejects the Annie Lennox CD from the car's stereo and inserts the Indigo Girls. Jay says he's bisexual, but the only time he ever kissed a man he found him too hairy. He says that he prefers women but he'd be open to the right guy if he met him. Katie met Jay at the Y one night when she was lifting weights and trying to be stronger. They saw each other at the Y for three months or so, and then they started to meet for coffee sometimes. Jay's been single for six months now. Vick doesn't like Jay. Katie thinks it's because he reminds her that Katie used to date boys.

Jay pretends to open the automatic doors for her with a grand gesture. Katie can't smile. She's not sure if she can survive the grocery store tonight, although she respects Jay's idea that keeping her regular schedule will bring healing. Groceries on Tuesday is not a ritual, but perhaps it should become one. She enters the store, taking a deep breath.

Jay is speaking, as he patiently untangles a cart from the mess of wire and wheels. "This is very Zen, you know—healing through ordinary things, just the everyday habits of life. It's an act of worship. A little magic. Not to let any one event take over your life, you know. You can go ahead to the produce aisle—I'll be there in a sec."

Katie interprets this as a command. She walks toward the produce aisle, feeling completely alone. She stares at the floor so she won't step on any cracks by mistake. A cold draft strikes her back, sending shivers under her tank top. She feels like an invader from the summer outdoors as she glances at the produce aisle. The fluorescent lights wash the vegetables to harshness. The vegetables themselves lie stiffly in their trays like corpses, toe tags beneath listing prices. $3.99/lb, 1.99/lb, all odd, number patterns that aren't safe—Katie rounds off in her head. Four dollars. Two dollars. Selling produce is like selling the dead, Katie thinks, and her arm hairs quiver in the cold.

Katie knows she's imagining, but she can't stop. Her rituals are breaking down around her, and she doesn't know how to keep herself safe. She sees danger in every direction, threat and danger and death as the lines knot around her. Here she passes the long-bodied cucumbers in their crypt, cool and oblivious to the passage of time. Here are onions, mummified in their mesh bags, shedding skin-like testaments on the floor. White bean sprouts are maggots swarming under the yellow light. Katie stops at the grimy brown potatoes, rough with earth, speckled with eyes. She needs eight potatoes, eight to ward them off, eight to be safe. She takes a plastic bag and reaches for a potato. Thousands of eyes watch her without blinking. If she takes one potato, she has to take them all. Katie pulls her hand back and drops the bag. She's trying to count to eight, but the price tags confuse her. She's trying to hum Bach but she can't remember how it goes. A scream rises up in her and is swallowed before it flies free. She must not tell, she must not show fear, she must keep her silence.

And suddenly Jay is saying, "How many potatoes do you need, hon?" He's picking up potatoes and they're just potatoes, nothing more, she's safe, Jay's here.

"Eight," she whispers.

He glances at her face, and nearly drops the bag. "God, Katie, you look like a ghost. Oh, Katie, hon." He sets down the potatoes and hugs her. He's warm and gentle against her. His body heat is a white flame forcing the gray lines to pattern. "I didn't know how bad it was. I thought you hated Vick. She was so cruel to you."

Katie can't say the real problem, can't speak of her secret. "I miss her anyway," she whispers. She's told Jay all the mean things Vick has said to her, but she hasn't told him the joys. This is why Jay thinks Vick hurts her, Katie tells herself.

"Do you just want to go home and talk?" he asks.

Katie looks in his eyes. A lock of hair has escaped his short ponytail and hides the left side of his face. "Let's get some groceries, and then go back," she says. "Healing through ordinary moments, daily habits. That's what you said. Magic."

And this is the closest she has come to telling Jay of her rituals. Tuesday night groceries is now a ritual. Katie notes it to herself. She's never counted rituals, she realizes, and decides she should start. She must have an even number at all times.

Katie once read about OCD when she was in college, the semester she dropped out of school. She'd taken Intro to Psych as a filler course, around her advanced mathematics and classical voice lessons. She read with interest about people who wash their hands over and over, and who must lock and unlock their doors three times in a row before they leave their house.

Katie remembers this now, as Jay drives her home, and wonders again how this relates to her rituals. Clearly it is not the same thing—Katie likes dirt, and gardens, and rows of symmetrical flowers. She doesn't need cleanness. And why would anyone lock and unlock a door several times before using it? That would be inefficient, since the door's already unlocked the first time. These are patterns that disturb people's lives and prevent them from living peacefully.

But a glass of water—a person must drink it anyway, so why not hear the music in patterns of eight? Her rituals aren't hurting her life. If she drinks water in patterns of eight, how does that hurt her? If she's careful to stand on the bathmat when the toilet finishes flushing, she can't be hurt—unless perhaps there's a fire in the building. But Katie is smart. She'd leave a burning house. The rituals are not mandatory, not compulsive, which is why Katie knows she doesn't have a problem. No one else can see them, or even know she is performing them. They're magic to keep her safe.

Jay pulls into her parking spot—Vick's spot, Katie only has a bicycle—and kills the engine. "I'll bring the groceries in," he says. "You go unlock the door." It's dark now, and Katie must perform a ritual to enter her house. Darkness requires special rituals, especially since she forgot to turn on the porch light before she left. Katie starts by pulling out the three keys to her door—color-coded in rainbow order, red-yellow-blue—and touches each key in her hand, in order. Then she glances left, to the large shrubbery, where a rapist may hide. She unlocks the three locks—door knob, deadbolt, deadbolt—and swiftly steps inside, right foot first. She turns on the kitchen light and pours a glass of water to complete the ritual. One, two, three, four (breath) five, six, seven, eight. Katie relaxes. She's safe. And Jay's here.

Jay enters with groceries in his arms. A loaf of wheat bread topples out of a bag. Katie catches it. Jay says, "I'll put these away. Man, it's hot in here. You should open a window."

Katie doesn't open windows. There are no screens, and she's on the ground floor of the building. She sets the bread down and says, "Thanks for giving me a ride to the store."

"My pleasure," says Jay. "Do you still want to talk?"

"No," she says. "I just want to go to bed."

Jay regards her sadly. "All right," he says. "Do you want anything? I could stay here if you'd feel safer. I could crash on the couch out here. I don't have to work tomorrow."

Katie doesn't know if there is a place for Jay in the rituals. But she fears the worst if he doesn't stay. Vick might come and kill her. The rapists might finally find their way in.

"I'd like that," she whispers.

Jay's quick to say, "If you need anything, I'll be out here. I won't bother you—I'll just be here if you want to talk. I came here straight from class, so I've got a change of clothes in my gym bag. You go get your pajamas on. I'll put the groceries away. Frozen stuff, you know."

Katie slips into the bedroom, and shuts the door. She hears Jay rummage around in the kitchen. She sits on the bed and removes her sandals (first left, then right). She unbuttons her tank top (from the bottom up), and tosses it in the laundry basket. She notices Vick left clothes in the laundry, which means she'll be back. Katie unhooks her bra (bottom hook first) and tosses it onto the tank top. Bare-breasted, in jeans, she reaches for her pajama top and pulls it over her head. Her feet don't touch the ground as she undresses.

She emerges from her room and enters the kitchen. Jay glances up. He kneels in front of the crisper in the fridge, his hands full of vegetables. He puts the carrots in the drawer and closes it. "Do you always wear jeans to bed?" he asks.

"Yes," she says. She's lying. This ritual is for when anyone new is sleeping in her home. She discovered it when she was nine and her uncle stayed with the family. That was the last time she ever wore a nightgown.

Jay says, "That's really weird. Why?"

"I just do."

Jay looks like he wants to ask her about it, but he doesn't. Katie is glad.

Katie dreams of gray lines in motion. They thread in and out of her vision until she can no longer tell where they are. They transform from the straight lines of musical bars into a gray fog that seeps through her ritual walls. Katie counts to eight, but her wall is already compromised. These are new dangers, ones she cannot predict, ones she cannot stop.

The fog condenses back into millions of lines tied in complex knots. She can't see a pattern. Ani purrs in her lap and then leaps away, scratching Katie's thigh. Ani runs along a gray line until she vanishes. As Katie reaches for her, Vick appears and levels a gun at Katie. Katie leaps up and runs away to a grocery store. The doors won't open, so she presses her face against the glass. Inside, Jay is practicing taekwondo. He repeats the same patterns of movement so his body will remember them. Katie bashes her fists on the door. "Jay! Please, Jay!" The gray lines bind her wrists and ankles to the door.

He glances at her and smiles. "Ordinary things, Katie," he calls through the glass. He picks up his gym bag and leaves out the back. Katie presses against the door. She looks over her shoulder and sees Vick running towards her. All the lines of danger point to Katie. She pounds and pounds but the door won't open.

Katie sits up in bed. Her room is a tangled maze with no solution. She's screaming inside but there's no sound, she's quiet, all quiet. Katie knows she'll die soon. She'll die before she's thirty-two. She knows this. The rituals are breaking down. She can't defend against so many onslaughts, so many assaults.

She checks the clock. 2:44AM. This is a safe time, this is a good time to touch the floor. She sets her bare feet on the floor and stands shakily. Her legs collapse under her and she falls. Katie cries out as her cheek strikes hardwood. She lies on the floor sobbing. Her door's opening, *oh God*, her door's opening—

The light comes on. "Katie?" Jay says. His voice shakes. He touches her shoulder.

"Don't touch me!" Katie shouts, lifting herself on one elbow. She scrambles onto the bed and dives under the covers. The sheets still smell like Vick. She fears she's pushed away Jay, her safety, her only safety. The sheets are wet with her sweat, and she curls in the heated indentation made by her body.

"Katie, what is it? You're scaring me. Talk to me, hon." The bed sinks as he sits next to her, on Vick's side.

She stays in her burrow. Katie's music is broken, in discord. Her numbers fall away from her like shed hairs from a cat. The gray lines ensnare her like bars. All that's left is Jay. She blurts out, "Why am I scared of everything?"

Jay's voice comes to her, soft and soothing. "I'm scared too, hon. Everyone is. We just get through it by doing ordinary things, just keeping the daily patterns going. Simple things, like making dinner or going for a walk. Can I see your face? Would you come out from under there and talk to me?"

He speaks as if she's six, but Katie understands that he means it kindly. "My patterns are broken," she says. She wants to tell Jay what's wrong, what's really wrong, but she isn't sure she understands what that is. Katie is sure Jay would understand. He understands everything. But she's silent, hidden under the covers.

"I'd like to give you a hug," he says. "If you'd like one."

Katie's breath is raspy, under the covers. She's in a hot crypt, mummified by her own body heat. Death isn't cold—it's burning. "I'm so scared."

"You're safe here," says Jay. "Please come out. Talk to me."

Because it's Jay, Katie obeys. She slowly rolls over, tangling the covers with her efforts. Eventually she escapes the blankets, and looks up at him. He's watching her, his body relaxed and ready. Katie whispers, "Yeah, I'd like a hug." Jay leans forward, and Katie lifts herself into his arms. He strokes her hair and gently scratches his nails into her back. Katie is soothed, and she counts his movements. He moves his hand up and down, over her back, and Katie loses count. She cries on his shoulder. Jay's narrow shoulders are taut with muscle.

"It'll be okay," Jay soothes, rocking her gently in his arms. "You're safe, Katie, you're safe."

Katie understands then what she has missed all this time. She loves Jay, loves the flip of his hair, loves his strong shoulders. And Jay loves her too, she sees it through everyday actions, ordinary things—the healing of rituals. Jay is her new ritual, keeping her safe, keeping her strong. He's stronger than numbers, stronger than terror. Katie tilts her head back and looks in his eyes. Jay glows with a soft white light, and all the lines shape themselves around him, aligned in magnetic fields.

Katie reaches for safety in the best way she knows how: she wraps her arms around Jay and kisses him, deeply, drawing him closer to her. She leaps into the unknown, but knows she's safe, here with Jay in her arms. Jay is startled, but after a moment he kisses her back, hugging her tighter than ever. Katie knows what she needs now, to complete this ritual, to keep Jay close to her. There are rules she must follow, and then he will stay. She must pull Jay onto the bed with her, so that his feet don't touch the floor—done—and roll on top of him while still kissing him—done—and straddle his hips while she takes his shirt off—

But he pulls away, pushes her off, rolls out from under her. Then he's off the bed, looking down at her though she still reaches towards him. Jay is frightened, so frightened, she sees it now, she has never seen him frightened before. She has lost her ottoman, she has no Bach, she has forgotten all her numbers, and now Jay is afraid.

He backs away, shaking his head. "Oh, Katie, no. No. I—" he stops. Jay swallows, and folds his arms. "Katie, you're my best friend, and you're so attractive, but no, we can't—"

Katie drops her arms to her sides. She's kneeling on the bed before him. "Please, Jay, I'm sorry. I thought—I was wrong—"

"You're so wonderful, Katie, but we can't. I wish it would work, but it won't. It just won't. I can't do this. I—I'm leaving."

"Please stay."

"No, I mean—I was going to tell you, but you were so upset about Vick—I got the award."

Katie's heart freezes. "So—"

"I'm going to Korea. It's a huge opportunity, Katie, I can't pass it up." He is leaning against the wall, looking down at her. "It won't work. I'm sorry, hon."

Katie stares at the wall. She hears: I don't feel that way about you, but it's easier to say it's Korea. She doesn't respond.

Jay shifts his feet. "Katie, I'm sorry. I find you so attractive, but—I don't think it's really me you want anyway. I think you'll see that, when I'm gone. You've made me into someone I'm not. You want ... something. More than I am. I don't know quite what you're looking for, but I can't save you."

Katie stares at the wall. Everything has been taken from her. Jay is uncomfortable. He says, "This is all so weird. I'm sorry. I'll just go home. I'll call you tomorrow, okay?"

Katie doesn't respond. Jay tucks his shirt into his pants, where Katie has pulled it free. "Katie, please. Please don't get this way. Don't make this harder than it has to be." Katie is unsure whether he means for himself, or for her. Jay picks up his bag, walks to the front door and says, "You may want to lock this behind me."

He leaves, and the apartment is empty. Just Katie. She doesn't lock the door. There's no point.

Katie stares at the clock. Each minute burns her eyes in flaming red numbers, glowing in the dark bedroom. 4:42. 4:43. In her imagination the numbers catch fire, the clock catches fire, the apartment burns down and she remains in her bed.

She thinks of Jay. Jay said she'd see that it wasn't him, wasn't him at all. Katie does see. She knows now that she never loved Jay except as a friend. But he was safe. He was the only thing left.

Katie rolls onto her back as the clock marks 4:44. A time she once loved, for its symmetry and fours. She is remembering Jay in the weight room, Jay in the coffee shop, Jay in the grocery store picking up potatoes.

She stares at the ceiling, hugging a pillow to her chest. It's dark in the room, but she knows there's a stain on her ceiling like a demon. Every night she wards against the demon, fearing it will drop from the ceiling on her face, and suffocate her at night. "I hate you," she says, and throws the pillow. It strikes the ceiling and falls back on her face, knocking her breath away. *Ordinary things*, she thinks. It's not drinking the water eight times, but drinking the water at all. That's the ritual. Magic.

Katie gets out of bed and walks to the kitchen in the dark. She flips the light switch, and the fluorescent flickers on. Katie pours herself a glass of water, and drinks it slowly. One, two, three, four, five, six, seven. She pauses. She sloshes the water remaining in the glass, watching it swirl. It seems wasteful to leave it. She lifts the cup to her lips. Eight. She is shielded. She's standing on the kitchen rug, drinking the water, and feels better already. Katie misses Jay, but she's changing her rituals. This is a step. Perhaps someday she'll find peace in ordinary things.

Double Time

by John Chu

Skaters in black practice outfits swerved around Shelly. Her music was playing over the PA system. She had right of way. A scattering of figure skating fans sat in the rink's hard, blue, plastic seats. Even to a practice session, some had brought their flags. Her mom sat near the boards and waved her US flag as though if only it had shook more fiercely last night, Shelly would have landed her triple Lutz-triple toe jump combination in the short program.

The arena twinkled. Flashes of gold shimmered into fans sitting near to their slightly younger selves. Apparently, something would happen in the next few minutes they wanted to jump back in time to see again. The Shelly who had just finished this practice skate stood by the boards with Mr. Song watching the current Shelly skate. She ignored all of that. If she didn't wrestle her attention back onto the ice, she'd miss the combination again. No one wanted that, least of all her mom. She set her mind back onto mustering as much technical excellence and expression into her free skate as possible. She was still jet-lagged.

Her music ended and the announcer called out the program length. Three minutes and fifty-nine seconds. In a competition, much longer than four minutes and she'd be assessed a time penalty. In a practice session, much longer than four minutes and the start of her practice skate would be too far in the past to jump back to watch. Mom insisted that Shelly witness her run throughs because video never gave a good sense of a skater's sense of speed or ice coverage and because Shelly never remembered what she'd actually done on the ice. Of course, seeing yourself skating live and in person wasn't even remotely creepy. Unfortunately, Mr. Song didn't see any harm. Shelly skated to the boards, ignored the four-minute-older version of her rushing back onto the ice, then squeezed the time jumper latched to her wrist. Its digital display started counting down from four and a half minutes.

The world flashed gold. It spun in one direction. Her stomach spun in the other. Mr. Song and the rest of the rink shimmered into being. He nodded then handed Shelly her blade guards. As she put them on, her name blasted over the PA system as the next to skate. Mr. Song and Shelly settled by the boards to watch her slightly younger self skate to the middle of the rink then strike the same opening pose as Michelle Kwan had in her iconic 1998 free skate to the same music, "Lyra Angelica." Shelly was just relieved

Mom hadn't insisted that she simply ape Michelle Kwan move for move. Free skate requirements had changed too much since then.

"I shouldn't be here." Shelly winced at her opening triple Lutz. "I'm not even supposed to be a Senior yet."

She was because, last season, Mom had made Shelly take her Senior-level test behind Mr. Song's back. When he found out, he wasn't angry. Mr. Song was never angry. He merely pointed out in his own wry way that Shelly had her work cut out for her. She had placed a miraculous sixth at Nationals and now here she was starting this season with a bye out of Regionals so that she could compete against the best figure skaters on the planet instead. Because that wouldn't lead to utter and all consuming humiliation. No, not at all.

"Don't worry about tonight's free skate. You'll do fine." Mr. Song folded his arms across his chest. "It's your first Senior international competition. Even your mom should understand you're not expected to do well. I mean, Michelle Kwan's first in 1993, she placed sixth after the short program and ended up seventh overall out of eight."

"Mom doesn't do pre-1995 or post-2000 Kwan." Shelly slumped, leaning into the boards. "As far as she's concerned, Michelle Kwan never placed lower than second in any competition."

"I'm sure she has a better—Hey, that's interesting." Mr. Song had a penchant for understatement. He pointed out Tatiana Mishina, both of them, spinning side-by-side on the ice. "She's going to do it."

The latest rule changes had just come into effect. All summer long, the rumor had been that the European and World gold medalist would time jump from the end of her free skate back to the start to skate the whole thing with herself in unison. Done wrong, the penalties would take her off the podium, possibly out of the top ten. Done right and well, the bonus points she'd rack up could make her unbeatable.

Dread slithered through Shelly's body. It coiled around her heart and lungs then squeezed. Tatiana had just landed a flawless side-by-side triple Lutz-triple toe combination earning Mom's rapt attention. Usually, Mom was busy scribbling down Shelly's mistakes. Right now, though, the gleam of the brilliant idea in Mom's mind was as impossible to miss as the flashes of gold popping across the arena as fans jumped back in time.

"Maybe Tatiana's just trying to psych out her competitors?"

Mr. Song looked at Shelly with the same incomprehension he did when Mom spoke in Mandarin too quickly. As though each sound made sense by itself, but not in sequence. Like Shelly, he was sort of fluent enough.

"Do *you* like going into double time?"

Just thinking about it made Shelly woozy. Besides, the amount of time you jumped back had to be made up with jumps forward. Lots of people did that at night just before going to sleep, but all those chunks of time added up. Between school work and practice, she got little enough sleep as it was.

"We can convince Mom that I'm not good enough to time jump back—"

"Actually, skating just the last two minutes in double time isn't a bad idea. You already train clean double run throughs—"

"But, Mr. Song—"

"Shelly, this is this future. Next season, all the elite skaters will do some part or all of their free skates in double time. We can train it and try it out at Sectionals. Even if it's a disaster, you'll still place well enough to qualify for Nationals."

Her music ended. The Shelly on the ice started skating for the boards.

"Can't talk about it now. I'm coming here. Meeting me would be way too awkward."

Shelly threw off her blade guards. She rushed back onto the ice, ignoring her four-minute-younger self.

By the time the Zambonis rolled onto the ice, Shelly had finished seventh like her namesake, Michelle Kwan, also had her first time out. A whole two skaters had placed behind her. However, while Mom wanted Shelly to skate like Michelle Kwan, this was not what Mom had in mind. Mom didn't share Shelly's relief at not placing last. For days afterwards, as Mom drove them to and from Shelly's three daily practices, silence hung in the car like the heavy air before a storm.

The car's headlights barely lit the empty street and Shelly's flashlight barely lit her AP Chemistry textbook. She was oddly grateful for the quiet. Not acing her chemistry exam would have made Mom about as happy as coming in seventh. The exam would have been easier had Mom allowed her to take regular chemistry first. She squeezed in classes between practices. Half days of school had its advantages, actually. No one really had the chance to call her a "ho" any more. Yes, it was her last name, sort of, but really? The name-calling had gotten old long before high school.

"Shelly, Mr. Song and I have had a talk."

Shelly sank into her seat. She'd hoped skating in unison with herself would be simple. A week where the two hers spun out of sync, didn't land jumps at the same time, not to mention didn't hit their end poses at the same time had changed her mind. Her unison had improved since but it couldn't possibly be perfect enough for Mom yet.

"Mom." Her ribcage seemed to shrink, squeezing the air from her lungs. "Isn't getting one international assignment this season good enough? Besides, Mr. Song said I don't need to skate in double time to win Sectionals."

"何穎珊." Shelly's full name. The only thing worse would be if Mom continued speaking in Mandarin. "Your father and I did not come to this country so that our eventual child could be merely good enough at anything. In any case, you won't be competing at Sectionals."

"I won't?" Shelly refused to get her hopes up. No way that Mom had decided Shelly didn't need to skate anymore. Figure skating was an expensive sport. Mom and Dad had already given up so much for her.

"No, the USFSA has given you a bye through to Nationals. You'll be taking Emily Takahashi's remaining Grand Prix assignment next week."

Emily had suffered a stress fracture a month or so ago during her first Grand Prix competition of the season. The reigning US National gold medalist, Four Continents gold medalist, and World silver medalist had expected to recover in time for her second Grand Prix. Apparently not.

"Oh." Panic forced the air out of Shelly. "And I'll be skating in double time during my free skate?"

"Of course." Mom signaled her turn into the rink's parking lot. "I expect you to win this."

Shelly knew better than to argue with Mom. She slipped her textbook into her backpack. Skaters who might make the podium at Worlds skated the Grand Prix series. So much for a tune-up event to test skating in double time.

The opening notes of Shelly's free skate filled the rink. She slid over the ice in quick, elegant arcs. Tonight, the music's ethereal joy washed over her as her heart pounded through her chest. She'd nailed her triple Lutz-triple toe combination in the short program and was in second place entering the free skate by a healthy margin. Against some of the world's best, if she delivered the skate she'd been practicing for the past month, she might end up third overall. She'd stand on the podium at a Grand Prix competition. And, finally, Mom would be proud of her.

That joy lasted until her first jumping pass. She two-footed the landing of her triple Lutz, then squeaked out only a single toe loop in combination. Her jumps went downhill from there. She rolled through her falls determined that they wouldn't disrupt the choreography or flow of her program.

In the second half, she singled her second triple Lutz in more ways than one. Her future self was late or maybe her present self was rushing ahead of the music. Only one of her was on the ice to attempt the jump when she popped it, turning only one revolution in the air before landing.

Shelly's slightly older self showed up just in time for the side-by-side triple loop. Older Shelly landed a triple. Younger Shelly landed a double instead. Even with the bonus for elements completed in the second half of the program, she was hemorrhaging points.

Her lungs burned. Her body stung from the falls. The ice felt like mud beneath her skates. She'd never been so relieved to reach the combination spin that ended her program. By the time the older Shelly hit her final pose and the younger Shelly jumped back into double time, she'd landed two clean triples out of seven including her final jump, the side-by-side triple Salchow.

She hadn't exactly covered herself in glory but figure skating audiences were always generous. Their applause thundered across the rink even when someone skated like a human Zamboni. Mom's disappointment pounded through her head though and she hadn't even gotten off the ice yet.

Flowers and product placements dotted the kiss and cry area. Shelly and Mr. Song sat on a bench waiting for her score. The backdrop showed mountains and a camera was trained on them capturing their reactions. Her humiliation had been and would continue to be broadcast worldwide. However, she refused to cry.

"Well, that was a learning experience." Mr. Song rubbed his hands together. "Day after tomorrow, once we're back home, we'll look at the footage and we'll try it again so we get it right for Nationals."

"Mom has to be so disappointed in me." Maybe Shelly would cry after all.

"Don't start." Mr. Song crossed his arms over his chest. "You never gave up and you fought for every point. If the entire skate had been like those last thirty seconds, you'd be looking forward to your score right now. I'm sure your mom knows that."

Her score boomed over the PA system. She'd tumbled from second place to last overall. Skating in double time was stupid. Only two other skaters had attempted it here.

After that free skate, of course what Shelly wanted more than anything else in the world was to be strapped into the seat next to Mom's on the plane trip home. Mom sat by the aisle reading some engineering journal on her ereader. Shelly sat by the window staring at her tablet. Words gathered in dense blocks covered half the screen while a keyboard covered the other half. She'd rather have been sleeping but an analysis of the macaronic language in the works of James Joyce wouldn't write itself. Shelly kind of wished it would. Taking AP English early hadn't been her idea.

"I'm sorry, Mom." Avoiding the free skate from hell any longer would have just made it worse. "I'll do better at Nationals."

"It's okay. I haven't been reasonable." Mom reached for her bag sitting under the seat in front of her. She exchanged her ereader for an eye mask and neck pillow. "I was in grad school when I fell in love with Michelle Kwan's skating. When you were four and decided you wanted to skate, I was so happy, but skaters like her come once in a lifetime. I shouldn't have expected you to— You won't skate in double time any more. I'll talk to Mr. Song when we get home."

With that, Mom shut off her overhead light then went to sleep. The drone of engines covered up any other whispered conversations, isolating Shelly within her pool of light.

Tears welled in her eyes. Air wouldn't stay in her lungs and it was all she could do not to sob. She had never wanted to skate in double time and now she didn't have to. For once, Mom had relented. Shelly should have been relieved, so why did she feel so awful?

Shelly returned to her tablet. Her fingers tapped the keyboard while she blinked away her tears.

It had been at least a decade since Mr. Song skated competitively but, in skates, he always looked as though he could land quad Lutzes as a warm up. On the ice, Mr. Song might have been a student waiting for his coach rather than a coach waiting for his student. Only senior-level skaters trained this early in the morning and, as they warmed up on the ice, Shelly took her time lacing her skates.

Even if she had just come back from a competition, she couldn't blame how long she was taking on jet-lag. She was stalling and she knew it. Nationals was only six weeks away. This wasn't the time to argue with Mr. Song but life didn't seem to be timing itself for her convenience.

She skated towards Mr. Song. He spotted the time jumper on her wrist then smiled.

"Are you sure you want to do this?"

"You were the one who said skating the last two minutes in double time wasn't a bad idea."

A mock seriousness spread across his face. "Your mother is not someone to be defied."

"Which is why we're not telling her."

"We hadn't prepared nearly well enough before. It'll be tougher this time." He spread his hands, showing her his palms. "Lots of unison work in double time. Do you have time elsewhere in the day to lose? Your mom's not going to notice that you're suddenly nowhere to be found for minutes at a time whenever you jump ahead to compensate?"

"Sure, I've worked it all out." In truth, she had no clue. She'd take her chances to jump ahead as she found them.

"And triple run throughs." If she could skate for twelve minutes straight in practice, she could survive skating six in competition.

"I know."

"Well, let's get started then." Mr. Song grinned as he rubbed his hands and Shelly started cross-stroking around the rink.

The next six weeks lurched by like the stick shift that she couldn't drive. Between school, all that skating in double time and the sleep she wasn't getting, Shelly didn't have time to wonder if she was doing the right thing.

The less Shelly thought about her short program at Nationals the better. The judges had rather generously placed her sixth, about ten points behind a still recovering Emily Takahashi in first. For the free skate, Shelly had drawn last in the skate order. Her free skate seemed more like a formality they had to plow through than anything to do with deciding who would advance to either Four Continents or Worlds.

The crowd cheered as she skated to center ice. They gasped when a human-shaped flash of gold on the ice turned into Shelly's future self. Emily Takahashi had backed off skating her entire routine in double time to spare her healing toe, skating only the back half that way as Shelly had also planned. The time jumper on future Shelly's wrist counted down from just over four minutes. Future her had gone too far back in time. Years seemed to pass before the world stopped teetering for either of them.

The referee signaled a warning. If Shelly didn't start now, she'd be disqualified.

Future Shelly shrugged as if to say, "Well, nothing to do about it except to think of this as the second half of a double run through." Future Shelly should have known how this skate would go having already skated it with herself. Realistically, though, if she ever remembered how she skated, Mom wouldn't have made her watch her own practices. They struck their opening poses then the music started.

Michelle Kwan once said that to skate "Lyra Angelica" she just went onto the ice then thought of angels. Shelly, on the other hand, focused on one element at a time, ticking each off her mental list then pretending it never happened, especially if it hadn't gone perfectly.

The two Shellys skated as one, hitting every jump and spin in unison. They glided across the rink etching intricate patterns in swift arcs on the ice. Her lungs burned and her legs grew rubbery. For three minutes and fifty-nine seconds, she was the avenging angel. Her every edge and gesture was determined to prove that her short program was an aberration, that she could too skate. She refused to implode on the ice. Not again.

Finally, the two Shellys hit their final pose to the last beat of the music and the younger disappeared with a flash of gold into the past. She might have under-rotated her triple Salchow and skipped some steps in her footwork. The Technical Caller would sort that out via slow-motion video replay after her skate.

The audience exploded into generous, even for Nationals, applause. Flowers wrapped in cellophane, teddy bears, and other stuffed animals fell like thick hail on the ice. Tiny girls, ten years old at most, swarmed the rink collecting it all. Everyone in the audience appeared to be ... standing?

Shelly bowed. Every breath flayed her lungs and her legs felt like water. Getting to the kiss and cry felt as difficult as her eight minutes of skating. Relief that this horrible season was finally over pushed her off the ice.

It wouldn't be enough to please Mom, but she'd done the best she could. As far as Shelly was concerned, this skate meant more than any medal at Nationals. If she left the sport now, it'd be on a high note. Maybe she would quit. Now that her season was over, she'd have some time to think about it.

Mr. Song sat next to Shelly. He steepled his fingers, an amused expression on his face.

"You forgot to recalibrate your time jumper after this morning's practice session?" His amusement broke into a smile. "You realize now that the judges know what you're capable of, they're going to expect this every time."

"That's not funny." She'd look peeved at him except they were under the glare of a camera, waiting to catch her reaction to her score, if they ever got around to announcing it. "At least I'll never have to do that again."

"Excuse me?" Mr. Song stared up at a scoreboard that steadfastly refused to update with Shelly's scores. "Come Monday, we work on your short program and fine tune this free skate. We gave away a few points you'll need for Worlds."

Her scores boomed over the PA system and scrolled onto the scoreboard. They were too high. She'd won the free skate, beating Emily Takahashi by just under ten points, and placed second overall with no one left to skate. If she'd only fully rotated that Salchow, she might have won the whole thing. The audience exploded into applause again.

Her hands covered her mouth in surprise. She stood and waved to the audience before sitting down again.

"How?" The inevitable fell on Shelly like a boulder. The USFSA was going to send her to both Four Continents and Worlds. So much for quitting.

"Well, you didn't win because you didn't quite fill the short program sized hole you'd dug for yourself." Mr. Song shrugged. "In any case, Ms. Takahashi will decline her inevitable Four Continents assignment. The USFSA will want her to fully heal so that she can skate her entire program in double time at Worlds. That means you, Shelly, are now America's best chance to defend its gold medal at Four Continents. Congratulations."

"Oh." The world lurched beneath her. She gripped her chair for support.

"You look so disappointed. Yes, we both know you could have won this, but placing second and being named to the Worlds team in your second season as a Senior is not a bad thing." Mr. Song gently patted Shelly's back. "Don't worry about your mom. She'll see that."

Winning this thing had been the last thing on Shelly's mind. And she'd given up on the notion of pleasing Mom.

A reporter came up to Shelly. Then another. And then another. Suddenly, everyone wanted to interview her. She found herself wishing that Mom would barge in to tell her what to say.

After the medal ceremony, Shelly jumped ahead to compensate for the double time during her free skate. It cost her only a moment to create four minutes when no one could find her. By the time she sneaked out of the rink, the crowd was breaking up. People were heading to the parking garage, to the subway, or to the shuttle back to the hotel. Lamps, benches and piles of snow lined the way. Sparks of gold twinkled in the distance undoubtedly from people time jumping back to catch the shuttle. Mom and Mr. Song sat on a bench scanning the crowd. Shelly hid herself in the stream heading down the path. Her silver medal still lay cold in her pocket. It ought to have a chance to warm up before she faced Mom. Not only had Shelly disobeyed her but she had done so in spectacular fashion and on national TV. If she'd won, she might have gotten away with it. Stupid triple Salchow.

“Shelly.” Mr. Song waved then jogged to her. Mom pushed against the tide of the shuttle-bound in the distance. “You don’t need to avoid your mom.”

“Um... I—”

“You know she’s so proud of you.” He smiled at the disbelief on her face. “Really, she was just saying—”

“何穎珊, don’t worry me like that. I’ve been looking for you everywhere.” Mom planted herself next to Mr. Song. “You skated your entire program in double time.”

“Yes, Mom.” Shelly stared at her feet. The time of reckoning for disobeying Mom had come.

“What has Mr. Song told you about your triple Salchow? You could have beat Emily Takahashi.” Mom paused to catch her breath. “He and I were just talking about the rest of this season and the next season. A gold at Four Continents is a given but Worlds—”

“Hey, that’s Emily.” Shelly pointed at a clump wearing thick, hooded coats. One of them might have been Emily. “I should go congratulate her.”

She ran off before Mom could say otherwise. Time was awasting if she wanted to check out what Mr. Song had said. The time jumper couldn’t take you back any further than about five minutes. She circled around to hide behind the pile of snow next to the bench where Mom and Mr. Song had talked, then squeezed the time jumper latched to her wrist.

Her gaze faded from gold into benches, lamps and piles of snow although the air still glittered with time jumping. Mr. Song sat on the bench. Mom paced around it, marking a ring of cement on the snow-dusted path. Shelly caught them in middle of small talk about the weather, Dad, and Mr. Song's boyfriend. Eventually, the conversation drifted to Worlds, Mom's plans for global domination of ladies' figure skating, and Shelly.

"I've known she was up to something for weeks. She can't hide her jumps forward in time as well as she thinks she can." Mom stopped pacing and her arms fell to her sides. "I couldn't be prouder of her. Even that first novice competition, she was so awful but she tried so hard. She's everything I could have asked for in a daughter."

Mom had never spoken those words to Shelly, ever. As Mom nattered on, Shelly's hand moved to the time jumper on her wrist, waiting for its display to count down to zero so she could jump back in time again. Even though she was now the favorite to win Four Continents, Mom's words to her were about her under-rotated triple Salchow and losing to Emily Takahashi. The only way she'd ever hear how proud Mom was of her again in person was to jump back in time before the moment slipped too far back for her time jumper to reach.

Shelly looked down the path. Another Shelly hid behind a street lamp, listening.

Welcome

by William Alexander

Antonio sailed to the moon.

His craft passed over the tidal bridge of two seas touching. Once monthly the moon and the world moved close enough together to scrape air and share water. Each time the two seas touched, Antonio sailed between them.

Once on the moon, he sailed from the sea to the marshland. Then he tied up his sail and paddled slowly. His whole body hurt. It always did. But here on the moon he hurt less.

The world filled up most of the sky. Antonio navigated through marshy byways in the dark. He knew the way by memory and by the constellations of city lights above him, bright on the surface of the world. He refused to turn on any lights of his own. The Coast Guard didn't bother to patrol much these days, but Antonio still smuggled by the rules.

Lucía sat waiting on the long wooden dock behind Abuela's house. She dangled bare feet over the side, even though she knew she shouldn't. Gators could leap high above the waterline in lunar gravity.

"You're late," she said, annoyed but not worried. She never worried about him. Lucía was ten years old, and Antonio seventeen. A brother so much older was invincible to her, above all harm—but not above reproach.

"Got lost in the marsh," he told her as he tossed the first line.

She tied the line to a docking cleat. "You don't ever get lost." It wasn't a compliment the way she said that. It was just a given, and another rebuke for being late. "Lala is up and waiting."

Antonio untied the tarp that covered up his cargo—boxes of plastic-wrapped letters and double-wrapped cigars. Then he tied it all back down. "I'll unload later," he said.

"Obviously." Lucía looked up at the sky. "We've had nothing but night crossings all year," she complained. "I'd like to actually see the bridge sometime."

"It should last until a little after dawn," Antonio told her. "We'll watch it collapse. If we can stay awake that long."

"We will," she said. "No choice there. Lala's up and wants to talk." She turned on her flashlight and bounded away, up the trail from the hidden pier.

Antonio knew he should scold her about the flashlight. He knew he should teach her how to smuggle by the rules. But he didn't bother.

He followed slowly. He needed to acclimate to weighing less than he had yesterday, down on the world, and he needed to get used to hurting less. Every part of him hurt, always, but here that hurt seemed further away. His pain was an argument between other people, overheard but not shared. His pain was a violent movie on TV playing somewhere else in the house. His pain was information that he didn't need to pay attention to, highway signs that he didn't have to look at because he wasn't lost and never got lost. His pain wasn't so painful on the moon.

The kitchen smelled just like it usually did. One breath buried all the time he'd been away.

"Abuela," he said.

"Gordo," she called him, took both of his hands, and kissed both of his cheeks. It may have looked affectionate, but to Antonio it felt just as formal and disciplined as a military salute.

She poured him coffee from the stovetop espresso-pot into a tiny mug already half-full of sugar. He took it, sat, and sighed—half-content and half-annoyed. He already knew that he wouldn't be sleeping tonight, but even knowing that he had still hoped for sleep.

Abuela noticed his annoyance, of course. She missed nothing. She could sense the mood swings of mosquitoes.

"Almost dawn, Gordito. And you know the best way to get over bridge-lag is to suck it up, put off napping and just act like you've always been here. Your body should obey the local clocks. I always did. I never napped after a crossing."

They spoke Spanish. Abuela happily let all other languages atrophy inside her head now that most of the moon spoke Spanish. These days she needed no language but her own.

He took his small cup, pulled up a counter stool, and sat. It hurt. He held his breath until the shouting inside him faded back to background noise. Then he sipped his coffee. He didn't mind the strength. He did mind the sweetness, but didn't complain about it. This was what the word "coffee" meant in Abuela's kitchen: a tiny cup half-full of sugar sludge.

Lucía tried to pull up her own stool, but Abuela shook her head. "Back to bed with you, Gordita."

"Lala, it's practically morning!" Lucía complained.

Abuela didn't repeat herself. She never did. She never had to.

Lucía stomped up the stairs hard enough to skip most of them.

Abuela poured herself her own hourly cup. "Tell me about home." She said that with pain in her voice, and she savored the pain. It was sweet to her, somehow.

Antonio told her how bad it was down in the world, because that was what she wanted to hear. He told her about the tiny rations, about the un-secret boasting of secret police, about peeling paint and rusting cars, about her favorite musicians playing outdoors for pennies beside deaf old men hunched over domino games. He told her that the storms were getting worse.

All of it was true, or true enough. It was the sort of truth she wanted, the wound she needed to poke. Abuela wanted to know that the world she missed was worse off since she'd left it, exiled.

She needed to know that the revolutionaries were in every single way inept at governing what they had taken. Maybe that was true. Regardless, Antonio knew his duty and helped her make it true.

She listened. She sighed several times. She shook her head, aggrieved and satisfied.

"There's some talk of lifting the embargo," Antonio said after he told her about the storms. He sipped coffee slowly to give himself something to do besides look at her face.

Abuela slapped the counter top. "Never," she promised. "Not while I'm alive."

"Yes, Abuela," Antonio said, as though this made sense to him. It didn't. Abuela had spent two thirds of her life breaking the embargo. She had been the first to sail the bridge, and she still stood first among smugglers now that Antonio had inherited the actual sailing. Every envelope of cash, every letter between exile-split families, and every single cell phone came through her. But she would make sure the law they broke stood firm for as long as she lived.

"Don't you just humor me," she told him, her voice soft, sad, and savoring its sadness. "We were betrayed. The moon will not do business with the world. Not while I live. But the families we left behind still need our support."

"Yes, Abuela," he said once more, with feeling.

She watched him for one long and uncomfortable moment, deciding something. He shifted in his chair and then held his breath until his spine stopped shouting from the shift.

Abuela tapped the counter, finally. "That was your last crossing. Oscar will take the sails from now on."

The shouting inside Antonio ceased to be background noise. He couldn't concentrate well enough to turn the volume down.

"No." He didn't mean to argue with her. He meant to negate what she had said, to insist she'd never said it. And she never repeated herself, so she didn't bother to say it again.

"You hurt too much," she said. "That happens, sometimes. I've seen it happen before. The world is heavy. It weighs you down if you were not born there. You should have been born there. But now you can't go back. You'll always hurt if this goes on for much longer."

Too late already, Antonio thought.

"I'm still a better sailor than Oscar," he said out loud.

"You're better than anyone," she assured him, proudly. She claimed most of the credit for that. "But here you'll stay. Join your Tío's campaign staff. We need him elected here. We need him to uphold the embargo."

"The one that we break every month."

"Yes. Good night, Gordo."

"It's almost morning."

She didn't bother to answer or argue. Instead she dropped empty mugs in the sink. They floated down with a soft clatter. Then Abuela left the kitchen.

Antonio went back outside.

He sat in the grass, too distracted to keep the pain volume turned down. He hurt almost as much as he did in the world.

Lucía climbed through her bedroom window and joined him.

"What's with you?" she asked in English.

"Lala wants me to do something other than the single thing I'm good at," he told her. "She's giving the bridge run to Oscar."

Lucía sat in the grass beside him. "That's stupid."

He agreed.

Sunlight peered around the edge of the world to find the moon hiding behind it. Then it touched the bridge.

Antonio held his breath, and not for the usual reasons. He hadn't seen the bridge daylit in several months.

"How much longer will it last?" Lucía whispered.

"Another hour or two, maybe."

"I'll sail it someday," she announced, certain.

"I know," he told her. "But I should be the one to teach you how. Not Oscar. He'll just try to impress you. And he'll be mad when you turn out to be better than he'll ever be."

Lucía hugged her knees in the early morning cold. "I'll just pretend he's better until I get the run all to myself."

Antonio shook his head. "You'll never inherit the run that way. Besides, there's no pretending on the bridge. There's never any fooling the bridge."

A shooting star streaked overhead. Antonio waved at it. "Welcome home," he said.

"What was that?" Lucía asked.

"Ghost ship. Probably someone who tried to fool the bridge. They fell off between here and the world. They drift in decaying orbits until they finally fall home again, spreading their own ashes. That's why the Navy doesn't bother to patrol it anymore. Most who try the bridge come home burning."

"How do you know which side was home to them?" Lucía asked.

"I don't think they care anymore," he said. He hadn't meant to sound so bitter. "Either side will do."

Dawn illuminated the full length of the bridge. They watched waves swirl across it like a spiral staircase.

"Tell me about the world," Lucía asked.

He told her everything good about the place, because that was what she wanted to hear. He told her about the food. He told her about the music on street corners. He told her about beautifully rusted cars that ran on light and vegetable oil, which made the pavement smell deliciously fried. Then he told her more about the food.

She listened. "How's the pain?" she asked when he was done.

"What do you mean?"

"I've heard that the world doesn't like lunar people. Or it likes us too much, and holds us too tight."

"We're not lunar," he said, automatically channeling Abuela's distain.

"Sure we are. Both born here. And I've never even been down there." She waved one hand at the world.

"We're exiles," Antonio said.

"Lala's the exile," Lucía insisted. "Not us. We're from here."

He shoved her shoulder. She floated away and then hopped

back. "I'm from there," he said, pointing. "Right there. You and I are both from the bridge." Then he started to say something else, but Lucía put one hand over his mouth.

Men with guns moved in shallow, cautious leaps across the lawn. They wore thick black vests. Four white letters on each vest spelled NAVY. They closed in on Abuela's house.

"Move," Antonio whispered. He took Lucía's hand and led them down the hidden trail to the hidden pier and the sailboat that was still his.

"We're running away?" she asked, indignant, as though they had the option to stay and fight.

"We're hiding the evidence," he whispered back at her. "We're keeping the cargo away from Abuela. They'll be watching the main pier, but they haven't found this one yet or they'd be here already. Cast off."

She untied the line from each cleat, shoved the boat away from the pier, and then made a long, running jump to land inside.

They both paddled hard.

"We need to get out beyond the marsh," he told her.

"Won't we get caught up in the spiral wind?" she asked.

"Yes."

Lucía stared at the sparking bridge water. It swirled up, all the way up, until up became down. "But nobody's ever crossed the same bridge twice."

Antonio hoisted sail. "Not until now. This right here will be the very first time."

She grinned at him, a wild and crazy grin. "You'll be famous!"

"Nah," he said. "You're going to be the best and most famous bridge sailor in history, and they'll remember you for a hundred years after they've forgotten me. So pay attention. This is your first lesson."

They caught the spiraling exchange of air and sailed up onto the bridge.

The moon grew small behind them and the world grew large ahead.

Everything hurt. Everything shouted.

"Welcome home!" Antonio shouted along with everything else.

About the Authors

Tansy Rayner Roberts is the author of *Love and Romanpunk*, the Creature Court trilogy and *Ink Black Magic*. She won the Hugo Award for Best Fan Writer in 2013. You can find her blog at tansyrr.com and follow her on Twitter as @tansyrr.

Ken Liu (http://kenliu.name) is an author and translator of speculative fiction, as well as a lawyer and programmer. His fiction has appeared in *The Magazine of Fantasy & Science Fiction*, *Asimov's*, *Analog*, *Clarkesworld*, *Lightspeed*, and *Strange Horizons*, among other places. He is a winner of the Nebula, Hugo, and World Fantasy awards. He lives with his family near Boston, Massachusetts.

Ken's debut novel, *The Grace of Kings*, the first in a fantasy series, will be published by Saga Press, Simon & Schuster's new genre fiction imprint, in April 2015. Saga will also publish a collection of his short stories.

Sean Williams writes for children, young adults and adults. The author of over forty novels, ninety short stories and the odd odd poem, his work has won awards, debuted at #1 on the *New York Times* bestseller list, and been translated into numerous languages. His latest novel is *Twinmaker*, the first in a new series that takes his love affair with the matter transmitter to a whole new level.

Gabriela Lee has had her fiction and poetry published in the Philippines, Singapore, and the United States. She is currently an assistant professor at the English department of the University of the Philippines. You can find her online at about.me/gabrielalee

Jim C. Hines' latest novel is *Codex Born*, the second book in his series about magic-wielding librarian with a laser blaster, a motorcycle-riding dryad, and a spider who sets things on fire. He's also written the Princess series of fairy tale retellings and the humorous Goblin Quest trilogy, along with more than 40 published short stories. He's an active blogger, and won the 2012 Hugo Award for Best Fan Writer. You can find him online at www.jimchines.com

Alena McNamara grew up in Minnesota, where lakes are regular features of the landscape, and now inhabits Massachusetts (where they aren't). She's a graduate of the 2008 Odyssey Writing Workshop and Viable Paradise XV, has a B.A. in Physics, and works in a library next to a river. Find her at alenamcnamara.com for links to other stories and a pleasing variety of social media.

Faith Mudge is a Queensland writer with a passion for fantasy, folk tales and mythology from all over the world. Her stories feature in the anthologies *To Spin a Darker Stair*, *One Small Step*, *Dreaming of Djinn* and *The Year's Best Australian Fantasy & Horror 2012*. More of her work can be found at beyondthedreamline.wordpress.com

Tim Susman has published over a dozen novels and numerous short stories under various names, writing about fantastical creatures with human problems. He has researched both animal and human behavior and has worked as a database analyst, a project manager, and a product manager in the high tech world of Silicon Valley. Currently he lives with his husband in California and blogs at timsusman.wordpress.com.

E.C. Myers was assembled in the U.S. from Korean and German parts and raised by a single mother and a public library in Yonkers, New York. He is the author of the Andre Norton Award-winning young adult novel *Fair Coin* and its sequel, *Quantum Coin*, as well as numerous short stories in anthologies and magazines. You can find traces of him all over the internet, but especially at ecmyers.net and on Twitter: @ecmyers.

Dirk Flinthart is an Australian writer of speculative fiction who lives in Tasmania. Notable to date mostly for short stories, he is also the editor of the *Canterbury 2100* anthology, from Agog Press, and has the distinction of sharing a Ditmar award with Margo

Lanagan, which he is quite proud of. His first novel, *Path of Night* was published by FableCroft in 2013 and was nominated for an Aurealis Award for Best Horror Novel.

Karen Healey writes books and teaches high school, currently in Blenheim, New Zealand. That's where the good wine comes from.

Sofia Samatar is the author of the novel *A Stranger in Olondria*, winner of the 2014 Crawford Award. She has been nominated for the Hugo, Nebula, Campbell, Locus, and British Science Fiction Association Awards. Her short fiction, poetry and reviews have appeared in a number of places, including *Strange Horizons*, *Stone Telling*, and *Lightspeed*. She is a co-editor for *Interfictions: A Journal of Interstitial Arts*, and teaches literature and writing at California State University Channel Islands.

Sean Eads is a writer and librarian. He's originally from Kentucky, but now lives in Denver, Colorado. His first novel, *The Survivors* was a finalist for the 2013 Lambda Literary Award in the science fiction/fantasy category. His work has appeared in *Shock Totem*, *Waylines Magazine*, *Pseudopod*, *The Journal of Popular Culture*, and various other places. When he's not writing or answering reference questions, he tries to be on the golf course.

Amal El-Mohtar is the Nebula-nominated author of *The Honey Month*, a collection of poetry and very short fiction written to the taste of 28 different kinds of honey. She has twice won the Rhysling Award for Best Short Poem, once received the 2012 Richard Jefferies Society Poetry Prize, and is presently a finalist for the Dwarf Star and Aurora awards for poetry. Her short fiction has appeared in multiple venues online and in print, including *Apex*, *Strange Horizons*, *Lackington's*, *The Thackery T. Lambshead Cabinet of Curiosities*, and most recently in the special "Women Destroy Science Fiction" issue of *Lightspeed* magazine. She also edits *Goblin Fruit*, a web quarterly dedicated to fantastical poetry, with Caitlyn A. Paxson. Presently she lives in Glasgow with her fiancé and two jellicle cats, and has visited the Scottish Owl Centre in Polkemmet Country Park so many times she's begun to freak out the staff ("aren't you bored of us yet?" they ask, warily). Find her online at amalelmohtar.com or on Twitter @tithenai.

Shveta Thakrar is a writer of South Asian–flavored fantasy, social justice activist, and part-time nagini. She draws on her heritage, her experience growing up with two cultures, and her love of myth to spin stories about spider silk and shadows, magic and marauders, and courageous girls illuminated by dancing rainbow flames. When not writing, Shveta makes things out of glitter and paper and felt, devours books, daydreams, bakes sweet treats, travels, and occasionally even practices her harp.

Holly Kench is a writer and a feminist, with a classics degree and a fear of spiders. She lives in Tasmania, Australia, where a lack of sun provides ample opportunity for hiding indoors and writing off-kilter stories. Holly writes about her life as a stuffed olive on her blog *Confessions of a Stuffed Olive* and manages the website *Visibility Fiction*, promoting and publishing inclusive young adult fiction.

Garth Nix is an award-winning author of more than 25 novels and over 50 published short stories. His work has been translated into 40 languages and has appeared on the bestseller lists of *The New York Times*, *Publishers Weekly*, *The Times*, *The Australian* and *USA Today*. He lives in Sydney, Australia.

Vylar Kaftan has published over forty stories in such magazines as *Asimov's*, *Lightspeed*, and *Clarkesworld*. She won a 2013 Nebula Award for her novella, "The Weight of the Sunrise," an alternate history in which the Incan Empire survives into the 19th century. She lives in the San Francisco Bay Area, where she founded the science fiction convention FOGcon. She dreams in color.

John Chu designs microprocessors by day. He writes fiction, narrates for podcasts, and translates fiction from Chinese into English by night. His stories have been published or is forthcoming in *Boston Review*, *Asimov's Science Fiction*, and *Tor.com* among others. His story "The Water That Falls on You from Nowhere" has been nominated for the 2014 Hugo Award for Best Short Story.

William Alexander won the National Book Award in 2012 for his first novel, *Goblin Secrets*, and the Earphones Award for his narration of the audiobook. He has since written two more novels for Middle Grade audiences: *Ghoulish Song* and *Ambassador*. The latter is about Gabe Fuentes, a boy who becomes the ambassador of our planet just as his parents get deported from the country. Will studied theater and folklore at Oberlin College, English at the University of Vermont, and creative writing at the Clarion Workshop. He lives with his family in Minneapolis.

Alisa Krasnostein is editor and publisher at independent Twelfth Planet Press, a creative publishing PhD candidate and recently retired environmental engineer. She is also part of the thrice Hugo nominated Galactic Suburbia Podcast team. In 2011, she won the World Fantasy Award for her work at Twelfth Planet Press. She was the Executive Editor and founder of the review website Aussie Specfic in Focus! from 2004 to 2012. In her spare time she is a critic, reader, reviewer, podcaster, runner, environmentalist, knitter, quilter and puppy lover. And new mum.

Julia Rios is a Hugo nominated fiction editor at the online magazine, *Strange Horizons*, and is co-editor with Saira Ali of *In Other Words*, an anthology of poems and flash fiction by writers of color. When not editing, she writes, podcasts, and occasionally narrates audio stories and poems. She's half-Mexican, but her (fairly dreadful) French is better than her Spanish.

A Note From the Editors

In the winter of 2012, while she was doing errands in Western Australia, Alisa was listening to an episode of the Outer Alliance Podcast (which Julia hosts). It was a panel discussion about the lack of QUILTBAG characters in YA dystopian novels, and it made Alisa wish there were more YA stories with diverse characters. Later that day, she sent an e-mail proposing an anthology. Julia read the message on a hot summer day in Massachusetts, and so our time and season-crossing collaboration began.

We've always been interested in promoting diversity. Julia is a bisexual woman of color, and Alisa is a Jewish Australian feminist, so in some ways this is a purely selfish drive: we want to see ourselves reflected in the stories we read. But it's not limited to that; we also want everyone else to have the chance to see themselves, and we want to see stories about people who aren't like us.

Reading the submissions and editing the stories for this anthology has been a wonderful experience, and we hope you enjoyed reading it as much as we enjoyed making it. We'd love to make more books like this one in the future because there are so many more stories to tell.

Best,

Alisa Krasnostein and Julia Rios

Acknowledgements

This book would not be possible without the support of many people. We'd like to thank everyone who backed our Pozible fundraising campaign, especially Daniel Franklin, to whom this book is dedicated. Thanks also to everyone who helped us spread the word about why diverse books are important. Sunil Patel, Vylar Kaftan, John Chu, Guadalupe Garcia McCall, and Kyell Gold were kind enough to appear in our short videos about diversity, Thoraiya Dyer, Sue Isle, Shveta Thakrar, Fabio Fernandes, Sherwood Smith and Rachel Manija Brown wrote essays about the importance of diversity for the Kaleidoscope blog. Thanks also to Tansy and Alex of Galactic Suburbia, Sean Wright of Galactic Chat, John DeNardo of SF Signal, Shaun Duke of The Skiffy and Fanty Show, Tor.com, C.S.E. Cooney and John O'Neill of Black Gate, Tehani Wessely of Fablecroft Press, Timmi DuChamp of Aqueduct Press, and Holly Kench and Joyce Chng of Visibility Fiction.

Books are not made in vacuums. Behind the scenes we had invaluable help from Charles Tan, Elizabeth Disney, Terri Sellen, Amanda Rainey, Jonathan Strahan, and Garth Nix.

Finally, we could not have done this without the support of our families. Thanks to Jill Rios, Moss Collum, Chris Bobridge, Ruth and John Krasnostein, Daniel Bobridge, and Jenny and David Bobridge.

We'd like to thank our Pozible backers who include:

Niall Harrison
Georgina Coghlan
Simone Wilhelmy
Jess Bridges
Robert Hoge
Christina Le Galloudec
Alicia Cole
A H
Fran Wilde
Joey Shoji
Bryn Dickinson
David Cake
Krysta Chauncey-Allen
Kevin J. Maroney
Lynne M. Thomas
Rachael Acks
Jennifer Davis
Sarah Lee Parker
Mark Blevins
Stu Ash
Elise Matthesen
Samantha Rea
Ruth Turner
Stephen Dann
Mary Borsellino
Emma Wearmouth
Karen McKenna
Satima Flavell
Jessica White
Shiyiya
Moss Collum
Ben Peek
Deanne Fountaine
Erin Hoffman
Jess Liotta
Lisa Bolekaja
Greg Bossert
Laura Wilkinson
Joy Deborah Robinson
Marion Engelke
Joris Meijer
Kelly Lagor
Gretchen Treu
Emily Wagner
Deborah Green
Kirsty Sara
Daniel MacBride
Yukimi Ogawa
Deborah Kalin
Sidsel Pedersen
Tehani Wessely
Em
Rose Clarke
Mitenae
Ju Transcendancing
Jess I
Aviva Galaski
Zara Baxter
Jetse de Vries
Curt McNamara
Sally R.
Susan Loyal
Rob McMonigal
Carolyn Lamb
Fred Kiesche
Kate Gordon
Kirstie Olley
Scott Pohlenz
Jay Watson
Linda Sengsourinho
Suzanne The Librarian
Helen Stubbs
Joe Monti
Rudi Dornermann

Kari Sperring
Howard Copland
Victoria Hacker
Tania Reid
Fabio Fernandes
Christine Gordon
Keziah Dreaver
Laura Dean
Ariane Branch
Chris Bobridge
Caroline Mills
Sunil Patel
Ann Leckie
Lara Hopkins
Cory Day
Tsana Dolichva
Katharine Cooney
Jill Rios
Daniel Blum
Darcy Keller
Mindy Friend
Caitlyn Paxson
Delia Sherman
Anthony Phillips
B. Egli
Lisa Hannett
Jen White
Lenora Rose Patrick
Duncan Gilmour
Shaun Duke
Marianne de Pierres
Elizabeth Alpert
Todd Rowlands
Amanda Wrangles
Pam McMillin
Nicholas Whyte
Miriam Mulcahy
Mindy Johnson
Karin Landelius
Peter Hollo
Caitlin Nicoll
Rivqa Berger
Melina Dahms
Daniel Franklin
David Fiander
Catherine Schaff-Stump
Mirabai Knight-Lascoutx
Kate Heartfield
John Devenny
Alex Pierce
Shane Nixon
Joanna Kasper
David Annandale
Jess Lethbridge
Jack
Louise Williams
Claire Brialey and Mark Plummer
Sharyn November
Terri Sellen
Tansy Roberts
Catherine Macdonald
Elanor Matton-Johnson
Stephanie Gunn
Lisa Nohealani Morton
Laura E. Goodin
Catherine Green
Cliff Winnig
Mark Webb
Shannon Prickett
Ian Mond
Catriona Sparks
Nivair H. Gabriel
Jed Hartman
Catherine Davie
Cheryl Morgan
Julia Miriah Hetherington
Katharine Stubbs
Helen Merrick
David and Jenny Bobridge

The Company Articles Of Edward Teach

Thoraiya Dyer

Angælien Apocalypse

Matthew Chrulew

The Company Articles Of Edward Teach

Two teens thrown back in time, to another body, a different world.

Both raised in orthodox families - Layla, a Muslim, resenting the dominance of her father, the control others have over her life. Avi, Jewish, and railing against the future his mother has mapped out for him.

A chance encounter for wish fulfilment - both thrown into bodies in a different time and place.

Angaelien Apocalypse

Reports had come in as the revolution erupted: myriad rotating discs approached Earth at speed. Panic and joy spread around the planet in viral waves. Few needed any help to identify these flying objects. They were the angælic vehicles.

And at the helm of the lead saucer was the Man himself. Jesus Christ.

Bad Power

Deborah Biancotti

Hate superheroes? Yeah. They probably hate you, too.

'There are two kinds of people with lawyers on tap, Mr Grey. The powerful and the corrupt.'

'Thank you.'

'For implying you're powerful?'

'For imagining those are two different groups.'

From Crawford Award nominee Deborah Biancotti comes this sinister short story suite, a pocketbook police procedural set in a world where the victories are relative and the defeats are absolute. *Bad Power* celebrates the worst kind of powers both supernatural and otherwise, in the interlinked tales of five people—and how far they'll go.

If you like *Haven* and *Heroes*, you'll love Bad Power.

'These appetisingly wicked stories give you the perfect taste of Biancotti's talents.' — *Ann VanderMeer*

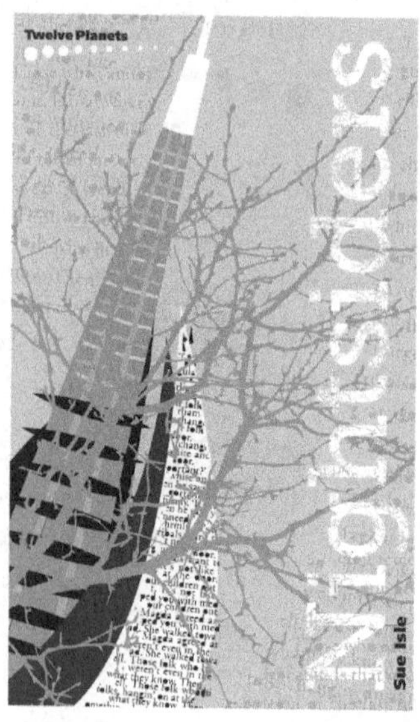

Nightsiders

Sue Isle

In a future world of extreme climate change, the western coast of Australia has been abandoned. A few thousand obstinate, independent souls cling to the southern towns and cities, living mostly by night to endure the fierce temperatures and creating a new culture in defiance of official expectations.

A teenage girl stolen from her family as a child, a troupe of street actors who affects the new with memories of the old, a boy born into the wrong body, and a teacher pushed into the role of guide, all tell the story of The Nightside.

'… [Isle's] writing is uniquely hers, direct and honest and crowned by a deft ear for dialogue.' – *Marianne de Pierres*

2012 Tiptree Long List Finalist

2012 Norma Hemming shortlist

Twelve Planets

Love and Romanpunk

Tansy Rayner Roberts

Thousands of years ago, Julia Agrippina wrote the true history of her family, the Caesars. The document was lost, or destroyed, almost immediately.

(It included more monsters than you might think.)

Hundreds of years ago, Fanny and Mary ran away from London with a debauched poet and his sister.

(If it was the poet you are thinking of, the story would have ended far more happily, and fewer people having their throats bitten out.)

Sometime in the near future, a community will live in a replica Roman city built in the Australian bush. It's a sight to behold.

(Shame about the manticores.)

Further in the future, the last man who guards the secret history of the world will discover that the past has a way of coming around to bite you.

(He didn't even know she had a thing for pointy teeth.)

History is not what you think it is.

THE CAFE LA FEMME SERIES

JOIN TABITHA DARLING FOR BOOK TWO OF THE CAFE LA FEMME SERIES

LIVIA DAY

DROWNED VANILLA

It's the beginning of a hot, hot summer in Hobart. Tabitha Darling is in love with the wrong man, and determined to perfect the art of ice cream.

Playing amateur detective again is definitely not on the cards—not even when her friends try to lure her into an arty film noir project in the historical town of Flynn.

But when a young woman goes missing from a house full of live webcams, and is found drowned in the lake outside Flynn, Tabitha is dragged into the whole mess— film crew, murder victim, love life and all.

There were two girls using the internet pseudonym French Vanilla, and only one is dead. So where is the other one? Why is everyone suddenly behaving like they're in a (quite specific) Raymond Chandler novel? And how the hell did the best kiss of Tabitha's life end up on YouTube?

Even ice cream isn't going to get them out of this one.

BOOK ONE AVAILABLE NOW